The
Remnant

Covenant

The Remnant

A Novel

Keith C. Terry

and

Wesley Jarvis

Covenant Communications, Inc.

Published by Covenant Communications, Inc.
American Fork, Utah

Printed in the United States of America
First Printing: November 1996

03 02 01 00   0 9 8 7 6 5 4 3

Library of Congress Catalog-in-Publication Data

Terry, Keith C. (Keith Clavin), 1933-
    The remnant / Keith Terry and Wesley Jarvis.
        p. cm.
ISBN 1-57734-056-6
    I. Jarvis, Wesley. II. Title.
PS3570.E698R46 1996
813' .54--dc21   96-49371
                                                          CIP

To three lovely ladies—Evelyn, Dorothy, and Josephine

ACKNOWLEDGMENTS

I wish to acknowledge my father, Erastus Leon Jarvis, and great-grandfather, George Jarvis, without whose help and guidance I would never have undertaken this study.

Wesley Jarvis

My sincere thanks to Jerry St. Vincent for his assistance.

Keith Terry

CHARACTERS

The Man With a Quest:

Samuel H. Meyers—*widower, retired lumber executive, former mission president. In search of the location of the remnant of the Nephites.*

The Recovering Professor:

Dr. Peter Polk—*recovering from a stroke, perpetual scholar of the Book Mormon, sets up a gathering of selected members of the Church to identify the seed of Jacob spoken of by the Savior.*

The Assistant and Wife:

Stephen and Anney Thorn—*both new members of the Church. Stephen works as assistant to the Book of Mormon Foundation Dr. Polk directs.*

The Widow:

Katherine Moore—*wealthy widow of the late televangelist Robert Moore, seeks to learn how she and Moore can be married in the next life.*

The Man with a Quest:

Todd Thorn—*Stephen and Anney's son, a recent convert.*

Max Williams—*a homeless computer whiz, converted with Todd.*

The Investigator:

Karry—*Australian steward*

The Sweetheart:

Brenda Thorn—*daughter of Stephen and Anney, sweetheart of Max.*

The Captain:

Captain Montgomery—*captain of the yacht,* the Free Eagle.

The Peers:

Maria Almansar—*professor of religious, studies at BYU, questions Meyers authority.*

Takahashi Samura—*seminary coordinator in Tokyo, Japan, invited to bring his wife, Noriko.*

Eric Kumani—*Hawaiian restauranteur, joins the cruise with his wife, Carol.*

Manuel Rodriguez—*bank executive from Oaxaca, Mexico and his wife, Carmen, have troubled feelings.*

The First Officer:

Officer Stone—*young, arrogant, inexperienced yachtsman.*

Out of the Past:

Charity Barker Mellon—*ancestor of Maria, finds the Church in England.*

Fujita Toko—*great-great-grandfather of Takahashi, has the impression that something good is coming*

Kumi Kumani—*progenitor of Eric, taught the gospel by Joseph F. Smith.*

José Manuel Rodriguez—*forebear of Manuel, one of the first Lamanites baptized in Mexico in latter days.*

Contents

CHAPTER ONE

A New Insight

Provo, Utah

POLK HAD ARISEN BEFORE DAWN like a kid on Christmas morning. He managed his own toilet and dressed comfortably in brown slacks and a light blue cotton shirt that he had pulled down from the closet with some difficulty, bending the wire hanger in the effort. He even drank a can of Ensure in his light, cheery kitchen, the room his wife had so lovingly designed four years ago, just before she died. He was satisfied that he was improving daily, perhaps hourly. A stroke for any person is debilitating, but for a seventy-one-year-old man an attack can be incapacitating for the remainder of his life.

Polk had arranged for Stephen to pick him up in the car before sunup. When they arrived at the mouth of Rock Canyon in Provo, the sun was casting diffused light from the east, but it still hid behind the peaks. Soon it would rush through the canyon between the jagged rocks and splash warmth all across Utah Valley, as it had every morning for aeons of time. Polk loved it.

It had taken some effort for Stephen to pry himself out of bed in his room at Day's Inn before 5 A.M. He could hardly believe some of the things Dr. Polk required of him, though he had to admit, they usually made sense once he got involved.

After he had settled himself to enjoy the sunrise experience, Polk took the time to fill Stephen in on the plan for the upcoming gathering. Simply a gathering. A vital meeting of carefully selected participants. The sort of shoulder-rubbing that Polk found stimulating and rewarding. He had not used the term *conference* this time.

It was to be a small gathering of interested, hand-picked individuals, all members of the Church who would uncover a long-forgotten promise that the Lord made to his covenant people the Nephites.

"An old friend came to see me while I was still recovering," Polk said. "He told me something very interesting. I didn't mention it to you sooner because I didn't want to distract you while the youth conference required your full concentration. For the past three months, my friend and I have been in touch frequently, mostly by phone. The more he talked to me, the more intrigued I became. His name is Samuel Meyers, and he has been scouting for something all over the Pacific Rim. He has come up with some startling information. I confess I am captivated with all he has learned. Sam and I go all the way back to college years together. Anyway, he has worked out a theory about the Nephites in the Book of Mormon. It's incredible. Wait till you hear it.

"Anyway, when I was visiting with your father-in-law's widow—to express my condolences—we got to talking. I mentioned that I wanted to have a little gathering and was searching for a suitable, secluded location. Without a blink, she suggested we use her time-share on a yacht she has part ownership in. At first, I couldn't believe she could be serious. She doesn't really know me at all, except through you. But she was absolutely earnest in her offer. So we have set up a conference on Katherine Moore's yacht and . . . well . . . there and one other location. I've invited eight or so people—carefully selected people—to attend a sort of week's confab, and some of the guests will bring their wives. I need you to check out the accommodations."

Peter Polk's bushy eyebrows twitched above his expressive eyes and his voice revealed his enthusiasm. "Stephen, the concepts my friend Sam has shared with me are beyond anything I have encountered in the Book of Mormon—in literally years. I just have to pursue this with him and come to some resolution on the matter before I die. Does that make any sense to you?"

Stephen smiled and gently punched his friend's shoulder. "What do you mean, before you die?"

"Don't be light with me. I know that dying is part of the plan of our existence. I came close this last time. You know that as well as I."

Stephen knew that Dr. Polk was referring to his stroke. Although Polk looked gaunt when compared to his former rotund self, Stephen sincerely believed that his mentor was on the other side of that experience and gaining strength every day. His ruddy face still reflected a zest for life, and the keen eyes that were focused on Stephen left no doubt that this perpetual scholar had found a new adventure to pursue—the whereabouts of the Nephites.

As a relatively new member of the LDS faith, Stephen had accepted the things he had been taught over the past year. He had not yet gone into much depth on the relationship between the Nephites and the Lamanites, and in the area of the two nations in the Book of Mormon, he had no strong opinions. But obviously Polk did.

Polk was silent for a moment as he gazed out over the valley before him. Perched on the ridge above Provo this August morning, with the sun streaking over Squaw Peak, it seemed like the dawn of civilization as the growing brightness gradually swept over the mountain to touch them and warm the morning air. At the moment, they were merely two men—one in his early seventies and the other in his mid-forties—seated on the edge of Rock Canyon with the newly risen sun warming their heads.

For the moment, Polk's plans were set aside and the two sat in silence, watching the sunrise—Dr. Polk in his wheelchair and Stephen seated on a folding lawn chair—looking for all the world as if they were waiting for fireworks to begin on the Fourth of July. This heavenly panoply was far more enthralling to Dr. Polk than any man-made display. It was a treat from the Lord, reserved for the few who cared enough to sacrifice a little sleep to observe it.

Only after the sun had made its rise to full splendor across the valley and the morning air had begun to warm up did Dr. Polk break the silence to resume his discussion with Stephen. Even though his excitement over the new Nephite theory was apparent, he set that aside and instructed Stephen, his assistant in charge of the day-to-day operations in a series of Book of Mormon conferences, in a rather matter-of-fact way.

Originally, Polk had planned to press Roy, his twenty-four-year-old computer guru, into service. Roy had been with him since the organization of the Book of Mormon Foundation three years earlier. The only problem was, Roy was committed to finishing his graduate studies at Brigham Young University and needed every spare hour to research, working closely with his chairman to complete all his assignments.

Stephen stirred uneasily at thoughts of directing yet another conference, or whatever Polk decided to call it. He hadn't anticipated traveling away from home again so soon. He wanted time at home with his wife, Anney, and his two teenagers, Todd and Brenda.

"You say a week?" he asked.

"That's right. Just six or seven days. I would expect you to go early and make sure things are in order on the ship; then Anney can accompany me, if she will. You can bring along your kids for all I care. I want you both to be part of the discussion we'll be having on this subject. Okay? I know you'll need to discuss this little matter with Anney, but can you give me an answer by this evening?"

Stephen nodded yes. He had expected Polk to request an answer by noon. My goodness, but he was getting patient these days. It would take some rearranging to squeeze this little journey into his schedule, but Stephen could manage it, particularly since Polk had encouraged him to bring his wife along. Somehow that eased the assignment. More than once Stephen had admitted to Anney that in his new line of work he would have to remain flexible, which by inference meant that Anney had to be flexible as well.

Living in the Bay Area was becoming awkward. Stephen had been flying to Provo, Utah, the home of Dr. Polk, more and more often lately. Now it appeared that Stephen would either have to move to Provo or work out a better computer system to make it possible to run the operation by e-mail, fax, phone, and the Internet.

With his incredible skills, Roy was always coming up with ideas on how Stephen could live most of the time at home in Lafayette, California, and still remain close to the expanding projects they had planned. For all his youth, Roy was a near-genius with anything remotely connected to computers. But fine-tuning a system for directing the foundation at a distance would have to wait until after his orals.

Sensing Dr. Polk's barely suppressed excitement about the

Nephites, Stephen asked, "What did your friend . . . what's his name . . . Sam . . . ?"

"Sam Meyers. Best friend I ever had."

"What did he tell you about the Nephites in the Book of Mormon that's so interesting? I really don't know enough about Lehi's family to understand why your friend would spend time around the Pacific Rim checking into the whereabouts of the Nephites. I thought they were killed off as a nation. Am I wrong?"

Polk shaded his eyes to shield them from the direct sunlight as he glanced over at Stephen. "No, you're not wrong. It's just that we tend to think because they no longer exist in the Americas as an easily identifiable nation, there no longer are Nephites on the earth. The whole Church has the same concept of the total destruction of the Nephites as you do. I've had to change my thinking on this matter since learning a few things from Sam. Yes, they were destroyed as a nation upon this land, but apparently groups of righteous Nephites escaped the final destruction."

"I thought they were annihilated at the Hill Cumorah when Moroni escaped and hid the plates. I can't remember the exact date, but it seems like it was around 400 C.E. Am I right?"

"You're close on your dates, but not all the Nephites were destroyed. Those at the Hill Cumorah and across the continents of North and South America, yes. All those people were indeed destroyed. But years earlier, some Nephites had left the area by ship."

"What you're trying to tell me is that there are Nephites on the earth right now. Does your friend Sam know where they are?"

"He has a pretty good idea. If his theory is right, then we ought to take a serious look at those people and know what's coming. No one likes surprises that hit you between the eyes. That is exactly what is going to happen in our day if we are asleep to the prophecy we've been given."

"That sounds serious," Stephen responded. "You're way ahead of me. You know better than anyone that I'm a novice at these things, so go slow. Tell me what you know."

Dr. Polk smiled and tilted his head in the enigmatic gesture that Stephen had come to know so well. It seemed to imply, "I know something you don't know," and Polk always did.

"Sam told me something that I had never pieced together. I found his premise intriguing."

Leaning over to grab Dr. Polk's elbow with a playful tug, Stephen probed, "Enough mystery. What did he tell you?"

With exaggerated resignation, Dr. Polk sighed and said, "I quote you, more or less, what he told me. He said, 'I know as well as I live that the Nephites did not all perish, but that a segment sailed away to other shores, where they have continued to live and proliferate until this day. The popular idea that only the Lamanites survived is now suspect. The Nephites still have a great destiny before them, which they will most certainly fulfill.'"

Stephen had been involved in studying the Book of Mormon for barely more than a year, and he knew his limitations. He did not know all that much about the complex interplay between the Old Testament, New Testament, and modern-day scripture. He was the first to admit it. But he had learned a great deal about the Book of Mormon, not only because he was intensely interested, but also because he had been thrust into a concentrated study of the book to give him background for the conferences in which he had taken part.

Stephen scrutinized the older man's face. "Are you going to tell me, or do I have to wait till the conference to find out just which nation—or nations—is made up of Nephites?"

"No, I'll tell you," Dr. Polk laughed, "but please make every effort possible to go to the conference anyway. You will find it most enlightening. I'll tell you a little more about what my friend told me, but first, let me quote you something in 1 Nephi 10:19."

Stephen had been with Dr. Polk long enough and discussed the scriptures with him often enough to know that the retired religion professor could recite whole sections of scripture from memory.

"It says, 'For he that diligently seeketh shall find'—the key word here is *diligently*—'and the mysteries of God shall be unfolded unto them, by the power of the Holy Ghost.'"

Polk gave Stephen's arm a fatherly pat. "What that means is that you can have the mysteries of God unfolded to you personally through the power of the Holy Ghost. What a promise! I believe that scripture, Stephen. I believe it with all my heart. It doesn't mean that I will be given to know the mysteries to direct the Church. That is reserved for the living prophet. It does mean, though, that I can discover things for myself and know certain doctrines in my own heart. I can even share them with my friends as postulations, but not as Church doctrine. Do you agree?"

"Sure, you've told me that before, and I believe I can have things revealed to me to guide and direct my own life."

"Good. Well, what I'm saying is that any sincere person, as the Prophet Joseph Smith said, can search the scriptures and gain understanding . . . including the mysteries." Polk nodded with emphasis as he spoke. "Sam says he has found overwhelming evidence in support of the idea that the Nephites were not all destroyed, but that they live on as a people and don't even know who they really are. But they will. Yes, my boy, they certainly will know their true identity!

"He called me a few days ago, Sam did. He'll arrive in Pago Pago to join us on Thursday, along with the others. Anyway, he mentioned a couple of things he has discovered in his research. Do you know anything about blood typing?"

"Not much. Why?"

Polk glanced up at the sun over his shoulder, putting his good left hand to his brow. "It's getting warm. Let's go back to my place. I have a fax from Sam with a summary of material he wants to present. He also included some of his latest discoveries. He wanted to bring me up-to-date on some of the things he's uncovered."

In Polk's study, Stephen helped the aging professor slide from wheelchair to desk chair. Settled for a moment, Polk fumbled among the stack of papers and pulled up the fax Sam Meyers had sent the day before. "Here, let me read it to you," he said.

The fax covered a wide-ranging study of evidences Sam had uncovered in his months of traveling around the Pacific Rim. Near the conclusion of the five-page document, Polk read aloud,

"'Blood types are revealing in nations and among tribal groups. As you know, there are several blood types: O, B, A, AB, etc. The most common blood type in western Europe is O; the most common type in Asia is B. Strangely, among the American Indians, blood type O is most common.

"'Let's compare blood types to see the most scientific method for determining a strain of people and perhaps their origin. Taking all of the Pacific Rim, it is interesting to note that on the eastern side of the South Pacific, the predominant blood type is O, the same as the American Indian blood type. On the western side of the South Pacific, beginning among the islands such as Tonga and Samoa and extending all the way into the deep regions of the Orient, the blood type is predominantly B.

"'This is all very well until blood typing reaches Japan. On the very rim of the Asian continent, surrounded by nations whose blood type is mostly B, the predominant blood type in Japan is O. This means that the Japanese, who are considered by most standards to be Asian, have a blood type that does not fit. Where did the Japanese people get type O blood in a sea of B-type blood among all its neighbors?'"

Polk looked up and touched his reading glasses. "Sorenson had this to say in summary when he completed his studies of blood typing in the Pacific: 'The blood-type evidence seems to link the classification of the Polynesian and Japanese unquestionably with the American Indian.'"

Polk resumed reading from Sam's fax. "Here are two examples among several Sam will present. These deal with agricultural products. 'When we study the cotton grown in the Polynesian islands, we note that it is a unique strain, different from that in the Orient. In the islands, cotton has twenty-six chromosomes; in all the rest of Asia, cotton has thirteen chromosomes. The twenty-six-chromosome cotton is identical to the cotton grown anciently in the Americas.

"'Sweet potatoes originated in Central America. Most scientists in the field agree that the plant stemmed from that region of the world. There is little dispute on the matter. The sweet potato was unknown to Europeans prior to the Age of Discovery. Yet the sweet potato was a common vegetable in the Pacific Islands and New Zealand long before Captain Cook ventured into those regions.

"'Along the lines of explorers by ship, Polynesian origins appear to stem from the east (the Americas) to the west. Some recognized authorities such as Heyerdahl, who made a monumental voyage from east to west in the Pacific, maintain that the Polynesians received at least some of their culture from the Americas. Keep in mind that migration must have been possible among Book of Mormon groups. There are recorded accounts of three main groups who came to the Americas at one time or another. The Jaredites, Lehites, and Mulekites all came by sea, as nearly as we can determine. It is likely that a vigorous sea-trading enterprise existed among these early founders of the Americas. The Book of Mormon indicates that there were people who occupied the seacoasts. We know that Hagoth, in about 50 B.C.E., was active in trade along the Pacific Coast with settlers moving into the North by seagoing vessels. We know that they kept up a shipping line and supplied those early settlers who were in the land northward. I really doubt that the ships were canoes and dugouts. Nephi constructed a ship large enough to bring Lehi's entire family across the Pacific.'"

Sam's fax ended with a personal comment. "'I think Hagoth and other shipbuilders had the same skills as Nephi. It seems logical that throughout the history of the Book of Mormon the people of Lehi had an active involvement with the sea."

Polk looked up from the paper he held in his hand. "Now then, this is only a small part of what we will delve into to show that, indeed, there is seed of the Nephites along the Pacific Rim." He sighed, as if he had taken some of the burden from his shoulders and placed it onto Stephen's. "I want you to be part of this little meeting. We only have the rest of this week to finish our plans.

"Check on the airline connections and reservations for all of us. I have the names and addresses of those to contact and how much I have budgeted from our funds to pull this off. The participants have already been informed and have agreed to attend. I think you can have everything whipped into shape by this evening. You can easily make any follow-up arrangements from your home in California."

Chapter Two

Search for Evidence

Nara

SAMUEL MEYERS HAD COME AT LAST to the hilly country in the central-most part of Japan to view the Seven Blade Sword. He had repeatedly pondered the sword's significance while undertaking a study of the seven tribes of Lehi. Was there a connection? Clearly there was a connection in Samuel's mind between what he had seen in South America and what he hoped to view here.

A youthful-looking Shinto priest stood quietly beside Samuel as he sat on the steps near the temple courtyard, pulling on straw sandals. Samuel arose, bowed to the priest, thanked him for providing the sandals, and then repeated his request for an audience with the head priest. Not with just any ordinary head priest, but *the* head priest, the elderly priest who officiated when the imperial family visited the wooded hills in the heart of Japan's most ancient capital.

As the American stood, he met the priest eye to eye. Both men were short-to-medium height by American standards; Samuel always felt about the right physical size in Japan, as he did now with the priest. At one time he had been five feet nine, but at age seventy-one, he admitted that he may have shrunk an inch or so. He had never been overweight, and under his white Arrow shirt his muscles were still firm and taut for a man his age. But each succeeding year seemed to require working out hours longer to maintain the edge. It remained to be seen how long he would continue to be vigorous and healthy—two wonderful blessings he had enjoyed all his years.

Samuel Howard Meyers loved the Japanese culture, though he

was totally western by nature and imbued with an assertiveness and drive true to his heritage. That heritage included a good deal of German blood in his veins, as well as some Danish and a drop or two of English on his mother's side. It was the German genes in him that dominated his appearance. His hair had once been blond and his facial features were clearly Teutonic. The Meyers family had immigrated to Utah just after the first flush of conversions to The Church of Jesus Christ of Latter-day Saints. His German ancestors had accepted the message of the gospel brought by the poorly funded American missionaries who walked the cobblestone streets of Frankfurt.

In his native dialect of the provincial, central Japan area, the young Shinto priest invited Samuel and his two companions, Junko and Komae, to follow him through the entrance to the head priest's reception room just off his private living quarters. Samuel understood the Japanese language. He had spent more than five years in Asia or among Asian people. First as an LDS missionary, a young man fresh from World War II; later as a mission president; and then during a host of repeated visits to the country. He knew the customs and language as well as any American diplomat ever assigned to the Japanese islands. Better than most.

Samuel had traipsed over a vast area of Asian sea and land and visited numerous ancient shrines and museums across the Pacific Rim—all in the past several months of intense travel. His quest had engulfed his waking hours and led him to such places as this hallowed temple. This was yet another shrine, except he knew culturally as well as spiritually that this holy ground was special. It was the shrine that housed the sacred Shinto relic known as the Seven Blade Sword.

A month earlier in his wide-ranging travels, mostly by air, he had made a special trip to South America to inspect a carving of a similar object—also known as the Seven Blade Sword. Some ten years before, Samuel had seen a *photo* in the Church Office Building in Salt Lake City, of an enormous depiction of the sword, which had been carved on a cliff in Paracas Bay in Peru.

With Junko and Komae close behind him, Samuel stepped into the head priest's quarters, brimming with charm and mindful of his good fortune to be here. After escorting the three to a side room, the young priest again indicated to Samuel that the head priest was a busy man. "Do not be alarmed should it turn out that he has no time to give you an audience," he warned in Japanese.

At his words Junko reached for the brown leather purse slung over her shoulder. Her wealthy husband owned a chain of Chinese restaurants in Japan, and the evening before she had set aside funds to offer as a donation—the equivalent of two thousand American dollars on the international exchange. She handed the bundle to the priest, whose face lit up at the sight of the cash. He left the room, inviting the guests to be seated. He would see if the head priest had a moment to spare and would also make out a receipt for the donation.

The inner quarters looked very much like a western living room. The low walnut coffee table and the upholstered couches of brown leather were western in style. Samuel knew custom, tone, manner, and place in Japan. He was aware that Americans were welcome to visit, but they were always considered foreigners, and even intruders, although no one at this moment would be able to detect the least degree of condescension from the white-robed priest who had left the room.

The three visitors sat down on the sofas provided and awaited the return of the young priest, and perhaps the head priest as well. Junko whispered to Samuel that she had no doubt, considering the amount of the donation she had given, that the head man would find a moment to speak to them.

She was right. The head priest soon appeared. He was a thin, small man, bald and robed in white. He was tiny, even to Samuel. He bowed as he entered, and Samuel noticed liver spots on the shiny crown of his head as he lowered it in salute. The priest's face seemed more youthful than Meyers had expected of a man in his eighties. His wet lips seemed to push the Japanese greeting from his mouth which, more than any other aspect of the head priest's person, revealed his advanced age. The younger priest followed, carrying a tray laden with small, exquisite cups of fragrant tea, which he placed on the table and withdrew.

The interview rushed by for Samuel, who had prepared a mental list of questions too numerous to answer in one sitting. He saved his most pressing question for the last few minutes, hoping to extend the time by his urgency to know. He asked if this particular shrine was the depository of the Seven Blade Sword, although he knew from his study of the shrine that it was.

The head priest nodded, then peered suspiciously at the American, as if he were the sole owner and protector of the ancient, rusted relic that Samuel had come to see.

"I should like to view the sword, if it is not contrary to your custom." Samuel's head bent forward in a reverent half bow. "Please do not think me rude. I merely want to confirm that it is here on these grounds and to see it for myself."

The head priest clapped his hands together. Instantly the younger priest who had escorted them to the quarters appeared from beyond the sliding paper doors adorned with murals of bamboo trees.

The head priest whispered in the ear of the younger man. The youthful priest bowed as he moved backward to the open paper doors. Samuel was not certain what was to come next. The guests watched as the head priest picked up a small ceramic cup of steaming tea and put it gently to his lips, silently sipping the pale green substance. Samuel, however, allowed his proffered drink to cool on the tray in front of him.

At length, the youthful priest returned, holding a four-foot-long wooden frame, the front of which was encased in glass. He handed it to the head priest with a bow and stepped back. The head priest took the framed case, turned it about, and (to Samuel's chagrin) displayed a full-scale, poster-like, color photo of the Seven Blade Sword for Samuel to study.

Samuel examined the image of the rusted metal and sawtooth blades which had been damaged through age and abuse. He noticed the way the six curved blades branched off the main shaft, like a saguaro cactus in the Sonora desert of the southwest United States. Though disappointed, he held his peace. After years of living among Japanese people, he knew that any sign of irritation on his part would not be culturally acceptable. He could see that he would not be allowed to view the actual relic—not on this first visit. He would have to bide his time. Still, it was interesting to see a life-size photograph of the object of his interest, especially the Chinese lettering that had been etched into the rusted steel by some scribe long after the sword had been discovered. Samuel knew that Chinese scholars had introduced Chinese lettering to the Japanese people in the eighth century C.E.

"Yes," he breathed. It was the very same design as the one in South America. Both swords must have originated from the same culture.

Of all the evidences in the Pacific Rim, Samuel recognized that this was as valid in expressing the origin of the Nephite nation as any he had studied. He was more convinced than ever that the Seven Blade Sword symbolized the seven tribes of Lehi—of which four tribes, the Nephites, would one day reclaim the promise and be the lead group to build the New Jerusalem. Stunning information . . . that was yet to be revealed.

* * *

EASING BACK IN A LOUNGE CHAIR, luxuriating in the warm evening breeze that wafted over him, Samuel gazed out at the forest-covered hills surrounding the small valley. Junko and Komae had left Samuel at an authentic Japanese inn eighty kilometers south of the Shinto temple. He had enjoyed a rigorous workout at the inn's full-service spa—lifting weights and swimming twenty laps in the nearly deserted pool before relaxing in the hot tub. All services were superb, including those of the matronly woman who gave his back a scrub to relax his muscles. During all these months of travel in the Orient, he had not missed a chance to work out, wherever he roamed. Tonight he planned to have an early dinner of rice and fish, and retire to his very Spartan room, which was supplied with a mat for sleeping on the gleaming straw floor. Nothing western tonight, thank you. This evening he desired what was considered in this part of the world to be the finest accommodations available—all strictly Japanese, including the meal he planned to eat. Early tomorrow he would fly from his present location and stop off in Tokyo to visit his younger sister and her diplomat husband, as well as an old and dear friend at the fish market.

Samuel had seen a good deal of the world in his lifetime, much more than any of his ancestors ever dreamed of seeing. But they had paved the way, and he was grateful for all their efforts through the years. He never took his ancestors for granted.

Early in the era of Church settlement throughout the west, Samuel's grandfather had somehow made it to the northwestern part of Idaho. In the next generation, Samuel's father had enmeshed himself in the hard-but-profitable timber business. Samuel, the first college-educated son, had jumped into his father's footsteps and supplied tons of seasoned lumber to the vast housing market of California in the 1950s and 60s, when the burgeoning population swept away virtually every remaining fruit orchard in the coastal communities of the Golden State.

Twenty-three years before Samuel's birth, his father, Elder Mark Herbert Meyers, had served a mission in the Orient. It was that introduction to the Japanese culture that sparked Samuel's lifelong study of the people.

Samuel was one of eight children born into the Meyers household, all active members of the LDS Church. Born near the end of the family, he was the first child his parents could support in college after the Great Depression. In the early 1940s, his father had prospered beyond anything they had dared to imagine. By 1943, when Samuel entered Utah State Agricultural College at Logan, Utah, the timber industry of Northern Idaho had taken hold, making wealthy men of those who had endured the hardships of a few years earlier. Herbert Meyers had risen with the industry.

Samuel had met Peter Polk in the fall of 1943 in the dorm at Utah State where they had been assigned as roommates. Peter hailed from a small town in eastern Idaho called Blackfoot. Like Samuel, he was a freshman as well as a celebrated wrestler in his hometown region. Both young men dressed in the style of the day and sported wise-guy grins. The silly freshman girls ignored Peter and fell all over Samuel. Though shorter than Peter, he had the look of Frank Sinatra, the singing idol of the day. Peter liked to kid Samuel that it wasn't his looks that attracted the girls, but the new fire engine-red, canvas-topped 1941 Ford V-8 convertible he tooled around campus in.

Samuel Meyers was in the Pacific a year later, a fighter pilot knocking down Japanese Zeros, his Ford convertible and the girls he left behind just a distant memory. In those glory days, he recoiled from the thought of pasting his hits on the fuselage of his Navy Corsair as other pilots did; it turned his stomach to think of the men he had killed. Whereas others in his squadron saw all Japanese through the caricatured grinning Jap posters, Samuel saw them through the eyes of his father as decent human beings. But Samuel obeyed orders and excelled as a pilot. No one in the high command detected his secret admiration for the ordinary Japanese people who were being misled by their military leaders.

When the war ended, he accepted a mission call to Hawaii. Then, mission behind him, he resumed his studies, only this time at Brigham Young University in Provo, Utah. It wasn't long before he married Margaret, "the loveliest girl in the whole Salt Lake Valley," whom he met at school. She was a sophomore; he was technically still a freshman. After graduation from BYU, he forged into the lumber business with his father in Boise, Idaho. Then five years later he abruptly decided he wanted to teach in the growing seminary and institute program of the Church Education System, a decision which came soon after he met the dynamic director of seminaries and institutes of the Church.

To qualify to teach, Samuel crowded his wife and three children into a small apartment in Provo and earned his master's degree in eighteen months. Then he plunged directly into a teaching assignment at the UCLA Institute of Religion. Twelve years into his teaching career, the Church called him to take his growing family and serve as a mission president in Japan.

With the unexpectedly rewarding three-year mission presidency completed by the mid-1970s, he returned—not to a teaching assignment as he had been promised and would have taken—but rather to the family's lumber business. His brother had suddenly died, leaving Sam's eighty-four-year-old father with the full load of running the business. Sam, as good at business as he had been at teaching, took the family lumber company into upscale prefab construction in the 1980s and increased the family fortune tenfold.

Now his two married sons and a nephew handled the day-to-day lumber operations while Samuel kept his hand in the business as chairman of the board of directors. He would let that position go in a year, then devote his time to a deep study of the Pacific Rim and the gospel's impact there. He had been looking forward to another mission with Margaret until she died two years ago. Part of him had fled with her. Life seemed devoid of warmth now. He knew a vital something was gone, but he was stymied as to the best way to get it back, if that were possible. Which he doubted.

He seldom worked through an entire day without thinking about Margaret, regardless of where he happened to be. Home for Samuel was Idaho, but it was no longer the same in Boise without her. His large home, a stately, comfortable retreat just off the ninth hole of the Plantation Country Club, was more a burden of memories now than the place for exciting family gatherings it had once been. He knew full well that he lacked Margaret's talent for entertaining children and grandchildren when they came to visit. For meals, he either ordered out for food, or his daughters or daughters-in-law fixed a passable spread. Either way, much was missing. Their visits were nothing like the radiating, high-decibel events they had been while Margaret was living. She had been hostess, wife, mother, grandmother—in short, the very heart of the home. It had all changed quickly after her mercifully brief bout with cancer, which ended in a painful death. She didn't deserve that.

The Brethren had recommended that Samuel find another lovely woman and remarry. The last "encouragement" to marry had come a few weeks ago when he dropped in at 47 South Temple to visit with his long-time good friend and General Authority, Robert Farnsworth, a member of the Seventy. Samuel assured his friend that he was looking for someone to marry. "She just hasn't shown up yet, Robert."

"Get her to show up," Elder Farnsworth had urged in his sterling, resonant tone.

It was three months to the day after Margaret's passing that Samuel had decided to pursue the question of where a remnant of the Nephites had fled. His father had insisted that Nephites were alive and gaining in world influence in the Pacific Rim. In a concerted effort to put his grief behind him, Samuel purposefully took up the torch and began tracing the Nephite travels his father had described before his death. Assembling the records and writings his father had composed, Samuel plunged into the research.

His friend Peter Polk had entered the picture when the two had had dinner at the Roof Garden in Salt Lake City a year ago. Before Peter's stroke laid him low, he had been eager to assist Samuel in the search. Now that his health was coming back, the two had concocted the notion to invite a handful of individuals—members of the Church from a variety of cultures—to join them on a luxury yacht for a week's private cruise and intense skull session on the blessings that had been promised to the Nephites, in the flesh, in the day of the Gentile. In other words, now.

It had become a personal search for Samuel to locate the remnant of the Nephites. He felt certain now that he had found substantial evidence that, yes, a Nephite nation was alive and powerful who, when the Lord was ready to make good his promise, would return and claim its rightful inheritance in the Americas. Samuel was convinced that the remnant would return and spearhead the creation of the New Jerusalem. The pieces had now come together.

Samuel sat in trunks and a t-shirt emblazoned with the words "WORLD CLASS GRANDPA." Scott, his grandson, had given him the shirt when he had turned seventy-one the month before. Samuel steadfastly maintained that it allowed him the stamina to keep up the pace he had set for himself after Margaret's death, and the teenager admired his grandfather for maintaining his rigorous training program.

Samuel drank in the beauty of the moving waters of the pleasant sea surrounding the inn on two sides. In this venerated but overpopulated land, the people retained the will to resist overrunning its natural beauty. Nothing in Japan was left to chance. All the available plots of earth were cherished and preserved for the nurturing of plant life. The forest was cultivated as meticulously as the rice fields—each living plant growing in its appointed place because someone intended it to be there. What a land of enchantment! Samuel recalled that Pearl Buck, the Nobel Prize-winning author, had called it "a cultivated paradise on earth."

Tonight, with all his latest discoveries as to the whereabouts of the Nephite nation, Samuel felt as if he had climbed Mount Everest and was up there shouting to the sky that he had made it to the top.

At that moment a muffled ring from inside his black leather gym bag brought him back to reality. Reaching inside, he pulled out the cellular phone that fit snugly within the palm of his hand. He had programmed the cell on his first visit to Japan three months ago. He unclipped the mouth piece, pulled up the antenna, pressed the red plastic button, and said, "Hi, Pete." He knew it must be Polk; he had left this number with no one else.

"You got it. It's me. How is your trip going, Sam?" Polk chirped, excited as a kid.

Samuel could detect the slightly slurred quality of his old friend's voice, but he was getting used to the idea that Polk might never completely recover from the stroke he had experienced less than a year ago.

"I tell you, Pete," Samuel declared with exhilaration, "I have tramped from the Polynesian Triangle, across the underbelly of New Zealand, to the mainland of China, on here to Japan, and even to South America for a peek at the seven blade sword I told you about. I can't wait for you to see the notes I've made on what I've uncovered. Did you know the words *Hagata* and *Hakate* in Java are originally a Japanese name—and both translate to *Hagoth*?"

"Hagoth as in shipbuilder?"

"That's right." He rushed the next words without waiting for another question from Polk. Their rapid-fire conversation was that of a couple of ten-year-olds on a camp-out. "I have lists of city names that were originally Hebrew or a derivative of that language, and you won't believe what I came across at the Shinto temple. I was there today. This trip has been so fantastic . . . Anyway, how are you doin', buddy? Still up to our little cruise?"

"I sure am. Nothing short of another stroke can stop me from coming. I can't wait to hear all you've learned. You haven't told anyone else about all this yet, have you?"

Samuel detected concern in Polk's voice. "No, but I can't see where it's any secret. I'm not with the CIA, you know."

"Right, but I'm kinda jealous—like your favorite sweetheart. I want to be first to hear the whole thing. And, besides, I think we need to talk about how we will present this whole matter to the Brethren before it becomes common knowledge. Also—and this is very important to me—I really want to see the first reactions of the group who will be with us on the yacht. What do you say?"

"No problem. I'm ready, boy am I ready. But I do intend to mention what I've been doing for the past few months to my little sister and her husband tomorrow evening at dinner. He's with the diplomatic corps in Tokyo, you know. I'll be flying there tomorrow."

"Oh, sure," Polk agreed. "I just don't want you to make any official report on your findings until we've talked."

Samuel was suddenly uneasy. "Do you know something I don't?" he asked.

"Nope, just wanted you to know that I'm thrilled with what you'll be presenting at the gathering. I want the group to come to their own conclusions about the Nephite nation, sort of discover it themselves without us telling them everything we know right off the bat." There was a pause on Polk's end, then, "You still plan to lead out in the discussions, don't you? I'm not up to talking for very long at a time."

"Oh, sure. No problem." Speaking before a group had always been one of Samuel's strong points.

"Good. By the way," Polk suddenly recalled, "my assistant, Stephen Thorn—you remember, the fellow who helped me this summer with that Book of Mormon youth conference in Park City? Anyway, he'll be arriving the first of the week in Pago Pago to tie down all the details of the arrangements, supplies for the yacht, and so forth."

"I know who you're talking about."

"You'll like Stephen. He joined the Church last year. Actually, his wife was baptized too, a few months after him; and at the youth conference, if you can believe it, his son was converted, too. The family is from the Bay Area. They have two college kids: the boy I mentioned and a girl. Stephen is very committed to his work in the foundation . . . Make him feel good about what we're doing. I've pushed him along on several projects, and he may need some boosting. Don't get me wrong; Stephen is a self-starter, but I've really been leaning on him. Okay?"

"Sure."

"Are you flying directly from Tokyo to Pago Pago?"

"No, I'll be going through Honolulu. I want to take a picture of the statue on the temple grounds in Laie, and see a couple of old friends." Samuel chatted for a couple more minutes with his friend, then dropped the cell phone into his bag. Leaning back on the lounge chair, he sucked in the warm August air that flowed in off the rocky shores of the point and thought about spending some time on a yacht. He loved the South Seas any time of the year. He could hardly wait to launch into a discussion with the group about his marvelous findings along the Pacific Rim. He felt certain he had broken the code. He was ready to unseal the documents and peer into the future of the Nephite nation.

CHAPTER THREE

The *Free Eagle*

THE MOMENT STEPHEN STEPPED ABOARD the *Free Eagle* docked at the wharf in Pago Pago, he knew that the accommodations for the group would meet anyone's discriminating demands. At 192 feet in length, shiny white and polished, ready for inspection, the sight of the sleek craft sent a ripple of excitement through Stephen's body. He had not expected such a magnificent vessel. He had read the flyer Katherine, his wife's wealthy stepmother, had handed him when they met a couple of days before at her home in San Francisco, but he had not expected anything so large and impressive. This was world-class yachting with all the amenities.

Stephen wasn't entirely sure of the details in Katherine's part-ownership of the yacht, but he understood that her first husband had invested in the ship as a moneymaker within his portfolio of investments. Upon his death she, of course, was heir to all his investments. Katherine mentioned that she sometimes scheduled a week of the year aboard the yacht, though for the past few years she had not chosen to use her time-share. She and her second husband, the late Bob Moore, had planned to use the ship this year during the last week of August. But those plans had changed abruptly with his unexpected death. Dr. Polk had quickly accepted the offer that Katherine so generously extended for his projected gathering. What an opportunity to seclude the group from the world and make the most of their study, all the while enjoying a luxury cruise.

The captain, erect in his heavily starched, white uniform, held out his large hand and welcomed Stephen on board. Stephen guessed they were about the same age—in their mid-forties—though at about six feet five, the captain had the advantage in height by some four inches. The lines of tanned skin that crinkled about his eyes gave him a strong, weathered look. Although his lips were chapped, his face was handsome and his body muscular and well-proportioned. *A man certainly looks more impressive in a uniform*, Stephen told himself. This man looked very impressive.

"Captain William C. Montgomery," the captain barked. "I'm at your service." The accent was definitely English.

"Thank you, Captain. I'm Stephen Thorn, project director for Dr. Polk, and I'm pleased to come aboard your marvelous ship." Stephen wondered if he had said that right. He had never been on a yacht of this class and certainly never sailed under such splendid conditions. But he had been sure from the moment Katherine extended her invitation that it would be a unique experience, to say the least.

"Welcome." The captain seemed to relax a bit. "I would like to show you about, if you'd care to accompany me on a brief tour. I'll have the steward take your things below to your stateroom, if that meets with your approval."

Stephen nodded. A tangle-haired blond steward, who couldn't have been more than twenty years old, stepped up to Stephen's luggage and nodded, "G'day," in a cheerful Australian manner that Stephen found infectious.

"Karry," the young man continued, introducing himself.

"Nice to meet you, Karry. I'm Stephen Thorn."

The captain began Stephen's personal tour on the aft deck, where fresh orchids adorned the oak-topped round table that could seat up to ten guests. From that point, Stephen got the full Cook's tour. Like a child at a toy store, he looked around him in wonder. His blue eyes hardly blinked. Though he had to admit he knew little about luxury ships, this was an utterly incredible craft.

"The *Free Eagle* is one of the most eye-catching yachts in the world," the captain offered, "with up to eighteen guests and nine staterooms with en suite baths in all of them. We have an elegant main salon that I will show you presently. My experienced crew and I are well versed in these waters and will provide you with excellent service. Your guests should have an enjoyable time. We offer the comforts of a four-star hotel."

As they descended below deck, the captain became more technical. "She is a motor yacht, launched in 1967 by Alkmaar, Holland, to a Witsen and Vis design. In the past five years, she has been totally rebuilt, repowered, and refitted: all new electronics, machinery, plating, decks—the works. She has twin 764-horsepower diesels and does thirty knots on the high seas—a marvelous craft to command." He patted the bulkhead in the engine room before grasping the metal railing that ran up from the stairwell.

On top, he pointed out the helipad, sun pads, spa pool, an easily accessible bathing platform with adjacent gymnasium, and water toys galore. Then they squeezed into the galley where the captain introduced Stephen to the swarthy chef. Karry, who had deposited Stephen's luggage in his stateroom, was now standing in the galley.

"Thanks, Karry, for taking care of my luggage."

"Yes, sir. I'm at your service, Dr. Thorn."

"Just call me Stephen. It sounds like you are from New Zealand or Australia."

"Australia, sir. Outback country."

"I've not been there, but I hear it's a lot like our Arizona."

"Right, though I haven't seen your Arizona, sir."

The captain next directed Stephen to the lower levels, leading him from the galley to the narrow stairwell that descended to the storage room. "Below we have a large freezer that can store up to a three-week supply of the best meats and other makings for the tastiest meals in the South Pacific."

All Stephen could think as he toured the vessel was how excited Anney would be. One of his delights in life was sharing everything with Anney. He smiled at the thought of the fun they would have basking in the luxury of this magnificent floating masterpiece together.

The captain showed Stephen two of the staterooms, each with its own full bath, an entire wall of mirrors, and a twenty-seven-inch color television set with the capability to receive over two hundred channels from the small dish on the sun deck.

"Do I understand correctly?" the captain began. "The fax I received from the charter agency that represents Mrs. Moore's interests indicated to me that you would arrive today and that most of the rest of your party will be boarding between 10 A.M. and 3 P.M. on Thursday. Is that correct? Are you expecting any other guests besides those you have listed on the fax?"

"One correction," Stephen replied. "My wife, Anney, and another guest on your list, Dr. Peter Polk, will arrive tomorrow afternoon from San Francisco. Will that be okay? We had hoped to convince Mrs. Moore that this cruise would be uplifting for her, but she backed out. I don't suppose she will change her mind, but if she should decide to join us, I would like you to reserve the master suite for her. Please leave it unoccupied, okay?"

"Should I place flowers and fruit in that suite?"

"No. I really doubt she'll make it. If she does come, I think she'll come with my wife. It's an iffy thing at the moment."

"We would be very pleased to have Mrs. Moore join us. It is very much like having royalty on board when she graces us with her presence. She lends such a breath of . . . what should I say? . . . elegance to any voyage."

"Yes. Yes, I think you phrased that very well," Stephen laughed. The captain was right. There was no one quite like Katherine. Elegant she was.

"Very good, Dr. Thorn. Then all will have arrived by 3 P.M. Thursday afternoon. What time would you like to set sail from this port?"

"Any time after that . . . by 3:15 if your crew is ready."

"Oh, we'll be ready, sir. We are a punctual lot."

The captain excused himself and returned to his duties. Stephen found his bags stacked near the closet of his stateroom. The queen-sized bed looked inviting after so many hours in transit. He would check out the planned menus with the chef, maybe stroll around Pago Pago for a bit, then come back on board and take a nap.

He unzipped his large, soft, nylon black bag Anney had packed before he left. On top of his trousers in the bag was a small envelope. He opened it and smiled as he read:

Handsome Husband, I know I will be joining you in a couple of days, but I wanted to say I love you. Maybe we can slip off to an isolated paradise island, if there is such a place on our itinerary . . . hmmm?

I will bring the good professor with me in one piece. He says that you have done a great job finalizing the arrangements. He is very excited.

My only regret is leaving Brenda and Todd. Face it, I'm on the verge of a full-blown case of empty-nest syndrome. Why, I don't know, since I have you.

Love you,
Anney

It suddenly swept over Stephen how involved life had become . . . knowing Dr. Polk and getting so wrapped up in the sheer excitement of probing every angle and concept of the Book of Mormon—and getting paid for it. This latest gathering had come so suddenly on the heels of the Book of Mormon youth conference that he had hardly had time to evaluate its effectiveness. Fortunately, this gathering would be brief—five days—and, as they would say in Book of Mormon jargon, *exceedingly* exciting.

* * *

"WELL, MATE, I SEE WE HAVE AN ADVANCE MAN to check out the ship," Karry, the nineteen-year-old Australian steward commented while seated on a small, stainless-steel stool in the galley of the *Free Eagle*. Karry had a rich, Australian bronze tan. The deep hue of his face enhanced the whiteness of his teeth that flashed when he smiled. He could have passed for one of the lifeguard racers at Farrin's Beach in Perth.

The lad (as he was called on the yacht) directed his remarks to the chef, who stood over the sink. The master of the galley was a thick, coarse man. His white cap covered stringy hair and his voice had a smoker's gravelly huskiness. The chef was not noted for his good nature—at times his manner even turned ugly. But at the moment, with no guests to please and not pressed to serve one of the full dinners he would have to stir up in another couple of days, he was unusually cheerful and spoke his version of Italian-cluttered English nonstop to Karry. He had come on board the *Free Eagle* at Côte d'Azur, a French port, where he had last cooked for a Riviera-based yacht. He was highly schooled in Italian and French cuisine, lately with a touch of the Polynesian/oriental flavors picked up in the Pacific where the *Free Eagle* had chartered for the past three years.

"What sorts are chartering her these next couple of weeks?" Karry asked, knowing that the chef knew everything about what was happening in port and on board the vessel, especially since he was in tight with the first officer, a prissy lad from England who had no dealings with Karry. Also, the chef and the captain played cards late at night and discussed all the happenings of the day. Though the two key members of the crew were worlds apart in culture, the two made great opponents at the card table.

"Not party people, you can be sure. It looks like a dull time we're going to endure. It's the old lady's turn—you know, that Mrs. What's-her-name from San Francisco. You know who I mean."

Karry didn't know who Mrs. What's-her-name was. He had only been aboard ship for a year, and he couldn't recall anyone vaguely answering to that description.

"Maybe you don't know. Anyway, she has invited some of her snooty friends. The captain says she recently lost her second husband, a telly guy who made big dollars preaching on the tube. It takes all kinds in this crazy world. She's not much fun—too quiet. Besides, that Thorn fellow just told me to lay in a supply of juices and soft drinks. Seems like we're about to get a bunch of teetotalers."

Karry knew that in fact most charter crowds were wealthy party types out for a good time. The drinking and sex that went on had been an eye-opener for a kid from a family sheep station in the Outback. He would never admit it out loud to the chef, but an ordinary group would be a welcome change. Personally, he hated cleaning up after drunks. Clean-cut people who had a few morals were fine with him. His parents had done a good job of teaching him.

CHAPTER FOUR

Father and Son

Tokyo, Japan

SAMUEL MEYERS KNEW FROM YEARS OF INTERACTING with the people of Japan that he was having lunch with one who understood the old ways, a man with a sense of the emotion in certain situations. Kondo Samura was a man who upheld the dignity of his heritage. As good as he was at the fish business—where he had risen to be numbered among the outstanding fish marketeers of the *Tsukiji*, the world's largest fish market, located at the far end of Tokyo—his greatest skills lay in understanding his business associates. Kondo Samura did not consider himself a wealthy man, though he did manage to make a handsome living, along with his first son and two nephews, in the market place. His power rested in constant influence in the trade.

Their lunch of thinly sliced bluefin sushi and rice, with Japan's ubiquitous tea, steaming hot this August noon, was excellent. Samuel's tea remained in the cup, untouched. But then Kondo knew from years of associating with this special friend from America that he would not touch the tea, and he respected him for it. The sushi delighted Samuel and satisfied his taste for raw seafood delicacies. He thoroughly enjoyed acting the gracious host to Kondo at the table in the Takahaka restaurant in downtown Tokyo.

They had been freely conversing in Japanese about their sons and all that they shared in common. Kondo's two sons regarded their father as having a preindustrial, religious mentality— supremely loyal to family and, above all, devoted to his ancestors. Kondo did honor his ancestors, though he felt disappointment (if not shame) for the actions of one in the line of his forefathers, actions committed over 130 years ago.

If asked about his religious leanings, Kondo described himself as Shinto and Buddhist. He was true to those ways of life that rejected any claims of exclusive universality, such as that claimed by followers of Christianity or Judaism or, for that matter, the LDS Church.

It was in the Shinto realm of ancestor worship that he derived the greatest pleasure in his beliefs. He frequently expressed to his sons the importance of honoring one's ancestors, which carried along with it the necessity of living so that one deserved the respect of one's own descendants.

"Never shame the family." That had been the motto of Kondo's life. Such a thing had happened once long ago. Kondo kept the awareness of that dishonor in his heart, both to condemn his great-great-grandfather and as an example of what would become of him or his sons should they dishonor their family in like manner. He rarely spoke of the disgrace, even to his older brother who knew the ancestral history as well or better than he. Like Kondo, his brother seldom spoke of the event that had been so painful to their great-grandfather as a child.

For twenty-five years Samuel had been a friend to Kondo. He never came to Japan but that he paid the man a visit and invited him to lunch or dinner. When Samuel first visited Japan, it was Kondo who had befriended him because Samuel had met his sister while serving a mission in Hawaii in 1948. Kondo's sister had moved to Hawaii after the war to be with her husband, an American naval career officer. Though their sister had mildly disgraced the family by marrying a foreigner, the family was finally able to resolve the issue after twenty years. The two brothers had made a special trip to Honolulu to forgive and reunite with their sister.

When Samuel became president of the Tokyo Mission, one of the first people he called on to pay his respects was Kondo, as the sister had requested him to do.

Samuel had attempted to teach the gospel during his first visit to Kondo and his family, but the man had politely rejected all over-tures to gospel involvement. His two teenage sons, however, listened to Samuel and the young missionaries, and willingly accepted the new religion that seemed so familiar to them. Their mother favored joining the Church as well, but declined baptism out of deference to her husband. Kondo had resisted further attempts to involve him in anything that might distract him from his devotion to his ancestors. Although his sons insisted that of all churches, The Church of Jesus Christ of Latter-day Saints did more to revere their ancestors than any religious group on the earth, Kondo gave a deaf ear to their logic. He never turned against Samuel; he was never rude, never loud. He simply refused—as Japanese males of the old order often did—to discuss religion with Samuel.

It was Kondo's way to communicate in silence and to refuse the gospel in a wordless exchange that Samuel came to understand. Kondo knew that social decorum allowed him to employ the best tool available: silence. If Samuel attempted to communicate his beliefs using verbal methods, then Kondo would not accommodate him.

Kondo's sons were entirely different. It was as if they possessed the deep-seated qualities of the older Japanese, yet were willing to change with the times. In fact, they were eager to move into a modern era, which included American schooling and missions as part of their commitment to the gospel. In the process, they left their father behind in their day-to-day activities. To their credit, they retained one all-important aspect of the old order: they always showed deep respect for their father.

Samuel knew that Kondo would circumvent speech that dealt directly with the LDS religion. So on his frequent visits, he never tried to impose his beliefs on the honored Japanese father. He understood clearly that his good friend Kondo would rather not discuss religion, at least not Samuel's religion.

Kondo was talkative about other subjects and spoke endlessly of trivia when he visited with Samuel, whom he admired greatly. Today their conversation was lively. Samuel knew that Kondo's attitudes, feelings, intuition, and emotions took precedence over mere reason. So on this visit, he decided to tell Kondo the purpose of his trip to Asia, including Japan.

"Kondo-san," Samuel began. He held his chopsticks in midair

as he addressed the man in Japanese. "I have been doing a great deal of traveling lately. I have been in search of something you may be interested in hearing about."

Kondo nodded. Samuel read the mood to be one of interest on the part of his friend. "Kondo-san, I am attempting to locate a lost group of people who left a history of their ancestors in the Americas in the book that your fine sons read."

Not giving the title of the book, Samuel described how he had come to realize that some of those people mentioned in the book had escaped the destruction which had came upon the land in the Americas. He was now searching the Pacific, he said, to determine their ultimate destination after their departure from the Americas.

"These courageous people departed from the American continent hundreds of years ago, when Japan was ruled by its first emperor."

Interested, Kondo listened carefully to the explanation of the type of people they were and the tragedy that they had left no record. He could discern his friend's genuine concern as to where they might have resettled. "Do you think there is a connection between my ancestors and the children of the people you speak of?" he asked curiously.

Samuel knew from Japanese history and culture what Kondo meant by the word *children*. It was clear that he was referring to the posterity of the lost people who could by now—two thousand years later—be an entire nation, or nations, of children.

"I cannot say for sure. I only know that there are people in the Pacific nations who may qualify. I should like to know more, so I have done a two-year study to satisfy myself of their whereabouts."

"I wish you well in your pursuit. I am afraid that a person of my limited knowledge would be of very little help to you in discovering these people. But if I can be of assistance, please feel free to call on me."

"I'm not certain just what information I may need or where I should probe. I have, however, narrowed my search to a specific people." Samuel left it at that, concluding with, "I appreciate your offer of assistance. Your son Takahashi will be of help to me. I thank you for being the father of such a fine young man."

Kondo bowed his head. His body language said "thank you" without his uttering a word.

"May I be so bold as to request that you accompany me on a visit to my temple this afternoon, Kondo-san?" Samuel spoke softly and with great respect for this man of dignity. "I wish to show you what it is we do there. It will only take an hour for us to make the visit."

"I have seen your temple. My sons have taken me there. It is perhaps a little difficult today," Kondo said, giving a faintly pained look, which Samuel realized meant "no." Kondo would not be so rude as to bluntly say no. That was not his way, nor the way of most anyone else of his generation. Samuel, however, got the message.

Chalk that up as a strike-out. Samuel's old American reality crept in as he changed the subject abruptly and asked Kondo about his family.

* * *

"WHAT DID YOUR FATHER WANT this afternoon?" Noriko, Takahashi Samura's wife of twelve years, asked as she cleared bright-colored bowls from the table. The boys had hungrily eaten their dinner of rice and fish, the latter from a large plastic platter of sushi that Takahashi's father had sent home with him after their meeting. Always keeping abreast of current trends in foods, the family enterprise had shifted into ready-to-eat fish dishes that they marketed throughout Tokyo. "A lucrative market," Takahashi's father had reminded him while they spoke together in his office.

The boys had devoured over half the sushi. Noriko covered the rest with plastic wrap and placed it in the small refrigerator next to the long counter in the kitchen/dining/living room. The primary living space of the apartment was centered in this all-purpose room, the walls of which were lined with tasteful built-in cabinets that stored books, videos, sound equipment, and a couple boxes of games. Takahashi had fit a small computer desk into one corner of the living space and wore earplugs when he worked to block out the sound of the TV. Space was always at a premium in the Samura apartment which, beyond this room, held only two bedrooms and a bathroom.

"He is feeling old and will retire soon," Takahashi said in answer to Noriko's question. "He wants to take my mother and go to Hawaii this year for a visit. He says my mother has wanted to go there since I was a little boy. I never knew that. I guess I never knew a lot of things."

"How wonderful that they are going!"

"And . . . they want the whole family to go along at his expense."

"Oh, my! Did you tell him where you and I are going next week? Can you get off to go a second time with the family?" Noriko asked, excited at the thought of going on not one, but two, extravagant vacations.

Takahashi glanced over at the boys, who knelt on the mat before the television set. "I couldn't bring myself to tell him. He was so excited about taking the whole family that I just didn't have the heart to make it seem less than significant to me. I will try my best to get the days off. The Church Education Department will probably understand. But still . . ." His voice trailed away.

"Well, the cruise *is* business, you know," Noriko reminded him, "at least for you. He would have understood. When is he thinking of taking all of us? That is costly for your parents."

"In three weeks."

"Three weeks? Does he think you can get off on such short notice? It's not like him to make such spontaneous decisions. Why hasn't he told you sooner?"

"I don't know, I didn't ask. It's crazy." Takahashi shook his head, still concerned about taking the time from work.

"He needs to know your plans."

"Maybe I'll tell him this weekend. But I know my father. Even if it is business related, he won't be pleased if the cruise keeps us from joining the family in Hawaii. I'll tell him this weekend or maybe Monday while he's at work. I have caused my father so much disappointment that when these little bumps in the road pop up, I try to soften them."

"You haven't changed your mind, have you?" Noriko wanted to know. "We are going on the yacht, aren't we? Sister Keiko is coming to stay with the children. I've already made all the arrangements to be gone for the week. Have I acted in haste?"

"Oh, I haven't changed my mind. The tickets and reservations are waiting for us at the airport. But that is a puzzle, too. I don't know what Dr. Polk has in mind while we're there."

"I'm sure he has nothing in mind for me, and I want to enjoy the pleasant breezes as we sail. Oh, Takahashi, Hawaii sounds wonderful, too. I could visit Agemaki."

"Who?"

"My girlfriend Agemaki. She married a man named Sukero from Hawaii. I would love to see her."

Takahashi wondered what Dr. Polk was trying to piece together. Dr. Polk had told him that President Meyers would also be going on the cruise, and Takahashi knew that the former mission president was interested in the origin of the Japanese people. With a sigh, Takahashi dropped the question from his mind and slipped down beside his two sons, ages nine and seven, both absorbed in their favorite show.

He told them that there was a good ball game coming on and asked if they wanted to watch. He got sour looks from both.

* * *

KATHERINE MOORE, A LADY OF MEANS and charm, knelt at the side of the headstone as the early morning fog gradually lifted. She carefully placed two dozen white roses in the receptacle at the base of the newly cut, gray granite stone. Though she could easily afford the finest, most ornate monument to memorialize her late husband, the Reverend Robert Moore, she had opted for a simple, elegant stone. And though she had desperately wanted to bury Bob in San Francisco's Holy Mother of Mercy cemetery, next to a plot reserved for her, she had bowed to the feelings of her daughter-in-law, Anney, and allowed the televangelist to be laid to rest beside his first wife, Nadia, in the plot that he had purchased for himself some years before.

Anney, Moore's daughter, would never know how it pained Katherine and how excluded she felt looking down on the two graves. It was as though her own marriage to Bob had been declared null and void. Katherine's lips trembled as her grief welled up, threatening to overcome her carefully controlled emotions.

Katherine had worn casual clothing to the graveside: canvas pants, a simple white shirt, coat, and loafers. She wasted no time wondering what people would think of her attire. Her grief was inside her heart and mind. It was not something she cared to display for the world.

Anney, standing next to her, wore her blond hair smoothed back behind her ears. She, too, was casual in a jean jacket and loose-fitting cotton knit pants that revealed her still-slim body. Her jacket felt snug and warm against the cool, foggy air that would disappear in minutes as soon as the August sun became stronger. It was always fascinating to Anney how the sun could evaporate the mist like a giant torch.

Katherine and Anney had driven to the cemetery together this morning. They both keenly felt the loss of a man they loved dearly, but for essentially different reasons. Katherine had found passion and strength and a deep sense of commitment to the man who had been laid to rest three weeks earlier. Anney, the minister's daughter, had for most of her life felt an awed reverence for her father, the Bay Area's master televangelist. To her he had been a holy man, endowed with a voice to match his great spirit. Working in her father's office, Anney knew the grief of literally thousands of worshippers who tuned in every Sunday morning to get their weekly helping of Christian spirituality from his sermons. Until recently, Bob Moore had seemed to be more than a mere man. But surprising disclosures had revealed that he had, after all, been made of clay—a mere mortal—subject to the same temptations and faults as others. She now thought of him as little more than simply her father and the grandfather of her children. Such a change in a relatively short time!

After Anney had been baptized into The Church of Jesus Christ of Latter-day Saints, that, along with a growing awareness of her father's less-than-honest actions, had made the difference—dramatically so. Still, both women mourned his passing. Anney's invalid mother had died a little over a year before, paving the way for Katherine to secure the reverend as her own, even though it had been for only a few months. Nevertheless, even Anney had known that it was a wonderful few months for both Katherine and her father.

"I think the stone is beautiful, Katherine," Anney murmured.

When Katherine didn't respond immediately, Anney turned to look at her, noticing at once that she was struggling to keep from crying.

"Oh, Katherine, you *are* upset that we buried my father here." She dropped to the ground and slipped her arms around her grieving friend's shoulders and drew her close. "Oh, dear, I was afraid you were being too gracious and brave. You always try to do what is best for others. Katherine, you know that he loved you. And his spirit isn't here, anyway. You know that. His spirit has gone to meet the God he loved to preach about."

Katherine's thin shoulders shook as she sobbed silently. At last she raised her head and managed a weak smile at Anney. "I know, I know," she whispered tremulously. She bent down and adjusted the fern that graced the roses, patting her eyes with a tissue as she turned to meet Anney's concerned scrutiny. "I do feel him close to me at times." She sighed and let her gaze slip to the grave next to Bob's, where Anney had placed a bouquet of fall flowers. "It is just hard . . . so hard . . . to see him here with someone else . . . with no place for me. I feel so alone again, with no family at all. Oh, there's my brother in Chicago, but we seldom see each other."

Anney stood up, holding out her hand to assist the older woman. "But Katherine," she protested, "we're still your family! We all love you. You have been so good to us. You have been a mother to me, a mother I haven't had for years, and we want to remain very close to you. The children are delighted with you . . . surely you have seen that. Stephen admires you so much. And, come to that, except for the kids, you're the only family we have, too."

Katherine smiled at her stepdaughter. "I think that of all the words I hear lately, the ones from you and Stephen referring to me as family, and the kids calling me Granny Katherine are the sweetest. I love all of you."

Anney reached out again and put her arm around Katherine's waist in a friendly hug.

"Oh dear," the elegant widow sighed, "if I stay here any longer, I will be reduced to more tears. My makeup will melt away and my heart will be heavy, heavy for the entire day. I have things to do, so if you don't mind, let's go back to the car." The two women started across the still-wet grass.

As they made their way toward Anney's vintage BMW parked on the asphalt under two very large magnolia trees, Anney said, "Just think, I'll be leaving for Samoa soon."

"You're going on Thursday? Are you okay for money? You know your father's estate, when it's settled, will be in the hundreds of thousands. Have you seen the will? It will all go to you and Stephen. I certainly don't need any of it."

When Anney shook her head in embarrassment, Katherine pursued the subject. "Well, if you have time when we get back, I'll show a copy of the will to you. We've all been so preoccupied of late."

She patted Anney's shoulder. She didn't find it necessary to add that she had paid off all of the reverend's debts, which came to over two hundred thousand dollars, and had maintained a running balance in his checking account of an additional three hundred thousand for his own personal needs. Now those funds would go to Anney and Stephen through her attorney, who had taken steps several months earlier to make a living trust and avoid inheritance taxes as much as possible.

Anney knew that Katherine was trying to make life a little easier for them financially. Her father, she knew, had run his ministry from month to month with little, if any, surplus of funds. He must have listened to Katherine over the past year and taken her advice. Anney suspected that Katherine had become his banker and financial adviser, though now was neither the time nor the place to get into finances. She would sort it out with Katherine later and come to some type of compromise on what was hers and what was really Katherine's.

She smiled at Katherine and said, "To answer your question about leaving, I'm actually scheduled to leave Wednesday evening. Everybody will be on board by Thursday, and we will be out to sea by late Thursday afternoon, if all goes as Stephen has planned it— thanks to you. He called me yesterday and said the ship is incredible! He really likes the captain and crew. Actually, he loves everything about the yacht. It's more than he expected in his wildest dreams. The best part is that I get to go, too, once again, thanks to you." Katherine merely smiled graciously.

"I'll meet Dr. Polk and his assistant, Roy, at the San Francisco airport, and then Dr. Polk and I will travel on together to Samoa. He's still in a wheelchair, you know, and might need a little help.

"But, oh, I hate to leave Brenda and Todd. I feel like I haven't spent nearly enough time with Brenda this summer, what with the conference we held in Park City. I'm afraid she's felt a little alone. She did spend the last two weeks with us and that helped, but I need to devote the entire week to her after we get back. We need to shop and get her ready to return to school at Redlands."

Katherine stopped and took hold of Anney's arm. "I have an idea. Do you think Brenda and Todd would like to come over to my place in San Francisco next weekend? I have plenty of room, and I'd love to plan some wonderful things to do with the two of them."

"Katherine, I wasn't hinting for you to babysit my two college-age children. I was just telling you what—"

"Anney, I've been looking for a reason to have them over so I could get closer to them. What better time? How should I invite them?"

"Well, if you really want to do that, I'll ask them for you. Oh, you know what? That won't work. Max is coming up this weekend to visit. I'm not sure Brenda will accept your invitation."

"Well, Max is welcome, too. He and Todd can share the guest room."

"Are you sure? I know Todd is dying to see your penthouse. I heard Dad describe it to him while they were together early this summer. I know they have good friends in Lafayette and don't lack for things to do, but who knows? They may find it a real kick to stay at Granny Katherine's place. I'll ask them and get back to you."

Anney and Katherine were off the freeway and heading up Montgomery Street toward Nob Hill and Katherine's penthouse when Katherine spoke. "You know, your father and I had scheduled the yacht for next week," she said sadly. "We planned to spend a couple of weeks leisurely sailing from island to island. How wonderful it would have been . . . It breaks my heart even to think about it. I could never go alone, and I don't feel up to inviting friends to go with me. They don't understand how I feel—they all divorce their husbands. I am glad your Dr. Polk mentioned his need for a secluded gathering place to me. It is good that someone can use the time."

Anney's father had told her about the arrangements for their planned cruise several months before. He had even talked about the possibilities of filming a sermon for his weekly telecast using the locals on one of the islands. He was hardly the romantic Katherine was, Anney thought wryly.

"All I can say is thanks again for the use of your ship. For us, it is a very big deal."

"Well, it's not exactly my ship. It belongs to a syndicate that my first husband formed. For most of the year, the yacht is chartered. Believe me, that is the only way I would hold on to such an expensive piece of machinery. It's purely an investor's scheme, and, as it is, we barely break even." Katherine's hands made a gesture of dismissal as she said, "Honey, it's a business, and I happen to use it a couple of weeks a year. I don't want to go, so I'm glad someone else can make use of it."

"I wish you would reconsider going, Katherine. It would do you a world of good to be out on the ocean with us."

"You don't need me cluttering up your meetings. No, if your kids come to spend the weekend with me, that will cheer my spirits. I love being around young adults. They are so full of life and adventure."

CHAPTER FIVE

Family Discussions

Tokyo

TAKAHASHI WISHED HE HAD LEFT HIS OFFICE AN HOUR EARLIER. Working hard to get things in order so he could leave for the cruise, he had stayed late to speak with an instructor at the institute of religion and to finish his monthly reports. Even at that, they were still not completed. Now his car was stopped dead still in the late afternoon Tokyo traffic.

One of the perks of working for the Church was that he could usually avoid driving during rush hour, but he had needed to wait until the close of the class period to give directions to the young instructor. As coordinator and institute director, he could usually select the time of day he was on the road, so he seldom had to contend with the commuter gridlock. Although he loved his job, what he hated most about living in Tokyo idled all around him—five lanes wide and hundreds of cars deep.

Whiling away the moment, Takahashi wondered again why Dr. Polk had invited him to a gathering on a yacht. It sounded a little off the wall, but Dr. Polk had assured him that all expenses would be covered by a Book of Mormon foundation. So whatever the pressing business, at least he and Noriko would get a free vacation on the high seas. He had contacted his superiors in the Church Educational System and was pleased that the trip met with their approval. They knew of Dr. Polk and his studies of the Book of Mormon, and thought it would be a good experience for one involved in Church religious instruction to attend. They were more than understanding on such short notice.

Takahashi knew the gathering was neither job related nor a Church assignment. Dr. Polk had assured him of that. Then what was it all about? Why was the venerable religion professor so vague about the purpose of the gathering? That's what he had called it, a gathering—not a conference, not a seminar, but a "gathering."

And now his father had asked him to drop by his office again. Why today of all days when Kondo had summoned him only a few days before to tell him of the planned family vacation? But it would be extremely rude of Kondo's second son not to make an appearance.

It was a constant sore spot to his father that Takahashi had gone to a university—Brigham Young University—in the United States, then had not returned home to take his proper place in the business. Still, in spite of his father's displeasure, Takahashi knew that his father was proud of him for completing his master's degree. His father seemed even more pleased that he had married well and now had two children of his own. Takahashi's job was not a disgrace to the family; it was merely outside their traditional labors, disrupting the father-son tradition of the past three generations. Kondo did not pretend to understand his son's job with the LDS Church Educational System. He could not resist repeatedly reminding his son that he would have been much more pleased if Takahashi had brought his education back to the giant fish market and stepped into a management position like his brother. The implication was there: Suki honored his father.

Takahashi knew that had he plunged into the fish-selling business, he would be making twice the money he was earning in the Church Educational System. But money was not the dominating factor in his choice of a lifetime occupation. Though it was hard for his father to understand, Takahashi felt great satisfaction in his work.

Takahashi cast his eyes to the traffic far ahead of him and was relieved to see that at last it was beginning to inch forward. Only three more blocks to the off-ramp to the *Tsukiji*, the great Tokyo fish market. The traffic would probably clear out to a moderate speed by the time he left his father's office and headed home. He hoped so.

Takahashi had taken a different path than his friends. He had spent too much time in America to have maintained a close relationship with his former teenage school friends. He sensed that to his old friends there was something eerie about him. And though attitudes were changing, in Japan it was still thought to be an unhealthy sign if anyone truly mastered the English language. Japanese students all over town practiced their English on English-speaking tourists, but they were merely playing at the English language. Takahashi knew English well and spoke it fluently. He had spoken English with only a little accent long before he completed his LDS mission to New England; his English had improved even more when he had studied for his master's degree at Brigham Young University. In addition to his fluency in English, Takahashi was employed by Americans.

So, aware that others viewed him with suspicion, Takahashi was forever on his guard. He was careful to assume a quiet demeanor among his family and friends, especially those outside the Church who were constantly looking for what they interpreted as a change in his taste or behavior. Try as he might, Takahashi was never able to conceal his cosmopolitan manner and tastes from his father. Face it—he was now part western.

"Father, I should have told you last Friday that Noriko and I are going on a cruise. I am sorry you learned about it from President Meyers at lunch today. Truly, I am sorry." Takahashi bowed before his father, who had risen from his desk—piled with ledgers, orders, and other stacks of paper—to bow in response.

Takahashi's father was not a large man. Nor was Takahashi. Due to his slight frame, the aging executive looked even smaller than his five-foot, six-inch height. Dressed in a dark silk western suit, he looked like the minister of Japan. His hair was streaked with gray, and the lines in his brow and cheeks pronounced him to be what he was—a seventy-year-old man about to retire and enjoy the fruits of his labors.

"You knew about this trip when I invited you to go with the family to Maui. Why did you not tell me then that you were going away on a ship even before our proposed vacation to Hawaii? How will you be able to take time from your work to do both?"

"It was stupidity on my part, Father. When I came in last week, you were so excited about taking all of us to Hawaii that I didn't want to diminish your own plan. Does that sound like an honorable excuse? I meant no harm, and I am trying to find a way to do both."

"It is a minor thing, but it demonstrates poor character on your part. I think you have been influenced too much by those you work with."

Takahashi knew before coming to see his father that the older man would again shame him and imply disgrace on the family that he had not continued with the fish trade. He tried to take it in stride but felt the sting nevertheless.

"You are not too old to take counsel from your elders. I wish you to know that you erred in not telling me directly of your plans when they had impact on my feelings. Do not hesitate to speak up, even if it does 'diminish an old man's dream,' as you say. Forthrightness is the hallmark of our family."

Takahashi knew only too well that his great-great-grandfather had shamed the family in the last century when he refused to draw the sword at a *seppuku* ceremony. That was old history and Takahashi couldn't care less.

"You must not let your supposed feelings of gentleness interfere with your duty to be forthright."

"Father, I take your counsel." Takahashi bowed in reverence to his elder.

The father reluctantly accepted his son's apology. He grunted to himself as he bowed.

* * *

SAMUEL HAD HOPED FOR A QUIET EVENING and a simple American meal at his sister's high-rise apartment in Tokyo. Instead, his brother-in-law had rounded up a tux and convinced him that he should go along with them to the embassy—to a full state dinner in honor of the Director General of Nippon Corporation International. Samuel felt it was the price of having a brother-in-law high in international diplomacy.

The Americans were honoring a revered Japanese corporate head for his "dynamic vision" to construct one of the largest truck-manufacturing complexes in the heartland of America with total control of the new company residing in the corporate nerve center in Tokyo.

The embassy's black-tie dinner was the sort of affair that Samuel usually went considerably out of his way to avoid. However, since this was to be his only night in Tokyo with his sister, he would acquiesce to her request and suffer a few hours of paying tribute to the Japanese industrial takeover of America. As his Idaho congressman friend recently stated, "They already own Hawaii, Brazil, and Peru. What more do they want!"

The prophecy is kicking in, thought Samuel. Why not observe the initial fulfillment and watch the dazzled Americans pay homage to a nation of such spectacular achievements that they could only be described by the West as a people without flaws?

The western-style dinner had been served, the plates removed from the tables. Samuel knew he would have to pay the price of a good meal by enduring the oratory praises heaped upon the industrial giant who had condescended to build a megabuck plant in America. Sam patiently suffered through the hour-long tribute and was grateful when it appeared that the final comments by the Ambassador of the United States were in progress.

How much like sheep Americans are, Samuel thought, not that he disagreed with the hostile takeover that was coming. The Gentiles would have to become part of the covenant people or suffer the consequences. Parts of Asia were in clear pursuit of world economic power and wherever that power would lead them. It was incredible that such things could happen to a nation so blessed and prepared. Many saw it as a "clear and present danger" to the Gentiles of the Americas.

Samuel was aware that somewhere along the powerful and pervasive climb of the Pacific Rim countries, Japan being the center point, the West began falling all over itself to proclaim the marvel called the "Miracle of the Orient." Samuel listened as the ambassador lavished praise on Japanese management techniques and their technological skills. *At least some of the Gentiles are succumbing joyously to the marvel of the hostile takeover by the Orient,* he thought to himself as the ambassador droned on.

Samuel deduced that what the Japanese had failed to complete at Pearl Harbor by force, they were quietly accomplishing while bowing with outward regard for the preservation of a new century of worldwide economic growth. They would garner it through the international trade table, while other countries—the United States resting at the top of the heap—drowned in red ink. Around the Pacific Rim, funds were accumulating in the trillions and had been doing so for the past decade or more, particularly in this fair Land of the Rising Sun.

The West would soon rethink its exaggerated impression of the Asian might and wonder what on earth happened to cause Japan to become so financially powerful, Samuel thought. He evaluated the scene at the embassy from his vantage point of prophecy, as if he were watching a Greek tragedy. He saw all too real previews of coming events. Despite his awareness of what was happening to the West, he still loved the Japanese people. He embraced the culture, himself under the spell of dignity they brought to the world. He had learned to love them when he was yet a child. He still saw the nation of Japanese people through the eyes of his father. Samuel and his father readily forgave them their premature aggression in World War II.

Still, for all of Japan's extraordinary culture that formed its national character, Samuel felt he knew its intimate texture of life from years of living among the Japanese. He also understood that, as honorable and clean as the Japanese were, they possessed a few rigid characteristics: absolute hierarchy, as witnessed at the head table this evening where industrialists of lesser rank were required to bow and scrape to the noble few; conformity by the masses to a standard of conduct no matter how ludicrous; and the expectation of submission to group. They also possessed an insufferable sense of national uniqueness. But somehow it was these virtues turned into flaws that made them into the powerhouse that they had become. Were the members of the Church all that much different? After a searching evaluation of the LDS culture, Samuel thought not.

As he pondered life in the real world, Samuel shook his head. Indeed, there ought to be concern by the Gentiles of America for Japan's economic challenge to the West. Hey, they were taking over, and it seemed that nothing Americans did would stop that. What was it Christ had predicted in the writings of 3 Nephi as he stood on the temple steps at Bountiful?

> And . . . my people who are a remnant of the house of Jacob
> go forth among the Gentiles, . . . and shall be in the midst of
> them who shall be many; and . . . shall be among them as a lion
> among the beasts of the forest, and as a young lion among the
> flocks of sheep, who, if he go through both treadeth down and
> teareth in pieces, and none can deliver.

That's what he predicted, and that is surely what is happening, Samuel sighed.

Sitting in the long, black Buick headed back to Shirley and Nathan's place in northeast Tokyo, Samuel realized that he was weary to the bone from traveling continuously and sleeping in such a variety of beds. It would be strictly Western accommodations tonight, he knew. He had become so accustomed to a floor mat that he hoped he could sleep on an innerspring mattress.

"Well, you have really hopped around Asia these past several months, Sam," Nathan ventured, pulling away into traffic. "Did you solve your father's riddle of where the Nephites can be found?" Nathan's tone betrayed a slight edge of cynicism. Usually, Nathan was pure gentleman, smooth as the finest Japanese silk. The remark was intentional and hit somewhere lower than Samuel's belt.

Samuel sensed that what his brother-in-law really meant was, "How is your silly wild-goose chase progressing?" though he didn't say as much, of course.

"Been okay, Nathan."

Shirley sat listening from the back seat, not saying a word.

Nathan made a sharp turn up Shimizu highway and swept across two lanes to make a left on to Daidokoro, then headed straight for the basement garage under their building. It cost the U.S. taxpayers a hefty $1,200 a month to park Nathan's Buick.

"A little voice of caution, my dear brother," Nathan warned. "Whatever you've found out about all the predictions you claim are in the scriptures that are ostensibly being fulfilled, if I were you, I would tread lightly about how I release this information." Nathan had served as a mission president in Hong Kong ten years earlier and knew from experience the ways of the LDS Church culture. Nathan tapped the steering wheel nervously. It was obvious that it troubled him to speak so frankly with his brother-in-law, especially since Samuel was his senior by eight years.

"All I'm saying, Sam, is be careful. You know you do not represent the Church in any of these studies you've made. It is strictly you and your friend Polk—"

". . . Oh yes, Sam," Shirley spoke up from the rear, wrapped in a silk shawl and made up to look ten years younger than her sixty-three years. Not one to enjoy any sort of confrontational conversation, she hoped to turn the topic in a different direction. "How is Peter? Did he recover fully from that tragic stroke?"

"He's fine, Shirley, not a hundred percent, but doing pretty well. I spoke with him by phone last night. He has a little problem with his speech, but his mind is as sharp as ever."

Then, ignoring his sister, Samuel turned his head toward his brother-in-law, who was now within a hundred yards of the garage. "Nathan, don't worry about me. I'm as committed to sustaining the Prophet and the Brethren as I have ever been. I simply feel that what I have been uncovering ought to be given a fair hearing, at least in private. I will put it away immediately if I am asked to do so. But to hold a skull session with a small group of interested members is not so world shaking. Wouldn't you agree?"

"Perhaps, but in that group someone could surface who will not buy all that you are peddling. They could go public and distort the intent of the group."

"Are you worried about the family image, or me, or both?"

Nathan shook his large head as the Buick dipped into the lower-level driveway and stopped at the gate, which silently retracted for the car to pass through. "I've said my piece," he said shortly.

* * *

As HE FEARED, SAMUEL DIDN'T SLEEP WELL on the expensive American bed in the guest room of his sister's apartment. He got up finally before dawn and used the bathroom, then walked back to the small table near the window. Slumping into the narrow chair, he clicked on the bedside lamp and reached into his case to retrieve his Book of Mormon. He opened its pages to the marker he had placed in Alma the night before. It bothered him that Nathan would caution him about conducting a session to discuss the promises and the whereabouts of the Nephites today. First, it was not Nathan's affair; second, Nathan might be right. Samuel and Polk just might be overstepping their authority a tad.

"Nonsense!" he blurted out. It would be a private group involved in private communication on the scriptures. *After all*, he reminded himself, *the Lord commanded us to study the scriptures, particularly Isaiah.*

CHAPTER SIX

Eric's Concerns

Hawaii

WHEN ERIC KUMANI SAW THE LARGE MAHI MAHI beautifully served on the silver platter—rubbed with olive oil and garnished with lettuce, parsley, and lemons—he nodded his approval. Seafoods were his specialty, and no one among the finer restaurants along Supuro prepared seafoods with any greater care or love of the profession than Eric, whose father had done the same.

Attired in a traditional flowered Hawaiian shirt and light blue slacks, with thick, wiry, black hair and wide facial features, Eric, at thirty-seven, still retained the youthful exuberance he had flashed as a teen at surfing contests on Waikiki Beach. His roots plunged back five generations into the LDS faith. It was his great-great-grandfather who ran to the edge of the water and swam out to meet George Q. Cannon on that fateful day in 1852 when the Church missionaries came ashore to be greeted by the natives of this paradise on earth.

Often on a busy evening, Eric circulated among the restaurant patrons and made light talk, asking how the food tasted, if they needed more wine, was the shrimp delectable, were they enjoying their stay in Hawaii? It was that constant, friendly patter that Eric had refined since his early teens, plus excellent food, that brought patrons in the door and compelled them to return week after week to sustain this four-star establishment.

As the young waiter carrying the platter of Mahi Mahi passed in front of him, Eric smiled. Taking his thumb and first two fingers, he pressed them to his lips and tossed the hand in the waiter's direction.

"Tell me, Eric," one of the comfortable-looking tourists asked after Eric had inquired if the food was satisfactory and received an enthusiastic reply from the party of eight, "are you native Hawaiian?"

"'Bout as native as they come, sir."

"Where did the Hawaiians come from, anyway?"

"Straight out of heaven. We liked it so much, we recreated it right here, you know."

Eric's comment brought laughter from everyone near enough to hear his reply over the din of dishes, music, and conversation from the dozens of linen-covered tables that graced the large dining room.

Eric patted the patron's shoulder and moved on to the next party. It was a good evening, reservations only.

Even as he made his way among his patrons, Eric's thoughts returned to his family. He felt a little twinge of regret that he had been so sharp with his son Cory, who was fifteen and not doing all that well in school lately. Then there was the little matter of coming in late last night. Before Eric had left the house and driven to the restaurant, he had scolded the boy during dinner.

Eric made a point of eating dinner each evening with his family before coming to the restaurant. It made good sense to him, even though he could easily have dinner brought to his office located off the galley way at the back of the restaurant. Now he wished he had handled the matter with a little more diplomacy. Eric wished he had approached the problem differently, rather than chewing Cory out in front of his three younger sisters. *Nobody said it would be easy to be a parent, but it probably would be less of a hassle if I just had more patience with that kid*, he thought.

Eric stepped back into his office to phone home and apologize to Cory. It was never easy for Eric to make apologies. *Why? It makes me feel stupid? Maybe. Insecure? I doubt it. I just don't like to admit fault.* That was what Carol, his wife of seventeen years, had told him a couple of times: "Eric, it's your pride. Get over that and you'll do just fine as a father."

His own father was so mellow and easy to talk to. Why didn't he have that same relationship with his son? Was it just because the times were more intense? Eric pressed "1" and the pound sign on his memory telephone system. Within a few seconds Carol picked up the phone at the other end of the line.

"I'm sorry about this evening. I shouldn't have jumped Cory so hard about his studies. Sweetheart, would you tell him that I called and said I was sorry? You can do it better than I can," Eric coaxed.

Carol listened. "Don't you think you ought to talk to him yourself? Come on, Eric. Don't lay this on me. I agree you needed to pull him up short, but not at dinner and not with that loud, demanding voice you let fly. No, I think you ought to tell him yourself."

Eric sighed and agreed that she was right. Why was he shifting this thing over to Carol? Here he went again, protecting his pride. If she told Cory what he asked her to say, he could save face—very Japanese. But he knew he was not Japanese and, further, that Carol was not going to convey the message.

"Okay, get him on the phone. I'll talk to him."

"Before I do . . . just after you left the house, Dr. Polk called here from his home in Provo."

"Is there a hitch in the plans?"

"Oh no. He says the plans for the gathering are final, and he hopes you can still make it. He said it looks like the group will meet in Samoa and sail around the islands on a yacht."

"A yacht?"

"That's what he said, a yacht. I can take it."

"What else did he say?"

"He said the tickets are under your name at the check-in desk. Want to talk to Cory now?"

"Okay." Eric knew the conversation with his son would be short and guarded. He could run three restaurants with greater ease than he could handle this one son.

"Son . . . ah . . . I just called to say . . . well, to say I'm sorry I jumped you at dinner tonight. I still think we needed to talk, but I . . . I guess I picked the wrong time."

There was a moment of silence. Then the boy said, "Okay, Dad."

Eric detected no warmth, just a simple "okay." It wasn't okay. It took a lot for him to admit that he had been wrong in his approach, but sometimes the kid needed to be jerked up by his pants. How else would he learn?

"You mean, I guess, that you accept my apology?"

"Yeah, Dad. Sure."

Eric got the distinct impression that his oldest child wanted to get off the phone. Neither felt comfortable about the whole incident.

"Well, I just wanted—"

"Dad, you don't know how good I really am!" the boy exploded. Young Cory's voice cracked slightly as he spoke. "I don't do anything bad. I'm not into drugs or drinking. You jumped on me because I stayed out late with those guys. I didn't do anything wrong. We were at a movie—just a stinkin' ol' movie. It wasn't even a good movie."

"I know that now. But you should have called to let us know you would be a little late. We worry about you. Besides, you know you're the teachers quorum president."

"So? You're just afraid of what the ward will think! The bishop's kid is out after midnight. Wow!"

Eric had the urge to lash out at his smart-mouthed kid, but he held back and said instead, "Do you have any idea what it's like to have a kid out after midnight, cruising around with all that goes on these days? Just check in, okay?"

It was the same ground he had covered at the dinner table, only earlier he had raised his voice and made threats about making Cory stay home for the next month—grounded. Eric bit his tongue to keep from throwing out the ultimatum again. Again there was a pause, then Cory finally said, "Yeah, Dad. I know. And, Dad . . ."

"What, son?"

"Thanks for calling."

"Do you have any idea how much your mother loves you? You're her first. It ain't easy being a new parent."

"Bye."

"See ya."

Eric hung up. He sat looking out at the kitchen through the glass window that offered an unobstructed view of the gas ranges, the smoke, and the three chefs standing over them. He wished he had said to Cory, "Do you know how much *I* love you?" Why bring Carol into the picture? She didn't get into it with Cory. *He* did. And he should have had the guts to say so. But the wall that had sprung up between them was getting too high, way too high. He couldn't bring himself to say the words and reduce the size of the wall.

Eric sighed. All this was too deep to get into right now. He had a restaurant to run.

* * *

MARIA CHARITY ALMANAR, WIDOW, mother of one adult daughter, professor of Religious Studies at Brigham Young University, was strict, brisk, proper, and totally knowledgeable in her field. The men who had for centuries questioned a female's ability to lead hadn't met Maria. Her smile was disarming, but her ability to move a committee to action was legendary. In short, she was respected, if not admired, by all members of the department. Even the dean stayed on his toes around Maria. She had a way of making you feel you knew less than you thought you did.

Maria could intimidate, but Polk, during his years before retirement, had never allowed himself to spar with this woman of superior knowledge and quick wit. He was far too interested in the students and too little concerned about academic infighting to let anyone browbeat him. He and Maria had met often over the years at conferences, symposia, and other affairs. Polk admired her quick mind. She had never been a thorn in his side. But then, Maria had never dealt with someone like Polk who simply had no interest in the prevailing preoccupation of clawing to the top.

She liked Dr. Polk, though he had some irritating qualities. One that she especially disliked was his genteel way, which seemed affected to her. Another was his passive attitude toward pushing academic standards to a higher level. He was too absorbed in his own world, researching and studying, to make the department into what it should have been. But he was basically a good man. She had observed that while he was with the Brigham Young University Religion Department, he had a way of leveling the atmosphere among the professors and instructors. He was able to diffuse the prevailing academic jealousy so that prima donnas dropped their poses while in his circle.

Perhaps that explained why Maria had wholeheartedly accepted the invitation to attend a week's session with Polk and his group.

Whatever it was that he wanted to discuss at the meeting, he hadn't imparted it to her. She wondered what could possibly be so secretive about such a meeting. He had indicated that at least four others, plus a couple of wives, would be meeting in Samoa to begin a cruise on a private yacht. If anyone had asked, Maria would have confessed that spending a week on the ocean doing what she liked best—academic debate—sounded altogether worthwhile.

Maria liked teaching at BYU. She was even comfortable in Provo, Utah, and appreciated the small-town atmosphere. The mountains were so beautifully majestic any season of the year. From the front window of her small house in Oak Hills, she had a picture-perfect view of Mount Timpanogos. It was the one mountain she loved most in this world. At home, she frequently took the time to gaze out her window. But in her office on the ground floor of the Joseph Smith Building, she had neither a decent view nor time to spare. On average, she spent five and a half days a week in that building—researching, preparing materials, lecturing, or correcting papers.

A quick rap at the door to her office preceded the appearance of a head around the doorjamb. "Hey, Maria."

"Come in, Judy."

Judy occupied a small office two doors down the hall. She was relatively young—thirty-four—single, with a doctorate in LDS Church history.

"Can we talk?"

"Sure, sit down." It was early morning on Friday with no classes until 11 o'clock. Except for papers she had to correct, Maria certainly had time to talk with the young woman who had become her best friend. They shared everything, nothing held back—not that there was all that much to hold back. The two lived cloistered lives of research, teaching, and endless meetings.

"I heard that you've been invited to the Sanderson home for dinner," Judy said in her coy voice, knowing there would be some single men from other departments to meet, converse with, and perhaps date. Maria had already been that route. She was content with life as it was. Widowed for twenty-two years now, she knew that the flower of her youth had passed. So what? She liked her life in accelerated gear and her crowded academic schedule. She didn't need any more social contacts than she already had. She had a couple of gentlemen friends who squired her to special functions, such as academic dinners, concerts, and balls. She really needed no more. Nevertheless, people like Judy were constantly trying to "line her up" with some eligible single man.

Maria smiled. "Did I tell you that I've been invited to a small gathering—with who knows whom—on a yacht in a couple of days? One person we both know will be there . . . Peter Polk."

"I thought he died."

"Heavens no. He had a stroke. Judy, my gosh, don't go spreading such things."

"I haven't. I just thought he died last year."

"I spoke to the dean and have his blessing to be part of the gathering. We'll be sailing among the islands of the South Pacific for a few days."

Maria explained to her speechless department associate that Dr. Polk had invited her to join his carefully selected group. His foundation would pick up the expenses. "All he insists on is for me to come with an open mind."

"It must be fun to be in demand," Judy sighed with real envy.

"I wish I knew what it was all about." A small crease furrowed Maria's brow. "I'm going, but I'm not endorsing anything that goes against my grain."

Judy laughed and rolled her eyes. "I never dreamed you would. Heavens! What in the world could Dr. Polk present that would be hard for you to endorse, anyway?"

* * *

"MOTHER, HOW CAN YOU ASK US to spend the weekend at Granny Katherine's? My weekend's booked with the guys. I don't need to go to some relative's house while you sail around paradise with Dad." Todd pressed his point with his mother, Anney, while she sat with him, sharing a late-evening snack in the kitchen.

"Todd, I know you want to have your weekend for yourself, but think about it: she is so lonely and just wants to love her grandchildren. She was great to invite Max, too."

"Yeah, that's one bright spot. But Mom, come off it. Who are you kidding? She's not really our grandmother."

"She wants to be."

"Fine," Todd said in exasperation. He yanked the cupboard open, grabbed a box of cereal, then turned and leaned against the sink. "If you really want to know, I have a problem calling her 'Granny Katherine.' I like her well enough. She's cool and one of the best-looking grannies around, but get real, Mother. Spend the whole weekend with her and my sister?"

"You know, for a young man who suddenly felt humbled by what you learned at Park City and asked to be baptized, you sure have taken a different tack here at home."

"Mom, that isn't fair! Don't give me a guilt trip. I'm not buying that." He dropped the box of cereal down on the counter.

Brenda walked into the kitchen just as Todd uttered the words *guilt trip*. "Who's feeling a guilt trip?"

"I'm talking to Mom, Brenda. Butt out," Todd muttered, growling at his older sister. She was unfazed by his attitude.

Todd opened the refrigerator door and retrieved a half-gallon plastic jug of milk. He pushed the fridge door shut and turned on his mother. "I see this as something a guy ready to enter college should not be asked to do. Let me tell you, if it weren't for the fact that Max will be there as well, you could chalk me off."

"Oh, so that's what you're all steamed about. I think it will be great to spend a weekend in San Francisco," Brenda said sweetly.

"Well, I don't . . . and I think Dad would agree with me."

"Todd, I think you should go." Anney's voice had that maternal tone of command which Todd had heard periodically all of his life, and he recognized that he had not yet outgrown—if ever he would—the control his mother had over him.

In frustration he blurted out, "Man!" He reached up and lifted a large cereal bowl out of the cupboard, slammed it onto the counter, and poured a healthy portion of Apple Jacks into it. He took a deep breath and turned to look at his mother, swinging the jug of milk at his side. "Okay, you win. But, and I *mean* but, . . . we have to come home Sunday morning. I want to attend church. Okay?"

"Well," Brenda insisted, "you'll have to come home on your own, because I want to stay until Monday morning. I'll be seeing Max off later Sunday evening. It's so exciting to think of spending the weekend with Max." Brenda turned her flushed face toward her mother and asked, "Do you like Max? I mean . . . you know . . . really, *really* like him?"

"Yes, I do like him. He's so bright he scares me," Anney said, keeping up the conversation.

Satisfied with her mother's endorsement of her boyfriend, Brenda chattered on. "Have you seen how large the windows are in Granny Katherine's penthouse, especially in the bedroom? At night you can look out over the whole northeast section of the city and see the lights of the Golden Gate Bridge and—"

"You can also see Alcatraz," Todd interrupted, "and that's exactly the way I see that place—my weekend prison."

"Oh, you're not going to stay at her place all the time," Anney beamed. "She wants you two to make up a list of places to go and things you want to see."

"Great, I take my sister and my granny along with me to some hot place. That ought to look swell."

"The people won't know Brenda is your sister," Anney consoled him. "It will look like you have a beautiful date for the evening. Anyway, I've had enough of this. You had better pour your milk before you drop that jug."

Todd knew he had pleased his mother by consenting to go. As his frustration abated, he realized that going out on the town with a wealthy granny didn't sound half bad, but pride kept him from admitting it.

CHAPTER SEVEN

Proud Heritage

Oaxaca, Southern Mexico

AT FORTY-THREE, HE HAD RISEN TO BECOME a man of means and influence, not only in his business of banking and finance, but in the LDS Church as well. The community accepted José Manuel Rodriguez as a man of his word and a careful financier; in certain circles, they also respected his religious beliefs. In the Oaxaca Valley of southern Mexico, Manuel's roots plunged deep into the cultural background of the valley. As near as anyone could tell, his Zapotec blood (lightly sprinkled with that of a Spaniard or two along the line) had sprung into prominence hundreds of years before and represented a proud heritage.

Manuel knew from tradition and legend that his family was never eminently important in the valley, but their Lamanite blood flowed back hundreds of years. The Church taught that his people were those who punished the Nephites for disobeying God's commandments. It was his people who remained on the land, in place, ready to receive the gospel in these last days from the Gentiles who had the book. Yes, Manuel's was a proud history.

Manuel's Aereo México Flight 56, still on the ground in the capital, was bound for Oaxaca terminal. It stood parked at the ramp like a perched eagle with its two Rolls Royce jet engines purring. Delays again. Manuel had boarded the plane half an hour before at Gate 62 of Mexico City's crammed international airport. He had earlier feared, as he rushed to the airport, that he might miss his flight home to Oaxaca. What a laugh!

He had learned minutes ago that the governor of Oaxaca, a friend of Manuel's and an influential man in the capital of Mexico as well as at home, had been delayed at the President's council meeting. And so, naturally, the large jet aircraft waited at the gate while the governor made his way to the airport from downtown Mexico City. Once he was on board, the plane would take off immediately. If there were other flights ahead of the governor's plane, they would be held on the tarmac while the governor's flight took first position.

That was the way things were done in Mexico. Influence was everything. Political figures of the governor's status were accorded favors that semi-ordinary citizens like Manuel never experienced. It would be unthinkable for the pilot not to wait for the governor.

As Manuel sat impatiently in his window seat and watched the flight attendants bustle about to keep the passengers calm with beverages and smiles, he wondered how it would feel to be so powerful in government. He had had a slight taste of it as an assistant to the Minister of Finance two years ago when he had agreed to serve in Washington, D.C., among Mexico's powerful banking lobbyists.

He had been selected in part because of his ability to speak excellent English. Not only had he studied the language while attending San Diego State College twenty years ago, but he had also served a two-year mission for the Church in London. These experiences had allowed him to converse easily in precise English with American legislators. Manuel's stint in Washington lasted two years. When the doldrums set in, he and his wife decided that the pressure of Washington politics was too rich for their Latin blood and they came home.

An occasional advisor to the finance minister, he could always tell the political bureaucracy exactly what he thought on issues since he had no political future at stake. There was no chance that his paycheck would be held hostage if his opinions were not shared. The finance minister was constantly asking him when he would move to Mexico City. He had all the potential for a high government job— connections in the States, a knowledge of the workings of Mexican finance, and a compatible friendship with all the powerful bankers from El Paso to Ecuador. The finance minister had urged Manuel to join them.

"We need an honest man like you," he told Manuel.

Admiring the finance minister's roomy office, Manuel nevertheless shook his head. "You don't want an honest man like me; at least some of the financial heads in this country don't."

"The Presidente has his eyes on you. I know, I meet with him nearly every day. Think about it, Manuel. The pay will be good, and you can return to your precious Oaxaca in a few years and be a powerful man."

"I am a powerful man in the valley already. Ask the workers in the fields around Oaxaca. They'll tell you that José Manuel Rodriguez *es muy rico y un hombre bastante grandísimo.*"

"A very rich and great man," the finance minister had laughingly repeated. "Yes, indeed!" Manuel had joined in his laughter.

"*Cuidado,*" the finance minister had said and touched the corner of his right eye, body language for *be careful.* "El Presidente has asked very specific questions of me about your qualifications. What could I do but level with him? I told him you are one of several bankers who are *banditos* that, sooner or later, will rob the country blind. That ought to hold him at bay, so you can go on enjoying your precious Oaxaca."

They parted at the office door with handshakes. Little did Manuel realize that the two would never meet again.

Seated on the plane, Manuel slipped back to reality. *Where is the governor? How could he be so thoughtless as to hold up a hundred people while carrying out some small business of state? More likely, they are deciding when to throw a high-level bash in Oaxaca.* Governors and presidents never explained anything to the public.

Manuel sighed in frustration. He remembered an LDS book that he had picked up in Salt Lake City at the Crossroads Mall. Its theme was patience and how to manage one's emotions to allow for this marvelous gift from the Lord. In the scriptures, the Lord had actually instructed the members to be patient. The words of the book came rushing back to him, and he found that he could actually relax and accept that the world would still make its normal revolutions whether the governor arrived soon or late.

Manuel's main concern at the moment was for his wife, Carmen. He knew she would be waiting at the Oaxaca terminal for who knew how long due to his flight delay. If he were still inside the terminal, he would have called her, but once on the plane, it wasn't easy to convince the flight attendants that he needed to leave for a few moments to call his wife about the delay. He couldn't bring himself to ask. So he simply leaned back in his seat and waited for the governor. He would come, eventually, and would be seated regally in the front section of the cabin where six seats, all abreast, were reserved for the dignitary and his aides.

Manuel's thoughts shifted to his own business interests and the reason for his trip to Mexico City. He wished he had been more persuasive at the banking meeting held earlier in the commerce building at the government plaza. He was stymied by the international group of bankers who had come to cluck their tongues at the inefficient Mexicans. The American bankers were especially condescending. He was not intimidated by their remarks—merely angered.

He had grown up in the Church, dealt with American LDS missionaries all his life, and felt comfortable during his numerous visits to the United States. But, still, it was never easy to face those international bankers and have them make demands on performance for all the funds they were extending to his country.

Manuel wondered for the thousandth time how he could be so bitter toward some of the Americans and yet honor an American prophet in Salt Lake City. He knew there was a vast difference between the Prophet and the American businessmen. And he thanked God for that.

The very fact that some of his fellow Mexican bankers, particularly those who dealt with the international monetary system, would do something so stupid as to cheat the Japanese and Americans on small, under-the-table deals frustrated him. Some of them were caught in schemes to defraud their own government, which affected the international sector through high-level manipulation. All of it bothered Manuel, especially now when the teetering financial world of Mexico hung in the balance. It was disloyal of them to commit such white-collar crimes. Even worse, it was unfair to Manuel and his fellow bankers in Mexico who were striving to be as honest as they knew how.

How is it that some of us try so hard to make Mexico into a nation respected by the business communities of the world, especially the American and Japanese, and yet fall so short of the goal? Manuel had no immediate answer to his own question.

He glanced up after a few minutes of contemplation and was relieved to see the bulky governor enter the front entrance of the cabin. He watched as the man smiled his politically correct smile at the passengers and waved his large hand. Then, in a true politician's voice that projected to the rear of the cabin, he apologized for the delay. Manuel had frequently watched ol' Governor Moreno disarm an entire plaza crowded with people from all over the valley. If he could effectively mesmerize thousands, then appeasing this simple group of passengers on a half-hour-delayed flight was a piece of cake. The governor's eyes roamed over the passengers. When he spotted Manuel, he winked and nodded his head toward the banker. In that fraction of a second, Manuel realized that the governor had been talking at length with the President of Mexico about the deplorable banking situation. He knew instinctively that he would have to meet with the governor soon and reassure him that Oaxaca banking was not affected. Manuel nodded his head in response to the governor's unspoken concern and mentally forgave him for the flight's delay.

"It is the same story all over again, Carmen *querida*. I get up there to the meeting and help hash out the problems and what happens? The government is only willing to slap the hands of those capital thugs in fine silk suits. If I were in power, I'd have those guys in federal prison. They deserve it." Manuel sighed, relieved to be heading home in his wife's car. "And, by the way, you remember the Minister of Finance?"

"Of course I know him. What did he say?"

"He warned me that El Presidente has his eyes on me."

"You don't mean that!"

"*Sí, es verdad.* Jorge thinks he's sizing me up for a federal job or something. Maybe he wants me to head up a group to represent Mexico at the International Bankers Meeting next month in London.

I wouldn't mind that assignment. It has been noised about."

"Is that what you want? To serve as chairman of that group? You would surely tie yourself to the capital. You know we would have to move to Mexico City." A wide grin crossed the small features of Carmen's face. "That would be fine with me. I wouldn't complain. I love it there—so much culture and the temple and all. But you don't," she sighed. "Yes, I could live there. At least I would be released from my calling, which is getting me down. But you would be released from the stake presidency. I wouldn't like that."

"Hold on. It's just talk. Besides, *los bandito-bankers en el capital no les gusto*. But that's only right. I don't like them either. They disgrace the very institution that they ought to go out of their way to defend and uphold. I wonder if the day will ever arrive when our people will truly be responsible? Do we actually have the character to build our nation to such great strength that we can fulfill our destiny? God will only bless us if we do our part."

Carmen turned onto the main highway to town and sped along. She shook her head at Manuel's latest comment. "You're too philosophical for me, especially at this hour." Manuel detected weariness in her tone.

Carmen had waited for Manuel nearly an hour in the lobby of the small air terminal that serviced three commercial airlines, plus some private commuter planes. She knew the delay was not Manuel's fault, but the tension inside her had risen as she waited. She had said her *buenas noches* to the governor, who had remembered that she was Señora Rodriguez. He even thought to inquire about the family. Then the large but regal, gray-haired governor had hurried off with his entourage to his limousine, which was waiting outside the terminal at the curb.

She had endured a day every bit as frustrating as her husband's. What snapped the straw was the condition of her house and the fact that there was no dinner for the children when she got home. Her maid, Emilia, had sent word that she had "*la grippe*" and would not be in to help with the housework. *How do you get the flu in August?* she thought angrily.

Emilia had also informed her that she would not be available to care for the children while she and Manuel were away. In a panic, she had called her parents and pleaded her case. As usual, they had been more than willing to have the children stay with them. They always assured her that they loved little visits with the children, but Carmen hated to put them out again. This time she had been sure she had all her bases covered—but that was before Emilia had come down with "*la grippe.*" Then, to top off that news came Manuel's flight delay, which took an extra forty-five minutes of her precious time.

Carmen looked away from the road, turned toward Manuel for a moment, and sighed, "I can't tell you how badly my day has gone."

"My goodness, *querida*, you are upset. I'm sorry I have added to your problems."

"Oh, it wasn't your fault. It's just that everything seems to be falling apart. The whole day has been discouraging. I went to the orphanage for my usual assignment before meeting with Alicia's teacher. When I got home, expecting to find Emilia there and the house in order, I found a note telling me that she was ill. Don't worry. Papa and Mama have agreed to keep the kids, but the house is a mess and I still have to pack. We'll just have to leave the house as it is."

Manuel reached over and gently massaged his wife's tense neck and shoulders as she drove. "That will be the day when you leave the house a mess. Don't worry. You can relax on the plane."

Carmen shook her head as she sent the car onto Boulevard Central. Darkness had swept down on the city by then. Many people were out walking in the fresh evening air. Earlier in the day, a mild westerly storm had sprinkled the ground and settled the dust that had been stirred by unseasonable wind over the past week. The pedestrians who were dressed in dark colors were hard to see where there were no streetlights or where the lights were out.

Tonight it was hard to make out the green fields along the highway from the airport to the outskirts of town, but Carmen and Manuel could smell the wildflowers and the freshness they loved about their town. Oaxaca was never without the scent of tropical flowers that bloomed year round, but fresh grass and water in the streams came only during the rainy season.

Carmen looked out on the crowded, dimly lit street as their Toyota sedan nosed its way toward the eastern hill section of town.

The Rodriguez family lived in a large, flat-roofed home perched on the shoulder of the eastern mountains that led toward the main highway to Monte Albán, the monument that housed the remains of Manuel's ancestral culture going back at least 1,500 years through Mexican history. It was a noble history that Manuel took great pride in relating.

"Oh, Manuel, I almost forgot. Your secretary called me late this afternoon to tell me that you had a call from Dr. Polk. His Spanish was never great, but with his stroke she said he speaks very slowly and slurs his words a little. The poor man. But he got the message across."

"And?"

"He wanted to make sure we're still planning to join the group in Pago Pago."

"Of course we are. Why are you looking at me like that? Don't you want to go? I thought you were looking forward to it."

"Oh, I do. I am just so tired. But it's more than that. I feel like he is asking me along merely to be nice, and it's expensive for him."

"That's all right. I want you to go with me." Manuel smiled and the touch of his fingers on his wife's neck altered slightly, from massage to caress.

Carmen's lips curved to match his smile. "Good," she replied in a slightly husky voice. "I'm going to love getting away."

"*Mi querida*, why don't you take the express route by the bus depot? I want to drop off the attendance reports for Carlos. He has to have the stake report in to the area brethren by tomorrow afternoon. I meant to drop it off this morning."

The mood inside the car changed abruptly. "Manuel, how can you do this to me? I don't have time," Carmen protested in a staccato barrage.

"Okay, okay. Let's go directly home. I can take them over early tomorrow. No problem."

"Now that makes me feel guilty. No, I'll drive you by."

"Okay, I'll make you a deal. We go by Carlos' right now, and I'll help you clean and pack when we get home. Okay?"

"You . . . help clean the house?" A teasing smile crossed Carmen's lips.

"Sure, of course I will. I wasn't always an important man in the Valley."

They both chuckled as Carmen sped to the right and directed the car toward the south side of town.

* * *

WHEN ERIC KUMANI LOCKED THE SIDE DOOR of the restaurant and walked to his Prelude convertible in the parking lot, it was after midnight. It was always after midnight when he closed his doors, though it was not every night that he came to the restaurant. He made it a policy to take off Saturdays and Sundays and whenever there was a youth activity in the ward. He never wanted to slight the youth. Tomorrow was Thursday; tomorrow he and Carol would fly to Samoa to begin their cruise with Dr. Polk and his group.

Eric's body cried out for sleep, even more than usual. He would try to get a full eight hours, if the family would cooperate. For some reason, the thought of one of his ancestors crossed his mind as he pulled away from the parking lot.

Life must have been easier for his great-great-grandfather, that first Hawaiian boy who joined the Church in the previous century. Life was much simpler for everyone back then.

Eric tried to recall the stories of his great-great-grandfather as he slipped the key into the ignition. What was his name? It bothered him for the next five minutes as he crossed Honolulu, gliding through amber lights on his way. Kumi! Yes, that was the name, Kumi. Why, of all times, was he thinking of him now? Eric knew he was tired if he had nothing else to ponder than a great-great-grandfather, but he was grateful all the same. To think that the little boy had had sense enough to join the Church. Eric smiled in the darkness at the pleasant thought.

* * *

MARIA WOULD HAVE DENIED IT, would have been offended at the suggestion, but she was a manipulator of the first order. In every facet of her life, she rearranged circumstances to suit her own needs.

In this case, she opted for stopovers both in Los Angeles (to visit her sister) and Hawaii (to cushion jet lag), finally heading for Samoa on Thursday morning.

She wondered about the wisdom of boarding a yacht she knew nothing about, except that she did receive the promotional charter flyer by fax. Even in a black and white photo, the yacht looked like a floating hotel. She had already made up her mind to enjoy the cruise, and why not? It would be a new phase in her ever-expanding experiences while attending conferences.

The trip from her sister's home to LAX gave the two of them a chance to chat about family matters. She liked being with her only sister, and she didn't see her nearly often enough. As Maria sat calmly in the passenger seat of the Ford Taurus, her sister wove smoothly through the seven o'clock traffic. Janet was making excellent time, considering the hour. For some reason, the freeway was not as crowded as she had anticipated although Maria was struck by the similarity between California freeway drivers and ballet dancers. She decided wryly that Utah drivers must never watch good ballet.

"Why did they invite you to this meeting . . . because you're a woman and they needed to balance the group of scholars?" Janet asked. Her face was thin and drawn. Her sixty-five years showed in every line, but her mind and body were alert and agile.

"My, my. We are catty this morning!"

"Don't mind me. I always have my doubts as to the intent of men when it comes to including professional women. You do consider yourself a professional, don't you, honey?"

"No more than you."

"Ha! I've been a hausfrau all my adult life. And now, even as a widow, I will remain that. But I do enjoy my name extraction mission at the center."

"I'm glad you have something interesting and challenging to do now that Fred is gone."

"Well, Maria, it's been nice to have you spend the night with me. Call me if you decide to come home this route and want to stay over again."

"I'll let you know."

"Oh, I almost forgot what I wanted to tell you. We talked so late last night that it completely slipped my mind."

"What is it?"

"Our family history. I was doing some research last week, and this kindly little brother, who happens to be working a couple of hours a day on name extraction, was talking with me about his extractions in England. We compared notes then I pulled up some records back when our ancestor Charity Barker Mellon came into the Church in Manchester, England. I thought you might be interested, since your middle name is Charity. I copied an entry of the baptism and some brief notes on some church business and how she converted. You might want to read it. She told her conversion story to someone who recorded it. Reach back there and grab my folder."

Maria turned and retrieved a leather day planner.

"I'll get it out when we stop. You can take it with you. I made a copy for you."

As Janet pulled into a three-minute unloading slot on the departure level of United Airlines, Maria pecked her cheek, pushed open the door, and stepped to the curb. Opening the back door, she pulled out her rolling, forest-green bag while her sister unzipped her day planner.

"Here." Janet reached back over the car seat with the photocopied document in her hand.

"Bye . . . and thanks," Maria called over the traffic noise. "You're a doll to bring me to this madhouse of an airport. Bye."

Janet pulled away, waving as she eased into the mainstream traffic.

Maria glanced out the window of the United Airlines 747, still on the ground at LAX as the maintenance crew completed their careful inspection. Leaning her head back, she closed her eyes, wondering what Book of Mormon topic Peter Polk could be analyzing now. Then she reached over, opened her bag, pulled out the document that her sister had given her, and began to read. Her imagination and knowledge of history filled in the sketchy account. Soon she was absorbed in the story.

Charity worked for the slubber at the end of Manning Street on the outskirts of Manchester, not a stone's throw from the new rolling coaches that ran on iron rails. Everything appeared to be changing in 1842.

Charity had friends who talked all day long at the carding mill about America. Everyone wanted to go to America. She was too young at seventeen to think about such things. Where would she ever get enough money together to make the trip, even if she wanted to go? She had no parents to support her. She and her older sister were all that was left of her family. The previous year consumption had taken her mother, who had been a widow since Charity could remember. It was life. Charity herself had worked in the mills since she was ten—first the one where her mother sent her, two miles west of their flat, and now the smaller mill that hired only "older girls" who had experience running thread through the spools to make linen cloth. In one way it was a relief to work here. She no longer had to listen to the sobs of little children working twelve hours a day, the slubbers beating them with straps to keep them awake and at the job.

Charity made her way each day to the mill from the flat where she lived with her sister and her sister's family. She was fortunate; it was no more than half a mile away. Many days during her usual twelve-hour shift, all Charity could think about while she worked was sleep. With her niece crying half the night with the croup, it was no wonder she was sleepy at work. As soon as she finished her shift, she planned to hurry home, have some bread and mush, put on her night clothes, and go to sleep in that cramped little space at the top of the stairs. She was so tired.

When the foreman shouted, "Day's work finished, me ladies," Charity thankfully grabbed her threadbare cloth cape from the rack, tossed it about her shoulders, and scurried out of the mill onto the cobblestone street. The rain had stopped, leaving puddles of rust-colored water pooled in the depressed areas of the roadway. She easily skirted those. Though it was May, the weather could still be nasty. But it would soon be summer. She loved summer. Warm days and nights were so comforting.

Charity crossed the intersection that bustled with carts, buggies, and people on foot. From the far corner, she saw two men shouting at passersby, no doubt trying to sell something. She could not make out the words they were shouting. More and more, it seemed, the streets were filled with people, and more often than not someone would be selling goods on the corner. She paid no attention since she hadn't a pence to spare. With her meager earnings, she never entertained the thought of purchasing a trinket or whatever the laddies were hawking.

As Charity neared the corner, she heard one of the fellows shout out, "You, young lady. Would you stop for a minute and let us speak to you?" Looking up, she noticed that the fellow was addressing her.

The man was dressed in a long, black coat and sported a wiry brown beard. He sounded nothing like the people around Manchester. His was a strange, clipped brogue she was not familiar with—maybe Irish. She had heard that there were more and more of those types coming through Manchester of late.

In spite of her fatigue, Charity paused. Nor was she alone, as a half-dozen other homebound workers had stopped as well. A broad-faced, pipe-smoking man hesitated beside her and listened for a moment to the speaker's shouted words, then muttered as he walked away, "Blimey, it's those Mormon missionaries. I ain't got time for such things." Charity stared after him curiously, then returned her attention to the bearded man who had called out to her.

As he finished his general message, the man walked directly up to Charity and said, smiling, "Thank you, Miss, for stopping. Here, I'll give you this notice."

Charity took the thin sheet of paper the man handed her. She could recognize a few words in print; she knew her numbers, but she could not read well—not that she was going to let this pushy chap know that. She looked down at the paper. The tall young man with the beard stuck his finger in the center of the paper and said, "This is your invitation to come to one of our meetings this evenin' at Holly Square. We will be meetin' in an hour. If you come, I can promise you that your life will change, and you will hear the most important message of your life."

"Be off with you," Charity said in a tone of dismissal. "I'm too tired to go to anything. If the king himself was to show up, I wouldn't have that much interest." She snapped her fingers, then thrust the sheet of paper back at the insistent fellow who, she couldn't help but notice, seemed quite charming. She knew no men well, not even her brother-in-law who spoke civilly if he needed to communicate with her, but that was seldom. Other than the foreman of the mill, she seldom had contact with men at all.

It was the kindness in the man's voice that touched a hidden section of Charity's heart. His penetrating eyes and easy manner compelled her to remain a moment longer than she knew she should.

"I'll tell you what, Miss," he persisted, wrapping her fingers back around the scrap of paper. "You come to the meetin' tonight, and I will personally guarantee that you will hear somethin' that will fulfill your fondest dreams. We will be talkin' about the Savior himself. Have you ever felt that you were meant to do something or hear something very special that would open up an entire new world to you? I promise you that the message we have will give you a new direction in your life, and you will understand the Lord Jesus Christ as you have never, ever known him. Please come." His appeal was sincere.

Charity didn't say she would or she wouldn't. Without another word, she clutched the thin paper, whirled about, and hurried briskly down the street to her flat.

Her brother-in-law could read. He had been four years to school as a child. Charity produced the sheet of paper and hesitantly asked him to tell her what it said. He read it silently, then laughed. Handing it back to her, he told her that it gave the time and place where the missionaries would be meeting that evening. He had nothing good to say about the Mormons, those strange Americans who were out in the streets shouting for the people to listen. "The only good thing I know about the lot of them is that they are helping the people who accept their religion get passage on ships in Liverpool sailing to America."

America!

After supper, sitting on the side of her cot in her tiny cubbyhole, Charity held the paper up to the one small window and studied it in the fading light. The words meant nothing, but the thought of being part of a group that offered hope and perhaps a chance to actually go to America engulfed her.

Charity didn't exactly pray. But thoughts and questions were buzzing around in her mind, when as clearly as if someone were on the stairs outside her door, she heard a voice. Her door was open. She heard it clearly. "Charity, go listen to the fellow you met on the street. He has a marvelous message for you. Go now!"

Charity looked around her, startled at the voice. It was a man's voice. She jumped up, grabbed the sides of the door frame, and peered out and down the stairs. No one there. Not a soul in sight anywhere who *could have spoken those words. Silently, wonderingly, she said to herself as she stood leaning out of her room, "I'll go. Yes, I will go."*

She grabbed her one good dress that hung from a hook on the wall, quickly put it on, and ran downstairs. She splashed cold water from the bucket on the back porch over her face and combed her hair before an old cracked mirror above it. She left the flat without saying a word to her sister. She wanted to see for herself if that fellow on the street corner could actually show her a new life.

Charity had recorded her conversation years later, and in her recollections she had included her thoughts as she scampered up the street to attend her first meeting with the Mormons. She had wondered if it was possible to hope for something better than years of working twelve hours a day, every day except Sunday. Was there something out there that would change her life? And why had she heard a voice? What did it all mean? She was determined to find out.

CHAPTER EIGHT

Gathering of the Peers

Thursday, late afternoon,
Pago Pago

AN AIR OF EXCITEMENT PREVAILED on the *Free Eagle*. Over the past six hours, all of Polk's invited guests had boarded the yacht. First came Maria, Samuel, and Eric, who had met in the airport in Honolulu. All three had taken overnight layovers before making their connecting flights on to Pago Pago, American Samoa. Then Manuel and Carmen had arrived from Auckland, where they had made connection with a flight to Pago Pago. Takahashi and Noriko came through Fiji's international terminal, where they caught a commuter line to Pago Pago.

Unpacked, refreshed, and now out to sea, the group met at Dr. Polk's request for an introductory discussion session in the main salon. Polk welcomed this small, hand-picked group of Church members from his wheelchair, which had been strapped to the leg of the dining table. He wanted to get right to the matter at hand. He knew that his travel-weary peers could only endure a short discussion before their minds would begin to shut him out, and he would lose his effectiveness with the group. Stephen stood by for a moment, then pulled up a dining chair to be at Polk's elbow. He was grateful everything had come off smoothly so far. He felt responsible.

At the front of the salon, in a corner, stood a small work area of electronic equipment. The yacht afforded round-the-clock communications with the world. It was all there: phone, fax, computer, color printer, and copier with all the essentials. They had available a modem, a connection to the Internet, and access to the Worldwide Web. Of course, Polk had brought along his books on CD and a few very special videos.

The light, open room was simple and elegant. Long, curved, wooden sashing enhanced the beauty of the windows without interrupting the view of the blue Pacific beyond. Brass railings were everywhere along the walls and stairwells. The room had been decorated with sunshine hues that made it seem like an airy garden. The motif of tropical splendor carried a brightness throughout.

Lounge chairs and other comfortable furnishings were plentiful, laid out by a designer to give that casual-yet-expensive look. Stephen feared that the group would become so relaxed in the opulent atmosphere that they might very well be dozing off soon. It was Polk's and Meyers' job to keep the interest high so that wouldn't happen—a rather stiff order in this setting.

Before meeting and talking to Meyers, Stephen had been uneasy that Polk's former roommate was scheduled to lead the discussions. He hadn't been all that certain of Meyers' abilities, as he was of Polk's. But Polk certainly gave his friend high marks and, after all, the man had crisscrossed the Pacific Rim in pursuit of information he considered vital to the whereabouts of the Nephite nation. He ought to be on top of his subject.

Stephen wondered if he would ever feel up to the assignments Polk tossed his way. He simply did not yet have the background to dispense the kind of information that Polk found so electrifying.

When Stephen had spoken to Samuel Meyers just two days before, Samuel told him that Polk had begun to set up this meeting when he first became lucid after his stroke in late fall of the previous year. Samuel had reported to him on his findings in the Pacific and discussed critical verses in the Book of Mormon in preparation for this weekend session. Nothing, but nothing, was going to halt this gathering of knowledgeable people on a subject that needed some type of closed forum.

The agenda Polk and Meyers had outlined was for present company only, to be presented in a study-group setting. It was as close to a top-secret meeting as any gathering of individuals could be expected to be within the Church. But the subject matter was still too sensitive for any sort of open sharing with a larger body, even if some sort of symposium could have been arranged. And had Polk and Meyers *wanted* to open it to a large forum, both agreed that Church policy demanded that it not be done—not yet. No, Polk and Meyers wanted everything discussed in this gathering to be private and confidential—not exactly secret—and offered as evidence only, not as doctrine. Truth was, they wanted a little off-Broadway review before their major opening.

As Polk addressed the group, his excitement was evident. He was sure that this propitious moment would not likely come again for him, and it had come none too soon as it was. He had all of his players lined up. It would be Meyers' research and presentation, but Polk's genius behind the dialogue. Polk felt that he and Meyers made a good team.

For Polk, however, poor health was suddenly his worst enemy. Though he had turned seventy-one just two months before, which was young by today's Utah obituary standards, he sensed that the Lord was not going to grant him many more years. The gathered information would have to come out now or never. Not that he would protest if death should come soon. He had more reasons to be on the other side than he did on this. He longed to be with his wife, who had passed away four years before. The spirit world didn't sound half bad to Peter, except that he would miss being a father and grandfather. "When the time comes, I'll be ready," he often said. But until that time, he would do what he wanted to do for the promotion of the Book of Mormon, a book he considered the finest missionary tool ever placed in the hands of the covenant Gentiles.

Here, surrounded by his peers, was where Dr. Polk wanted to be, fully able or not. He found little joy in sitting around his house, isolated from discussions of the Book of Mormon. He seemed to gain strength from this sort of involvement. And what a discussion this would be! This, to Polk, was the real stuff of life—this delving into areas of doctrine, pulling in scholars to share their views, filling up the mind with the depth of what the Lord had in store for his people, for those who would truly study and ponder the Book of Mormon. Wasn't it President Benson who, when he was the prophet, declared that the Church had come under condemnation because the membership was not reading the Book of Mormon, though they had been commanded to do so?

Dr. Polk had waited all year to be part of this little conclave. He was here now and would stay until the very end of the discussions. That was all there was to it. He was not yet exhausted. His great mentor had been President Kimball, who had the drive that Polk admired so much in a man. If President Kimball could give his all until his body completely gave out, so could he.

CHAPTER NINE

First Session

On the Free Eagle

FINGER FOOD AND DRINKS came up the stairwell from the galley. Karry, the steward, arranged the assortment of snacks on the long, cherrywood coffee table and handed each person a fruit punch drink made with a sparkling lemon base. The tall frosty glasses were garnished with sprigs of spearmint leaves and served with pink straws.

After handing out the drinks, Karry stepped back to stand against the walls of the salon where, unnoticed, he observed the group and listened to their discussion. He was curious about these people. This was not the usual yacht crowd. Their choice of drinks had made that clear right from the time of their boarding. Karry had quickly surmised that the invalid in the wheelchair was really the man in charge. He liked Dr. Polk immediately for his easy manner and soothing voice as he spoke to the group.

From the upright chair across from Polk, Maria, ever critical, scrutinized her old college associate and felt concern. She hadn't seen him since shortly before his stroke, and the change was apparent. His altered speech was the most notable change. Then, on closer observation, she noticed that his skin tone had gone from a rosy, British pink to pale gray.

From the opposite side of the room, Manuel likewise considered Polk's physical deterioration. The sight of the wheelchair alone gave him a start. He always envisioned Polk as a jolly, robust man, older but alive with activity. The wheelchair seemed to confine Polk.

Takahashi had bowed to Polk and extended his hand when he entered the salon. The mutual respect and affection were still present, but Takahashi did not feel Polk's usual strong grip. Dr. Polk, he sensed, was weak from months of confinement, but he was glad to be tutored by the master once again. Takahashi had never before met a scholar like Dr. Polk who blended such strong doses of human compassion, humility, and intellectual brilliance—a rare combination among academics.

Stephen noticed that Polk was revitalized and ready for mental combat, or whatever he planned to do in this salon for the next few days. Perhaps because Polk was personally in command he hadn't shared the details with Stephen as he had done in the last conference. That was okay; in fact, it was a relief. Stephen wouldn't be expected to know anything about the subject at hand. That essentially let him off the hook.

"So we meet, and now we begin," Dr. Peter Polk said, his voice slightly slurred. He touched a handkerchief to the right corner of his mouth and patted the saliva that tended to drain there since his stroke. Anney had bought him ten new linen handkerchiefs at Macys in downtown San Francisco a few days before; after washing and pressing them, she had stashed them away in the top drawer of the dresser in Polk's stateroom. She had an extra one in her lap to hand him if he needed it.

Polk motioned with his outstretched left arm, waving it limply as he spoke. "Stephen, would you wheel that blackboard closer to this side of the room so President Meyers can use it more effectively?"

Stephen had made arrangements for the small blackboard and a few other props from the quartermaster on board. It had arrived, with chalk, minutes before.

After inviting the members of the group to introduce them-selves briefly, Polk launched into his opening remarks.

"Don't worry, Sam," Polk smiled at his old friend. "I'm not up to one of my two-hour lectures." He paused, trying to catch the eye of every member of the group. He knew every one of them well. "The fact is, my dear friends, there is positive scriptural evidence that a remnant of the Nephites has been preserved." He said no more for thirty seconds.

The *Free Eagle's* twin diesel engines hummed as silence prevailed. The members of the group waited for Dr. Polk to resume his introduction. One or two eyebrows twitched, but no one expressed surprise. "I mean," he continued, "there are living, breathing Nephite people out there." He pointed west with his good left hand. "They are alive and well and strong. I don't mean that they are mixed with the Lamanites. I'm convinced that they are not in the western hemisphere, nor are they space aliens. They are on earth and appear to be somewhere in the Pacific Rim. I say again, they are out here. The evidence that we will present will cast a very bright light on this whole subject." He held up his good hand as if to ward off controversy. "I know, I know. You are thinking, 'Has the old fellow lost what little he had left?'"

That brought a little burst of laughter.

"Laugh if you will," Polk smiled, then continued seriously, "we are going to present some rather startling evidence that will require explanation at some point. We bring this discussion of living Nephites to your attention as information and not as doctrine. There is a difference. Since Sam and I have been piecing this together, we felt that it might serve us well to bounce what we've discovered off a carefully selected group—that's you.

"In this room, all of us are members of the House of Israel—some by adoption, others by true lineage. We have at least one Lamanite here who is clearly of the lineage of Joseph." Polk smiled at Manuel, then cleared his throat. "And we may have one or two Nephites in the room as well." All eyes in the room bore into Polk's.

"You have all been hand-picked to attend this little confab. So please indulge us for a couple of days, and you may never read certain scriptures and comments by the authorities in quite the same light as you do now." He paused again, looking intently into each face before him.

"I beg each of you to listen carefully and weigh the evidence that Samuel Meyers has amassed. You all know him. We're a small group, so please feel like family while we're here together."

With that, Polk stretched out his hand toward Meyers. "Sam, it's yours. If I say any more, I'll just steal your thunder."

Samuel Meyers straightened his shoulders, looked down at the notes in his lap, then faced the group. Suddenly he experienced a moment of panic, as if he were speaking before a large crowd in the BYU Marriott Center. He was a little surprised that after all these years of speaking before large groups of people he would suddenly feel nervous.

He nodded at his old friend, cleared his throat, and moved into his subject. "What I have to say will not set well with everyone in this room. It may not set well with most of you. Nevertheless, we have invited you here to draw upon your wisdom and experience, and also to evaluate your reactions to what we have uncovered.

"Now, we have come together to discuss—and hope to arrive at a basic understanding of what is contained in—the Book of Mormon, along with other evidence available in the Pacific to substantiate a certain hypothesis."

Samuel stood up and scribbled rapidly on the blackboard:

A. NEPHITES NOT ALL DESTROYED.

As he wrote, he verbally expanded the topic. "We will show that not all of the existing Nephites were present at the last battle at the Hill Cumorah. Consequently, the Nephites—as a people—were not utterly annihilated."

Samuel continued to outline his hypothesis.

B. PROMISES MADE TO NEPHITES – NOT LAMANITES.

"We'll look carefully at the scriptures that tell of the Savior's promises and see who he was talking to. We'll also check out Isaiah and see how he verifies these promises."

Moving his hand down, Samuel wrote again.

C. PROMISES TO THE NEPHITES:
    1. INHERIT THE AMERICAS.
    2. SPEARHEAD BUILDING THE NEW JERUSALEM.

"The Nephites were promised that they would inherit the Americas in the days of the Gentiles—that's today, and that's most of us who are Gentiles. Evidence indicates that the Nephites will receive the gospel and take their rightful place, leading out in the building of the New Jerusalem. Startling, isn't it?" It was a rhetorical question. He was not inviting discussion yet.

Next, he wrote:

D. LOCATION

"We will show that the Nephites are to be found in a nation that exists today and that it is somewhere in the Pacific Rim."

Samuel turned back and scrutinized the faces before him, looking for a reaction. Foreheads were furrowed and all eyes were fixed on the blackboard.

It took a moment for the words to register. When they did, Manuel nearly came up off the sofa. "What? What are you saying? You don't mean Nephites! Those promises belong to the Lamanites."

"Perhaps this is the most startling fact of all," Samuel replied softly, empathetic to Manuel's concerns. He had expected such a response, but he was still uncomfortable. He shot a quick glance at the calm sea out the window. They had been underway for over an hour and he could feel the movement. The ship left a trail of white foam as it plowed along at thirty knots—full speed—on its way to Juno Island in the west.

Samuel returned his eyes to look directly at Manuel before continuing, though he did not address his concerns. "For years we have all assumed this honor belonged to the Lamanites. But when we look at the evidence another way, we see that we have all misunderstood who would spearhead the building of the New Jerusalem. Therefore, this will be the focus of our discussion—the promises made to the *Nephites* that are to be fulfilled in our day. If you think for a minute that this shift in future events does not impact your life in some way, you are wrong. When the Nephites return, as they surely will, they will come through the Americas like a lion among lambs. The message is clear."

In a caustic voice, Maria scoffed, "Samuel, Samuel." Her voice held a note of exasperation. "This is highly suppositional, bordering on delusional. Where's your proof?"

Eric, also agitated, but for different reasons, spoke up: "If they're alive and well, then where are they? Or should I ask, *who* are they?"

Samuel thrust out his hands like a traffic cop signaling STOP. "Hold on, hold on. We'll get to all that. We'll answer every question you have . . . all in good time. But for the sake of a clearer understanding, please hold your questions for a bit." Samuel reached for his Book of Mormon. "I think we should start at the beginning and clarify the premise—that the Nephites were not totally destroyed. First, open to the introduction to the Book of Mormon."

Pages rustled as fingers found the right spot.

"Take a look at the second paragraph, last sentence, where it clarifies the background of the inhabitants of the Book of Mormon land. It says this: 'After thousands of years, all were destroyed except the Lamanites.' This undoubtedly means that all the other tribes or nations that we know of in the Book of Mormon writings were killed off. The question is, does this phrase mean that there were no more Nephites on the earth? Or can it mean that there simply were no more Nephites in the land of the Americas? It makes a world of difference how we perceive this statement."

Maria spoke up again. It was her nature to plunge directly into the issue at hand and resolve it as quickly as possible. "Sam, aren't you twisting the meaning of this statement to suit your position!"

"No. I call your attention to it because we will soon compare it to other scriptures and statements which would nullify this one, if you read it without expanding your understanding."

"It states categorically that ALL were destroyed," Maria said with exaggerated patience, as if correcting one of her students.

"Well, as we get into the writings and teachings of some of the prophets of this century, such as Joseph F. Smith and David O. McKay, you will see that they have invalidated that introductory statement—that is, if we interpret it to mean that every last remnant of the Nephites that ever lived was wiped out in the last great battle or the cleanup that followed."

Maria was not convinced, but she said no more. She was as

curious as any in the room to hear what Sam and Peter had done with their research into this subject. She was sure they would have something to back up their statements. They were too steeped in scholarship to build a theory without careful research. Yes, it promised to be interesting—not that she expected to accept all they had to say. Still, she did not want to hinder the presentation. She decided to hold off judgment until a more appropriate time presented itself in the discussion.

Samuel said, "It might be well to indicate that the Book of Mormon's introduction was not part of the 1830 edition to the book. It was written later by editors—"

"But, as I recall, it was approved by a living prophet when it was issued," Maria insisted, then caught herself. She was trying not to disrupt, and had intended to remain silent and let Meyers finish. But it was her nature to challenge every statement with which she disagreed. She would have to try harder to hold back.

"Another good point, Maria. We are not challenging the statement in the introduction. I, too, think it is correct insofar as it describes those Nephites who were destroyed when their nation had fallen into transgression, to the degree that Mormon and Moroni describe in their writings."

Karry, the Aussie steward, hated to leave the group and return to the galley. He had caught a signal from the Hawaiian guest, the big Polynesian guy, that the glasses around the room were empty, and that meant fetching more drinks from the galley. Although Karry was intent on learning about these people, his job nevertheless required him to serve.

"More fruit juice and 7-Up," he shouted in his thick Outback accent as he rounded the door to the galley below the main salon.

The chef was off duty and Myron, who hailed from New Zealand, took the order and began combining juices to be taken up to the salon. He had been trained a year ago to tend bar on the *Free Eagle.*

"Any of those blokes ask for a beer or something stouter?"

"Nah, they're a religious bunch. But that's okay, mate. I heard that Thorn fellow—you know, the chap who came on board first before the others—say that they were all Latter-day Saints. Some folks calls them Mormons. Ya ever heard of the Mormons, mate?"

"Yeah, sure. A couple of those young fellas in ties and white shirts came around our place once. Me old man kicked 'em out. Mormon, eh? Pity we didn't land a crowd like that last party bunch. They had girls with 'em, and not too bad lookin'. Not that it did us any good. I have to say they kept me busy with spirits flowing like a waterfall in a storm. Plenty busy. These believers are a bloody boring lot, wouldn't you say, mate?"

"Whatever they are, they sure like your fruit punch upstairs. Just keep mixin' it. I want to get back up there. It's pretty darn interesting."

"What? They got you involved in all their amens?"

"Not on your life. I'm just servin' the punch and cookies."

"What about tea? It's getting on in the afternoon. Did anyone want tea?"

"You heard the cap'n tell us that these Latter-day Saints don't drink tea, and don't go fixin' coffee for them, either. They don't drink it any more than they drink tea."

"What do they drink besides water and punch?"

"You got me. Don't know. Maybe I can find out."

"Sounds ta me like you like being up there listenin' to 'em. You didn't get too excited with that bunch o' bankers from Hawaii a couple o' weeks ago. If you'd a listened to them, you might a picked up on some way to make a pile." Myron reached under the bar for the punch syrup bottle. "Be careful, now. They might get you involved in this church stuff."

"Not on your life. Just hand me the tray and I'll be off."

"Hold on, my eager lad. You might drop the ice in the glasses to help out."

"Sure thing. Be glad to."

Meyers cast a shrewd glance at Maria. He had already come to the conclusion that nothing was getting past Maria Almanar, Ph.D. He knew from earlier encounters with her at seminars and forums at Brigham Young University that she held to a legalistic point of view, both in life and with the scriptures. That was okay. In fact, they had wanted to test every sort of response, but he would have to hold her in check if the group was to make any progress at all.

Resuming the discussion, he said, "The fact that all Nephites in the land of the Americas at the time of the battle of Cumorah were destroyed does not invalidate the possibility of an earlier departure from the land by a segment of Nephites, or even a departure by Nephites at the time of the Cumorah battle, the site of the annihilation of the Nephite nation. It does categorically tell us that, as a nation, the Nephites were destroyed. I don't think anyone doubts that. I'm sure most of the Nephite stragglers left at Cumorah were hunted down and slaughtered or coalesced into the Lamanite tribes and thus became Lamanites."

Samuel reiterated his point. "So, if the statement in the Introduction that the Nephites were destroyed is fact, then there must not have been any Nephites left upon the lands of the western hemisphere right after the battles at Cumorah. It appears to refer to the deaths of those Nephites who remained in the land and were ripe for destruction, not to those who may have escaped by leaving earlier.

"The question is, were there groups of Nephites who escaped the final destruction of their people because they were righteous and guided away from the evil of that environment? Were some led by the hand of the Lord to safety in a more distant land prior to the destruction of the nation of Nephites by the Lamanites? Was there any promise that they would be led away? Is this not the method the Lord has used time after time to preserve selected groups? Yes! Yes on all counts."

Meyers moved back to the blackboard, erased his previous outline with a few swift strokes, and with a fresh piece of chalk wrote in bold white letters:

WERE NEPHITES LED AWAY PRIOR TO DESTRUCTION?

He answered his own question by writing one word—a large "Yes."

He repeated the question, this time underlining the word *prior*.

"And if they were led away, did those Nephites who escaped and survived become lost at sea? Or did they obtain another homeland?

Are they, in fact, a great nation that exists somewhere today? That is the question. I say again, it is what I hope to resolve with you before this cruise is over."

Several in the room were rapidly flipping through their scriptures as pertinent passages came to mind. Seeing this, Samuel said, "Now, before we go into a deeper discussion, I think you all deserve a little time to do some research on your own. I can see that you would like to think about what we have suggested. So at this time I'll ask Stephen to distribute some references to you. You'll see some scriptures listed, as well as a brief historical overview of some of the people we'll be discussing. Look it over, check out the scriptures, or take a nap if jet lag gets to you. Then we'll try to get together again later tonight.

"Keep Hagoth's ships in mind. Hagoth sent out shiploads of Nephites. Be sure to read Alma 63 and pay attention to verse 8. And, by the way, don't confuse Lamanites with Nephites. Hagoth was a Nephite."

Samuel reached over and picked up a stack of stapled papers from the table and handed them to Stephen who was already on his feet, holding out both hands to receive them, ready to pass the papers out to the group.

The handouts contained summaries of the Nephites, the Lamanites, the Gentiles, the Jews, and the lost ten tribes of Israel, plus scriptures and other information. The writings were brief, but still required twenty-odd sheets of paper.

Polk had been unobtrusively watching the faces of his friends. He knew that Samuel had piqued their interest. He also knew that more than one of the participants hardly needed any background information on the various groups mentioned in the Book of Mormon. But it wouldn't hurt any of them to review what was contained in the handouts.

* * *

NORIKO UNFASTENED THE CLIP holding her thick, black hair and set it on the cabinet. Preparing to change her clothes for dinner, she loosened her casual, wraparound skirt and let it fall to the floor.

She had already slipped out of her shoes at the door, in typically Japanese fashion. She tossed her hair about, letting it wave across her cheeks and said to Takahashi as she relaxed, "Well, what profound things did you learn at the feet of the master this afternoon?"

"I learned humility."

"You mean we flew all the way here just so you could be instructed in humility?"

"I'm kidding. I learned that the Nephites as a people are alive and well, but I don't yet know where they are located."

"What do you mean?"

Takahashi dropped his khaki walking shorts then, grasping his sand-colored Gap t-shirt at the back of the neck, pulled it over his head. Next he sat on the edge of the bed and pulled off his socks. His sandals stood like two soldiers next to the stateroom door. He looked forward to a shower before dinner.

"The entire session today was on the Nephites as a surviving people. And you know . . . President Meyers was very convincing. He showed us in the Book of Mormon and the Doctrine and Covenants—at least he showed my nonscholarly mind—that the Lord promised that the Nephites would be preserved in the flesh, meaning in this life, to be around in our day and in the future to be . . . what did he say about that? I can't quote it exactly. Anyway, the upshot of the whole session today was the fact that the Nephites are alive and functioning right now."

"I always thought they were all killed off at the end of the Book of Mormon. Is our Japanese Book of Mormon different from the English version?"

"You've been misinformed, Noriko—that is, according to President Meyers."

"You mean he and Dr. Polk are saying that isn't so?"

"Well, it is partly true. And President Meyers is doing most of the talking, by the way. That point came up about the destruction of Nephites that is so clearly documented in the Book of Mormon. And he said that yes, the Nephites as a nation were wiped out in those battles at Cumorah. But earlier—and this is the key—a group of Nephites got on board ships near the Narrow Neck of Land on the West Sea and cut out onto the high seas, caught the California

Current, and swept west to the Orient. According to the notes President Meyers handed us, those Nephites that left evidently escaped about fifty years before the birth of Christ. They went on a Hagoth ship. At least, that's one theory."

"A what kind of ship?"

"Hagoth. It tells us in the Book of Mormon that a large body of Nephites left by ship about that time. Hagoth was a shipbuilder. It is primarily that group who left by ship that President Meyers was talking about. He thinks they became a whole nation of Nephites and are still around today. Isn't that amazing? I had read about their departure to the north, but never thought about it as an escape for their preservation. Amazing point of view! I have to think about that. The idea is pretty new to me."

"Do you think he's right?"

"Believe me, if you read the scriptures he listed, you would be surprised. It sure sounds like it could have happened that way."

"Then, where are they—the Nephites, I mean—today?"

Takahashi flopped back on to the soft bed. "President Meyers hasn't told us yet. Oh, man. Jet lag is getting to me. It's hard to change time zones and have to adjust. My mind doesn't function that well when I don't get enough rest."

"Anney Thorn seemed very charming and kind to me, even though we had to use sign language to communicate. I do wish I understood more English. I so want to talk with her."

"I'll translate for you."

"It isn't the same. You will run out of patience with all the questions I have to ask her. Don't worry about it. We'll understand each other well enough."

Noriko looked through her few clothes hanging in the closet, sliding each outfit aside as she tried to decide what to wear. As she searched, Takahashi told her that the ship's phone system connected to the world so that they could call home and check on the children. Noriko nodded and said she would call later, then returned to the question of a Nephite escape.

"Well, if Nephites left before the destruction at the Hill Cumorah, where did they go?"

"Some settled the land northward; others were never heard from again. The scriptures say no one knows what happened to them. Helaman wrote that they could have been drowned at sea. Who knows? I have the handout. It's right there on the bed."

Noriko picked up the loose-leaf folder. When she opened the cover and saw the printed words in English, she let the folder drop to the bed cover. Her forehead creased with concentration. "In all my life I have never heard of this idea about the Nephites surviving the destruction at Cumorah. Have you?"

"Well, I've heard some of the old members in Tokyo insist that some of the Hawaiians have Nephite blood. That doesn't make up a nation, but . . ."

Takahashi leaned across the bed to the nightstand where he had placed the Book of Mormon when he came in. He picked it up and thumbed through the book to 2 Nephi 9:53. He wanted to share with Noriko what he was learning about the Nephites. "Here it is. This is the reference in the notes."

"Nephi's younger brother Jacob, a great prophet, said, '. . . And because of his greatness, and his grace and mercy, he'—*he* meaning the Lord—'has promised unto us that our seed'—*seed* meaning the Nephites—'shall not utterly be destroyed, according to the flesh, but that he would preserve them; and in future generations they shall become a righteous branch unto the house of Israel.' That's what it says."

It was hard for Noriko to pick up on what her husband was quoting. "I guess I missed something in your reading. I suppose it's important."

Takahashi grew serious. "Of course it's important. Jacob, the prophet, is speaking to a group of Nephites and recording this for us. He is saying that the Lord promised the Nephite seed—Jacob, the younger brother of Nephi—that their children would survive in the flesh and at some point become righteous in the house of Israel."

"That's news to me."

Takahashi's dark eyes twinkled. "So, my little precious one, somewhere, as we sit on this floating hotel about ready to go have a delicious dinner—at least by Western standards—there are Nephites lurking about, and who knows who or where they really are? They're out there and they might just get you."

Takahashi pushed the Book of Mormon aside, reached out and grabbed Noriko by her tiny waist, and pulled her to the bed, smothering his face in her neck and nibbling on the soft, fair skin that tasted so delicious to him.

Chapter Ten

A Surprise Weekend

San Francisco, California

"WELL, YOU DIDN'T HAVE TO COME. You could have stayed home and gone out with your buddies," Brenda chided Todd as they moved from the lobby of the Nob Hill Park Place to the doorman's desk near the elevators. "Since you did come, quit grumping."

Brenda smiled at the gray-haired, black-suited keeper of the lobby and said smoothly, "We are here to visit our grandmother, Mrs. Katherine Moore. We're Brenda and Todd Thorn."

"Oh yes, Mrs. Moore left word with the desk that you would be coming. The elevator will take you to the top floor."

Inside the elevator, Todd pressed the brass button that sent them twenty stories up to the penthouse.

"I'm not trying to stonewall this little weekend outing with Granny Katherine, Brenda," he sighed in the elevator. "It's just that I'm leaving for school in five days. Come on, I have friends I haven't seen since last fall, that's all. You make it sound like I don't like her. I do. It's just that I don't really know her. You've hung out with her. Besides, you get along better in this kind of situation. I mean, I wouldn't mind going out to dinner or something. But spend the whole weekend with her? It's not exactly my idea of fun, you know what I mean?"

"Frankly, I wish you had just been up front with her and said what you feel," Brenda replied. "But you're wrong if you think she's a stuffy old lady. You're right; you don't even know her. This way you'll get acquainted."

"Oh, I don't think of her as a 'stuffy old lady,'" Todd retorted. "I think of her as a stuffy old *rich* lady."

"I don't know why you're so rude about the person who gave Granddad nothing but the best during the last year of his life."

"Okay, I'll put on a smile and just hang."

"Well, it won't be all that bad. Granny Katherine has plans for us this evening. It'll be exciting. I know. I've been with her. Todd, she needs to feel like she has family around, especially at this time when she's so lonely for Granddad. I don't think you have the foggiest idea what it's like to lose someone you love dearly."

"Maybe not," he shrugged, and added sarcastically, "You do, of course."

The elevator made an abrupt halt and a muffled bell sounded as the light above the door indicated the twentieth floor. Todd stepped out first with the shoulder strap of his bag hoisted over his shoulder. The bag had seen lots of wear in the past year with all his travels. He held the door open as Brenda pulled her larger bag on rollers out of the elevator and crossed the marble floor. There were two penthouse apartments on the top level. Brenda pointed to the one on the left. Todd slowly followed her through the luxurious passageway. Yep, the tall, ornate, arched doors even smelled like money.

Brenda punched the doorbell while Todd took in the gold foil wall coverings, floor-to-ceiling mirrors, and ficus trees in large, ceramic planters. He nodded toward the large, framed, original paintings on the walls of the foyer. "Pricey place," he murmured. "Real pricey. Granddad hit the jackpot, didn't he? He told me life was great up here. Now I see what he meant. Granddad, you fox!"

"You're so irreverent," Brenda shot back.

"Oh, come on, Brenda, lighten up. Granddad would have been the first to agree with me."

Brenda pursed her lips and shushed Todd. "Do you want her to hear you?"

Katherine opened the door. Dressed in slim black trousers and a matching short jacket, she stood back with her arms wide open. "Oh, you two are so handsome. Come in, come in. I have been excited all morning anticipating your visit."

"Hi, Granny Katherine," Brenda smiled as she stepped into

Katherine's outstretched arms.

"Hi . . . uh, Granny Katherine," Todd echoed, finding it awkward to call his grandfather's wife Granny Katherine. He caught Brenda's eye, hoping she wouldn't embarrass him with some dumb comment. Katherine restrained herself and extended her hand to Todd. One day they would embrace.

Katherine had never been a grandmother—or a mother, for that matter—but she was charmed by her late husband's two grandchildren. From the day they had returned from Europe, she'd insisted that they call her Granny Katherine. Todd had resisted. Today he uttered the name for the first time. And even now, his tongue had stumbled over the words. It was no wonder: this elegant woman was the absolute antithesis of his mental picture of a corncob-smoking granny.

When they had first protested that the title hardly fit, she had laughed and said, "Oh, I love the title 'Granny.' It's a tradition in my family. All the grandmothers for generations back have been called granny. Since I have not been blessed with children, I was so afraid I would never have the privilege of hearing that title refer to me. So you two are a special gift. What grandmother gets two ready-made, beautiful grandchildren—trained, educated, and pleasant to be around? And, at last, I am a genuine granny."

"Where's your boyfriend . . . Max, is it?" Katherine asked as she ushered the two young people into her apartment with its vaulted ceiling and stunning furniture. She was surprised he was not with them.

"He's taking the red-eye from Los Angeles this evening. He hopes you don't mind him arriving at midnight. It's cheaper that way. I'll drive out to pick him up later."

"Not at all. We'll still be up. This is a festive time. He can arrive any time he wants. What a lively weekend I have planned!"

Watching Todd as they lunched, Katherine recognized the strong jaw and grin that had been her late husband's trademark. It was simply amazing how certain genetic traits skimmed through human bloodlines as with thoroughbred horses. Just amazing.

"I appreciate both of you coming over to be with me for the

weekend. Now that you know the plans I have for this evening, please don't feel you have to stay with me. I remember how it was to be young. So if you want to go somewhere by yourselves, please feel free."

"Granny Katherine," Brenda said, "we came to be with you and see the city. We don't really care what we do. It's just fun to be in such a gorgeous penthouse as yours. I'll bet Granddad loved this place."

"He did," Todd chimed in. "He told me it was great living here." Todd's eyes shot Brenda a message: *Not to worry*. He wasn't about to reveal that he had really wanted to go with his buddies to a concert. Oh, well. There would be others. He could see that his sister found it exciting to hobnob with such a wealthy person. She loved the trappings of wealth—the doorman and the maid who served lunch. The whole scene for Brenda was really uptown living.

The conversation shifted to Todd's plan to head for school in Provo the following week. It bothered Brenda that Todd, a bright student who could have enrolled at Stanford, was settling for what she thought to be a lame school in a provincial town. She fought her inclination to put down the college again. She had already expressed her opinion two days before when he received his official letter of acceptance. Todd had finally walked out of the room while she was still railing on him about low-life colleges. But she hadn't changed her opinion that he would never make it in the real world as a graduate of a podunk college.

Todd had reminded her that he was only going to Utah Valley State College for a year. By then, he hoped to get accepted to study at Brigham Young University. Besides, who knew, maybe Max would like to go to school there next year.

"Is Brigham Young University any better?" Brenda had wanted to know. "And besides, I doubt that Max would want to go to school in Utah." That was when Todd had walked out of the room rather than get into it with her.

Brenda let it go. She had no desire to get into a confrontation on schools with Todd here at Granny Katherine's. If Todd didn't care about attending a name school when he had the option, what business was it of hers?

* * *

THEY STOPPED AT BEN & JERRY'S to cool off and rest their feet after traipsing through the auto show at the convention center on the south side of San Francisco. Going to the show had been a concession to Todd. Brenda and Katherine knew he wanted to see the hot new cars.

With the first taste of their favorite ice cream, all three sighed with pleasure, in full agreement that Ben and Jerry's ice cream was the best. It was only three blocks down Nob Hill from Katherine's place, so she had sent the car home. They would walk up the hill.

The tiny ice-cream shop was always lively. "I haven't been in here for months," Katherine observed. "My figure can't take it." She suddenly looked pensive. "I was here in March with your grandfather. Yes, it was March." Katherine did not want the tears to start flowing again. She quickly changed the subject. "Has your mother called you?"

"Oh, yeah," Brenda replied. "She left a message on the machine. I need to call her back this evening. Actually, they are a few hours earlier than we are—on the other side of the international date line."

"You're welcome to call her right now. It's no hassle to call the ship; it's set up for international calls. I have my cell phone in my bag."

"No, that's all right." Brenda hardly wanted to call her mother in front of all the people around her. Besides, it was too noisy.

Todd didn't notice that Katherine was on the verge of tears when he said, "Did Granddad show you all the great dessert spots around the city? You know he was great on desserts and treats. Mom used to get so mad at him for bringing us treats whenever he came over. He—"

Todd felt the kick on his shin from Brenda, who had realized that this talk about their grandfather was causing Katherine sadness. She could see that much more would send her to the rest room with a Kleenex to her nose. Todd got the hint.

Katherine noticed Brenda's concern and Todd's quick look at

her. "It's okay, Brenda," she said soothingly, patting Brenda on the arm. "I think Todd needs to talk about his grandfather. And even if I'm emotional, I do, too. He was such a part of our lives that I want to remember him. They say it is part of the grieving process to recall the fun times we shared with him. Don't be embarrassed if I cry sometimes. I really do get some comfort reliving those special times with him, and I'm sure you do, too."

Todd looked at Brenda, down at his ice-cream sundae, then up at Katherine's somber face. He could see that she really was trying to be brave.

"Ours was a fairy tale romance," Katherine sighed, her voice barely audible. Seeing disbelief on the faces before her, she couldn't help but chuckle. "Can you imagine that at our age? Bob made me laugh. I felt so . . . so alive again, in a way that I never thought possible after the death of my first husband. I just wish that your grandfather and I had been younger. We would have had a child. I'm convinced of that."

Suddenly Katherine said in a burst of exasperation, "I wish . . . I . . . well, I wish I had the faith Bob had. Religion wasn't really a part of my whole life like it was to him. If I truly felt that I would see Bob again in heaven, I would be able to get through the rest of my life much easier." Katherine moved her head from side to side with animation as she talked. "The way I feel now . . . you know, when we finally decided to remove the life-assist equipment . . . and you were all so kind to let me be alone with him when he finally went . . . I wanted to go with him. I didn't want to stay another minute on the earth without him." Katherine pressed her slender fingers to her lips to stop them from trembling. The noise of dishes rattling and loud voices at the counter smothered the sounds of Katherine's ragged sobs as she struggled to regain control of her emotions.

Todd looked furtively around the room. He hated it when women cried. But he thought Katherine should know what he had recently learned about death. Finally, he reached out awkwardly and patted her hand. "You know . . . uh . . . Granny Katherine, I really believe you will see Granddad again. I think we all will."

Katherine dabbed at her eyes and cleared her throat. "What a wonderful thought that is, Todd," she smiled wanly. "But I have to live in the real world now. In my world, it is hard to visualize anything beyond this life. I have been convinced of that for years. However, now I seem to be open to anything that could possibly sway my present stance on the subject. Oh, I loved to hear your grandfather preach of a glorious heaven, but I never really believed it. All I was interested in was him. He was my god, my love, my all. Now he's gone.

"Goodness! Listen to me." Katherine brought herself up short. "What am I talking about? You two are so young, with life ahead of you. Let's get off this before I sit here like a sobbing idiot and make you miserable."

"But one other thing, Granny Katherine." Todd took a deep breath, pushed his sundae to the center of the marble-topped round table, and said, "I can't leave it at this. I have learned things this summer that I never knew about . . . about what happens to us after we die . . . you know, in the eternities. I really am convinced that we will see Granddad again. We will. I listened to Dr. Polk—you know Dr. Polk . . . you met him. Anyway, he talked about marvelous events that will happen after death."

Brenda tried to stare down Todd, but he refused to make eye contact with her. Next, she put her hand on his shoulder and while squeezing it, looked at Katherine with a weak smile. "Granny Katherine, I'm sure you don't want to listen to a blow-by-blow description of how Todd converted to the Mormon faith." Brenda hoped Todd would catch the hint and lay off. It was completely out of place talking about what he experienced in Park City.

"Oh, but I do want him to tell me. Have you heard this, Brenda?"

"No." She released her grip on Todd's shoulder, knowing that any further effort on her part to move the discussion away from Todd's enthusiasm for what he had discovered in Park City was hopeless. She sat back and folded her arms, trying to control her emotions at her brother's determination to tell all.

"Actually, Brenda," Todd said, "you may be interested. I converted the same time Max did. He was the one who pushed me along, really he was."

"Please tell us, Todd, what happened." Katherine was sincere in her request, and both Thorn children sensed it.

"Well, I think the real clincher—you know, about our conver-sion—came the day we decided to fast. Polk had told us that one of the most positive ways to get a spiritual confirmation of anything is through fasting and prayer, done for the right reasons with the right spirit. So we experimented."

"What do you mean 'experimented'?"

"Just that. I mean Max and I decided to fast for twenty-fours and also to pray a couple of times during the fast to see if what Dr. Polk had told us would have any effect on us."

"You mean you guys actually went twenty-four hours without eating anything, no food at all?" Brenda was incredulous. Max had not told her.

"Or liquids of any kind. I mean zip." Todd nodded. "Nothing touched our lips except a toothbrush, and it was pretty dry. We didn't even swallow.

"It was more Max wanting to try the experiment than me, though I went along with it. I'll have to admit that about midnight, while Max was sleeping in our room, I got out of bed and started to go out into the hall to the little room on our floor where they have ice and pop and candy in the vending machines. I was dying for something cool and refreshing. I didn't think I could take fasting another minute. I felt like a wimp. Then I said to myself, 'What is the purpose of all this if I'm not going to stick it out?' So I didn't sneak out. It was then that I woke Max and asked him to kneel beside the bed and pray with me. I needed all kinds of support at that point. He got out of bed, and I knew he was as thirsty as I was, but he was so good about it. We knelt there in our room and really poured out our hearts. I guess I had never really prayed for anything in my life like I prayed for some kind of answer."

"How did it come to you?" It was a foregone conclusion of Katherine's that Todd had managed to capture the Spirit and felt the Lord nearby.

"It was no biggie. That is, I don't recall any special . . . you know, strange feelings or even a tingle. Still, I got the same impres-sion Max did. We both knew, when we compared insights, that it was right, that we ought to join. Don't ask me exactly how those thoughts came to me. It was like I knew it all along, but now I had a clear signal that I should be baptized. If there is such a thing as a signal, a word, a touch, a sense of right, I had it. Man, did I have it! So did Max. He told me later that he had received an impression that it was right to join the LDS Church before we began our fast, but he wanted me to have that same experience. And I did. Really, it was just like that."

At that, Todd changed direction in the discussion. He felt odd going any deeper about the way Max claimed he saw his deceased mother nodding to him in his mind. That little insight was strictly between him and Max. At the moment, Todd's mother flashed into his mind and he said, making a 180-degree turn in the discussion, "Did you know that Mom and Dad are going to the temple in Oakland to be sealed to each other pretty soon?"

Brenda wanted to shout, *Shut up!* to Todd. She tried to send a fierce message with her eyes. *Not now. Don't get into this crazy Mormon stuff. Not now, not when Katherine is so fragile. Cork it, kid,* she wanted to scream. She didn't. It would merely inflame the issue and upset Katherine even more. But Katherine was a lady, able to conduct herself as a lady under any circumstance. Brenda was convinced of that.

"Sealed to each other? What are you talking about, Todd?" Katherine seemed puzzled but interested.

"In that temple in Oakland, it is possible to be married for this life and the life in heaven, too. And that isn't all. Dr. Polk told me that the LDS Church members are the only people on the face of the earth who can marry husbands and wives to each other even though one or both have already died."

Katherine had never heard of such religious practices. Her eyes opened wide at the thought. She peered searchingly at the young man. She could see that Todd was serious. More than that, he seemed personally convinced. *Would it be possible to have Bob as my husband after this life? Well, that would be assuming there is some kind of life after death.* The minister in Krakow who officiated at their wedding apparently had not had the power to perform a marriage to promise the couple that they could be together after death. In fact, as she searched her mind for memories of weddings she had attended, she could not remember any such promise ever being made to a bride and groom.

"Listen, Granny," said Todd, his tone becoming earnest, unaware that he had shortened her title. "If God made marriage where families could be together in this life, wouldn't it be cruel if he didn't make it possible for them to be together in the next life as well? Dr. Polk taught about this from the Bible. Dad and Mom were so excited when they heard it."

Katherine leaned forward with interest. "Do you know where such a statement is located in the Bible, Todd?" *Could it possibly be so?*

"Well . . . uh . . . not exactly." Todd flushed with embarrassment. He had opened this discussion and did not know enough to complete it. "But Dr. Polk does. Why don't you call him in the morning and find out from him? You said we could call the yacht if we wanted to. He's supposed to be with Dad and Mom. But you know that—it's your yacht."

"Oh, my!" Katherine said, her voiced tinged with growing interest. "I wish I could sit down and talk to Dr. Polk. I had no idea such a thing was possible. Do you know your parents repeatedly urged me to go with them on the cruise? I should have gone! I declined because I didn't want to be extra baggage for them . . ."

Katherine's mind was churning with ideas as they walked into the entrance hall of her apartment. In a rush of words, she blurted out, "I have a great idea, if we can make it work. Brenda, do you have a valid passport?"

Puzzled nod.

"Todd?"

Another nod.

"Does Max have one?"

That drew blank expressions from both.

"Hmmm. That could present a problem." Katherine reached into her bag and retrieved her cellular phone. On second thought, she hurried into the kitchen and sat down at the oak-and-white bar next to the white telephone. Calling out to Brenda, she asked, "Where is Max right now? Can we reach him by phone?"

"At work, I guess," Brenda answered, following her into the kitchen, "That is, if he hasn't already left work to get packed to come up here tonight . . . Why?" Brenda felt a little uneasy.

"I have an idea, that's all. Call him. Do you know his number?"

"Sure."

She handed Brenda the receiver. Todd wore a baffled expression. Brenda dialed the work number she had memorized weeks ago. She reached him just in time. Max told her he was about to leave work. "Is something wrong?" he asked, holding his breath.

"Let me talk to him," Katherine said, eagerly reaching for the phone. She had met Max at dinner in Park City. Other than that, she didn't really know the young man.

"Max, Granny Katherine here. I hope you're still planning to stay at my place for the weekend."

He was.

"Do you have a valid passport?"

He did! He had worked in Panama two years before and had needed one then.

"Next question: Can you get off work until Monday? That is, if you don't mind going somewhere with us. We won't be back before Monday evening? Okay?"

Max hedged. He wanted to know where.

Katherine didn't want to divulge that. He might decline the offer. "Just come, dear. We'll talk about the details when you get here, but bring your passport. That's essential. Bye."

Katherine handed the phone back to Brenda. Brenda assured Max she had no idea what was going on. "See you at midnight," she said lightly. "Don't miss that red-eye. Bye."

Stunned into silence, Brenda and Todd sat mesmerized, watching this impetuous woman of means. Within the next ten minutes, Katherine had called her travel agent and made reservations for Max, Brenda, Todd, and herself to take the earliest flight in the morning to Pago Pago. Then she asked for a charter flight from Pago Pago to Juno Island, where the yacht would be moored Friday evening—Saturday, their time. Katherine knew the yacht's itinerary. She had gone over the route with Anney the morning they returned from the cemetery, eager to tell Anney little details about the South Sea islands they would visit.

Arrangements were made.

"If you kids agree, then let's spend the weekend in the South Pacific."

Brenda looked at Todd, and Todd, mouth open, stared at Katherine. Then Brenda burst out with an exhilarated laugh. "Why not? Let's surprise Mom and Dad!"

"No, no. I'm going to call your mom and dad to let them know. Come on. They deserve to know before we just show up. Besides, we need to be sure there is room for all of us. But let's surprise Max. He's telling his boss that he may not be back until Tuesday. They'll survive without him. We'll have to stay out of your parents' hair, of course, but it will be fun. I hope they don't kill me for this, but they did beg me to go with them. This is just a little delay, a slight change in plans, and a couple of extra guests."

The shocked expression on Todd's face quickly changed to one of pure pleasure. He didn't understand this unlikely little granny one bit, but he sure liked her style.

"I want to know what your parents know about a marriage in heaven and, if I can, meet with Dr. Polk," she explained. "We'll take it from there."

Katherine was a woman of action—always had been. Money had made it possible. From her penthouse she called the *Free Eagle* and got the bridge—all due to a marvelous satellite connection. In turn, the first officer transferred the call to Stephen and Anney's stateroom.

When Anney entered her stateroom after touring the yacht, the phone was ringing. Stephen was down the passageway helping Dr. Polk get settled for a rest. She was a little surprised that the phone would actually ring in their stateroom. Maybe the steward had a question. It had not occurred to her that a call from San Francisco could actually connect to a stateroom on a yacht in the Pacific Ocean. "Yes, hello?" The voice she heard was sweet and clear and excited.

"Anney, this is Katherine."

"Katherine? What's happened?" Anney stood paralyzed with

fear for her children. No one called a ship in the middle of the ocean without a darned good reason.

"Oh, nothing's wrong. Don't get alarmed. Brenda and Todd are right here with me. We've been having ice cream at Ben & Jerry's. We're just fine. How do you like the boat? Plush, isn't it?"

"It's gorgeous, of course. But I didn't expect anything less."

"Aren't you the spoiled one? Remind me to make you swim home . . . Anyway, honey, I want to ask you something, and please tell me frankly if I'm overstepping my bounds."

Anney sat down suddenly on the edge of the bed. "What do you mean?" she asked.

"What was that all about?" Stephen asked. He came into the stateroom while Anney was ending the conversation with Katherine.

"You'll never guess."

"Then tell me."

Anney crossed her legs on the bed and threw back her head. "It's Katherine," she shouted. "I can't believe that woman! She wanted to know about how people who have died are married to each other in the temple so they can still be married in heaven."

"What does that have to do with her?"

"She is flying out here with the kids and Max early tomorrow and will be on Juno Island not too long after we arrive there tomorrow evening. She made her plans, charter and all, and called me to see if it was okay with us. What am I going to say? 'No, you can't come use your own yacht?' They're coming by charter from Pago Pago, if all the connections hold."

Glancing up at Stephen's face, Anney giggled with delight. "She really is, honey. She's coming . . . tomorrow!" Anney threw up her hands. "She promises not to interfere with anything that is going on here. But get this . . . she just *has* to talk to Dr. Polk, the man she thinks has an inside track on eternal marriage. She wants me to line up a few minutes with him tomorrow evening so he can explain this new and exciting concept to her."

Stephen shook his head and said, "That lady! There is no one, but no one, like her." Suddenly both burst out laughing. "Isn't it great?" Anney smiled at Stephen, "I mean, the kids are coming for the weekend. Everything is going to be perfect!"

"Well, yeah . . . I suppose. It sure is making you excited, anyway." His brow furrowed in thought, he said, "Yeah, that's great . . . I only hope Dr. Polk is up to it tomorrow. Did you notice he is coughing a lot? He doesn't seem to know what is causing it, but his chest is tight. The cough had calmed down some when I left him, but I'm a little worried about him."

CHAPTER ELEVEN

A Cultural Feast

Thursday Evening

THE CAPTAIN SAT AT THE HEAD of the oval dining table. It would be the only evening he would be dining with the group as host. Dr. Polk would assume that role for the remainder of the cruise.

Captain Montgomery, striking in his white uniform, spoke in his impeccable British manner as the food was served from the galley. "I asked our chef—who, by the way, is perhaps one of the finest I've encountered on a ship—to serve native island food this evening. In Pago Pago they have some excellent traditional foods, and we thought perhaps you might enjoy a touch of Samoa."

A murmur of pleasure could be heard around the table. It was a congenial gathering, which included all the guests, plus the captain and the first officer.

"The chef and two Samoan natives prepared this special menu for you," the captain went on. "Some of these specialties were prepared on shore and brought on board before we sailed. I think you will enjoy the meal, but if you don't care for a particular dish, please feel free to decline it."

The stewards began to place colorful, beautifully garnished platters of unfamiliar foods in the center of the table. Karry was the least formal of the two stewards. Not only had he conversed with several of the guests as they settled in, but he and Stephen had become friends since that first hour when Stephen boarded the ship.

The captain seemed to take pride in naming and describing the dishes before them. "Here you have breadfruit, fish, taro, opened *palusami*, and, of course, the main attraction is coming right up."

Karry retrieved the main fare from the galley below and entered the dining room with it held high above his head on a silver platter. Anney glanced over her shoulder to watch him carry in the platter, but it was too high for her to see what it held. Karry lowered the platter between the captain and Anney, then slid it carefully to the middle of the table. He stepped back with a flourish, and the dinner guests exclaimed with surprise and delight.

Except for Anney. Shock would more accurately describe her reaction. There before them was a small roast pig, laid out with full pink hibiscus and white orchids covering the ears. The little brown roasted pig was resting like a small puppy on its belly, with its legs tucked under and a smile on its snout.

"Roast pig is a must at a traditional island feast," the captain said with relish.

Anney, who loved Honeybaked Ham at home, had never envisioned the entire pig as she ate it. All she could think of was the movie *Babe* and this poor little pig they had slaughtered to prepare a meal for her and the others. The sight abruptly spoiled her appetite. Suddenly queasy, the mere thought of consuming a lovable little piglet turned her stomach. She had no intention of eating a bite.

On the other hand, the others around the table had no compunction about feasting on pork. All took hefty servings as the captain began slicing into the rump. "It is fantastic, Anney," Stephen whispered. "Try it."

She refused. Not until the remains of the roast pig had finally been removed from the table and a luscious coconut cream baked in taro leaves was served did Anney regain enough interest in food to test the dessert.

During the meal, Stephen looked across the table at the first officer, who couldn't have been older than his mid-twenties. He asked the young man, whose name was Stone, how he happened to be an officer on the *Free Eagle*.

Like the captain, Officer Stone was British, tall, angular, and bright. He was also dressed in a white uniform that made him appear official. "My parents wanted me to have a stint on board a charter vessel. My family has been yachting for many years. I wanted a year at sea after I graduated from Cambridge. When I return to Liverpool, I will read law and become a barrister."

"Yes, a fine young officer this man has become," the captain bragged. "I trained him myself."

"Then," Stephen asked, "you are in command when the captain is resting or ashore?"

"Quite right, sir. The rest of the crew are not truly skilled yachtsmen. They are stewards and maintenance crew, though one of the crew members is training in navigation and, of course, he spends a good deal of time on the bridge. Actually, he's a marvelous help up there." The first officer pointed the tines of his fork skyward to indicate where the bridge was located. "The others . . . well, let's say they care for the needs of the ship and the charter guests. Not that such services are not essential to the cruise; it's a matter of—"

The young first officer caught a sharp glance from the captain and fell silent.

"You must have a good deal of experience to land such a weighty assignment at your age," Stephen continued.

"Well, as I said, I was raised on yachting in Europe, sir. My father is a championship sailing yachtsman. He has taught me much of what I know, as well as Captain Montgomery here. I have learned a great deal on this ship."

Anney noted the pride and snap in the officer's voice, as if he knew everything there was to know about sailing a world-class yacht.

"Well," the captain cautioned, "there is a lot to navigating a yacht of this caliber, but this young officer is learning rapidly. There are some things he has yet to experience—the challenge of rough seas is one. We try not to be at sea in rough weather, so those experiences are not necessarily part of training a young officer. Passing from island to island as we do on charter, we make port almost every evening. And we stay in close touch with the weather advisory. When it promises to get nasty, we make sure we are safely in port."

Anney ate her fill of the coconut cream and complimented the captain on the dinner. "This is certainly an elegant craft," she complimented him. "However, I'm not much of a sailor, so if things get rough—you know, wind and rain—just put me ashore until it blows over."

"I'll remember that, Mrs. Thorn," the captain laughed.

Polk had a thing about formal dinners. This first evening together would set the tone for the following evenings. During the day, all other meals would be catch-as-catch-can, with buffets set up on deck at breakfast and lunch time. Those who preferred to breakfast in their staterooms had but to call the galley and order whatever they wished. But dinner was reserved for the group to come together, dressed in their island best. The meals would begin with someone offering an evening prayer and blessing on the food, then Dr. Polk, as had long been his habit, would speak briefly on some vital point in the Book of Mormon. Then the food would be served.

* * *

MAX CAUGHT THE CITY BUS two blocks from the small apartment house in East Los Angeles where he and his street buddy, Tony Alvarez, had lived for the past three weeks.

Thanks to his stipend received at Park City four weeks earlier, he had made the deposit and paid the first and last months' rent. Then he asked Tony if he wanted to vacate their digs under the Los Angeles Interchange east of the city where they had set up two tents and a common eating area beneath the pepper trees that were dusty from the long summer without rain. Tony had been a little apprehensive, but on the strength of his trust in Max had finally agreed to move his few possessions and sleep under a roof for the first time in many years.

Before that time, Max had walked over two miles to work each day. But that was no problem for him. He had known nothing but an altogether difficult existence. Perhaps the easiest part of his life had began when he escaped his father's verbal and physical abuse and took to the streets of Texas. He wound up hitchhiking I-101 along the California coast for a year until he followed a lead and got a year's job with a shipping firm in Panama. Then he returned to find steady work in the low-rent industrial section of East Los Angeles, west of the interchange. Now, at twenty-one, Max worked hard as a shipping clerk in a furniture factory.

He had been hired as a flunky, planing wood and sweeping sawdust, but it hadn't taken his boss long to figure out that Max was a computer natural and had put him to work doing billing and shipping. Max had eagerly absorbed everything he could learn about computers. Because Max had few expenses (living under the freeway as he did), he had been able to save enough money to buy an old, used computer, then a year later, a powerful, sophisticated, new PC. Alert to all the latest advances in cyberspace, he worked his way onto the Internet, developing electronic skills on his own that few in the industrial park understood.

Although Max's salary increased steadily, he had continued to live in a tent to support his obsession with the computer: he could buy more equipment if he had no monthly rent to pay. It had worked for him for the past year. Tony had guarded his computer and printer equipment during the day while Max was away at his job.

Tony's crippled legs kept him from venturing very far from his own tent, and Max paid him to guard his possessions. Despite the fact that he was physically handicapped, Tony's scarred face looked menacing enough to warn off any would-be thieves. Tony's main expense was for food. The two men maintained separate tents, but shared meals. Tony knew that if he were just legal, he could apply for welfare assistance from the State of California and would receive shelter and food, plus a small living allowance, as many did. He was a Mexican national, however, so there would be questions. He had been in California long enough that Max was pretty sure he would qualify for citizenship and could apply to remain in the country legally. But Tony was afraid he would be deported, so he refused to surface.

Not until Max met Brenda in Park City, in June, did he have any desire to get an apartment and live like a normal bachelor. When he accepted the teachings of the missionaries and joined the Church shortly after he returned to Los Angeles, everything had changed. The missionaries had actually sat in his small tent and taught him the gospel, a novel experience for them. The mission president had had his reservations about the two elders riding their bikes to the brush area under the interchange, first to teach Max, then to continue fellowshipping him. The week following his baptism Max rented the apartment. No one was more relieved than the mission president.

The only problem with the apartment was its location. The rents were certainly cheaper in East Los Angeles than anywhere else, and that had been his primary consideration when looking for a place. The major drawback was that it was in the heart of gang territory, with its attendant risks of theft and drive-by shootings. There had been no shootings in the immediate vicinity of his apartment, but the risk was there all the same. As to theft, Max was most uneasy about all of his precious computer equipment. He knew that to the gang members, it was worth only what it would fetch in a pawn shop. But even that might well be worth their attention. So as he gradually moved the component parts into his apartment, he hid them as well as he could in old boxes beneath his other scanty possessions, heaping his most threadbare clothes on top.

Tonight, as he sat near the Southwest boarding gate, his mind was not on his computer. He was pondering his relationship with Brenda. He had acquired two very bright spots in his life this summer: Brenda, and his membership in The Church of Jesus Christ of Latter-day Saints.

Max had experienced a whirlwind romance in Park City, all due to Brenda's grandfather's illness and her flight to Salt Lake City to visit him, then her stay at the lodge where her parents, the Thorns, and her brother, Todd, had set up their conference. Otherwise, Max doubted that he would ever have met the woman of his life.

Brenda was beautiful, small but athletic, and filled with enthusiasm for life. To Max, there was an almost visible glow about her. He had felt his whole being reach out to her from the first evening she was at the lodge. In some ways, she had been a major distraction to his explorations into the Book of Mormon.

Before being invited to Park City, he had entered a chat group on the Internet and was soon committed to the concept of finding out about the Book of Mormon. The chat led to a rather timid application for acceptance to the Park City Book of Mormon Youth Conference that was held in June. To his amazement, he had qualified and was accepted. The fact that he had hitchhiked all the way from Los Angeles to Park City confirmed the interest he held for the project. In turn, the sponsors of the conference had paid the expenses for lodging, food, and transportation home. Max was also compensated $2,500 for his three weeks in attendance.

After having taken off that extra week, Max had been frankly surprised that his boss at the furniture factory wanted him back He had called to ask for the extended time off, but it would have made no difference whether the boss agreed or not. Max would have taken the week, even if it had meant the loss of his job. It was that important to him to stay the extra time with Brenda.

His boss had growled at him, but, in truth, he would have consented to nearly anything to keep Max in his employ. The girl who had attempted to take his place had been little help. In fact, shipping was so fouled up when Max returned that he had to work extra hours to put things right on the computer and adjust the accounts.

The financial compensation Max was given for his participation in the conference went toward rent, some used furniture, more equipment needed for his computer setup, plus the beginnings of a small savings account. It also helped pay for this weekend trip to the Bay Area to visit Brenda. Southwest Airlines had offered a late flight to San Francisco at a drastic discount. Max felt lucky that he had been able to reserve a ticket from his computer connection. It had been the next-to-the-last seat available on the red-eye flight.

What was there about Brenda that fascinated him so? He longed to be with her. He told himself it was crazy. He had avoided relationships with girls all of his life. It wasn't at all like him to attach himself to anyone. The reasons were subconscious, but any therapist could have told him he was afraid to get hurt. Hurt, pain, longing . . . loving—those were emotions he had tried to shove out of his life.

Brenda knew nothing of his real life. She knew he worked in Los Angeles, that he was a computer whiz for a furniture company, but that was the extent of her knowledge of the real Max Williams. He would have to fill in the gaps sometime, but not yet. He simply could not lose her by revealing too much of his former lifestyle. He didn't even have a high school diploma. Far from it. Max had never attended high school at all, and he feared she would never want to see him again if she knew.

Brenda. Oh, Brenda. Max was gripped with concern and yearning. Then, too, there was another issue: Brenda didn't yet understand the Church. She had been pretty disparaging about it, even bitter that her whole family had accepted it. In his heart he felt sure that she would convert to the Church, given the same exposure that her parents and brother had experienced. He worried, though. It wasn't so much that she was a holdout. It was more that she had no interest—period. She hadn't shown any signs up to now that she would change her mind, but he would convince her that it was the right thing to do. Surely he could. How, he didn't know.

He hadn't seen her since he kissed her good-bye at the Salt Lake airport four weeks ago. She was bound for home in Lafayette, California, and he for Los Angeles, with the promise that he would make this trip for the weekend—to be together and review their lives. He would tell her this weekend all about his crummy background. He felt he had to. Would it make any difference? She came from such a stable, happy family of respectable people. He had no family. Maybe she wouldn't see that as a total negative. At least she wouldn't have in-laws to contend with.

He wondered about her family. When he called Brenda later from his computer phone, she had told him that her grandmother had invited both of them, as well as her brother, to her penthouse in San Francisco for the weekend. She assured Max that he was welcome and that he could share the guest room with Todd.

At first Max was keenly disappointed. He had wanted Brenda all to himself. He also felt some concern that he would be imposing on her grandmother, but he reluctantly accepted the invitation anyway. Now the woman had called asking if he had a passport. What on earth for? Waiting to board his plane, Max shook his head in wonder when he thought of where he would be staying in San Francisco. *Me, in a penthouse? Strange things do happen.*

Soon the flight attendants began preboarding passengers. Next, numbered card-holding passengers began filing onto the aircraft. Max stood, shifted his backpack, and headed toward the line of passengers behind the plastic rope. He could see that most of those passing through the gate with boarding passes were young, excited, and definitely going to the Bay Area for a good time. So was he.

* * *

THE DRIVE FROM NOB HILL through the quieting streets of San Francisco went smoothly. Reaching the freeway, Todd gunned up the on-ramp, easing smoothly into the light traffic that still plied the freeway at midnight. He enjoyed zipping along in his mother's vintage BMW—always had. Todd and Brenda were alone in the car. They had left Katherine pulling suitcases out from the back of her room-sized walk-in closet, talking to herself about what clothes she would need.

"So, you think this thing with you and Max will last if you don't even take a look at the Church?" Todd probed Brenda for the tenth time in the past week, his tactless approach one that only a brother could get away with.

"I didn't say I wouldn't look at it," Brenda said in a huff. "Just because you've all turned into such fanatics doesn't mean I have to believe it."

"Come on, you know what I'm talking about. We're not fanatics, and it isn't something we just happened to stumble onto, either."

The two drove in silence for a few minutes. Todd could tell that Brenda was fuming, but he couldn't let the subject drop. "Listen to yourself, Brenda. This flippant attitude of yours will cause Max to take a hike." Todd glanced over at his sister to gauge her response and tried to decide whether or not to pound away further about the Church.

Not long ago he wouldn't have cared one way or another what Brenda believed. In fact, he could understand her resistance. A few months ago he had been just as irritated when his dad had tried to get him to check out the LDS religion. But two things had changed. First, he had learned for himself that the gospel of Jesus Christ was true. It had opened a new vista of life itself and had given him a perspective of what it was all about. Second, he had found a wonderful friend in Max Williams. And would you believe it? Max had fallen for his own weird sister. The thought that she might blow the best chance she was ever going to get—to have both the Church and Max—was too stupid for words.

Brenda looked straight ahead at the taillights flashing brightly as vehicles braked for the night construction ahead. A mobile sign on a small trailer read: CREW AT WORK, LEFT LANE ONLY. Todd pressed lightly on the brake pedal.

"I hope this isn't going to be one-lane all the way to the airport. Max'll be at the curb in ten minutes," Brenda muttered, glancing at her watch one more time.

"Nah, I think we're okay. . . . Well, you still didn't give me a straight answer. I'm serious, Brenda. I'm telling you, if you don't open the Book of Mormon and take a good look at what it's all about, or talk to me, or better still, some missionaries, this thing you've got going with Max isn't going to take. I'm serious."

"I know you're serious, but get off my case, Todd. I'm sure Max would like me to join the Church, but he doesn't bug me like you do. I have a life, and I have to make up my own mind. Okay?"

"Okay, I'll back off, but first let me just say that the Church is very important to him. He and I really got into the Book of Mormon while we roomed together at Park City. We both stayed up late—night after night—talking about the Church."

"Then you joined. I know, I know."

"We did all this studying, and we were both convinced it was true. That was before you ever showed up. It may sound like we sort of flipped, but it wasn't like that. I'm telling you from the deepest part of my soul that the Church is true. Besides, I'd sure hate to see you throw away a guy like Max. He's different . . . like . . . I don't know; he has depth or something. You'll regret it forever if you pass up this chance."

Brenda felt trapped. Why couldn't she have met Max at some other time, some other place where religion wasn't an issue? Why, all of a sudden, was she surrounded by these religious zealots?

To her, religion had never been comfortable. Her mother had known this about her by the time she started junior high and refused to go with the family on Sundays to listen to her grandfather preach. She had loved her grandfather dearly, but couldn't bear to sit through another one of his "Christ and Power" sermons. If they only knew . . . it sort of gagged her to listen to any of the preachers she had been exposed to. They were all pretty much the same—all the television hype, the makeup, prepping the overflow audience in the studio, even her own grandfather's dramatic performance. No, if that was religion, then she wanted no part of it. She would never understand why people fell for it.

It wasn't fair that religion had to be an issue here, not when she had fallen so completely in love with Max. He was like a gift to her, so good, so perceptive of her needs, and like Todd said . . . so deep. The miracle was that he loved *her*—plain ol' Brenda, nobody special. He was the first guy that ever really meant anything to her. She felt that she had been waiting for him all of her life, and she loved him completely. When she thought about it, it seemed strange that they had known each other such a short time. It seemed much longer.

Brenda turned her head away from her brother and watched the cars out the window. *Why did Todd have to bring all this up? We don't need to talk about religion this weekend, for heaven's sake!* Even though it made her angry to admit it, she knew that Todd was right. Max, as sweet and patient as he seemed, was no doubt mulling over the situation, wishing that she could feel as he did about the Church. *Why can't he just accept me as I am? We can each do what we want to do on Sundays. I can sleep in while he goes to church. I can't see any problem with that.* She leaned her head against the back of the seat and sighed. Yes, there was a problem here, and she knew it as well as Todd.

The traffic began speeding up as they reached the end of the single lane, the bright orange cones slipping behind them. Todd looked at his watch and pushed hard on the accelerator, sending the small BMW into the inside lane. They would make it in time.

* * *

"YOU KNOW, I'M STILL LEARNING THINGS in the Book of Mormon . . . well, in all scripture for that matter. I've become aware of that fact time and again." Stephen was seated on the twin bed across from Dr. Polk, who was reviewing his notes for the next day's session. Dr. Polk had retired early to study, propped up on pillows, and Stephen had come in to say good night and to talk for a minute before going to his stateroom. Or perhaps he would wander up to the aft deck to watch the guys speeding around the yacht on the two Jet Drive Nauticas. The crew had flooded the water surrounding the yacht with lights. Stephen could hear the buzz of the toys out the porthole of Polk's stateroom. Polk put down the papers and raised his eyebrows.

"So what can I explain this time? I know something is bugging you."

"Not bugging me. I just need some enlightenment, so I'm asking the guru of all Book of Mormon knowledge a simple question."

"Shoot."

"You and your friend Sam have both mentioned the concept of the Nephites building the New Jerusalem when they return. I'm not familiar with the concept of a New Jerusalem. It sounds like it's to be built in the Americas. But in my mind, I always thought it would be the Jews who would return to the Holy Land, as they are now doing, and rebuild that city. Did I miss something? Where is the New Jerusalem going to be built and why?"

Polk turned onto his side and remained propped on his good elbow as he spoke. "Good question." He coughed for a moment, trying to clear his throat. "Umph . . . Let me tell you what I know about this whole concept. First, the New Jerusalem will be built in the Americas; second, it has to be built before the Second Coming. It will be the city where the Lord will come in all his glory. In the official history of the Church, there is a phrase that fits exactly what we're talking about. As a matter of fact, now that you bring it up, I think I'll quote it tomorrow in our discussion." Polk turned his head toward the small desk in the corner of the stateroom. "Would you mind getting something for me? I need it run out anyway. *The Ultimate LDS Library on CD*, as you know, has the complete *History of the Church*. Would you slip that CD into my lap-top and pull up *History of the Church*, volume one? I don't remember the exact page, but try searching under 'Zion' or 'cut off.'"

Stephen got up from the bed and brought over the lap-top and the CD. He sat back down and inserted the CD, searching the key words "cut off."

"I think this is it on page 316."

"Start reading where Joseph Smith is telling about 'Zion, et cetera, et cetera.'"

Stephen adjusted the screen away from the bedside lamplight and read: "'Zion is the place where the temple will be built, and the people gathered; but all people upon that holy land being under condemnation, the Lord will cut off, if they repent not, and bring another race upon it that will serve him.'"

Polk said, "Now don't be confused here. Any land consecrated by the Lord is holy land. Okay, look at what our own history says, sanctioned by the Prophet Joseph. It tells us about Zion. It is the place where the temple will be constructed and the righteous people of the Lord will gather. Also, as you look at that quote from the official history, you see that the Lord has an alternative plan if the people—the Gentiles—do not become righteous. They will be removed and another race—race, mind you—will come in and build the New Jerusalem in *this* holy land, not the Holy Land in the Middle East."

Polk rolled to his back, then used his good hand to reach down by the side of the bed and retrieve his scriptures. It was amazing how adept he had become with one hand. Thumbing through the Pearl of Great Price, he stopped at Moses 7:18 and read, "'And the Lord called his people Zion, because they were of one heart and one mind, and dwelt in righteousness and there was no poor among them.'

"Here the Lord is revealing to Moses a Zion society, a group righteous enough to live the law of consecration. But Zion is also a literal city. The Jaredite prophet Ether wrote about the city of Zion."

Once again Polk turned pages rapidly. He found Ether 13:4-6 and read: "'Behold, Ether saw the days of Christ, and he spake concerning a New Jerusalem upon this land.' Or the Americas," he added.

"'And he spake also concerning the house of Israel, and the Jerusalem from whence Lehi should come—after it should be destroyed it should be built up again, a holy city unto the Lord; wherefore it could NOT be a new Jerusalem, for it had been in a time of old; but it should be built up again, and become a holy city of the Lord; and it should be built unto the house of Israel.

"'And that a New Jerusalem should be built upon this land'—
again, the Americas—'unto the remnant of the seed of Joseph.'

"Now then, Joseph Smith had revealed to him that the very
heart of the New Jerusalem—the city itself, with the temple in the
center—would be built in Jackson County, Missouri . . . 'the center
stake of Zion.' Joseph Smith must have seen in vision the New
Jerusalem because he described it when he said that it would be a
great group of cities, a sort of megalopolis. The Doctrine and
Covenants further tells us in Section 64 that the New Jerusalem will
be an ensign to the nations of the world . . ." Polk found the scripture and read it as he spoke: "'And the day shall come when nations
of the earth shall tremble because of her'—that is, Zion—'and shall
fear because of her terrible ones.'

"Stephen, it will be a literal series of cities, glorious and beautiful, awaiting the arrival of the Lord. And who shall build it? In
D&C 52, at the beginning of the revelation, it says this—hold on
while I get it—it says, 'Behold, thus saith the Lord unto the elders
whom he hath called and chosen in these last days, by the voice of his
Spirit, saying: I, the Lord, will make known unto you what I will that
ye shall do from this time until the next conference, which shall be
held in Missouri, upon the land which I will consecrate unto my
people, which are a remnant of Jacob, and those who are heirs
according the covenant.'

"When you read Jacob, here again it is the remnant of Jacob,
son of Lehi, that it has reference to. He makes a distinction between
the remnant of Jacob and the heirs, or Gentiles, who are the covenant
Gentiles that were promised the right to be first in the last days. The
Nephites and the covenant people of the Lord will join together in
building the New Jerusalem. It will be a great honor. But as I read it,
the Nephites will do the actual supervision and leadership of the
construction of the New Jerusalem."

Stephen set the lap-top to one side of the bed and said, "You're
ahead of me, Dr. Polk, but I'm beginning to see that the Nephites
have to surface sometime before the contracts are drawn up on the
New Jerusalem."

"Exactly."

Chapter Twelve

A Walk on the Shore

Friday Morning
Juno Island

WITHIN A FEW HOURS THE EARLY MORNING SUN would focus on the tin-roofed stores, creating intense heat. At the moment, it crept slowly across the rooftop of the Bay Haven Hotel as Stephen and Manuel secured the tender to a tie-up on the wharf. They had risen early and decided to come ashore in the small motor craft and stroll the white, sandy beach that formed a crescent on Juno Island—a speck on the map in the Pacific's vast expanse.

Samuel had mentioned to the group the evening before at dinner that they could sometimes find floating glass balls that had been lost from fishing nets in the Sea of Japan, if they got up early and walked the beaches. Stephen's sleep time was off anyway; he was up by 5 A.M. Seeing Manuel on deck, he had asked him if he wanted to hunt for glass balls with him in the early morning light.

The air and water were as warm and pleasant as a mild Turkish bath. The two men strolled along in shorts and wild Hawaiian floral shirts, combing the beach for any sign of the gray-green balls Samuel had described. In their search, they shuffled along the fine sand and glanced out into the bay where they could see the *Free Eagle*, a thousand meters from shore, where her crew had dropped her hook. She was radiant in the morning sun, the rolling waves of the bay gently rocking her.

The seawater lapped at Stephen's bare feet as he sauntered along the curving beach. He caught his breath in awe as he let his eyes drift along the sand. The scene looked for all the world like a page from *Travel Magazine*—sand, water, and a glorious sunrise in the tropics. It was incredibly beautiful.

"Stephen," Manuel said after a few minutes of silence, raising his voice to be heard above the lapping waves. Stephen smiled at the slight Spanish touch he gave to his name so that it came out sounding more like "Esteban." "How long have you been working with Dr. Polk on his projects?" he queried.

"Over a year," Stephen answered easily. "Why do you ask?" He had become friends with Manuel last fall when he and Roy had gone with Dr. Polk to Oaxaca, Mexico, prior to Polk's stroke. They had enjoyed dinner at Manuel's home, and Manuel had shown them the town that evening. Stephen recalled buying some black ceramic pieces of art from a vendor on the street.

"I don't know, exactly. Do you sense a change in his attitude?"

Stephen studied Manuel's face, then turned to look out at the waves. He was not certain what Manuel was driving at, but he sensed that it was not a positive probe of Polk.

"Please don't think I am critical of Brother Polk." Manuel could see that he may have struck a tender spot . . . a bit close to Stephen's loyalty to the professor. "I have known him since I was a student at San Diego State. You know, I graduated from there. I met him when he came to lecture on a Know Your Religion tour. He spoke at the Church Institute while I was taking a class in Book of Mormon. After that initial meeting, we saw each other off and on over the years. I helped him with several of his tours to Mexico and even went with him and some of his students as they explored among the ruins of southern Mexico. I have admired him all these years. More than admiration, I respect him. We have been friends a long while."

Stephen kicked sand in front of him and kept his gaze on the beach, ostensibly looking for the glass balls. "Having been friends that long, you may know Dr. Polk much better than I do," Stephen replied. "I don't know exactly what it is that you see as a change in him. Oh, I know that the stroke has taken its toll on his body, but I see no change in his attitude and how he approaches things."

"I do. Oh, yes, I do!" Manuel spoke with a degree of passion surprising to Stephen. "Maybe it is the influence of Brother Meyers," he went on. "The two are so caught up in this Nephite nation business that I feel he has veered from his usual Book of Mormon studies."

"By that I presume you mean his interest in traditional Book of Mormon lands. I can see where this whole discussion might be a little disconcerting for you. You feel that the promise of an inheritance of the Americas, made in the Book of Mormon, is reserved for the people of the Americas, the Lamanites, or the Indians, don't you?"

"Well . . . yes, I do."

Stephen was quiet for several minutes, seeking inner courage and wisdom to answer Manuel's concerns. Finally he replied, "All I can say after listening to the presentation yesterday is that it seems possible to me that it may not be just that way. Frankly, I don't have enough background, nor do I know enough about Brother Meyers, to make a judgment call on his attitude, or, for that matter, on any influence he might have on Dr. Polk's. I do know that both of them are heavily involved in this quest to find the location of the Nephite nation in the world today. But I really don't sense a change in Dr. Polk, insofar as my involvement with him is concerned. He has been trying to help people understand the underlying truths in the Book of Mormon since long before I met him, I'm sure."

Manuel took a new tack. "It's me . . . I know it's me."

"What do you mean?"

"I mean—and please excuse my concern, I am Latin, and the Latins are very open with their emotions—I came here to help Dr. Polk in any way I could with matters concerning the Book of Mormon. Surely you know of my love for the Book of Mormon. However, I feel a shift in the air. I think there is a movement, beginning with men like Brother Meyers, to replace the traditional view of the children of Lehi in the Book of Mormon. He is highlighting a new set of people that may or may not exist."

"I see," Stephen said, remembering Manuel's reaction during the first discussion. "I can understand what you're saying. You feel that they are moving away from the emphasis on the Lamanites in the last days—shifting to the Nephite people, if they can be found. Of course you do." Stephen's expression became empathetic. He had observed how certain members of the group were reacting to the information Meyers was dispensing. It was now coming in loud and clear that Manuel at least was concerned—more than concerned, maybe offended was a better term—by the new theories.

"Let me ask you," Stephen felt his way cautiously, "do you consider yourself a Lamanite?"

"But of course! *Sí*, absolutely. I have a drop or two of Spanish blood in my veins, but I have much more Indian—Mayan—that is certainly Lamanite. I consider myself a Lamanite as much as any of the pure Indians in Mesoamerica. It is for this reason that I am concerned about the shift I detect."

"Are you concerned that Brother Meyers could have enough influence to cause a shift in the mission to the Lamanites? He is not a General Authority of the Church, you know. He is just one man with an idea . . . who happens to have amassed a pack of evidence to support his claims, that's all."

"Yes, but it is a powerful idea, with astounding evidence. Whether mere theory or not, these things have a way of shifting people's thinking. I am convinced that this is the beginning of a movement to involve people of the Pacific region of the Church through a greater understanding of their heritage. It feels like a move from the Day of the Lamanite to the Day of the Nephite. Am I wrong?"

Stephen shook his head lightly, signaling to Manuel that perhaps he was carrying the possible repercussions of the new evidence too far. "I'm not so certain that what we are discussing here this week will have any impact on anything. You see, Manuel, the object of Dr. Polk's promotion of the Book of Mormon is a rather simple one. I know for a fact that he doesn't care where the reader comes from, or what his heritage is, so long as our studies have impact and convince people of the testimony of Christ and the witness of that testimony, which is so much a part of the Book of Mormon, and that it is a book for our day. If the Lamanites are true to their commitment to the gospel, then they share in the fruits of the last days, the same as the Gentiles. There are no restrictions on those who can come into the Church and receive all the blessings of the Lord. There is nothing to fear on the part of any group, so long as they covenant with Christ. I really think your concerns are groundless."

Silence hovered as they walked a few more steps.

Stephen spoke again. "I also know that it is easy for me to say this because my role is different from yours. I'm not Lamanite. Your whole view of these matters has a different base. If I'm right, you desire to save an entire people, the Lamanites, and see them inherit their blessings. I just worry about my immediate family—at least thus far in my limited study of the gospel. And, believe me, that is all the responsibility I can handle at the moment."

"You're right. I fear for my people. We are a childlike people, very sensitive to change and withholding of affection. We run on emotions much of the time."

Stephen glanced over at Manuel, took him by the arm, and said, "I don't know anyone who loves the Latino or the Lamanite like Dr. Polk. I know. I've traveled with him among the ruins, and I've listened to him talk about your people."

Stephen stopped, cupped his hand to shade his eyes, and looked down the beach at the curving shoreline. "I also think we had better make for the tender and get back on board the ship. I've got to check on Dr. Polk." Stephen kicked again at the sand, glancing at his troubled friend as he turned about. "It looks like luck didn't favor us today with any glass balls."

Retracing their path along the shore to the tender, the two men edged deeper into the warm, pleasant water. The beach hotel and tender were now bathed in the morning light. Stephen squinted his eyes and wished he had remembered to wear his sunglasses as Manuel had.

"No, I think your fears are misplaced," Stephen concluded. "I read the other day in the *Church News* that the majority of the members of the Church are Spanish speaking. Now, that tells me that the Spanish-speaking nations are outnumbering the rest of the Church."

"Perhaps so, and I too am aware of that news, but do you know something? Many of those who speak Spanish who are coming into the Church in Latin America are predominately of Southern European extraction—that's Gentile stock. It means that the

Lamanites are not coming into the Church as rapidly as everyone seems to think. The fact that members, lots of members, speak Spanish does not necessarily mean they are Lamanites. Look at Argentina, Uruguay, even Mexico. A majority of the members—and in some Latin American countries, *most* of the converts—are predominately European, not Indian. I have seen the figures." Manuel released a heavy sigh.

"I'm not a Gentile, but they are. Look at my skin." Manuel placed his deep-brown bare arm next to Stephen's light freckled skin that was sparsely covered with blond hairs. "I am Indian. Fortunately, I came from an educated family, and I had a grandfather who was Spanish. Otherwise, in my country, I perhaps would not be a banker. We do have a class structure in my country that places most pure Indians at the bottom of the social ladder. They deserve a great blessing from the Lord." He clenched his teeth in frustration. "I want my people to be allowed to move to the top of the ladder, especially in the Church. I don't want the Church to get distracted by a new emphasis. We are making progress, slowly but effectively. Really, we are!"

Stephen mustered his courage once more. "One word of counsel, Manuel," Stephen cautioned, placing his hand on Manuel's wrist once again in a reassuring gesture. "One of the things that attracted me to the gospel when I joined last year was certainly the Book of Mormon. But as I listened to the elders explain about a living prophet, I was convinced that the Lord would work through that man. Since joining, I have been taught this principle very firmly. I have an even deeper conviction that the living prophet of the Lord is directing matters today through inspiration. Nothing is going to shift in the preaching of the gospel without the approval of the Lord through his living prophet. I truly believe this. So why don't you set your mind at ease and enjoy this free trip with your wife?" Stephen pointed to the *Free Eagle* floating in the center of the bay. "'Kick back and let the information flow. You don't have to swallow it whole.' Do you understand that phrase?"

No smile crossed Manuel's face. However, he sensed a kinship with Stephen and felt he could converse freely with the man. He lifted his right hand and waggled his fingers back and forth in a *más o menos* response. Manuel was not yet convinced that what they were reviewing in the group was sound. He shared the conviction of his fathers that the Lamanites were a greatly blessed people. He had too much tradition in the Church ever to accept the idea that the Lamanites would not surface and become (as he was sure the scriptures indicated) a rose—a beautiful, full and glorious, blossoming rose. He had been taught this all his life. It often sustained him when he became discouraged with the members of the stake in Oaxaca who were so often uncommitted in their Church duties. He was grateful that he had come from a dedicated, untiring family, going back to his grandfather, who was the first to join the Church.

* * *

THE RODRIGUEZ FAMILY HAD LIVED *in the Oaxaca Valley as far back as family legends were repeated. It was precisely this fact that made Manuel's great-grandfather, also named José Manuel Rodriguez—who in 1909 was sixteen, almost seventeen—familiar enough with the surrounding ancient ruins to be of assistance to the gringos from the north who had ridden into town with fine saddle horses and pack mules.*

It was after the rainy season that the two professors from the Brigham Young Academy and two other interested, self-styled, explorers— all Latter-day Saints—arrived in Oaxaca to obtain supplies and two or three guides. The professor, Mendenhall, spoke Spanish fluently; the others had picked up a sort of "border Mexican," having spent the past three months in Mexico touring the ruins in and about Mexico City.

When Professor Mendenhall approached the town square looking for two or three young men who knew the terrain and wished to make a few pesos, José surfaced. José knew how to sell himself, and did anything and everything to make enough each day to help his father support their family. On the day that Professor Mendenhall appeared in the plaza looking for help, José had been shining shoes. His dusty brown skin and large black eyes and hair projected youth and health.

Mendenhall evaluated the youth carefully. He thought José a little young for the job of guide. "Usted es un poco joven, muchacho," he said.

"Tengo dieciocho años, señor," José had lied about his age.

Fortunately, Mendenhall had liked José from the start. For the following two weeks, José and one other young man from Oaxaca became guides to the explorers as they trudged among the ruins in the valley. José had never enjoyed work so much. He dreaded the day the wonderful venture would stop and the gringos would leave. Professor Mendenhall was a man of great honesty, kindness, and generosity, three qualities of character José had not often seen—and never had he seen all three in one individual, not even in his father.

Although José's father was a good man who cared for his small plot of earth on the edge of Oaxaca, José faulted him for having no ambition to make more than the small amount the family needed to survive. José was the opposite. He took every opportunity to ingratiate himself with the businessmen and their commercial ventures in the heart of the subtropical city of Oaxaca. He especially curried favor with the three local bankers who always sought out José when they crossed the plaza to have their shoes shined. He took great care to spit-polish the tips of their fine black leather Oxfords. While José was out of town during the two weeks he and his compatriot guided the Americans on their tour of the ruins, he made sure that he came back to town twice a week to rush into the three banks and shine the owners' shoes. He refused to lose his clientele, especially the bankers. It was José's opinion from sheer observation that where the money was deposited was the site of economic power in the valley.

Life for José was strictly the Oaxaca Valley. He had never been beyond its hills. He did not care. For José, the entire world revolved around the central part of the city, and gravity secured the three bank buildings to the edges of the central plaza.

At least that was his orientation until Professor Mendenhall began to explain to him the purpose of his visit to the valley. He spoke to José of the Lamanite heritage. In two weeks José, whose keen mind absorbed knowledge as if it were a giant sponge from the deepest crevasse in the Gulf of Mexico, had learned a new concept; he learned who his people really were.

Mendenhall taught José from the pages of the Book of Mormon, translating the words into Spanish. José could read, but there was no Book of Mormon in Spanish available in Oaxaca. All the knowledge José gained during the two weeks he spent with el grande profesor came from Mendenhall's vast background of the gospel.

The concepts José repeatedly begged Mendenhall to retell were those of the promises to the Lamanites in the last days. Mendenhall retold José of the covenant the Lord made with Enos about the future of the seed of Laman, Lemuel, and Ishmael. He spoke of the great knowledge that would come to their children in the last days. He pointed out to José a number of times and assured him that he was truly a Lamanite, and that the Lord loved him and would greatly bless him and his people . . . that one day they would blossom as the rose.

The teachings had sunk deep into José's soul.

Five years after Mendenhall and his associates returned to Utah, José made his way to Mexico City, where he accompanied Oaxaca's leading banker on a business trip. By this time, Indian though he was, José was the banker's assistant and knew banking better than any young man in the valley.

In Mexico City, José eagerly searched out the missionaries. In a letter to José, Mendenhall had written the address of the mission home in the city. During the ten days he spent in Mexico City he was with the missionaries, older men who had come from what he learned were the LDS Church colonies in Northern Mexico; they were elders and they spoke Spanish as fluently as José himself. He listened once again to the great promises extended to the Lamanites by the Lord. He did not have to be taught faith in the Lord Jesus Christ. He had always believed in Christ. The elders baptized him the day before he returned to Oaxaca.

If there were other members of the Church in the valley at that time, José didn't know them. In time, the Church dispatched missionaries to the region; by then José, who now was a part-owner in the bank, became the first branch president of the Church in Oaxaca. He had married, had eight children, and raised them in the Church. He lived a long and fruitful life and, before his death, instilled in his young great-grandson—his namesake, Manuel, a good, honest boy who showed great promise in the banking business—that one day the Lamanites would be so numerous and righteous that they would lead the Church to fulfill its promise to usher in the Millennium. Manuel believed that with all his heart.

* * *

MANUEL AND STEPHEN CLIMBED BACK on board the *Free Eagle* in time to take a quick shower, have breakfast, and relax a moment before the discussion resumed in the main salon.

The breakfast special this morning featured eggs Benedict. It was Stephen's third breakfast on board; each had been a great treat, served on the aft deck of the yacht where its clean, water-resistant, hardwood flooring offered true luxury. The indoor/outdoor wicker furniture, with white-and-green striped cushions, was surely equal to the poolside comfort of any four star-hotel—whatever that was like, Stephen thought as he sat down to eat.

Eggs had never tasted so good. The fork-split English muffins— toasted and buttered, topped with eggs and warm hollandaise sauce, along with slices of Canadian bacon—were out-of-this-world delicious. It was *bon appetit* all the way on this yacht—although Stephen had met with the chef when he first arrived and found that he wasn't nearly as warm and inviting as the food he prepared. In fact, he had seemed cold and aloof, resentful of Stephen's suggestions regarding the tastes and limitations of the religious group he would be cooking for. That didn't bother Stephen as long as he kept those delicious meals coming. That was what the chef was hired to do.

Chapter Thirteen

Session Two

Friday Morning
Juno Island

SESSION TWO GOT UNDERWAY AT 9 A.M. SHARP. After the marvelous dinner the evening before, it had been plain that Dr. Polk was too exhausted to stay up for another discussion. All had agreed to postpone coming together until morning. Stephen was sure he had detected relief on all their faces. At least they had not protested.

Samuel stood before the group to begin the discussion. "Brother Meyers," Eric said eagerly, his wide, Polynesian face glowing, "before you begin, let me tell you all something. When I was thinking about our discussions, I remembered that one of my ancestors wrote an account about a blessing that Joseph F. Smith gave to a brother in their new little branch of the Church when President Smith was the prophet and came to visit the members in Hawaii. In the blessing, he told the person that he was a Nephite."

Takahashi raised his hand, nodded his head in a brief bow from his chair, and said, "If I may also say something. I found the information about the explorer Heyerdahl, which you included in your packet of information, very interesting—especially his observation that many of the Polynesians had borrowed certain foods and other aspects of their culture from the Central Americans. I'm afraid we have all assumed that the Nephites were a rather simple people, when actually they must have been highly skilled to build ships and trade as they did."

"I have not thought of them as simple," Meyers interrupted.

"Yes . . . okay." Takahashi nodded. "I agree, why couldn't some of them have resettled in other parts of the world? After all, we know that in the Book of Mormon several groups left Jerusalem, or that region of the world, and made their way to the new world. In this account, we have knowledge of three: the Nephites, the Jaredites, and the Mulekites. I, for one, can see that the first part of your premise is at least possible. Of course, without strong evidence that does not mean it happened."

Manuel slumped down in his seat, a scowl on his face. "Well, you haven't proved it to me," he mumbled, barely audible. Then his voice grew louder, "I say that this is all a ridiculous theory."

Caught up in the drama being played out in the room, Anney had no intention of participating, though she was engrossed in the teachings of Christ found in the Book of Mormon, which she had come to love since hearing and accepting the gospel eight months before. Suddenly aware that the tension was building in the salon, she waited with interest to hear the new facts presented by Samuel Meyers. Like most recent converts to the Church, she was eager to learn all she could and discover new insights into the gospel. However, like Stephen, she had no opinion on whether the Nephites were alive and returning, or whether they were destroyed. She had centered her new faith on a much more pressing and, to her, more vital issue—the Book of Mormon as a second witness that Jesus Christ was the Son of God. But it wasn't hard to see that there were those in the group who held strong views on the subject of the Nephites and Lamanites. Anney listened as Meyers spoke.

"I'm glad to see that all of you did your homework. Perhaps we will leave the first part of our hypothesis for now, though, and proceed to the next. But be assured, we will come back to it and tie it all together before we are finished. Today, let's talk about the recipients of the promises the Savior made. As you know by now, Dr. Polk and I maintain those promises were made to the Nephites, not to the Lamanites.

"And why did the Nephites receive the promise? Look at the logic here. Think for a moment exactly who the Nephites were."

Samuel took up a fresh piece of chalk and wrote the word

Nephites on the board. "The Nephites were the righteous nation that Nephi set up after they divided off from the Lamanites. The Nephites were the ones who were faithful to the Lord most of the time throughout the thousand years that they were a civilization. The Nephites kept the record and had numerous prophets. They may not always have been righteous, but until they were destroyed as a nation, they did have prophets among them, and they retained the covenants of the Lord for most of that time. In other words, they obeyed the Lord throughout the history of their nation. We also know that they were of the House of Israel."

Alongside the first word, Samuel added the word Lamanites.

"Now, what were the Lamanites doing? For the most part, they were nomadic, bloodthirsty, constantly going after the Nephites. In short, they were savages. They kept no scripture; they disobeyed constantly. They lived out that thousand years trying to destroy the Nephites and their record. As a matter of fact, except for several brief but very bright times, we see only destruction on the part of the Lamanites."

Manuel was quick to add, "But the Lamanites were also of the House of Israel. Don't forget that."

"Right you are. Oh, and I know . . . there was Samuel the Lamanite, a great prophet, and all the people of Ammon who had been Lamanites. They were truly committed to the gospel. Let's call them the 'covenant Lamanites,' though when they joined in with the Nephites, they actually *became* Nephites. Those Lamanites who joined the Church and were faithful enjoyed the eternal blessings promised any child of the covenant. And those Lamanites who were righteous after the appearance of Christ and became part of the Zion society, they, too, were part of the covenant. But when I speak of the Lamanites as a nation, a total people, I refer to the multitudes, the main body, the hordes who were rebellious.

"Among the Nephites, most lived the gospel. True, near the end they were destroyed because they turned against the Lord. Yet does this warrant total eclipse of the promises given them in the Book of Mormon? Why would the Lamanites, who were predominately unfaithful, be so blessed in the last days and no blessings at all be given to the Nephites, who were consistently a righteous people? I'm speaking of a *people*, a people to whom I believe promises *have* been given that will be fulfilled in the Lord's own due time . . . maybe in the not-too-distant future." Meyers sensed he was preaching. He silently told himself to lighten up.

"Now for some evidences in the scriptures. As I read the words of Isaiah, either quoted by Nephi or by the Savior when he appeared to the Nephites, and read the words of the prophet at the temple after the great destruction, I see that nothing slipped past Isaiah as he was writing about our world today, the 'Day of the Gentiles.' I mean, he understood it all."

"What are you getting at, Brother Meyers?" Takahashi asked, a little confused. It sounded to him like Meyers was running together Nephi, the Savior, and Isaiah in some new pattern of explanation. Samuel was glad to see that Takahashi was beginning to feel more relaxed with the group and more free to speak out.

"Let me show you this in relationship to the subject we are discussing about the promises to the Nephite nation. It seems that without the teachings in the Book of Mormon, there are parts in the writings of Isaiah that simply cannot be fully understood. The catalyst for their comprehension is not found in the Bible—only in the Book of Mormon."

Maria, true to her nature and training, decided to speak up, "You're saying that we have information in the Book of Mormon from the writings of Isaiah that the rest of the Judeo-Christian world doesn't have?"

"Right. That's part of the beauty of the Book of Mormon. It opens a whole new dimension to the scriptures. We all know this to be so. Every one of us. This is especially true in at least two comments made by the Savior when he appeared at Bountiful to the Nephites after that terrible destruction.

"Christ was emphatic when he said that he spoke that which his Father had commanded him to say regarding those writings of Isaiah. Did you hear that? It came as a command from the Father. So, under the direction of the Father, as he made the introduction to those verses of Isaiah, Christ said to the Nephites . . . now let's see . . . turn to 3 Nephi 16:16–18." A pause, then Meyers read:

Verily, verily, I say unto you, thus hath the Father commanded me—that *I should give unto this people this land for their inheritance.*

"That refers to the Nephite people, not the Jews at Jerusalem. Then Christ said—and please stay with me, because if you don't, you'll miss it as I missed it for many years—

And then the words of the prophet Isaiah shall be fulfilled, which say—

"You see, first Christ gives the land to the Nephites as an inheritance, as we see above, then he follows up with Isaiah's words:

Thy watchmen shall lift up the voice; with the voice together shall they sing, for they shall see eye to eye when the Lord shall bring again Zion.

"Dr. Polk will explain the concept of Zion and the New Jerusalem in a minute. But look what we have here. Christ is speaking not of Jerusalem, or the Holy Land; rather, he is speaking directly to a branch of the house of Israel—the Nephites—explaining in detail the time when Nephites shall be given this land for their inheritance. The land—the Americas—will be primarily for the Nephites. It will happen when the Lord shall bring again Zion.

"Now the next question. What is meant by 'Zion'?"

"Wait!" Manuel blurted out. He could bear his frustration no longer. Meyers and Polk glanced up from their scriptures. "I can't believe you think this says that the Americas were given as an inheritance to the Nephites. What about the Gentiles and the Lamanites? I've always understood it to mean that the Lamanites would get the land of Zion for their inheritance. I still think they were the only people left, and the ones who were given the blessing. I've been taught that all my life. You'll have to make those verses a lot plainer to me before I accept what you're saying." Manuel immediately regretted that he had spoken so emphatically.

"Manuel," Samuel said quietly, absolute empathy in his voice.

He had sensed how these ideas would affect this proud Lamanite. "Manuel, who was the Lord speaking to on the temple steps in Bountiful when he appeared after the great destruction?"

"I always thought it was both Nephites and Lamanites," Manuel replied insistently. "Didn't they join together when the Savior came from out of the heavens? There are legends about this in Mexico. Surely you're not going to tell us that my people were not around!"

"Well, the Lamanites who converted to the gospel had the curse lifted from them and were numbered among, or *became, Nephites,*" Samuel answered. "It was one of the greatest miracles ever. Do you think the warring Lamanites were in the Land Bountiful shortly after the destruction? Bountiful was deep within the Nephite region, according to the geography of the Book of Mormon lands. I don't think there were warring Lamanites present. The Lamanites appeared to be in their own lands. There is no indication that they showed up at the steps of the temple. Again, I will say they were in other areas of the country. We have no record of just what was happening with the Lamanites during the destruction.

"As near as I can tell, the cities that were destroyed according to the record were Nephite cities. The Lamanites were in another part of the land. This doesn't mean that they did not feel the destruction. I'm sure some of the Lamanites were ripe for destruction as were the Nephites, but there is no record of it. The Lamanites didn't keep a whole lot of records, remember, at least not much scripture. If they did, we don't have them. The Book of Mormon as we have it is a Nephite record. Of course, it is intended for all the seed of Lehi, but it was recorded by Nephites in the time of the Nephites. When Christ appeared, the record made of those proceedings was intended for them. Show me where the Lamanites were present, and I will gladly accept that information. I cannot find anywhere that it was so."

Manuel was not satisfied with that answer. "Surely you have read our traditions and know that the Maya have many symbols depicting the Savior. I'm sure you are all familiar with the bird-god Quetzalcoatl, who many in the Church believe to be Christ. That is a Lamanite tradition. How can you prove there were no Lamanites in

Bountiful to receive Christ when he appeared out of heaven? No, Brother Meyers, I think you are mistaken in this very important matter. My people were there. I have felt this all my life. Now you tell me that my own people were not there when the Savior spoke, that they did not pray with him, or fall down and worship him. I have a hard time accepting such a view." Manuel was so agitated that he had to guard himself from slipping into Spanish.

Meyers had anticipated that Manuel might feel a sense of betrayal at this explanation of the circumstances that would prevail prior to the coming of the Savior, particularly concerning preparations for the ushering in. It was not surprising that Manuel flatly refused to consent to what he obviously regarded as nontraditional doctrine at best, even bordering on heresy.

"I have to agree with Manuel," Maria interjected. "He's right. We have all been taught that the Savior was speaking to all the people who survived, or at least to those who were around the temple." Her light brown hair swung freely as she shook her head insistently. "No . . . this isn't right. I'm sorry, I can't buy all this. Is it your opinion that the transformation of the righteous Lamanites was a lasting or a temporary sign?"

Meyers answered, "Well, 3 Nephi, chapter 10, verse 18 speaks of those who *had been* Lamanites and that they were to be participants in the manifestation of Christ. Had been is the key phrase here. This means that they were no longer Lamanites, but became Nephites . . . permanently. This manifestation of Christ came two decades after the Lamanites who had joined the Church were miraculously transformed."

Meyers felt no frustration, nor did he feel intimidation. He had expected such a response. He simply reiterated, "Christ is speaking to the Nephites when he quotes Isaiah. Logic tells you that. Even if there were Lamanites present, those present were the righteous ones who had survived the destruction and were transformed. No, those at the temple—the Nephites and the transformed or covenant Lamanites who were now considered Nephites—were the recipients of the Savior's promise, which he had been commanded by the Father to give.

"Think about it. Do you think the other Lamanites were even

aware of the writings of Isaiah? I don't. Christ is speaking to a right-eous body of people, not that there couldn't have been a righteous body of Lamanites in the land. I'm not saying that. But the main body of the Lamanites—and they were, by all accounts that I have read, savages—had not been taught the scriptures. They knew not of Christ.

"Now listen to what Christ says that confirms this. It's in 3 Nephi 20:11–14. He mentions those present:

> Ye remember that I spake unto you, and said that when the words of Isaiah should be fulfilled—behold they are written, ye have them before you, therefore search them—

"Don't you agree with me that the Savior was talking to a literate, scripture-reading group when he gave this counsel about *searching the scriptures?*"

"Of course he was," Maria agreed.

"Do you think the savage Lamanites had been taught to *search the scriptures?*"

Samuel looked around the circle. All eyes were down, intent upon their scriptures.

"I don't think so," Meyers observed. "The Savior goes on with his discussion of the prophecies of Isaiah in verse twelve. But I'd like to interject here that, later, the Lamanite nation became a Zion people and lived in harmony for nearly two hundred years with the Nephites. There is no evidence that the curse was lifted from those Lamanites. The curse—the color of their skin—was lifted earlier for a select body of Lamanites. If you recall in your handout, the curse was lifted for those Lamanites who joined the Church and fought side by side with the Nephites for their liberty prior to the destruction. Here is verse twelve:

> And verily, verily, I say unto you, that when they shall be fulfilled then is the fulfilling of the covenant which the Father hath made unto his people, O house of Israel.

"Once again, who are *his people?*"

"Nephites, you are saying," Takahashi responded quietly.

"Okay. Then we have verse fourteen, which is a repeat of what Christ said earlier in chapter sixteen when he said:

> And the Father hath commanded me that I should give unto you this land for your inheritance.

"I can't read anything else into that very clear statement by the Savior himself, except that the inheritance would go to the Nephites—the people he was speaking to—in the latter days.

"Manuel, as far as your statement is concerned—that you have been taught all your life that the promise was directed toward the Lamanites—perhaps there are two things I could offer.

"First, since it has long been accepted that no Nephites survived, it has been commonly believed that the only other seed of Lehi left to claim the promise were the Lamanites. But if we can show evidence that Nephites live today, do you see how it changes that concept?

"And, second, it might be interesting to note where the idea that the Lamanites were to be the recipients of the Savior's great promise first came about. Did you know that first Oliver Cowdery, then later Orson Pratt, started the whole concept? Oliver and several others had gone to a gathering of Indian nations to preach the gospel. While teaching them, Oliver and the others seemed to get carried away with promises. They told those Lamanites who were there what great things the Lord had in mind for them in the latter days. I have searched, but I can find no statement from the Prophet Joseph sanctioning their preachings . . . not one. Feel free to use the *Ultimate LDS Library on CD* and check it out for yourselves."

Samuel then turned to Dr. Polk and invited him to discuss the promise made by the Savior: that the Nephites, once they returned and received their inheritance, would be the driving force behind the building of the New Jerusalem.

Stephen turned slightly to see how the group had taken Meyers' information about Oliver Cowdery that was transmitted by Parley P. Pratt to his brother Orson Pratt regarding the day of the Lamanites. No one had stirred, and every face bore a slight frown. Clearly, what he said was news to them.

*　*　*

KARRY DIDN'T COMPREHEND THE DISCUSSIONS. He could tell that at times the interchange between Meyers, who seemed to be the teacher, and those seated around the salon was heated. Even if he didn't understand what they were talking about, it was stimulating to listen. Again, he felt something deep within him responding to the atmosphere of the gathering. Somehow what they were talking about seemed so compelling to him. What was it? This group was so different, so wholesome. Strange. They kept bringing in talk of the Lord, certain people, a promise. What was there about these nice, considerate people that attracted him so?

Taken on the surface, some of the comments made by the crew of the *Free Eagle* made sense to Kerry: "They are a religious lot who've locked up the liquor cabinet. Stupid!" Cruising was supposed to be for having fun, wasn't it? And all they really seemed to be doing was sitting around with their Bibles open, or whatever books they were using. Some of the women, he noticed, seemed to have more free time than the rest of the group. They didn't gather in the salon when the rest of the people had their discussions, but spent their time reading, napping in their staterooms, or visiting the island instead.

Karry didn't understand.

Contrary to the views of the rest of the crew, he considered that what the people were doing was not in the least boring. He found himself wanting to be in the salon with them. Even when they disagreed, there was a depth of belief—beautiful, yet different than he had ever known.

He decided, during the heart of one discussion, that he would speak to Stephen, the man who came early and prepared things on the yacht. At the moment, Stephen was seated by his attractive wife on the center sofa. He seemed like a man who might explain the whole nature of the atmosphere of the group. Karry wondered at himself. It wasn't like him to get involved with groups that came on board the *Free Eagle*. All most of them wanted to do was have a great time and get drunk. This bunch was decidedly different.

Karry wanted to know why.

* * *

STEPHEN TOOK THE BOTTLE OF SODA Anney handed him as she sat down on the weathered bench and stretched out her legs to relax. It was nice to be together, just the two of them. For weeks, they had been heavily involved with Dr. Polk's conferences and needs, with little private time together. Today, they strolled among the tourists on Juno Island; at least, they had for the past hour this late afternoon.

"Nothing makes me as suddenly tired as walking around souvenir shops and looking over the junk they expect you to buy," Stephen said, taking a swig of strawberry soda. "Here I thought this might be the deserted isle you suggested in your note. I'm flat-out disappointed."

"Me too," Anney grinned, leaning her head on Stephen's shoulder for a moment. She picked up two postcards and studied the brightly colored pictures, wondering who she would mail them to. Looking up at Stephen, she said, "You know, something is beginning to bother me about these group discussions on the yacht."

"What?"

"We're hearing all this talk about the idea that the Nephites weren't destroyed as a people. Rather, that they were killed off as a nation, but some escaped and are out there somewhere." Anney motioned with her arms toward the bay.

"So?"

"So doesn't it seem strange to you that none of the prophets have mentioned this in any of their talks? At least, that is what Samuel would have us believe. I mean, think about it, honey. Here is a major piece of news, and nothing has been said officially. Doesn't that strike you as strange?"

"Yeah, but I'm not troubled."

"Why? Do you have some private insight that I don't? If you do, please let me know."

"Don't get me wrong . . . I thought about this last night, too."

"Good. Then I'm not the only one asking questions."

"I haven't really taken it up with Dr. Polk or Samuel, though I may, but I figured . . . What the heck? First of all, Samuel made it very clear that this is information for a small group. Okay? Therefore, he's not broadcasting it as if he were the prophet."

"That's true, but—"

"But he's not. I think that is the most important thing about how he is handling this evidence. The other thing that struck me about this whole thing is that others have done somewhat the same thing."

"What do you mean?"

"Remember when I was first introduced to the Book of Mormon on that estate in San Diego? I remember hearing Dr. Polk discuss the concept of chiasmus in the Book of Mormon. You remember my telling you about chiasmus, that sort of inverted poetic form of writing that's found all through the Book of Mormon?"

"I guess so. You've told me so many things, I can't remember half the things we've talked about."

"Anyway, it was a kid on his mission—I can't remember his name; he's a professor of law at Brigham Young University now. The thing is, in the late 1960s this young missionary discovered that there is chiasmus in the Book of Mormon. He was so excited about it that he wrote a letter to his mission president explaining the concept, and the mission president sent it on to the First Presidency for them to see his marvelous discovery. I mean, to find this ancient method of Near Eastern writing in a book translated in the nineteenth century was astounding. It would have been impossible for Joseph Smith to write that form of expression. No one in the western world even understood the concept in the 1820s."

"So what are you saying?"

"The thing is . . . Dr. Polk says he has read nowhere that the First Presidency ever commented on that discovery by that young missionary. I don't think a one of them has ever uttered the word *chiasmus* publicly. I mean, they could do some heavy PR with that concept alone, if they wanted to, but they remain silent. I don't know why. Dr. Polk says it's because the Brethren speak primarily on the first principles of the gospel. For whatever reason, the information you find on chiasmus comes through F.A.R.M.S. publications. But then F.A.R.M.S. certainly hasn't stopped talking about it just because the Brethren don't mention it."

"Then you're saying that the leaders of the Church don't seem to get all fired up about these things?"

"All I know is they keep a pretty low profile when it comes to introducing concepts other than the fundamental found in the Book of Mormon or any of the other scriptures. Honey, there are plenty of researchers looking into the things that are supposed to take place in this era, but the ideas either remain in the realm of speculation or they're discussed by other researchers and written up.

"Even if Dr. Polk and Sam take their findings directly to the First Presidency, you may never hear another word about it. Nope, all they are charged to preach to the members is faith, repentance, baptism, and the laying on of hands for the gift of the Holy Ghost . . . and they stick pretty close to that responsibility."

CHAPTER FOURTEEN

Private Discussions

Juno Island

LATE MORNING, WHILE MOST of the participants were hard at their assignment to digest the material Samuel had given them in the latest session—a handout about Jacob, son of Lehi—Maria found Samuel stretched out on a deck chair with his notebook and scriptures open, reviewing some papers. She stopped a moment, then asked him if he would stroll around the deck with her, out of earshot of others. "Let's talk, okay?" He arose with a smile, dropped his notebook onto the deck chair, tucked his scriptures under his arm, and slowly began to walk with Maria.

Her fingers interlaced nervously.

"Okay," Maria said, glancing sideways at Samuel. "Here's the thing: I should never have consented to come. I'm not good for this group. The ride is great; the food and accommodations are superb, best I ever had . . ."

"But?" More fidgeting. Maria became even more serious.

"Samuel, this isn't working for me," she responded with quickened breath.

Her words didn't throw Samuel. He could have taught a course in creative listening. "You're trying to tell me that you don't buy this new insight into the idea that the Nephites have survived as a people?"

"I didn't say that." She shrugged, slid her fingers through her hair, and let the wind off the bow feather it smooth. She was grateful they were out in a full breeze.

"What do you mean, then?" Samuel persisted. He valued Maria's insights, even though he disagreed with her traditional stance on the issue of the Nephite peoples.

She shook her head. "I came here to learn. But I'm not an easy candidate for new concepts in the gospel, especially those that emanate from outside the usual channels."

Samuel managed a weak smile. *Cut to the core.* "Come on, Maria. You act as if I'm trying to impose my findings on the entire Church." He tensed as he was challenged—a rare event, especially coming from a woman. He turned and looked closely at her, measuring his response.

Maria's eyes closed and her chest heaved. She simply hated to be placed in the position of defender of the traditional faith, at least over something as seemingly minor as a small group uncovering evidence about the Nephites. Did it really matter, anyway? Of course it mattered. All details of the teachings of the Book of Mormon mattered. They mattered terribly.

"Well, if you're so uncomfortable," Samuel said at last, "you certainly don't have to stay with us. Do you want to bow out of the group sessions and just spend the time as you choose? Or you could catch a flight back to the States when we anchor in the morning, if it bothers you to be with us. You can take a commuter to Fiji and from there catch an international flight to L.A. or San Francisco."

Maria's shoulders bunched and her head shook again. Her voice was barely audible. She stared at him for a moment. He asked her to repeat what had been muffled by the wind.

She spoke louder, with a humorless laugh. "I'm not a quitter."

"I can appreciate that. Neither am I. Then you do want to stay with us!"

A nod came in agreement.

Meyers took a breath, then said, "Maybe I ought to say something that needs to be addressed at some point in this gathering. I think everyone in this group is aware of the great admonition given by our late prophet, Ezra Taft Benson, when he told us in very frank terms that we must study the Book of Mormon daily. I have quotes on the inside cover of my book to remind me of his concern. Here are two of his statements." Meyers pulled his Book of Mormon from under his left arm. Like some members, he carried the standard works constantly as he moved about, never knowing when he might need to read from them. He adjusted his reading glasses as they stopped near the bow of the ship on the main deck. "Listen. I know you know this one:

> Unless we read the Book of Mormon and give heed to its teaching, the Lord has stated in section eighty-four of the Doctrine and Covenants that the whole Church is under condemnation. . . . Now we not only need to say more about the Book of Mormon, but we need to do more with it. . . . The Book of Mormon has not been, nor is it yet, the center of our personal study, family teaching, preaching, and missionary work. Of this we must repent.

"The second quote is this:

> I bless you with increased understanding of the Book of Mormon. I promise you that from this moment forward, if we will daily sup from its pages and abide by its precepts, God will pour out upon each child of Zion and the Church a blessing hitherto unknown—and we will plead to the Lord that He will begin to lift the condemnation—the scourge and judgment. Of this I bear solemn witness.

"President Benson declared his warnings to us ten years ago. This great prophet left a solemn certainty that neither the condemnation nor the eventual scourge and judgment has been lifted in nearly 166 years, but that we as a Church are still shouldering this heavy burden. Am I putting too much pressure on us? I don't think so. All the leaders of the Church are asking us to do is read the Book of Mormon, study the Book of Mormon, and make it the centerpiece of our study of the gospel. That is really not too much to ask. I personally love to study it; it just comes to life for me. Maria, I don't want to hammer on something that has become my own personal commitment to the Lord. I want to get a fix on just what the scriptures are telling and act accordingly. Is that wrong? Also, I need you to continue commenting in the group as we go along on this discussion. That's why Dr. Polk invited you. The only way to know if the evidence will hold up is to have someone like you—knowledgeable, alert, and willing to give it your all and take nothing for granted."

Samuel felt clammy from the frank encounter. He smiled, squeezed her arm, and said sincerely, "Thanks."

But was Maria convinced or even appeased? He couldn't tell.

CHAPTER FIFTEEN

Personal Problems

Noon Friday

ERIC WAS GRATEFUL FOR the high-tech communications on board. He needed to call home and find out from his sister, who was caring for the children, how things were going. His greatest concern was for Cory. He knew it was not a good time for them to be away from the family. They had some real problems to work out. The phone on board ship was his only way to keep tabs on Cory. It might be just a teenage phase, but Eric saw red flags shooting up all over the place when it came to his oldest son. He seemed to be so easily swayed by his peers. If he would deceive his family about the earring, what about other things? Girls, for one. This latest trick was such a stupid, surface thing. But did it send a signal that something more threatening could be happening? What about drugs? Both Eric and Carol knew drug abuse could be devastating to any kid. As a bishop, Eric had handled two incidents with kids in his ward—both involved with drugs and both from good, active families. No way were LDS kids exempt from such things. He had seen that firsthand.

His experience as a bishop notwithstanding, dealing with Cory was Eric's first experience at being a parent of a teenager, and he was uptight about the whole scene. It was impossible to be objective and give patient counsel when it was his own son at risk. Maybe it was Cory's sneaking around and doing things without their knowing that caused Eric and Carol to worry so. It was this as much as anything that troubled Eric as he dialed home using the phone in his stateroom.

The whole situation with Cory had come to a head when Carol noticed that the boy had pierced one of his ears. She had been taking him to the restaurant where he worked part time for his dad and walking, out the kitchen door to the garage slightly behind him, she had spotted the tiny hole in his earlobe.

Startled, she had blurted out, "Cory, have you had your ear pierced? Do you wear an earring?"

Cory's left hand had reached for the ear in a reflex attempt to cover the tiny indentation.

"When did you get that done? *Why* did you? Cory, what's happening to you?"

"Mom, don't say anything to Dad, okay? You know how upset he gets. Please, Mom. I'll explain. Please?"

Making no promises, Carol had left Cory at the back door of the restaurant and stewed about him the rest of the day. When she picked him up that evening, she drove just a couple of blocks to a side street, then pulled the car over and parked beside a vacant lot overgrown with vegetation. Cory could tell by her set face that there was no way out of this mess but to lay out the truth—at least part of it.

Hunching down in the passenger seat, Cory glanced furtively out the windows. All he needed was to have someone he knew spot him here with his mother.

"Here's the thing, okay?" Cory said angrily. "Mike said all the guys in California have earrings. What's the big deal, anyway? I can always let it grow back. I don't see why you care."

Mike, it seemed, was a new *haole* from Glendale, California—a guy he had taken up with in school. His mother had moved with Mike and his brother to Honolulu where she now worked in a reservations center along Waikiki Beach.

At Carol's probing, Cory grudgingly revealed that Mike's mother was "cool." She laughed a lot and liked Cory. She seemed glad that Mike had made a friend so quickly. That friendship had begun a week before school was out for the summer. In the three months since Mike had arrived in Honolulu, Cory had learned what was really rad in the world, especially among the guys in southern California—skateboarding, earrings, even tattoos.

With dismay, Carol could see that this Mike had made quite an impact on her vulnerable son. But Cory sure hadn't brought him home to meet his family. He was no doubt sorry that she had noticed his pierced ear, but she could tell by the hostility in his voice that he was far from repentant.

Her mind braced against what she might hear, Carol finally mustered the courage to ask the biggie: "Cory, is Mike into drugs?" Was there the slightest hesitation before Cory answered?

"'Course not! Anyway, Mike's mom trusts him!" Cory bitterly spat out the words. "He doesn't have to be in at any certain time. You guys think I'm still a little kid."

Carol drew a deep breath. This was beyond the scope of her disciplinary skills. "Cory, I have to tell your dad. This boy is not a good influence on you. Just hear how you're talking to me. You're in need of some strong counseling. We only want the best for you, and someday you'll be glad we cared enough to be firm."

"Yeah, right!"

Cory wasn't home.

"He's not here right now," Eric's sister said. "But he's doing what you told him to do. He works every day with Lyle at the restaurant. I drove him over there this morning." Eric's sister sounded positive about the situation.

"Lyle's a good man. I'm sure he'll look after him and see that he keeps busy." Lyle was Eric's assistant manager, who was great at overseeing things in the restaurant while Eric was away. Lyle knew of Cory's rebellion and had promised to help if he could. Nonetheless, Eric could not deny that he felt a bit uneasy. He knew that Lyle was pretty casual about life in general.

His sister brought him up to date on things around the house and flipped back to the subject of Cory. "I'll have him call when he gets home. We can reach you on your boat, right? Oh, is Carol there? I need to ask her about the girls' dresses for Sunday."

"No, she's gone ashore with some of the other women for the day. I'll have her call you when she gets back on board . . . Say, Deb, tell Cory I called. Thanks for your help. I'll call the restaurant and talk to Cory if he's there, then I'll call you again this evening."

When Eric reached Lyle, he talked about restaurant business for a few minutes, then asked to speak to Cory.

"Cory's not here right now. You know he's been working. He's a good worker, so I let him take a break for half an hour. He said he needed to pick up something for his skateboard while he's in town. He promised me he'd be back in half an hour. Want me to have him call you as soon as he shows?"

"Yeah, Lyle. Do that. And Lyle, I told you he's on restriction."

"I know. Does that mean he can't take a half-hour break and do a little business?"

Lyle was good at his job, but he had no family. What would he know about raising a teenager? Panic began to rise within Eric's mind.

"So you don't want Cory going off alone. Is that right?"

"I don't expect you to be a policeman, Lyle. I'm sorry to put this extra burden on you. I just want him to do his job at the restaurant and stay nearby while he's there. Carol and I are just hoping he'll shape up."

"I understand. I'll watch for him and maybe go with him the next time he has an errand to run."

"Thanks. I appreciate all you're doing."

Eric sat on the edge of the bed in the stateroom and slammed both fists down hard on his thighs. He needed to be tending to the pressing needs of his family, especially Cory, not roaming around the South Pacific. He should have told Polk they couldn't make it after all.

Yet he had to admit he was interested in everything that was going on here on the yacht. He was learning so many concepts about his people that he never knew. At least, he felt they were his people. He didn't need Samuel Meyers to tell him that he was from the family of Joseph, son of Lehi. He knew about the large statue of Lehi blessing his son Joseph on the grounds of the temple in Hawaii. It seemed logical that the posterity of Joseph, youngest son of Lehi, was in the islands. Why else would they have depicted such a scene?

Eric knew he came from a rich background of family and the Church, beginning with his great-great-grandfather Kumi, who was a boy when the gospel was introduced to the people of the Islands in the 1850s. It was a proud heritage of conversion, one he had been told repeatedly by the older members of the family. In spite of his anxiety, Eric had to smile as he remembered his old grandfather's enthusiastic version of the story.

Ships docked at Honolulu Bay regularly in the 1850s. The sailors and passengers from the mainland enjoyed the lush growth on the island of Oahu that stretched from the mountains to the east all the way to the azure blue waters of the Pacific.

Young Kumi got out of bed and stepped outside the family's thatched-roof hut and relieved himself behind the coconut tree, which he could climb faster than any boy in the village. When he looked up, he saw a clipper ship anchored in the center of the bay. Forgetting that he was hungry, he dashed to the shore, eager to be among the first to get a job helping the passengers with their belongings. The dinghies would be coming ashore soon, but Kumi never waited until passengers stepped into the small, warm waves along the shoreline before he lined up a potential haole who would want him to carry his things to the hotel.

The sun was well into the eastern sky by the time Kumi dived into the surf and swam like a dolphin to the dinghies alongside the vessel. He couldn't remember a time when he couldn't swim in the pounding surf. Today the water was calm, except along the beach where the waves were curling three or four feet high. That was nothing for a fourteen-year-old boy with Kumi's swimming abilities.

Kumi's father had been dead since Kumi was eleven. He had been stabbed to death in a bar although the English sailor who cut up his father had suffered no punishment. The Navy sent him back to England—that was it. The family felt helpless. But then, who could fight the British Navy? They had guns, knives, and cannons. Kumi hoped the British would fail in their attempt to take over the island. What did they call these beautiful islands . . . The Sandwich Islands? Not a good name at all. Someone told Kumi the name came from the Duke of Sandwich.

At least this morning the clipper ship at anchor flew an American flag and was not a naval ship. That was good. Sailors never gave more than a penny for packing their things around all day. Americans gave as much as a shilling for a day's service. Kumi was one of three brothers who helped to support their mother and three sisters. He didn't mind earning money this way. He liked to talk to the passengers, whether British, German, French, or American. Kumi knew the key words to speak in all three languages though he had learned slightly more English than German or French. He liked the Americans who, for some strange reason, spoke more or less the same language as the dirty British.

"Sir! Oh, sir!" Kumi shouted from the top of his voice to the young man who stood in the warm morning sun at the railing of the upper deck. He looked down and smiled at the Hawaiian youth bobbing along the hull of the ship. "I help you, okay?"

Although the young American was formally dressed in a black suit and tie, he didn't look much older than Kumi himself. He cupped his hand to his ear and called down, "You want to help me?"

Kumi heard him clearly, "Yes, yes. I work for you, okay?"

In spite of his serious appearance, the American youth had a smile that softened his long, narrow face and prominent eyes. With his wholesome grin, he asked the boy in the water, "How much? How much do you charge? Do you understand me?"

Kumi understood clearly. He held up his index finger with salt water dripping off it and said, "One shilling for whole day. Okay?"

An older man, black bearded and rotund, came up alongside the youth and said something to him that Kumi could not hear. The young man seemed to challenge what the older man said. At length he leaned back over the side of the ship and called, "Okay. One shilling. You can carry my things to the Plantation Inn when we get to shore."

"Okay!" Kumi shouted back with delight that he had a day's work. He loved to bring his mother a shilling, especially when his two older brothers often came up empty-handed at the end of the day. He wanted her to be proud of him.

Kumi smoothly treaded water while the rest of the passengers settled on board the dinghy for the transfer to shore. He stationed himself directly below the American youth and spoke to him in a quiet voice, so as not to attract the attention of the two seamen whose job it was to row the boat to shore. If they noticed him, they would shout for him to get away from the boat. All seamen treated Hawaiian boys like they were puppy dogs— and mangy puppies at that.

"Sir, sir!"

The suited youth turned to the side and looked down into the water where he saw Kumi. "Oh, it's you. Did you swim all the way out here? Will you swim all the way back, too?"

Kumi wasn't sure exactly what the youthful passenger was asking, but he had learned years ago to nod yes to any question asked. He thought the young man had asked Kumi if he was going to swim back to shore. Sure he was.

"Yes, sir. I swim."

"Good, I guess. That is a long swim and I don't know how you can swim that far."

The passenger's comments went by Kumi for the most part, but he understood the kind tone and the eagerness of the young man to communicate. Kumi liked him. He was pasty white, but that was the way the haoli *always looked. This one, Kumi surmised, was too young to grow a beard, not much older than he was. Did he have family with him? Was the fat man with a beard his father?*

The American youth glanced over his shoulder at his large companion, who was also wearing a dark suit and tall black hat—the style in 1853.

"Brother Joseph, you may regret getting too friendly with the natives. Keep all of your communications with such formal and short."

"But Brother Cannon, aren't we here to teach the natives the gospel? I have to start somewhere. Besides, I like this young native. He's very friendly."

"Maybe too friendly. They all steal, you know."

"I'm not too worried. I don't have a lot to steal, believe me."

Kumi understood enough of the fat man's words to know that he was instructing the youth in the ways of the Islands. He heard the word steal *and responded to the youth, "Sir, I not steal, I not. Okay?"*

Elder Joseph F. Smith, almost sixteen years old (going on twenty-five with all his experience from Nauvoo to the Salt Lake Valley) grinned down at the youth, then turned back to Cannon and replied, "You know, Brother Cannon, I just might convert this native boy to the gospel. I certainly will try."

CHAPTER SIXTEEN

Katherine Arrives

Friday Night
Juno Island

KATHERINE, BRENDA, MAX, AND TODD gaily settled into their staterooms on the *Free Eagle*. Katherine had insisted on having a stateroom away from Polk's suite and the main group so she would not be a bother. She and Brenda would manage just fine with a queen-size bed. Katherine had made it clear that she planned to spend the weekend with the young people.

When Brenda had called her mother from her bedroom at Katherine's penthouse, she had asked for her mother's honest opinion. "What do you want us to do, Mother? We can't resist going along with Granny Katherine for the weekend. It's just too rad to turn down. You know how much fun she is to be with—and she's paying for the whole thing. You don't argue with Granny Katherine; you know how stubborn she can be. But what do you think? Is it okay, Mom?"

Anney had smiled with delight as she urged her daughter to come along. She wanted the family to be together for a little holiday, anyway. Park City had hardly been a vacation, and her father's death in Salt Lake City had added to the strain on the family's hectic summer. Anney was elated at the thought of the family having a couple of carefree days to enjoy each other. Both of the kids would be away at school in a matter of weeks. She was pleased that Katherine was bringing them with her, and having Max along was an added bonus.

From the chartered helicopter that brought the four of them from Pago Pago to the airstrip on Juno, they took a taxi to the wharf, where Stephen and Anney met them. Earlier, Karry had navigated the tender to the tie-up and waited in the fading twilight while the expanded group piled into the craft for the quick trip back to the yacht.

It was nearly dark as they climbed aboard the tender. Todd was amazed at the beauty and size of the *Free Eagle*. He hadn't known what to expect, but this was far more than his wildest imaginings.

He leaned over and whispered to Max standing next to him, "No waaay, man."

"Yeah, waaay," Max replied with a grin and a nudge.

Todd's hand shot into the air and Max flung up his own and slapped Todd's in a victory pat. It was as good as winning a jackpot— to think they would be spending the next couple of days on the *Free Eagle*. Todd had mentioned privately to Max on their flight over that with her kind of money and friends, Granny Katherine oiled lots of skids. Those connections had already kicked in before they ever left San Francisco.

To Todd, the yacht looked like a magnificent mirage, all decks alight, bobbing silently in the water as they tied up alongside her.

The crew would make one more excursion in the thirty-three-foot Intrepid Yamaha tender to pick up those who were still in town at the shops. By 9 P.M. they would lift the tender back onto the top deck with the crane and secure the other toys on deck. Todd and Max agreed that just watching the crew in action, readying the yacht to set sail, would be a kick.

As Anney walked down the passageway to be with Katherine and the kids, the thought haunted her that Polk should never have come. His cough was not getting better. When she had insisted that he go to bed immediately after dinner, he complied without a fuss. While Stephen helped him get ready for bed in the bathroom, Anney turned down the sheets and slipped out.

The first words out of Katherine's mouth to Anney after

learning that Polk had gone to bed were, "Is he still awake? Do you think he could talk to me? I really wanted to talk to him tonight." There was urgency in her voice.

"Oh, I don't know." Anney's tone was guarded. "I'm pretty sure he couldn't talk with anyone tonight. He's had a long day for man in his condition. . . he's really not too well, Katherine. I'm sorry."

Katherine tried to control her emotions, but when Anney, whom she had come to love as a daughter, denied her access to the man she had specifically come thousands of miles across the Pacific to see, it was too much. Her lips began to tremble.

"I need to talk to him," she whispered, then suddenly turned her back to Anney.

When she had herself in control, Katherine haltingly told Anney again why she had picked up the kids and come running. She desperately wanted Polk to tell her how she could be with Anney's father in the heavens forever.

Anney could see how vital this was to Katherine. She sat quietly, thinking of all the possibilities. Finally, she pulled Katherine close and said soothingly, "I'm sure he will be able to talk to you in the morning. Do you think you can wait until morning? Besides, you need to go to bed. You must be exhausted. Believe me, if he were well, he would see you. Stephen thinks he may have to see a doctor tomorrow, even though right now he is refusing to talk about it."

As Anney removed her arm from Katherine's shoulder, she impetuously checked her watch for the time. Her face glowed with an idea. "You know, I just thought of something. It's not very late. Maybe Brother Meyers would talk to you. I should think he would be as informed as Dr. Polk. Oh, Katherine, you'd like him. He's about the same age as Polk, but he seems a lot younger. He has a great deal of experience in the Church. I'm sure he would be able to answer all your questions. Why don't I run and get Stephen to ask Brother Meyers if he will come answer your questions tonight?"

Katherine hugged Anney with gratitude and hurried to the bathroom to repair her make-up.

CHAPTER SEVENTEEN

Samuel and Katherine

Friday Night
Set to Cast Off

MANUEL TOOK A LONG DRINK from the frosty glass, then pressed it to his forehead. He shook his head in agitation while Carmen dressed for bed. "You may not know what is going on here, but I assure you, *querida*, I don't like the direction this whole meeting is taking. Do you know what we have been discussing up there today?"

"I'm beginning to understand part of what is going on. I can tell you're not pleased," Carmen replied. Manuel hurriedly covered the gist of the day's discussion, explaining to Carmen that the group was in the throes of debating how the Nephites had somehow survived as a nation and the fact that they would return and gain their inheritance in the Americas. That much Carmen had heard. It was no earth-moving concept to her, mainly because she did not understand the extent of the discussion. But she was concerned about her husband's feelings.

"Now they are suggesting . . . what am I saying? They are hardly suggesting. They are stating as fact that the Lamanites—our people—will *not* be the ones to inherit the land of the Americas. They insist that the privilege is reserved for the Nephites, especially the four tribes of Lehi. Carmen, we're Lamanites, plain and simple. But this President Meyers appears to think that our nation will not be part of the building of the New Jerusalem. By that, I mean all of our people. Yes, you and I will and other Lamanites who have joined the Church—what he calls the covenant Lamanites—but not the Lamanites as a people.

"Do you realize they are saying that when the Savior appeared to the people of the Americas following the destruction that wiped out all of the great cities, that he didn't appear to the Lamanites, that it wasn't to them that he gave all those great promises? Meyers is of the opinion that when Christ appeared on the temple steps in Bountiful, he spoke exclusively to the Nephites and that the Lamanites were not even close by."

Manuel was beside himself. He set his drink down on the dresser, picked up the stack of handouts he had accumulated, and angrily slammed them down on the bed.

"I've never heard that. Have you? I assumed that our people were there. I know they became a Zion people right after that, because for the next two hundred years there was peace and prosperity in all the land."

Manuel angrily yanked the bedspread down to the foot of the bed, kicked off his shoes, threw a few pillows against the headboard, and flopped down on the bed.

Carmen looked at him in bewilderment, not understanding his anger. "*Perdón, peró yo no puedo entender nada,*" she said as she walked over to stand beside her husband, hands on her hips. "Is that all you're upset about? How can you get so riled up about something that is so far off? My goodness! We have so many real problems in Mexico right now, I don't see how you can get heated up over whether it's the Lamanites or the Nephites that are going to help build the New Jerusalem. My life will go on, and so will yours."

"You don't understand," Manuel sighed impatiently. "This is affecting my whole attitude toward the Church."

Carmen's expression became serious, and she slowly sat down beside Manuel on the bed, watching him intently. She didn't want anything to come between her husband and the Church. Too many times she had seen people in the stake get upset with something that was said, or not said, and abandon the Church. Surely her husband was not one to do that. He was a strong priesthood leader. How could his testimony hinge on such a little thing?

She listened.

"The Lamanites seem to be coming out in a different light than the Nephites. I'm really confused about what I have been told all my life . . . and comparing that with what I'm hearing from Meyers and Polk. Many of the promises in the Book of Mormon appear to be to the House of Nephi and Nephi's brothers—Sam, Jacob, and Joseph, along with Zoram. I feel like they are setting up the Lamanites for a fall. I talked to Stephen this morning on the beach about my feelings. He doesn't know much about the subject, but I felt better, so I said nothing to anyone else. Then today we came right back to this same issue of the Nephites taking back their inheritance. Maybe it is off in the future, but my mind is not settled on this."

Carmen listened. She knew her husband was a fighter for a cause. The very president of Mexico knew his determination to hold to his standards and insist on change. The same drive captured his thoughts this very moment.

"I asked Meyers what was to happen to us, and he made an interesting statement. He said the Day of the Lamanite had not yet come. Where have I been all these years, thinking that the reason the great work is going so rapidly in Central and South America was because the Day of the Lamanite had arrived?"

"Did he tell you when he thought that day would come?"

"He said they would discuss that tomorrow. I'm about ready to pack up and go home. I wish the whole confab were over. I would take off if it weren't for Brother Polk and the respect I have for him. Believe me, I would."

Carmen knew enough to let her husband blow off the steam. She hoped he would be calm by morning.

* * *

SAMUEL MEYERS MOVED ALONG THE PASSAGEWAY to Katherine's stateroom, the irritation plain on his face. He would do this out of duty to Dr. Polk; if Stephen hadn't pressed the matter, he surely would not have gone out of his way to appease this lady, at least not now when he was so caught up in the presentations at hand.

Stephen had approached him thirty minutes ago. At the request of Anney, he had asked Meyers to take a minute to meet with Katherine and explain the concepts of eternal marriage and the proxy sealing powers.

"Sam," Stephen had said, "she is recently widowed—four weeks ago, as a matter of fact. She is not a religious person per se, but she does believe in God, though her view of deity is rather broad. To her, God is everywhere as a spirit. She married my father-in-law, a popular televangelist who preached mainly in the Bay Area. He was beginning to be recognized nationally when he died suddenly from a heart attack. It happened while we were in Park City at that youth conference. That is, he wasn't with us in Park City, but he happened to be in Salt Lake City at the time, at the invitation of a minister there. Anyhow, Katherine wants to know all about the LDS concept of eternal marriage. Crazy as it sounds, she thinks that if she comes to the right person who can perform a celestial marriage, she can have her former husband in heaven."

"Do you think she believes the part about eternal marriage?"

Stephen shook his head. "No, not really. I think she wants to hedge her bets."

"Then why are you asking me to go down there and explain what I consider to be a sacred doctrine of the Church, reserved for those who sincerely desire to know the Lord's works?"

"Oh, Sam, you don't have to go. I can tell her as much as I understand, but it will come as a great disappointment to her if I show up. I'm family. I may be a member of the Church, but she doesn't see me in the same light she will view you or Dr. Polk. You have the brow and demeanor of a man of great wisdom and authority. You will comfort her, and she will accept what you say. Or, at least, she'll be comforted. She's truly a great lady who has been widowed twice. She is bereaved and miserable and wants to know what she has to look forward to in the life to come and who she can be with."

"She sounds a little confused. Okay, I'll go down, but I may or may not get into what I deem sacred doctrine that ought not to be cast before swine."

"Well, don't tell her she's swine, for heaven's sake. She has great self-esteem and plenty of money to help her feel that way. Her first husband was CEO of Chemcon Corporation before he died. She could buy and sell even you."

"Okay, I get the point. But you know God is no respecter of persons."

"Right, Sam." Stephen thumped the older man on the back good naturedly. "She's waiting for you to share your great wisdom."

Samuel knocked lightly on the door of Katherine's stateroom.

Katherine was bred to take her time answering the door. By the time the door eased open, Samuel was about to leave, thinking no one was in. "Yes?" Katherine asked. She was dressed in a pink flowered muumuu she had brought along from San Francisco. It was one she had bought the last time she was in Hawaii. Her hair was softly styled and emphasized her long lashes and oval face. The high-collared neck of the muumuu enhanced her mature beauty.

Samuel was taken aback. He had not expected such a strikingly handsome woman to open the door. His frustration eased a little. "I'm . . . Samuel Meyers. I believe Stephen, your son-in-law, told you I was coming down to try to answer a few of your questions."

Katherine flashed her most charming smile and pushed back the door, "Oh, yes. Thank you so very much for coming. Please come in."

Brenda appeared just then, dressed in faded jean shorts, a purple blouse, and sandals, her well-brushed auburn hair resting on her shoulders. Sparkling with youth and excitement, she introduced herself, explaining that she and Katherine were sharing the stateroom. Then she asked to be excused, picked up her bag, and left.

With Brenda out the door, Samuel offered to escort Katherine to the aft deck for a refreshing drink.

"Without alcohol, right?" Katherine queried. "You are a Mormon!"

"Yes, I am, though the official name of our church is The Church of Jesus Christ of Latter-day Saints."

"Is that right? Well, I know something about your temperance codes. All right. A cool drink would be nice." Katherine smiled, accepting the invitation.

The deck radiated with indirect lighting, and the music piped from the bridge was soft and soothing. Samuel sat for a moment observing Katherine as she admired the view. She was perhaps the most beautiful woman he had met in a long time.

Katherine turned then and looked directly into Samuel's eyes, saying, "I do hope you don't mind explaining to me about this concept of making a marriage on earth binding in heaven. My adopted grandson mentioned something about it to me the other day. I had never heard of such a thing before, but I loved my late husband. Very frankly, I want to perpetuate that marriage relationship. Is it really possible?"

Katherine's searching eyes revealed to him a depth of understanding that he had not anticipated. Stephen had said she was lovely, but he hadn't begun to do her justice. Samuel saw before him a person who was stunning in manner and demeanor. Unexpectedly, the words of Elder Wellington's final statement to him on the matter of remarriage—"Get her to show up"—echoed in Sam's mind like bells pealing from a garden terrace.

Samuel said nothing for at least a minute while he studied Katherine's face. It was as if he were trying to search her soul for the flaws that she knew lurked in there. Beginning to feel uncomfortable, she waited; her mouth curved in a faint smile. *Why doesn't he speak?* After all, he was the one who was going to explain how she could be with Bob in the next life. *Say something,* she thought, *anything. Don't just sit there and stare at me. Please.*

Samuel spoke at last, but his words startled him as much as they did Katherine.

"Who *are* you?" he exclaimed.

Katherine drew in a sharp breath of air. At last she broke the silence. She stared at Samuel. "What do you mean, 'Who am I?'"

"I mean, really. Who are you? You are so familiar to me. I have known you somewhere . . . I'm thinking maybe not in this life."

Katherine was shocked. She wondered if Stephen had lost it by sending this man to her. He was certainly good looking for man in his . . . what, early seventies? Unfortunately, he was not too tall, not as robust appearing as Bob. Still an altogether interesting man to say the least, but so strange in his approach.

"Are we going to get into reincarnation?" she asked abruptly, crushed with disappointment. "I studied that once and it doesn't appeal to me. Is that where this is going?"

Her question jarred Samuel back to reality. He relaxed his gaze from an intense study of Katherine's soul to a more normal glance at her person. His face flushed a deep red with embarrassment. "I'm sorry," he stammered. "I just . . . well, I can't explain what I'm feeling. I'm really not one to make such statements . . . You must think I am odd. Ask Dr. Polk. He'll tell you I'm okay, but I just . . . I don't know . . . Forget it."

Again Katherine was puzzled, this time over his discomfort. She gently reminded him of the reason he had come to see her. "Shall we talk about my situation with my late husband and the problem I would like to resolve?"

"Sure. Let's do."

CHAPTER EIGHTEEN

Which Jacob—Which Joseph?

Late Friday Night
At Sea

THE AFT DECK OFF THE GRAND SALON was nearly deserted as the *Free Eagle* made her way toward St. Paras where they would dock the following morning. Her final destination was to be the island of Fiji; she was scheduled to arrive predawn Monday morning. The breeze stirred the flaps of the canopy without a sound, and the lights of Juno slowly receded from view. Takahashi Samura and Samuel Meyers sat together in quiet conversation, enveloped by the solitude of the late night. Noriko and the others had gone below to the staterooms after an evening of happily locating all the constellations they could identify in the magnificent sky above. Out here nothing obstructed the view.

Suddenly the three newly arrived young people came running up to the aft deck before turning in, to enjoy brimming ice-cream sodas and the last of dinner's apple torte served up from the galley that was still open and taking orders. Laughing and joking about life on a world-class yacht, they invited Samuel and Takahashi to join in their banter. Tired as they were, they couldn't seem to settle down for fear they might miss something exciting. After a few minutes, they scurried away as noisily as they had come.

Katherine was asleep in her stateroom. To her, the yacht was not a novelty as it was to them, and the long hours in transit had finally forced her to rest.

It was near midnight. Still, Takahashi and Samuel felt a desire to talk and an energy that did not come uniquely because they were ahead of their Japanese time. As they reviewed the day's discussion, Takahashi looked out over the dark water where the running lights cast eerie shadows. The sounds of water, wind, and darkness seemed to engulf him.

He suddenly sat up, looked at Samuel, and swept his hands out toward the vast ocean. "President Meyers, please, I hope you don't think me odd, but sometimes I look at my life here on earth as if it were like this dimly illuminated ship, surrounded by darkness. I can see only the things that are close and bright. I have a difficult time looking into the distance. Do you ever get that feeling?"

"Often."

"I sometimes feel like my own country has no roots. If it weren't for the gospel, I would be without a rudder. You know, Japan has no real history that harks back to truly ancient times, like China or India does. I know that I'm obscure in my thinking when it comes to things that are not directly in front of me." He spread his hands across the white tabletop as if to indicate that it was the limit of his clear vision.

"It is the Japanese blood in you that makes you so philosophical," Meyers grinned. "What are you getting at?"

"I was just thinking about some of the things we have been uncovering in the Book of Mormon—or more precisely, things you have been telling us. They are still not entirely clear, though I'm beginning to realize that perhaps I do have an origin. In some ways, the points you make are very clear, yet vague. I . . . you may think me bold to say it, but I sense that perhaps the Japanese may be the seed of the Nephites. And if the blood of the Nephites runs in my veins, I would feel good about that. To have Father Lehi as an ancestor would be very comforting. Do you think everyone wants to know the history of their people?"

Meyers smiled like a Cheshire cat at Takahashi's leading statements, not quite ready to reveal all he knew. "I don't know about everyone, but I find greater meaning to life when I can point to my origins. Keep telling me your feelings. It's not often I get a Japanese male to look deep within himself and try to make sense of his world.

They may look, but seldom express it verbally—at least not to me, a Caucasian."

"What I am feeling is not merely Japanese. It's universal, I think. It's the human spirit and mind, no matter what one's race or creed. In my case, it is as if the Lord will allow me to see only those things in my immediate vision and receive glimpses of things in the remote past." Takahashi laced his fingers together on the table. "For example, while we were discussing the commandment in 1 Nephi that we search the scriptures and give great heed to prayer and study, I came up with this confusing thought: Why did the Lord allow two sets of important prophets to have the same name?"

"What do you mean?" Samuel was pretty sure he knew what Takahashi was driving at, but he wanted him to clarify his question.

"I mean, here we have confusion in the scriptures, or at least we have to rely on the Spirit to indicate which is which—which Jacob and which Joseph. In the western world, those are perhaps two of the most common names given to boys, at least Joseph is. Look at it. There was a prophet named Jacob who had twelve sons, and his name was changed to Israel. Then there was a prophet named Jacob who was the son of Lehi. Also, there was the prophet Joseph, the favored son of the Jacob called Israel—the same Joseph who was sold into Egypt; and, on the other hand, we have Joseph, the son of Lehi. Doesn't it strike you as odd that the two sets of prophets shared the same common name? Have you ever thought that through? That is, why did that happen?"

"Oh, yes." Samuel smiled, leaning back and lacing his fingers behind his head. "I have pondered that on my own and even discussed it with some of the Church leaders. Of course, I have my own personal opinion as to why the Lord arranged things that way."

"I'm curious. Why?"

"Well, think about it. The Lord expects us to exercise faith, to study and pray, and sometimes accompany our efforts with fasting in order to understand the scriptures. I could go into an entire discourse on the subject of how to study scripture, but I won't. Oliver Cowdery, a scribe as we both know, had a personal revelation from the Lord . . . you know, the one found in section nine of the Doctrine and Covenants. Oliver thought he could translate the characters on the plates and get the true meaning merely by asking—something we all need to keep in mind—and the Lord told him it didn't work that way. Apparently, the plan of salvation is structured to require our greatest efforts to achieve lofty ends. It doesn't necessarily mean that it has to be complex. It means making something our own through personal effort." Samuel leaned his head back far enough to gaze directly at the brilliant stars. "The Lord said to Oliver," he began,

> Behold, you have not understood; you have supposed that I would give it unto you, when you took *no thought save it was to ask me.*

Samuel brought his head forward and studied Takahashi's puzzled face. "This is lesson number one from the Lord, when it comes to discerning the scriptures: 'You have not understood.' There is so much wisdom in this scripture. Although in Oliver's case the Lord is referring to translating, I think the concept applies to understanding scriptures and the will of the Lord. If you recall, the Lord went on to reveal this additional bit of insight: 'But, behold, I say unto you, that you must *study it out in your mind*; then you must ask me if it be right.'"

Takahashi silently nodded his head in agreement. He loved being tutored by Meyers-san, who seemed to be a well of information.

Samuel leaned forward again in the deck chair, placing his thin hands on his knobby knees. "You know, for me it is fundamental that we get our act together before we ask for additional information. When I was running our family lumber company, it bugged me no end when men in supervisory roles—you know, bosses, foremen—would come into my office and ask me questions and want answers that they had spent no time trying to figure out for themselves. That is just sloppy leadership. I usually let them know that they needed to use their own minds and common sense to figure out a sticky problem, not to ask without studying the problem first. When they did that, often there was no need to ask. The solution would come to the sensible leader. Some never learned that fundamental leadership trait. Pity."

"I get some of those same problems as a seminary supervisor in Japan," Takahashi interjected. "Dumb little questions come up that the teachers should have figured out themselves."

Samuel agreed with Takahashi. "I think that is what the Lord wanted Oliver to do. Let me see, where was I in that scripture? Oh yes, I think I've got it . . .

> If it be right . . . then you must ask me if it be right, and if it is right, I will cause that your bosom shall burn within you; therefore you shall *feel* that it is right.

"It seems to me that the same thing applies, as I said, to a study of the scriptures," Samuel said thoughtfully. "If a person ponders and studies, then goes to the Lord with full intent regarding things that are important to that person—and maybe only to that person—I'm sure an answer will come. The Lord will reveal what it is the person wants to know. I'm not so certain that the person learns exactly every detail to the answer, although by applying this method, direction will come. It is the best method in the world for handling our own personal problems, as well as those of the kingdom."

Samuel leaned back again in the wide, white canvas chair and said, "If the Lord wants us to ponder and study the scriptures so that the words of the Book of Mormon—or whatever body of scripture he wants us to understand—are clear to us, then we have to get some of it through our own efforts. It's like a puzzle or a mathematical problem. What meaning does it really have to us if we already know the words to the crossword puzzle? It negates the challenge.

"I once had a bishop who said, 'Life is the only game in which the object of the game is to learn the rules.'" Samuel grinned, remembering his friend who had also been his bishop. "Takahashi, part of the excitement of the game of life is to work it out by ourselves, and then ask for help to get us over the rough spots. We want things in this life to be meaningful. The only way that happens is to struggle with the knotty problems and make the solution part of our lives."

"I follow you, up to a point. But . . ."

"You asked me why the identical sets of names of prophets? I'm not saying I know for sure. I once again point to logic and evidence, having spent time pondering the scriptures that tell us about those prophets. I have thought about those identical names—Joseph and Joseph . . . Jacob and Jacob. What I have to say is solely my own thinking at this point. I have to admit that I haven't gone to the Lord with this problem to get an answer. Up to now, I haven't made it a focal issue. But I'll share my thoughts off the top of my head, if you like. I don't plan to bring them up in the group and speculate among the others, but I will share this . . . sort of one-on-one with you, okay?" Samuel rubbed his fingers over the crown of his head and stretched his legs out in front of him.

"Jacob who was renamed Israel and Joseph who was sold into Egypt were among the prophets first named. In contrast, the sons of Lehi, Jacob and his brother Joseph, were both relatively obscure. Nevertheless, they had something in common: all four were prophets of the Lord. Still, it is interesting that Jacob and Joseph of the Book of Mormon have nowhere near the impact on the minds of scholars as do Jacob and Joseph of the Old Testament, not even among LDS scholars, who ought to give their names greater billing.

"You see, the world is not at all aware of this dual naming of prophets. We sometimes think along the lines of tradition, or of the world, while we're trying to solve a difficult problem."

Samuel sat up again, pulled his legs under the chair, and leaned toward Takahashi in earnest discussion. "Having obeyed the Lord's commandment to take his family out of Jerusalem—and at great loss of property to his family, I might add—Lehi never flagged, according to the record. True, we know of one slip on his part—he was only human, after all—when he became discouraged about Nephi's broken bow. Actually, Lehi showed great faith and prayerful obedience to the Lord. We know he kept his ancient covenants; he offered up sacrifice in the wilderness.

"While he was out in the vast Arabian desert, far from Jerusalem and trudging along at the mercy of the elements, the Lord gave Lehi two wonderful gifts, marvelous gifts . . . the most *important* of all gifts to a man who esteemed family above most things. He gave to Father Lehi two additional righteous sons—Jacob and Joseph. It was as if the Lord were compensating Lehi for the rebellious Laman and Lemuel, though Lehi never gave up on those sons, either.

"Lehi forever after referred to Jacob as 'my firstborn in the wilderness.' I think Father Lehi knew that the Lord had sent those priceless gifts to him and Sariah for their suffering and obedience, and to offer them hope in their old age. Which brings up another thought. Wouldn't you love to read the writings of Lehi in the 116 pages Martin Harris lost? Think of what might be in those writings of Lehi that are not available to us now! We might have learned more about those two sons born in the wilderness who became great prophets." Meyers glanced at Takahashi, caught his eye, and then said, "Do you know what I think?"

"What?"

"I think Father Lehi was *inspired* to name those two boys Jacob and Joseph. It makes sense. If the Lord wants us to figure out the hidden truths in the Book of Mormon, and especially in the writings of his favorite author, Isaiah, and to do a complete job of deep study—remember, he commanded us to do just that—then it is my opinion that the Lord inspired, or may even have *revealed in vision* to Father Lehi while in the wilderness, in a vision, the names he wanted those sons to bear."

"But why?"

"Why would the Lord do that? So it would require faith and study on our part to figure out which Jacob and which Joseph he and Isaiah made reference to in the Book of Mormon, which includes Isaiah's references to the remnant of Jacob or the seed of Jacob. Think about it. He is making it clear to us what is meant . . . If we are inspired to know by the Spirit which prophet is which, then we can get somewhere with this puzzle. I like to think we have a direct pipeline to the heavens when we do what we are asked to do."

"I think you're right. My great-great-grandfather had an experience that so impressed him—first with shame, then with peace of mind—that he asked his children, grandchildren, and even his young great-grandchildren to be alert to a great event that would come one day. It was never something clearly defined. We had to have the Spirit to know it. He mentioned that it was a great event that would happen in the family.

"At long last, I was the one who came to the discovery of what it was he insisted would happen. The great event, as far as I'm concerned, was the day my brother and I accepted the gospel. The whole family will benefit from our conversion. We have done our great-grandparents' and great-great-grandparents' work in the temple. Oh, that our father would join while still in this life. It is the wish of my soul."

Samuel caught his breath. "Takahashi, would you be willing to share the story of your ancestor with me?"

The younger man paused a long time, wondering at the significance of Meyers' interest. Finally, he bowed his head briefly and replied, "Brother Meyers-san, I would be honored to do so."

Sapporo – 1864

The condemned man was Taki-Zenzaburo, an officer of the Prince of Bizen in the nation of Japan. The era was late for such an act of self-inflicted death. In Japan they called it seppuku; *among English-speaking westerners it was labeled* hara-kiri—*either term meant disembowelment or stomach cutting and slicing of the neck.*

Seppuku as a means of regaining honor was demanded by the condemned officer himself, who had given orders to fire on the people of Hiogo (now Kobe, Japan). They were foreigners whom he felt deserved to die. But in a special tribunal, the government decreed that Taki-Zenzaburo had acted without authority and, therefore, he was ordered to commit seppuku, which the condemned officer agreed was the only solution.

In the temple courtyard, Satsuma troops, a host of foreign legations, and the seven kenshi (sheriffs or witnesses) all stood silently in the yard awaiting the condemned officer. Night had fallen, and the large, high roof of the shrine, adorned by dark-stained, wooden pillars, was lit up by a profusion of gilt paper lamps. The elevated platform was strewn with white mats and a scarlet rug. Candles atop wooden posts cast additional light on the scene.

As Taki-Zenzaburo stepped sharply to the mat, attired in ceremonial dress, there was no question that he was directly from the loins of nobility. The most noticeable item of clothing was his hempen-cloth wings, which were worn only on special occasions. Anciently, the condemned was dressed in white underclothing.

His kaishaku, a friend of his noblest years—Takahashi's great-great-grandfather—knelt as gentleman executioner with sword in hand. In reality, Fujita Toko, who was Taki-Zenzaburo's confidant, would act as second to the act. At twenty-one years of age, Fujita had been a pupil of Taki-Zenzaburo. He had demonstrated that he was the best of those Taki-Zenzaburo had taught the skill of swordsmanship. Ceremoniously, Fujita knelt to the victim's left. Outwardly nothing revealed the turmoil inside the young man.

Taki-Zenzaburo, with great dignity and pride in his demeanor, bowed ceremoniously to the seven kenshi. *They, in turn, bowed to him. Without haste, Taki-Zenzaburo stepped upon the raised floor and walked to the mat at the center of the carpet. With some effort he prostrated himself before the altar, then sat down on the red carpet, facing away from the altar. Three attendants brought forth a stand. Atop the stand was the* wakizashi, *the nine-inch sword (or dirk) that had been pounded into the finest steel edge by a smith who had heated it and pounded it, then heated it and pounded it one thousand times. It took many days to bring the instrument to the finest edge known to man. So sharp was the steel blade that a sheet of paper dropped on the edge would be sliced in two.*

One of the attendants took the small sword from the stand and, prostrating himself on the mat, reached out and handed it to Taki-Zenzaburo. The condemned man took hold of it reverently and placed the knife before him.

Taki-Zenzaburo opened his mouth to speak. With great sincerity, but without emotion, he uttered his final words: "I, and I alone, unwarrantedly gave the order to fire on the foreigners at Hiogo, and again as they tried to escape. For this crime I disembowel myself, and I beg you who are present to do me the honor of witnessing the act."

This type of witnessing by those assigned had to be made for this self-immolation to have eternal effect on Taki-Zenzaburo's soul. Anciently, those who committed seppuku did so to redeem their souls for some broken covenant or promise. They had the option of cutting the throat, piercing the breast, or disemboweling. All three forms of seppuku—*taking their own lives—were acceptable and honorable methods of atoning for wrongs committed.*

The victim was allowed to have assistance from a kaishaku, *a second, who would instantly administer the sword to the neck after the honorable victim pierced his own abdomen. This merciful act of cutting through the neck by a specially chosen servant was acceptable.*

The attendants removed Taki-Zenzaburo's garments from the girdle to the top of his head. He sat naked from the waist up. Taking a moment while kneeling, he stuffed the upper garments under his feet and lower legs. This tilted his body slightly forward. He did not wish to fall backward, but rather face-first onto the carpet. His hands were steady. From childhood up he had been taught the manner of seppuku. *He always knew that, should it be necessary to recapture his soul, he would have to go through with it. If it came to this ultimate act, he would muster all the dignity and strength of a noble ancestry and perform the ritual. The moment was at hand to go through with this greatest of all personal sacrifices.*

Gripping the dirk with his right hand, Taki-Zenzaburo carefully placed the tip at the left side of his firm, muscular abdomen. He looked down at the knife to be certain it was properly placed. Then, with satisfaction on his face, he plunged the knife deep into his side and drew it firmly and rapidly across the stomach to the center, where he drew it upward. He turned it slightly and, dropping back to a point parallel to the left side, made a clean sweep to the right side.

Not one expression of pain could be seen on the noble face.

He pulled out the dirk, raised his neck upward, stretching as best he could, while leaning forward. His kaishaku, *Fujita, was to jump up from his kneeling position when the knife started across the warrior's stomach. Fujita froze.*

It was obvious to the second kaishaku, *who stood at the rear of the raised floor, that Fujita was not going to raise the sword and cut the warrior's neck as was the custom.*

Was he too young to perform such an act? Was he a coward?

There was no time to judge. The second kaishaku, *with sword in hand, leaped forward and with the movement of a keen athlete brought the sword around the right side and sliced it across the warrior's neck at an angle. It was an irregular blow, and sliced completely through the tendons, tissue, and spinal cord at the base of the skull.*

Taki-Zenzaburo's severed head rolled onto the carpet with a thud and came to rest sideways, its open eyes staring toward the kenshi. *Life had fled.*

Fujita stood for a moment, staring at the head that had rolled to one side; then he had the presence of mind to bow to the body of his good friend who lay wasted on the crimson carpet. The second wiped his sword with paper and stepped back from the raised floor. He moved to the shadows of the wall and stared out at the officials. No one spoke.

Two officials from the palace stepped forward and, bowing to the seven kenshi, *declared that the sentence of death of Taki-Zenzaburo was accomplished, with no reference to the delayed slicing of the neck that Fujita should have administered.*

Extreme shame prevailed with all, and especially with Fujita as he left the platform and moved quickly from the court of the temple and walked out into the dark street. He felt a deep urge to join Taki-Zenzaburo in death. The terrible scene played repeatedly in his mind as he walked the lonely streets of the city and wondered at such strange, yet familiar, acts of men and felt overwhelmed by dishonor for not having the courage to terminate the agony of his warrior-friend with a swift swing of the sword. Why had he been reluctant?

Curiously, he didn't realize that he had been aimlessly crossing bridges, paths, and countryside roads for hours. At length he turned about and retraced his steps, arriving back within the city by midnight.

He knew he had committed an unpardonable act of shame by not acting as instructed—such an act was expected of one with his swordsmanship skills—but the horror of being part of such a ceremony had suddenly struck him as barbarous.

He re-entered the city by way of the Chamber Bridge, or the River Summa. It was late; there was no one in sight. He stopped at the arch of the bridge and looked out on the dark water that ran two miles to the sea. There must be a better life, a more noble life than this. Why do I suddenly feel so disenchanted? What other way is there besides *Bushido*—the way of the warrior?

It was then that an impression came into his mind. Perhaps only a thought, but a powerful thought. The mental impression carried a message that fixed on the forefront of his mind. The Spirit declared to him that one day—not in his day, but one day—those down the line among his posterity would no longer be adrift in this world of madness. They would have the truth. He sensed from his clear thoughts that those who would come after him would be wise and choose the correct course in life and eternity, and be favored of Deity. One day a great event would touch the lives of his posterity. One day.

Two years later and miles away, Fujita Toko entered the Shinto religion and took certain vows to become a priest. As it was permissible in his religious order to marry, when Fujita married and he and his wife had children, he passed along his deep conviction that life is precious and that the gods would send to his family something very special.

CHAPTER NINETEEN

Troubling Thoughts

Friday
Middle of the Night

"PLEASE EXCUSE ME . . . I heard you come into your room." Manuel stood outside Samuel's door, wearing a light robe and sandals. He had slipped silently out of bed, hoping not to disturb Carmen, and quietly crossed the hall where he knocked lightly and waited for Samuel to let him in.

The two men stood looking at one another. The only light remaining in Samuel's stateroom came from the shaded lamp next to the queen-size bed where the covers had been turned down invitingly. As the two men looked at one another, the ship swayed gently, reminding them that they were on the high seas, under ideal conditions inside and out.

"Can we talk, Samuel?" Manuel's speech was formal, precise, and direct.

Samuel groaned within. His long, searching conversation with Takahashi had left him drained, yearning to stretch out on that big bed. But Samuel had spent years as a priesthood leader in various assignments, many of which had required him to give impromptu counseling, and often in the middle of the night. Besides, he had been expecting Manuel to seek him out.

"Sure," he responded with an easy smile. "Have a seat."

The stateroom accommodated two large overstuffed chairs arranged at an angle, so that two people could face each other as they conversed. Manuel sat stiffly in the chair Meyers offered.

"I know I'm keeping you up and the hour is late, but I'm too agitated to sleep." Manuel rubbed his chin as he spoke. "This has not been a good day for me."

"I have sensed that."

"I know you have. That is why we have to talk."

Manuel sucked in a great gulp of air and slowly exhaled. "Throughout our entire stay on this yacht, I have been uncomfortable. It began yesterday with your first presentation. I came to listen and to learn and maybe throw in my opinion. Carmen and I actually came on this luxury voyage because we thought we would enjoy the fun and companionship with Dr. Polk and the others we have met. I never thought it would turn into a series of discussions where my people would be the object of such rejection."

Samuel decided to not interrupt, but to let Manuel speak his mind frankly before he offered any comment.

"Look at my side of your presentation. All my life, as I said yesterday, I have believed in the Church and have been told repeatedly that the Lamanites were a choice and blessed people, that they would come forth in the last days and be part of the great restoration of all things and lead out when the Savior makes his great return. Blessed, mind you."

Manuel's lips were dry and his throat was hoarse. He had stood up to presidents of nations, yet at this moment he felt such tension that even his speech was shaky. It wasn't Samuel per se who caused these feelings. What he had come to see in the scriptures had become equally clear to all.

"I thought all the Nephites were destroyed, that not one of them was left—none. I was taught that since I was a child. The position of the Church was always—in any discussion of Nephites and Lamanites—that my people were the choice people and the only descendants of Lehi to remain after the great wars. Now that I see the possibility of Nephite survival, I am having a very difficult time accepting this. If it is true, where have we been all these years with our thinking?"

"I'm glad you came in to talk to me," Samuel responded sincerely, as he felt himself catching his second wind for the night.

"Really, I am. But I have to speak frankly. I have to ask you . . . where would you and all of your people who have come into the Church because of the Book of Mormon . . . where would you be without it? And who kept the record which we call the Book of Mormon? Not Lamanites, not Gentiles, but Nephites. As the warring people they were at that time, the Lamanites would have killed the Nephites and, in fact, destroyed the record, given the opportunity.

"You must look at it from the right vantage point, Manuel. You and Carmen are *covenant* Lamanites. You have accepted the gospel along with all of your family, as I understand it. You are so needed to help the rest of your people become *covenant* Lamanites as well. You can't be part of a resentful attitude toward the Nephites when they inherit the land. Such an attitude is inspired of Satan. Don't let it get to you this way."

Samuel poked his chest with his thumb and said, "Where do you think *my* nation—the Gentiles—will be if they don't repent and humble themselves? They will be far worse off than your people. They will be removed from the land, and the Nephites will roll through them 'like a lion among lambs.' The Savior himself declared it.

"You ask . . . how did we get off the track on the Nephites and the Lamanites in the last days? I think I told you my view. Early Church opinion-makers spoke as if the Lamanites, or American Indians, were all that remained of Father Lehi's posterity. Nowhere do we find this idea confirmed by any of the prophets in this dispensation while holding office. However, whether right or wrong, the idea of total Nephite extermination took root and flourished, becoming an entrenched tradition.

"Over the past decades, heroic efforts have been made by The Church of Jesus Christ of Latter-day Saints to bring the American Indian into full membership and participation in the Church. I wouldn't for a moment take away from all that has been done for the Lamanites. Great men like Tom Swensen—a true saint among the Lamanites—have worked their hearts out for the cause. The effort has met with less-than-great success and appears not to have the emphasis it formerly enjoyed. If this upsets the Indians, it is most unfortunate but understandable. No institution keeps investing in relatively fruitless ventures.

"But look at you and the people surrounding you. You are the finest examples of those who receive the gospel, regardless of lineage, and come in with full faith and give unstinting service. I have nothing but admiration in my heart for you."

Manuel took stock of his situation. After a moment of silence, he said, "I have to make the adjustment, that's all. It is tough for me to do."

"You must fight this feeling of jealousy and antipathy toward the great people of the Nephites, my friend. Get a handle on your emotions. Don't let the Evil One cause you to stumble. You have great blessings awaiting you and your family and all those among you who are accepting the gospel and living the commandments."

Samuel knew that Latin people wore their emotions close to the surface. He held Manuel's eyes with his own and waited for the dynamic Lamanite to register acceptance of this concept on the position of his people. Manuel finally lowered his head and let his eyes focus on the carpet.

Following an inner prompting, Samuel finally asked softly, "Would you like to pray with me about this, Manuel?"

Seconds that seemed like minutes ticked by.

Manuel wiped the back of his hand across his dry lips, looked up to reveal moist eyes, yet said nothing. Again he looked deep into Samuel's eyes as the two men sat two feet apart.

"Yes," he managed huskily. "Would you offer the prayer?"

Heart beating rapidly, his mind pleading with the Lord to supply the words, Samuel quietly dropped to his knees beside his troubled friend. Both bowed their heads in silence for a long moment. When Samuel finally spoke, his voice was soft, but strong and true.

"Heavenly Father, we kneel before thee in humility. We know that thou lovest us. We feel thy love and concern that we may come to understand and do thy will. Tonight thy son Manuel is troubled. With all his soul he desires to know his place and the place of his people within thy kingdom. He desires affirmation that he and his people are accepted of thee, that through the covenants they make with thee, they may be a blessed people. Wilt thou bring understanding and peace to his heart? Wilt thou make him a light in the dark to his people, that through him they may come unto thee?" Samuel became too choked with emotion to speak. At last he was able to control his voice and he finished the prayer. "Please comfort and bless this good man, Father. He loves thee and needs thee now."

As Samuel looked up, he could see that Manuel's shoulders were heaving silently. He gently placed his arm around the younger man and squeezed him reassuringly.

When at last Manuel regained his composure, he spoke. "Thank you, Samuel. You are a fine person. I'm sure I have had the wrong spirit with me since our first session yesterday. You are right . . . the Lord loves us all. I feel that, too. And I know that if it is the Savior's wish that the Nephites be re-established in the land, then it will happen and it will be right. It's not going to set well with my people, but then most have no comprehension of the gospel anyway."

Manuel stood first. He reached out to shake hands with Samuel, who ignored his outstretched hand and took him by both shoulders to draw him to his chest in a bear hug. Manuel hugged him back, tears flowing freely down his face.

In a muffled voice Samuel said, "We both have to face the fact that our people will not enjoy all the blessings of the gospel if they do not repent. Go home and make yourself into an even stronger leader. Don't give up on your great service to the Lord and your fellowmen. What more can the Lord ask of you?"

Manuel opened the door and walked with a lighter step back across the hall to his stateroom.

* * *

NINE A.M. CAME EARLY TO SOME on the yacht. Samuel was a few minutes late making the first discussion session of the day. He came in sporting the brightest Hawaiian shirt in the room.

Without ceremony, he led out. "The question at this time is the current description of the Nephites. We know they will appear among the Gentiles, but where will they come from?"

"Aren't we overstepping our bounds?" Maria asked, letting her tongue slip in a little edge of sarcasm.

"What do you mean, Maria?" Samuel asked, knowing what she

meant.

"Look, we are not the Council of the Twelve or the Prophet. We are doing this thing without any approval. Doesn't it bother you a little to make such absolute statements?"

Samuel answered her question with one of his own. "Do you really think that we ought *not* to search this out in our minds?"

"I think we have our plate full when it comes to things we have been given by our prophet to delve into."

"Like what?" Eric asked, as if she had pinpointed his personal involvement at the gathering and was speaking directly to him, which she was not.

Samuel's mouth curved into his impish grin. His voice began with deceptive softness, then grew in volume as he warmed to his subject. "Did you ever challenge the F.A.R.M.S. group for all the dabbling they have done in the Book of Mormon? Aren't you a member of that group? I am. They do a great service. But what on earth are they doing sponsoring a dig in Wadi Sykes? They are eating up big bucks that seem to be pouring in from interested members of F.A.R.M.S. Have we less right to do a detailed study of what Christ and Isaiah had to say about the Gentiles, Nephites, Lamanites, and the House of Israel?"

Samuel had startled his group with his heated reply. They had not expected such a response. Seeing the surprise on the faces before him, Samuel toned down his words. Their impact, however, was still unmistakable.

"Come on, Maria. Be fair. I realize that Dr. Polk and I lack the certification to conduct such a study for public dissemination. We haven't passed inspection yet; F.A.R.M.S. has. They have years of experience and the approval of the 'Y' to conduct all the studies they are doing. But, hey, they're holding symposia on the BYU campus on a host of subjects that are not necessarily authorized by the General Authorities. I doubt that they would have been afforded such recognition fifteen years ago, when a handful of scholars decided it was time to take apart the Book of Mormon in an academic manner and properly document their work. We have more of a mandate than they did when they started out, or have even at the present time. Read again what the Savior commanded us to do. Basically, it is what we are about.

"Let's look at 3 Nephi 23:1. It's right at the top of some heavy things the Savior wants listed in the Book of Mormon record.

> And now, behold, I say unto you, that ye ought to search these things. Yea, a commandment I give unto you that ye search these things diligently; for great are the words of Isaiah.

"Maria, we are only trying to do what the Lord commanded in that scripture." He smiled, then raised and lowered his shoulders expressively. "I have searched the writings of Isaiah diligently. Why? Because I truly believe that the writings of that great prophet are true and insightful. As they say, his words are great. I fail to see that we have overstepped our bounds. We have come up with what we think is a clear explanation of the rise of the people of Nephi in the last days. The Lord has commanded us to search out these kinds of things, and I stand by the results of my study."

Maria refused to back down. "I think you are twisting the scriptures just a little."

None of the others cared to interfere in their academic sparring match.

"Please tell me where I have twisted these scriptures," Samuel said quietly. "I believe you said you agree that the Lord was making a covenant with Jacob, the son of Lehi, and his people. The problem we find is that none of the latter-day prophets have chosen to speak in detail on this issue of the Nephites returning to this land and literally taking over. It is *their* land, Maria. Even you have agreed that the Lord, when he met with the Nephites, was speaking to that particular group of people and no one else. The Nephites have been promised this land and the right to spearhead the building of the New Jerusalem.

"Christ himself has laid it out. Does he have to spell it out any clearer? He wants us to ponder and study these things. Do you know why the Lord wants us to dig on our own? Because he knows that the saints who will be of most value in the eternities are those who have been refined in fire. He wants us to search. The very word he used was SEARCH. When we *search*, we make a thing our own.

"I was mentioning this very concept to Takahashi last night. If everything is just handed to us, we don't feel like it is ours. Searching and finding are joyful things to do. It is more of a challenge. We truly *own* the knowledge we search diligently and find."

Samuel paused a moment before continuing.

"We now have an understanding that the Nephites are a group or a nation of people who will surface sometime before the millennium and take their rightful place, which is to lead out in the construction of the New Jerusalem."

* * *

LUNCH WAS SERVED AS A BUFFET. Maria avoided Samuel as she rounded the table with her plate, taking small portions of the delicious-appearing foods. Afterwards, she secluded herself in her stateroom to review the scriptures she wanted to bring up at the afternoon session. She wanted to show Meyers and the group that there was a traditional position, a stronger position than what Samuel had espoused up to this moment.

When the group gathered for the afternoon session, it seemed the appropriate time for Dr. Polk to direct a discussion of unique features of the Pacific Rim peoples and their background. Samuel felt as if a change of voice, a personality they all respected, would smooth the ruffled feathers.

What Polk had to share was pretty straightforward and scientific. He began to detail aspects of comparison.

Then Manuel spoke up. "What about the physical appearance of the Nephites? I can't see any group, except those of obvious European origin—the people of Australia, New Zealand, the Dutch in Southeast Asia—who are what you would call whites. It's my understanding that the Nephites were a "white and delightsome" people. That could even mean red-headed and blue-eyed. What about the Nephite people? What did they look like?"

Samuel stepped in to say, "I'm not sure that color of skin is an issue. First, there are no clear descriptions of skin tone in the Book of Mormon. We don't know exactly what they looked like. I doubt that they looked Swedish in skin tone. Besides, in later versions of the Book of Mormon, the scripture you referred to in 2 Nephi 30:6, which talks about Lamanites and Jews who are converted to the gospel becoming white and delightsome, has been changed by the Brethren to *pure* and delightsome. The people of Jerusalem, where Lehi's family came from, traditionally have had olive complexions. Who knows just what the Nephites looked like?

"Then, too, you must remember that the Nephites we are referring to began as a *remnant*. They apparently did not retain the same skin tone and original appearance that they had in the beginning, although we do not know exactly what that was. Except for the far northern regions of Japan, there are no brown-haired, light-eyed people in the Pacific Rim. It is my theory that the original Nephite group that left the Americas eventually intermarried with the local inhabitants. There were natives on all the major islands and subcontinents long before the Nephites arrived, and they must have mixed with the lighter-skinned Nephites that came seeking a new land. I maintain that there is still a great deal of the original Nephite blood in the people."

This information brought a round of comments coursing through the main salon, some protesting that if they were mixed, then they were not pure Nephites. Samuel countered with the example of Manuel. Manuel was not pure Lamanite, but claimed his lineage through that line.

* * *

KARRY FELT DEPRIVED. He had to man the tender as the chef went ashore to purchase fruits and produce. The demanding chef was always a bear with the natives. He insisted on the freshest and the best, always suspicious that the market vendors would try to pass off leftovers because he was foreign and did not know their ways. His eye was usually too sharp to take any fruit or vegetable not picked that day.

Karry knew he would miss the discussion that was being held at this very moment, and it irritated him. He had to talk to Mr. Thorn by this evening. He couldn't rest until he did.

CHAPTER TWENTY

Altered Plans

Saturday Afternoon
Docked on St. Paras Island

IT WAS DURING THE MIDAFTERNOON BREAK that Manuel received the call from Mexico. He had left Polk's stateroom and was making his way down the hallway with Stephen toward the deck for a short walk before returning to the group session, when a crew member found him and handed him a message from the bridge.

"Thank you," Manuel said. Reaching into his pocket, he took out a small roll of dollars on a clip, peeled off three bills, and slipped them into the young man's hand.

Stephen waited while Manuel studied the note, a shocked expression spreading over his face.

He looked up and said, "It says there has been an assassination attempt on the president of Mexico, and I'm to call Mexico City immediately. Excuse me. I must make this call."

"Sure. Go!"

Stephen stepped aside and Manuel moved adroitly to the door leading to a stairwell.

"Manuel, if I can be of any assistance," he called out, "I'll be in Dr. Polk's room. Let me know."

Manuel had trouble getting through to the private number he had been given. After four tries, he finally reached a secretary. She asked him to hold. Soon the very deep and official voice of the assistant to the President of Mexico came over the receiver.

"Manuel, *muy bien*. We have a serious situation here. An hour ago, while the presidente was speaking in Plaza Revolución, two would-be assassins tried to gun him down. He was not harmed, but two ministers were. Moreno and Martinez were both shot in the scramble for cover. Moreno is dead and Martinez is in critical condition in the hospital. We want you to stand by in case El Presidente needs your advice or assistance in some way. He told me to ask if you could make arrangements to be here by morning."

Without hesitation Manuel nodded his head to the wall in his room and answered, "*Si, ¿Como no?* Of course. I'll try to make arrangements somehow."

Manuel stood where he was, saddened, in shock at the turn of events. Jorge Martinez was Minister of Finance for the nation of Mexico. It puzzled Manuel that the president wanted him to be there. He was not that deeply involved in the financial affairs of the entire nation. There were others much closer to the powerful circle of government officials than he. Oh, he had advised Martinez from time to time and did sit on the financial board, but he was not part of his staff, and he certainly did not mingle with the inner group of ministers. That was reserved for the climbers, the political animals he sometimes detested. He knew little about the internal affairs of the ministry itself. Perhaps the president merely wanted the entire board to assemble in the city for a council meeting, since the minister was obviously unavailable to offer any advice to the president.

Manuel dialed Polk's suite and spoke to Stephen. He briefly explained what had happened in Mexico and asked if Stephen would mind scheduling emergency arrangements so that he and his wife, Carmen, could take the next flight out of Pago Pago. Stephen assured him he would get right on it.

One more session was scheduled before the group would break up. Earlier, Dr. Polk had requested that the phone in the salon be removed to avoid distraction from the discussions, but now the crew had replaced the phone specifically for Manuel, in case he were called by the Mexican government to answer some emergency situation.

Manuel had shared with the group his concern over the tragedy that had taken place that evening in Mexico City. They all felt the strain and anxiety of their colleague. A shadow slowly spread over the gathering.

As he opened the last session, Dr. Polk addressed the issue of the Lamanites, specifically mentioning the great blessings that would be poured out on the Lamanites. They would "blossom as a rose" and would be remembered by the Lord and allowed to come forth and be gathered to the completed New Jerusalem in the very last days.

Manuel knew that Dr. Polk was making a special effort to show compassion for him and his people. Though it came late in the discussion, he appreciated Polk trying to ease his feelings. He saw now that the scriptures left a wide window open for the Lamanites after the Nephites would have built the New Jerusalem and invited all the tribes of the earth—including the Lamanites—to come in and partake of the blessings. The Lamanites would one day be gathered to Zion and receive all the blessings promised them and more, if they were a righteous people and made the necessary covenants.

Polk was halfway through his comments when the phone rang, shattering the concentration of the group. All eyes turned to Manuel, who had the phone in hand on the second buzz. He spoke in rapid Spanish. The conversation was brief, but clearly serious. Seeing the unspoken concern on the faces around him, Manuel held his hand over the receiver and in a loud whisper said, "It's the president. He asks for my help."

Eyebrows raised. Looks were exchanged. All were surprised and impressed that Manuel would be contacted by the President of Mexico himself.

"Sí, sí, entiendo completamente, el Presidente . . . sí."

After listening again, Manuel quickly turned to Stephen and asked if he had been able to schedule a flight out of Pago Pago that night. Stephen had tried, but the only available flight would leave the next morning for Honolulu, and from there a 747 to Los Angeles and on to Mexico, if the connections held. Stephen knew enough Spanish to know that Manuel had repeated his flight schedule to the president and that the president did not find it satisfactory.

Manuel hung up the phone and turned to Stephen. "Thank

you for making the arrangements," he said. "The president will try from his end to get me back sooner."

Standing by the door of the salon, Carmen also understood the conversation. The president wanted Manuel back in the city—immediately! She even surmised why his return was so important. Attempting to glean all information possible about the true situation in Mexico City, she had called her sister and other friends at home, had CNN World blaring on the television set in their stateroom, and had tracked the events in every way possible.

Her sister had little to tell. CNN World had a better handle on the story, but their clip was brief and frustrating. The news at the top of the hour replayed the scene at the plaza during the firing of weapons and scrambling of dignitaries on the stand. Then they cut to the hospital, reporting that the Minister of Finance had taken two bullets to the abdomen and was still in surgery. With total disregard for Carmen's need to know, CNN's programmers cut next to a scene in London where a car bomb had disrupted the morning commute for thousands of Londoners.

Slipping over to the doorway where Carmen stood, Manuel quietly told her that he must discuss something urgent with her. Together they hurried to their stateroom.

"*Querida*," Manuel said breathlessly, as soon as they had closed the door to their room. "The news agencies have not been fully informed. Minister Martinez is not expected to live. The Presidente has informed me that he wishes to present my name to the council to be the new interim finance minister. How shall I respond?"

"I was sure of it!" Carmen exclaimed. She threw her arms around her stunned husband and gripped him fiercely. "Who else could he have selected? Who else is so completely honest and cares so much about our people?"

"Well, perhaps you are a bit biased," Manuel slowly replied as he held his wife close, rocking her slowly back and forth, grateful for her support. A heavy weight had suddenly dropped onto his shoulders. What a monumental task he faced! Would he prove strong enough for the job? So much corruption to overcome. *What was it President Meyers had prayed . . . that God would make me a light in the dark to my people, that through me they might come unto him?* Manuel closed his eyes in silent prayer, *Oh, dear Father, is this how I can reach my people? Please help me be a righteous example before them.*

With shaking hands, Carmen and Manuel hurriedly finished packing their belongings, wishing they had thought to bring along an extra suitcase for the souvenirs they had already collected on the islands. They moved automatically as they packed, too disjointed in their conversation to make much sense. As Manuel closed the last suitcase, another call came from the president. This time it was routed directly to the Rodriguez stateroom.

The president informed Manuel that Jorge had not survived the surgery. The two spoke briefly about the great service and fine character of the deceased finance minister, then the president advised Manuel that a five-passenger U.S. Naval jet was serviced and ready for him at the base in American Samoa. The President of the United States had offered to fly Manuel home as a courtesy. The U.S. Navy was also dispatching a naval helicopter to pick up Manuel and Carmen in two hours on the nearest island to the yacht. It was being prepared as they spoke. Everything was arranged to whisk them back to Mexico City, where Manuel was needed.

Stephen stood at the open door of the helicopter, which rested on the tarmac as it waited to carry Manuel and Carmen to the naval base in American Samoa. Amid shouts of good-bye, the temporary Minister of Finance of Mexico gripped the handle to climb into the passenger section of the aircraft.

Stephen patted Manuel's shoulder and spoke loud enough to be heard over the roar: "I know this has not been easy meeting with us, but believe me, we are grateful for your input at the meetings. Do your best. Make us proud!"

Stephen backed away from the door, then shouted from the asphalt pad, "Manuel, we'll be watching the news! I like having friends in high places. I expect royal treatment when I visit Mexico next time."

Manuel smiled broadly. His enthusiastic "thumbs up" said it all.

Carmen was already inside, perched on a bucket seat with her belt secured. The second pilot of the craft was Latin-American and spoke pleasantly to Carmen, as if he had known her for years. She was happy to be speaking her native tongue again to someone other than Manuel.

His clothing and hair whipping around him, Stephen backed away from the helicopter as the rotors began to pick up speed. As the awkward-looking, gray machine lifted off and circled away toward Pago Pago, he waved one more time before returning to the vintage taxi that had brought him to the airstrip.

Waiting patiently inside the taxi, Karry also watched the mighty machine lift off and disappear into the sky. He had come along to man the tender, but when Stephen had asked him to come to the airstrip with them and help with the Rodriguez luggage, he had willingly agreed.

In the taxi on the way back to the dock, Karry posed the question that had been haunting his thoughts since the evening before. "Mr. Thorn . . . uh . . . Stephen, sir. I've been waiting for the chance to talk with you about a serious matter."

Karry's tone startled Stephen. What could he have done to cause this young man such concern? The fellow was obviously uncomfortable in his request.

"I will say it straight out," Karry exclaimed. He self-consciously rubbed his knees as he spoke, "I want to have you . . . or someone . . . tell me about your church."

Stephen thought he heard a softly exhaled "there" following Karry's request.

"Okay . . . sure, be glad to," Stephen said, relieved that it was nothing more serious. He smiled at Karry, who seemed to be just as relieved. "You must have seen or heard something that has interested you. Can you be more specific about what caused you to be curious?"

"Oh, a lot of things. I'm not a religious person, not at all. I just want to know what it is about you people that makes me curious and, at the same time, have a good feeling. Can someone explain before you leave the ship? I may never have contact with your kind of people again."

"Sure. I can arrange it. How about tomorrow morning in the aft salon? Say 8 A.M. Can you get the captain to let you off for the morning?"

"I'll try. But I may need permission from the first officer. The captain has taken to his bed. He began feeling poorly this morning. That's what I heard on the bridge while I was serving coffee."

"Oh, I didn't know. I hope he's up and about soon. Keep me posted. Okay? Eight o'clock tomorrow morning. I'll have someone there. If you have a problem getting the time free, call me. I think I can help arrange it. But you try first. No sense going over anyone's head before you've tried."

Stephen wondered who he would get to talk to this young man. Polk and Meyers would be needed in the main salon, so they were out. Eric and Takahashi wouldn't want to miss the discussions. He'd have to come up with someone.

* * *

THE AFTERNOON SESSION HAD DISSOLVED in the stress of Manuel's crisis. Everyone had wanted to help Manuel and Carmen get ready to leave. Now that they had departed, Polk and Meyers felt the mood was not right to have further discussions until the next morning. Since the afternoon still promised a couple hours of sunlight, Samuel asked Katherine to go ashore with him and rent two little four-wheelers and climb the volcanic mountain on the narrow, gravel road to view the dormant crater and enjoy the scenic view.

"One of the crewmen told me that he made the trip to the top last time he was here and had a great time. We can talk more about the principle of eternal marriage, if you'd like," Samuel added for greater incentive.

Katherine laughed gaily as she asked, "Do they supply helmets?" Then she wondered about getting her hair flattened or windblown and generally ending up looking scruffy, but after thinking it over she replied, "Why not?" The opportunity to learn more about how she could be with Bob forever was too enticing to resist.

"I'll bring along some material I printed out from a book we have access to on CD-ROM. It explains the subject a little better than I've been able to."

True to her thoughtful nature, Katherine ordered a small picnic dinner from the galley and asked them to put it in a backpack for Samuel to carry.

A hand-drawn sign taped in the window of a rental office on Main Street offered the use of motor peds and four-wheelers for ten dollars an hour. After Samuel forked over forty dollars and signed on the dotted line for the machines, they listened carefully as the bored proprietor gave them pat directions to the crater. No doubt he had spoken those words a thousand times before.

They found that the little contraptions were simple enough to operate. Katherine was relieved to see that all she had to do was press on the accelerator to go forward and grip the hand brakes or the foot pedal to stop. She was a high-spirited lady, but she refused to go any faster than fifteen miles per hour. Dressed in jeans, a light short-sleeve cotton blouse, helmet, sunglasses, and light cotton gloves she had found in the stateroom, she was set for rugged terrain.

The rugged climb never materialized. When the paved road ended on the edge of town, the gravel road began. They passed groves of banana trees and several fields of pineapple, cane fields, and more cane fields as they climbed toward the top of the mountain. Midway, Samuel pulled off the winding gravel road, stepped off the four-wheeler, and turned completely around to take in the 360-degree vista. Katherine remained seated on her machine and watched Samuel enjoy the view. It was a brilliant late afternoon, offering the promise of a painter's sunset. Far to their right they spotted the *Free Eagle*, bobbing lightly on the shallow waves in the bay. She looked like a toy from high on the mountain.

At the crest of the crater, where the gravel road made a wide turn like the end of a cul-de-sac, Samuel and Katherine pulled to the side, got off, and began the short trek to the rim of the crater. It had been a hundred years since the volcano had last spewed out its fiery liquid. Black, long-cooled lava stone surrounded three sides of the crater; its center was a dark black hole. It was Katherine's first view inside a once-active volcano. Not greatly impressed, she turned her attention to the view below in the bay.

Removing the helmet, she hung it on the bars. The tradewinds played with strands of her soft gray hair as she slowly turned around, absorbed by the moving sight of sea and island with green, lush foliage all across the mountain. Samuel also took in the view, then turned slightly so he could watch Katherine, framed by the beautiful setting. It was refreshing to be so close to civilization, yet able to enjoy the sensation of total privacy afforded by such isolation.

Together they strolled from the crater to a patch of green grass that grew along the edge of the road. Samuel had dropped the backpack on the grass before venturing to the crater's rim. Katherine reached down, hoisted the backpack and unzipped the flap. Then she began to remove the contents, which included a small linen cloth and a mini-feast. The chef had provided a small loaf of freshly baked bread, cheese, cold sliced turkey, fruit salad in a plastic container, and two plastic plates. From inside the backpack, Katherine pulled out a small bottle of wine and two small plastic cups. Fortunately for Samuel, the chef had also packed a petite bottle of Perrier.

Katherine poured Perrier into one of the cups and handed it to Samuel. For herself, she poured a little wine. The grass felt cool and inviting to sit on as each made a sandwich from the available ingredients.

Katherine had already lifted her sandwich to her lips and was about to take a bite when Samuel asked if they could say grace. She was mildly surprised, but lowered her food to her plate. She understood the custom at a formal dinner, but out in the open on a mountain top, it seemed a little out of place.

"Okay, but you will have to say it. I'm not good at those sorts of things."

Samuel's was a brief thank you. Then they ate.

Between bites, he explained in more detail the concept of eternal marriage. He had told her the evening before that eternal companionship required certain prerequisites, such as Church membership. That was fundamental. He had then recited to her a litany of requirements beyond baptism, such as living the Savior's commandments. Now he attempted to answer Katherine's questions about last night's dialogue.

"You mean *your* church commandments?" she asked.

"I mean the whole gospel of Jesus Christ, with all its requirements and blessings. You see, Katherine, nothing is required of us by the Savior that doesn't carry with it a blessing."

"I like that. I think it ought to be that way. But how many of us

can muster the moral determination to live by those great requirements?"

"Everyone with a desire."

Samuel switched his approach and spoke philosophically of the
beauties of eternal marriage.

"I have another question," Katherine said after a bit.

"Go ahead."

"What if I were to become a full, card-carrying member of your
church and were sealed to my late husband, Bob . . . and then . . .
what if I wanted to marry again while I'm still here, alive? What
would happen to our . . . what do you call it?"

"Celestial marriage."

"Hmmm, I think that was what you called it last night, but you
used another term just now and so did Todd when he told me about
this concept."

"Eternal marriage?"

"Right. That's the word—*eternal*. That means forever. Anyway,
would I forfeit that right if I should marry again? Not that I'm planning on a marriage in the near future, but you know . . ."

Samuel explained companionship marriages and the opportunity two people who have been sealed to others would have to marry
for this life only.

"Interesting. As I listened to you explain these things, I began to
say to myself, 'This is exciting.' It seems that you have all the bases
covered, and I like that. However, as I have given some thought to
the matter . . . realistically, I know myself. I'm afraid I don't have the
right stuff to become a believing member of your church. Look at me
enjoying this delicious wine. I'm a woman of the nineties, so to
speak. I may not be downright wicked, but I enjoy so many of the
little . . . what? What you Mormons perhaps would call "little sins"? I
love cappucino. I enjoy wine with my meals. I frankly love my
lifestyle. Face it, Samuel, I'm a woman of the world."

"What are you trying to say?"

"I'm saying that, though it saddens me, I'm afraid I don't fit the
pattern."

"Katherine, you are talking of nothings."

"What do you mean, nothings?" she asked indignantly. "To me

they are important little touches to my life to make it a little more enjoyable and, at times, bearable. They are not just little nothings to me."

"Oh, but they are, Katherine. They're what real estate salesmen refer to as 'cosmetic' obstacles when trying to close the sale of a house that needs a little fixing up. If you were to understand the true meaning of membership in the Church of Jesus Christ, you'd have no problem aligning your life with the pure teachings of the gospel. Your little enjoyments, as you call them, would melt beside a magnificent conviction of Christ. Your life would become such a masterpiece of involvement in the wonderful, important things of life, you would find it easy to discard the little vices you now enjoy caressing." Samuel caught himself. Why was he getting so worked up? *Cool it. You're going to frighten this lady away—from the gospel as well as from you.*

"Katherine, you don't understand," he continued in a less agitated tone. "Before you ever try to alter your lifestyle, you will have a conviction deep in your heart that things are right and that you are part of the most wonderful way of life in the universe. It may not come quickly, this conversion that I'm talking about. We may have to work on the greater things before you make a mighty change."

Katherine set her plastic cup on a flat surface of volcanic rock, and her lips parted in a teasing smile. "Well, I think you are one of those squeaky-clean missionaries in disguise. You are using some very persuasive techniques to sway me to your beliefs. I don't think 'we' are ready to make that leap." She smiled, looking into Samuel's eyes, then wrapped her arms around her knees and gazed out into the bay in deep thought.

"To be frank with you, Sam, I never really got too caught up in my late husband's religion. He was so powerful in speech and body language, and heaven only knows I adored him from the moment I first saw him on TV . . . But it was the man who attracted me, not what he preached."

Katherine slowly shook her head. "You don't know what an impact that man had on my thoughts and desires. No one knows. But you're saying that in order to have Bob bound to me . . ."

"Sealed, the word is sealed."

"Okay, sealed to me. In order to do that, you are saying that I would have to come full circle into your faith. All I can say at this moment is, I'm not ready to make such a commitment. I say this without any malice toward you or any of the other members of your church I know. I'm simply not ready to make such a commitment."

Samuel fell silent, a dejected look on his face.

Suddenly, as if it had just occurred to her, Katherine asked, "And what about Bob? Would he also be required to embrace your faith, wherever he is?"

"Yes," Samuel said quietly. "Yes, he would."

"And you people have those bases covered as well." Katherine put her open hands flat on the grass behind her, threw back her head, and laughed. "Well, there you have it. Bob would never do it . . . not in a million years. In fact, if there was any group of people Bob maligned, it was the Mormons. For some reason your religion was offensive to him. I could never understand why it mattered to him one way or another. But it was almost his crusade. He seemed to get satisfaction from trying to expose your church as a fraudulent religion."

Katherine looked ruefully at Samuel. Finally, ending the discussion, she bent down, grabbed the backpack, and shook it upside down, saying brightly, "Well, it's going to be a clear day tomorrow." Seeing Samuel's quizzical look, she laughed. "That's what my mother always said when we ate every single thing she had prepared for a meal. I hope she is right this time."

Samuel feigned a grin, but his heart was heavy. He watched his gracious companion slip the empty containers into the backpack, then stand up.

"Thanks for coming up here with me this afternoon, Katherine. It has made me feel young again. I have longed literally for months to be in such a paradise . . . with a lovely lady to lay out a spread before me. You've given me refreshment in more than one way."

"Samuel, you're too much. Surely a man of your talents and charm doesn't have to sit around pining for companionship."

"Perhaps not, but it's true. I have been far too busy with my personal, self-inflicted assignment to take a woman on an afternoon outing. Besides, I haven't met anyone I wanted to invite before this."

"I'm glad I could help you achieve your fantasy," she laughed, keeping it light. Then she smiled regretfully at Samuel. "Can you believe what a changeling I am? Here I came all this way, so excited about the chance to be with my husband after this life, only to learn that it could never be. Even if I were of a mind to accept your beliefs . . . still, knowing Bob, it could never be."

Samuel knew it was time to descend the mountain and return to Katherine's yacht. He was disappointed, yet deep inside he hoped that perhaps Katherine was not closing the door entirely. It was just possible that she might want to learn more. There was that something in her spirit that convinced him that if she were to convert to the gospel, she would become a powerful force in the lives of many.

* * *

BRENDA PLACED THE GLASS OF JUICE on the glass-topped table. She let her arm slip around Max. She was always a little surprised at his thinness. His shoulders were wide compared to the rest of his body, but he had no bulk. All of her life, she had been surrounded by tall, masculine men who felt like ball players when she hugged them. It seemed odd to Brenda that she didn't mind Max's slender frame. She comforted herself that he had a manly presence, despite his thin body. His face, though smooth, was very masculine looking.

She was glad she had purchased a flowered Hawaiian shirt for Max during their stopover in Hawaii. Otherwise, he would still be wearing the drab gray shirt he had worn to meet her in San Francisco, or its twin that he had brought along in his backpack.

"I never dreamed I would be on a fancy yacht in the South Pacific, sipping juice, completely content, just lounging around with the girl I love," said Max.

Feeling his shoulders tense, Brenda looked up to see a slight frown on Max's face.

"What?" she asked.

"There is only one flaw: I don't belong here."

"What do you mean, you don't belong here? You have as much right to be here as I do. Neither one of us is paying for this little weekend spree. Remember, it's Granny Katherine's treat." Brenda snuggled down next to Max on the top deck, an array of stars dotting the backdrop of their romantic setting.

"No, you don't understand," Max sighed. "Brenda, I'm trash compared to you. You really don't know me. I feel like I've been playing a game . . . wearing a sort of mask."

Brenda tried to protest, but Max stopped her. "Brenda," he came close to shouting. All color had drained from his face and his eyes bored into hers. "You have to listen to me! I can't let you believe I'm something I'm not. Being here on this yacht has made me realize that I have to tell you." Max ducked his head and eased away from her.

Brenda could see that his hands trembled as he grasped the arm of the wide lounge chair they shared. Something told her to say nothing, to wait until he could muster the words he was trying to utter. In a halting voice, nearly whispering, Max slowly began explaining his whole miserable life—a life he considered a failure from the day he was born. Without looking up, he revealed that he had been raised in near squalor by a mother who had left him when he was twelve, a father who had kicked him out at sixteen, and that his was a life on the road, then on the streets of L.A. He frankly told her that he had tried everything, including one attempt at taking his life. He left nothing out. Painful though it was, he ended with a description of his recent life in a tent under the freeway interchange.

When he finished, Max paused, then looked up at the quiet girl. "You don't know me, Brenda. I'm really not the person you think I am. I know I ought to have told you in Park City . . . but you were so . . . you were the nicest thing that ever happened to me. I couldn't bring myself to reveal all this. I was afraid that you would just walk away."

Brenda listened, her heart pounding. Tears silently streamed down her face. When Max stopped speaking, she reached over and gripped his hand. All she wanted to do was hold him. For a moment she said nothing. She refused to be light about it. She did not have the words to express what she was feeling. All she knew was that she loved this brave man, and she yearned to soothe away all his past hurts.

Max spoke again before she said anything. He couldn't let her get into a relationship she would regret for the rest of her life. "Brenda, I love you. But you really need to think about what I have told you. I don't know how we would fit together once the thrill fades and we have a day-by-day life with all the usual problems married couples face. I really don't know if I can be a good husband. I'm so warped in some ways. I have pushed those terrible memories of my childhood right out of my mind. I guess you might say I had no childhood. I never knew an ordinary family like yours—love, fresh sheets, educated people. I didn't even graduate from high school. There is so much I have missed. I've got some dark gaps in my character development . . . big gaps."

Brenda put her fingers to Max's lips and pressed lightly. "Shhh. It's my turn." Reaching down, she pulled the hem of her colorful muumuu up and scrubbed it across her flushed face, wiping the tears away. "Darling, there is no such thing as missing a childhood. You were a child as I was a child. It's simply a matter of how you spent that childhood. My heart aches that things were so tough for you when you were growing up. I wish I had been there to be your friend. Don't you think I had my moments of unhappiness and feeling shoved aside by some people? Everybody does."

Max shrugged. "Not the same way as—"

"Wait, let me tell you how I feel. First, I know I love you, and you said you love me, too. That is an incredible thing." Brenda moved closer to Max and spoke very softly. "Since we do love each other, then isn't it a matter of adjustment from here on out? Look what we have in common. We were both raised in the latter part of the twentieth century. We're both Americans. We even grew up in the same state, at least in our teen years. We speak pretty much the same language. We both belong to the same race. You have blue eyes, I have blue eyes. Our skin tone is pretty much the same color, and we both love learning. I was thinking while we were dancing in Park City that your body fits mine perfectly. We're young and have many years to pull this thing off. I'm not expecting that we will be totally compatible right off the bat, but I do feel that in time we will come to understand and appreciate the experiences of one another. If . . . if I'm willing to live out my life with you and learn from your experiences, which I can see involved so much suffering, then why can't you, in turn, learn from my experiences and share the love of parents you can have at last? We just have to combine our experiences to gain the most from our lives together."

Max had never heard a husband-and-wife relationship described with more wisdom or sincerity. He searched Brenda's glowing, tear-washed face and felt a surge of intense adoration. Dare he hope that life could become that good? His emotions nearly blocked his ability to speak. He cleared his throat and said, "You mean, you don't think my life is worthless? You would still want me?"

Brenda was close to tears again. She gulped and nodded, squeezing his hand with all her strength. Max began to relax. His face reflected his gradual comprehension of her words. He gently cupped her face in his free hand and echoed her thoughts: "Then each of us will bring to our relationship our own experiences. Where I may have experienced a life of hardship, you have an abundance of love and secure feelings. Brenda, it won't be easy. Sometimes we may not understand where the other is coming from. But at those times, we will have to lean on each other. It makes sense. Oh, I love you, Brenda."

Brenda could wait no longer. She slipped both arms around Max as he pressed his hungry mouth to hers.

Max finally pulled away from Brenda, held her by the shoulders with his hands, and in the dim light from below, stared at her for a moment without saying a word.

"What?" Brenda asked, not wanting to play this staring game any longer.

"Brenda, I want you to have the missionaries teach you the gospel."

She hadn't expected him to be so direct about the matter. She was not prepared to answer yes. From her teen years on, Brenda had decided what she would believe. Independent and confident, she was not easily swayed by outside pressure to conform to a standard that anyone else had designed. She had made peace with the fact that Max had joined a church of his own choosing. She was sure that deep in her heart she could live with Max and respect his firm beliefs. She had even decided that if they should marry and have children, she would consent to let them be taught his religion.

Tears sprang up again in Brenda's eyes, but this time they were tears of frustration. She didn't deserve this blunt approach. How could he break the romantic spell that prevailed up to a moment ago? Besides, hadn't she been so willing to understand his circumstances and accept him just as he was? How could he, on the other hand, expect her to be anything more than she was? She knew he expected an answer.

"Max . . . oh, Max. Why are you doing this to us? You have your set of values and I have mine. We should be able to retain those and still love one another. Why do I have to conform to a set of rules and ideals that are yours and, by the way, fairly new to you at that?"

"Why? Because I love you and want us to be eternally happy. We can't be married for all eternity unless you accept the gospel. Brenda, you will love the gospel once you understand it!"

"I don't buy that," Brenda said in a burst of anger. She was not as fearful of expressing a firm opinion as she had been just one minute earlier. "I will go on loving you, and I hope you can love me as well, but don't ask me to become a member of your church. It is not me. I can't switch this thing on just to please you. Would you want me to do that?"

Max was suddenly sorry he had brought up the subject at all. He could see that he had approached the issue all wrong and Brenda was not ready. *How could I have been so blunt, so insensitive to her feelings? She's not ready for this. She deserves more time.* He saw clearly that she was still on a separate track from him, no matter what she said. This was especially true in the area of understanding the glories of the Savior's teachings as he had recently grasped them. *Back off. Don't push it.*

"Okay," he said with the same abruptness he had used in broaching the issue. "Okay, okay. I love you. I want to be with you. I will accept your right to remain as you are, but you must accept my convictions insofar as I wish to express them to others. I will back off, but I can tell you that this drive within me to have you sealed to me for eternity will not go away. It will only remain outwardly silent. Is that fair?"

Brenda took a deep breath. "Okay, we have a friendly truce on our hands. I can live with that." She smiled with relief. "Yeah, it's okay."

The deal struck, Max eased her head to his shoulder and leaned back in the lounge chair. He looked up at the stars, and in his heart he prayed once again for this girl he adored. Prayed for her soul.

CHAPTER TWENTY-ONE

Unlikely Missionaries

Saturday Night

THE PHONE RANG SOFTLY beside the queen-size bed in their stateroom. Eric and Carol were not asleep. They had been talking for the past hour about family, the cruise, and most particularly their son, Cory.

"Hello?"

"Eric? Lyle. I'm sure sorry to call you so late, but I think you ought to know what's been happening on this end."

"What is it?" Eric demanded. He looked at Carol, his heart on the verge of seizure.

"I'm still closing up, but I thought . . . well, I'd better let you know so you can call first thing in the morning before your boy goes off to church."

Carol raised up in the bed, gripped with fear. She leaned close to the phone, trying to listen to the voice on the receiver. She could faintly hear what Lyle was saying. Eric turned the receiver out from his ear toward Carol so she could hear better.

"What happened?"

"Looks like things could be turning around for Cory. He was here this evening helping me with some little chores I needed him to do. Since it was Saturday night, I thought he might be better off here than sitting at home. He's really not a bad worker and likes the money. He told me yesterday that if I needed help in the restaurant, he would come in. Anyway, about eight this evening he took a break and walked over to the mall. I said he could. Well, while he was coming out of the mall, he spotted a couple of his buddies in the parking lot. You know, the kid he was hanging out with—I don't remember his name—the kid with long hair and an earring. Anyway, I guess Cory was starting to walk over to those guys when a bunch of cops surrounded their car. Mind you, Cory was still near the entrance to the mall, but he saw the whole thing."

"How did you find out?"

"He came back all excited and told me the whole thing. So guess what happened, according to Cory? It was a big bust, a drug bust. Some of the cops must have been waiting for them. The kid that Cory had been hanging with was wrestled to the pavement, then cuffed and searched. Cory was smart enough to stay back with the crowd but he was close enough to see the whole bust. He said there was a crowd of people around. Anyway, they tossed that kid in the patrol car, along with a couple more guys, and had them out of there in no time."

"How did Cory react to the bust?"

"He was shaking like I don't know what. He came hightailing it back here, pulled me into the office, and told me everything. I'm telling you, it scared the daylights out of him. He kept telling me over and over again, 'Lyle, I almost sneaked out to go with those guys. Man, can you believe that?'"

Eric let out a long slow breath. Cory wasn't the only one shaking from the experience. Eric's hand was trembling on the phone. He covered his face with his other hand, weak with relief.

Carol had heard just enough to understand that there was no emergency, and she breathed a sigh of relief.

"How is he now?" Eric asked.

"Okay. He's okay. I took him home about an hour ago. I'm sure he's asleep by now. You know what he said in the car while I was driving him home?"

"What?"

"He said, 'Dad was right. Those guys are bad news.'"

"He said that?"

"Yeah. Honest, he did. He also said he was going to church in the morning, whether you and his mother were home or not."

Carol dabbed her eyes with the sheet; Eric was grateful it was dark. Tears were dropping off his cheeks, and he was so choked up he could hardly thank Lyle for his help before saying good night.

"Call him, Eric. Call Cory in the morning when he gets up. He really needs you to pump him up."

"I will. I will . . . And, Lyle . . . thanks, man."

* * *

"WHAT DID YOU SAY?"

"I want you fellows to take Karry aside and teach him the gospel."

Todd had stared at his dad in disbelief. Teach the gospel? That was what missionaries did. He didn't know enough about the absolute doctrinal facts to teach anyone else. He threw a glance at Max, who was just as dumbfounded. They could see that Stephen was dead serious.

Stephen had explained apologetically that all the other members of the Church on board were tied up in the final session. They, two brand new members, were the only ones available. Stephen explained that Karry had approached him, that he wanted to be taught now. Would they do it?

"Man, Dad. Man! This is too insane. What do we know about anything?"

Stephen held his son's terrified eyes with his own. Putting his warm, reassuring hand on the boy's shoulder, he spoke with love. "Do it, Todd. Do it for me. All you have to do is be sincere . . . please."

They agreed, but with great reservation. After all, they had only been in the Church for a couple of weeks. For the next half-hour they had pumped Stephen for information on how to present the teachings of the Church. Stephen showed them the CD-ROM computer setup in the main salon, where they had the LDS database, which covered most of the doctrinal teachings of the Church. Max was at ease with all the software, but they had little time to research, and in their anxiety they began to confuse what they were reading. Ultimately, they decided to wing it, to share what they had learned from their intense study of the Book of Mormon in Park City.

"Guys, listen to me. Teach from your strengths. Both of you have understood enough of the gospel to be convinced in your own right. Give him the testimony and insights that you have. That is all you can do. Then we'll pick up from there later tomorrow. I'm sure Sam will be available to give some assistance before we leave the ship.

"However, that's not really what Karry is worried about, you know?" Stephen said. "He's afraid we'll leave on Monday or Tuesday, and he'll be left hanging. He doesn't think he will ever meet another member of the Church again. So I promised him that we would teach him as much as we can. He wants to know, right now; he's that ready to learn. I've had to hold him off until morning, so please help him. You guys can do it."

Todd and Max once again agreed to give it a try. What did they have to lose? Plenty. With such novices attempting to persuade him that they had the gospel of Jesus Christ, the Aussie kid might throw up his hands and walk away in disgust. All of these concerns hung over Todd and Max deep into the night as they lay talking in the darkness of the stateroom they shared.

"The blind leading the blind," Max had commented as the two drifted off to sleep.

"Yeah, big holes. Big, big holes in our understanding, Max. Major ones. Who are we kidding?"

Finally they recalled that Todd's dad had given them one more piece of advice before leaving their room: "Pray, guys. Pray a whole lot while you're teaching him. The Spirit will guide you."

"Let's hope so," muttered Todd. "It did when we fasted at Park City."

"You know, you're right. That was some experience."

Fasting for Todd and Max had been more of an experiment than two young men seeking to understand the very meaning of life. The subject of fasting had come up when Max and Todd had visited Dr. Polk at his home in Provo one day during the youth conference. He had spoken strongly on faith and seeking the Spirit.

"Properly executed with deep humility," he had said, "nothing in this world can have greater impact on our minds and spirits than releasing our bodies for a short time from physical concerns and letting the Spirit take over, then bowing ourselves before our Heavenly Father with an awareness of our dependence upon him. It comes from hunger and faith. Try it. It won't kill you to deny yourselves food and liquid for twenty-four hours."

At Park City five weeks ago, Todd and Max had decided to try it together. Fasting was a new experience for both and they had to hit the sack early during the experiment because they were weak and dry. The experiment was taking its toll on the two. Fasting suddenly assumed a whole new meaning for Todd. It was harder than he thought.

It was Max who had suggested prayer that evening before they dropped their shaky knees into bed. Todd had been light and sarcastic, while Max had been touched by the Spirit. But sleep had eluded Todd, and before the night was over he, too, had received a witness of the power of sincere prayer.

That was last month. Now, here they were with Karry in the aft salon. Karry was all smiles, seated in front of his two instructors. He had received permission to be relieved of his duties for the morning—thanks to Katherine's intercession. Since the captain was too ill to be disturbed, she had spoken with the first officer, who had grudgingly granted her request The first officer had been in charge for more than twenty-four hours by now, and his temper was short. He was sharp with everyone this morning, even Katherine. But she had prevailed.

Todd and Max may have been the age of two young elders, but they both knew that dressed in t-shirts and baggy shorts, age was the only thing they had in common with the elders. More serious than the disparity in attire, they knew they were far from being as knowledgeable as the average elder. For this reason, both were tense and uneasy.

They huddled around a small table, surrounded by books, most of which none had read. But Todd and Max had some of their plays down: they would work Karry over for the next couple of hours with everything they knew about Jesus Christ, the Book of Mormon, and Joseph Smith—but maybe not in that order. They weren't certain of an order. If it went as planned . . . planned? Who were they kidding? There was no real plan. Karry would soon have all their meager knowledge—not too filling.

Max swallowed and looked his investigator in the eye. He was quick to let Karry know that they had never done this before, that they had joined the Church a few weeks ago themselves; but they would try.

"How did you come to ask my dad about the Church?" Todd asked as the three young men sat across from one another, heads almost touching.

Karry grinned and kept it light. These fellows were about his age, and he didn't want to seem too churchy to them. "Just curious. So I got this morning off and here I am. I'm bustin' to know what you fellows know that I don't. And don't worry, mates. I'm a fast learner, though I'm not a college-schooled guy. But just give it to me like you would anyone else and I'll listen. Got it?"

They got under way. Todd offered a prayer, all three kneeling on the soft carpet. He asked repeatedly that Karry would be touched by the Spirit. Back in their seats, Max started off with their planned approach.

Fifteen minutes into a brief look at the Church of Jesus Christ, as Max understood it in the time of Christ and today, Max began to grope for words. He quickly shifted to how he became converted through the teachings of the Book of Mormon. Abruptly he turned to Todd and asked him to relate how he became converted. Todd spoke for twenty minutes about how his parents explained things and how he also read the Book of Mormon and was convinced it was true. He finished and looked at Max for the next cue. Max drew a blank.

"Let's have another prayer," Todd sort of gasped, not knowing what to say.

This time Max prayed.

Todd took up the fight once again and launched into the Book of Mormon. He knew no other approach than to read the Introduction to the Book of Mormon. He followed that with a complete explanation, as he remembered it, of how Joseph Smith had a vision—he had marked that spot in the Pearl of Great Price scriptures where Joseph told his own account.

"Let's pray," Max suggested, after they read parts from the Joseph Smith story. Sweat was glistening on his forehead, and he couldn't help but notice how red Todd's face was.

An hour passed, and they could hear the group gathering on the other side of the wall in the main salon. They listened for a moment. Max looked at Todd, both hoping someone would come and take over, but no one disturbed them.

The three got down on their knees once again and Max prayed. His prayer was brief. Then he turned to Karry in a surprise move and said, "Karry, you pray now."

A red flush spread over the head and neck of the young Australian. "What? You want me to pray? Hey, mate, I've never prayed in my life. What do you pray for? How?"

Still on bended knee, Todd glanced furtively at Max, then at Karry.

Max smiled and said gently, "Just do it, man."

"How do I start?"

"I'll help you."

Karry's mouth went dry, and he gripped his knees with both hands, white knuckles evident. He shook his head, perplexed. "What do you mean, you'll help?"

"I'll say the words and you repeat them after me. Then, as you feel comfortable speaking to the Lord . . . you do believe in God?"

"Absolutely."

"Then talk to him. Talk to him in your own way. We'll just talk this thing through. It doesn't matter what you say, so long as it is your heart speaking to Heavenly Father. That's all I know about prayer. I just speak to my loving Heavenly Father and he listens. Try it. It works."

Max formed the words for Karry, and Karry repeated them, just as a four-year-old child would have. Beginning with "Dear Heavenly Father," Karry's lips moved, echoing every word Max uttered. It was Karry's first vocal prayer ever. After repeating a plea for understanding of what was being taught, Karry reached over and gripped Max's arm, then whispered, "Let me try it on my own."

Tears welled in Todd's eyes as he knelt there, head down,

listening to the totally sincere young Australian pour out his heart to his Father in Heaven. The simple, beautiful plea prompted Max to open his eyes in wonder, to study the young man whose blond head was bowed nearly to the carpet, his voice muffled with emotion. Max had never seen a person so completely open in word and thought. He knew as clearly as if he were standing in the very presence of Jesus Christ that Karry was speaking directly to his Father in Heaven, and that angels hovered there in the small salon. Max shot covert glances around the room, searching for the angels whose presence he felt.

Listening to the sincerity of the prayer, Todd wished he had more of the innocence and childlike feelings that Karry was expressing in simple Aussie English. He knew even then that it was a moment he and Max would recall again and again, and weave into their own lives and testimonies. Like bona fide, full-time missionaries, they were experiencing the delicious taste of teaching the gospel and watching a child of God respond. Both felt a rush that was more exquisite and precious—short of receiving their own testimonies—than anything they had ever known.

"I'm not a learned person, but I feel there is something about the lot of you that I want to understand. Am I making sense?" Karry had finished his prayer, asking his Father in Heaven to help Max and Todd teach him, and once again the three surrounded the table.

"Lots of sense, buddy," Max nodded, punching Karry on the arm.

"Let's talk about everyday things that you'll have to know and do if you want to be a member," Todd began with a grin, "like no more beer, booze, tobacco, girls—if you know what I mean."

Karry started moving his head up and down in agreement as Todd spoke. When Todd came to "girls," Karry turned sharply and asked, "What do you mean by girls?"

"I mean, you can't be fooling around."

"Oh, no sex, you mean?"

"Yeah, that's exactly what I mean . . . that is, not until you're married."

"Okay."

"Hey, you have to mean it."

"I do, man. I understand. Where I come from, they still more or less believe that sex is forbidden outside of wedlock. Not everyone, but you know, mate, I agree with you."

Todd continued with the list as he remembered it, then Max came in with greater detail about each topic brought up.

They kept at it for the next hour.

It was nearing noon, but Karry kept asking more and more questions. "Can I ask you one very important question about this gospel of Jesus that you have explained to me?"

"Sure," Todd said, now the picture of confidence. Max nodded, too, but more cautiously.

"What do you think makes your religion so special? There are lots of religions that preach about Christ. What is so different about your religion?"

"Lots of things," Todd said evasively. He needed time to think.

"But how is yours unique?"

Max offered, "Well, you heard us tell you that the true Church was brought back in the time of Joseph Smith."

"Yes, but what is really different from the others besides, say, your Book of Mormon?"

Max was still pondering the question. Todd waited for him to express himself, sure that Max would come up with just the right answer. He didn't want to say something amiss and spoil the moment.

At length Max spoke . . . this time in a new and more powerful voice. Somehow he seemed different, like he was really in charge or something. Todd stared at him as he listened to his friend speak.

"I'll tell you what is different," Max began. "I read this about the Church not long ago. We have the power to put you under water and baptize you, then confer the gift of the Holy Ghost upon you. This means that you can comprehend great and marvelous things about the gospel of Jesus Christ once you receive this gift. It is given at the time of your baptism, when you are clean before the Lord. That power to baptize and bestow the Gift of the Holy Ghost is called the priesthood, and as I understand from what I have been taught recently, it is the power to act for God here on the earth. You may know through the Holy Ghost that what we are telling you is true."

Todd was stunned by Max's response. His respect for the guy shot through the ceiling of the yacht and climbed skyward.

CHAPTER TWENTY-TWO

Conclusion

Sunday Morning
On the High Seas

STEPHEN'S CONCENTRATION WAS DIVIDED. He knew that in the aft salon Todd and Max were wading through the challenge of their lives. Had he been wise to have them try to convince Karry of the truth of the gospel of Jesus Christ? He had second thoughts, wondering if he should have put off teaching Karry until someone with experience could provide the answers. Stephen fidgeted within, but sat quietly listening to Polk introduce the windup session. At length Polk was ready to turn the discussion over to Samuel as he concluded his remarks.

With effort, Stephen finally zeroed in on Polk's earnest words. "This also means that all children of the covenant who are faithful will be blessed of the Lord: Gentile, Lamanite, Jew—it matters not. Any group or individual who comes in under the covenant will be afforded all the blessings of the House of Israel, regardless of lineage. Nevertheless, the children of four of the tribes of Lehi—known as Nephites—are clearly designated to receive the great blessing of inheritance that the Lord has reserved for them, since that promise was made to them by the Savior.

"As I read it," Polk continued, "as we move into the twenty-first century, the economic and political power of the world is shifting from the Gentiles to the House of Nephi, and there is little anyone can do about it. It was a promise made to that seed." With that, Dr.

Polk turned and said, "It's yours, Sam."

Meyers began cautiously. "While the summation I wish to present includes issues that may need to await further clarification and revelation, or additional, more positive evidence, one fact does remain. That is the positive scriptural evidence that the Nephites have been preserved; otherwise, all four tribes of the Nephites could not receive a knowledge of the Savior from the testimony of their fathers, which testimony is contained within the Book of Mormon. In that case, the very purpose for which the plates, which contain the Nephite records, were preserved would have been frustrated. That is something that does not happen with the Lord. As we are reminded in section three of the Doctrine and Covenants, it is not the work of God that will be frustrated, but the work of man."

Samuel asked Stephen to roll the video. Roy, Dr. Polk's young assistant who had done the filming, had taken care to make it as professional as possible. He had used a neutral background, secured his camcorder on a tripod, and placed large prompt cards out of view to refer to as he asked the aging patriarch the questions.

Samuel introduced the subject. "I want you to hear something rather interesting that we recorded a couple of weeks ago in Orem, Utah. It is an interview with the first patriarch ordained in Asia. He is nearing ninety. His name is Brother Watabe. He is fluent in three languages: Japanese, Chinese, and English. He was raised in China, where his father was a diplomat."

At a signal from Meyers, Stephen pressed the play button on the VCR. The scene began with Roy interviewing the patriarch of Japanese descent, who was now living in a small apartment in the home of his son in Orem.

The little man reminded Samuel of the head priest he had visited in Japan at the Shinto temple. His manner was reverent and polite, characteristic of the older generation.

"Brother Watabe," Roy asked, speaking as if he were a member of the Church (which he was not), "in 1980, during the dedication of the Tokyo Temple, the *Church News* quoted you as saying that up to that time you and another Asian patriarch had given 2,641 blessings to members of the Church who were of Japanese descent. Is that true?"

"Yes, that is true," came the quiet, heavily accented reply. "I also analyzed those figures," he continued. "Of the 2,641 blessings I pronounced on the heads of my countrymen, 1,372 had the lineage of Joseph—he who was sold into Egypt—and 444 were from Ephraim. Another 825 were from Manasseh. These are the direct lineage of Lehi. It is clear to me that the Japanese people who are members of the Church are predominately of the House of Israel."

Before Roy concluded the interview, the aging patriarch answered a dozen or more questions, mostly related to his life and his callings in the Church. Stephen stopped the video, and Samuel came back to the front of the salon to resume the discussion. He could tell by the group's total concentration that the interview with Brother Watabe had impressed them all.

"Now, I would like to share with you our findings to this point," Samuel remarked. "I made a summary of the criteria needed to identify the people who will possess the land of their inheritance— or the Americas—and I wish to convey these findings to you. None of this will come as a surprise to any one of you. We have spent these past few days concentrating on this very matter, and I'm sure most of you, if not all, have come to the same conclusion as Dr. Polk and I have."

"With some reservations," Maria said quietly.

Samuel acknowledged her comment, but continued without a response.

"For the sake of clarification, so that we all understand which people on the face of the earth possess more features of the promise than any other major nation, I would like to review with you the following."

Samuel placed the first of several large, hand-lettered, 18x24-inch poster boards on the easel Stephen had set up next to him. As Samuel read, he pointed to the poster board summary:

THE BOOK OF MORMON SAYS IN HELAMAN THAT SHIPS WERE LAUNCHED, AND SOME WERE LOST AT SEA.

"Ships of the Nephites were 'launched forth into the west sea,' or Pacific Ocean, taking their course northward. Under these conditions, they could easily have been caught in the mighty currents that flow around the entire Pacific Rim. A projected—and probable—landfall for such vessels would be somewhere within the Japanese archipelago, where many natural bays and inlets offer shelter and conditions conducive to disembarking. There is a plaque in the Hochiman Shrine above Yokahama Bay dedicated to the arrival of seven ships anciently."

He covered the first poster board with the second:

THE BOOK OF MORMON SAYS THE SEED OF THE NEPHITES WOULD BE AFFLICTED BY THE GENTILES AND THAT THE GENTILES WOULD BECOME AS A FATHER TO THE SEED OF THE NEPHITES.

"A basic and vital prophecy concerning the 'afflicting' of the Nephite seed by the Gentiles was fulfilled in World War II; the Gentiles afterward were to have their hearts softened. This would have been when General MacArthur became 'like unto a father to them' though the general had great cause to hate the Japanese. He learned instead to be like unto a father to them, administering their political affairs and providing them with a constitution only a little inferior to that of the United States."

The next poster board atop the first two read:

UNKNOWN HISTORY

"The Japanese do not know of their former ancestry, or of their language derivation, prior to their advent in the islands. They are unique in this situation among all other major nations. Thus, they may be the only logical candidates for possible Nephite parentage and recipients of all the Nephite covenants and prophecy."

The fourth poster board read:

SUDDENLY THE JAPANESE BECAME A NOBLE RACE IN ANCIENT

HISTORY.

"Time factors have been greatly modified as to the actual beginnings of the Japanese Empire. Traditionally originating in 660 B.C.E., scientific research now sets the date of their first emperor's birth at 60 or 61 B.C.E., his death at 1 B.C.E. If this is accurate, and with the Nephite exodus as we postulate it occurred set at 54 B.C.E., when ships were launched into the west sea and heard of no more, then their first emperor, Jimmu Tenno, could have been born in the Americas and taken by ship at age six or seven when the ships left the Americas. His uncle Ninighi, who set his nephew Jimmu on the Imperial Throne of Nippon (Japan) has a name pronounced very similar to that of Nephi by the Japanese. They pronounce the name of their country *Nippon*, even though we pronounce it *Japan*. Nippon, which name they still call themselves, is also a name that could have been derived from Nephi's name. Remember, the name Nephi became a royal title, like Caesar, to the Nephites."

The fifth poster board read:

RELICS FOUND IN JAPAN

"Artifacts that have been carefully researched and studied by such scientists as Meggars, Evans, and Estrada, commissioned by the Smithsonian Institute and assisted by highly regarded Japanese scientists, indicate that earlier patterns of the Jomon Ceramic Culture of Japan have been found in Ecuador in the Americas. They postulate that anciently Japanese fishermen brought these ceramic works from Japan to Ecuador. But this would have been very challenging for known small vessels to perform, traveling some 13,000 miles across the stormy Pacific Ocean, taking about eleven months for the crossing, and somehow making it through the westward turning of the mighty current now called the California Current. It is more logical for this ceramic culture to have been transferred from Ecuador to Japan aboard the great Nephite vessels leaving from the west sea. However, the scientists do show a relationship between Japanese and Central American cultural relics. Moreover, I recently had the opportunity to enter a Shinto temple in Japan and view a photograph of one of their most sacred relics, the Seven Blade Sword. Some ten years ago, one of the General Authorities photographed a large depiction of that same Seven Blade Sword carved on a cliff in Paracas Bay."

The sixth poster board read:

SACRED SYMBOLS IN JAPAN

"The Shinto religion, or way of life in Japan, has fostered the clean, cultured people that the Japanese are. The core of these beliefs is apparently based upon the laws of Moses and the teachings of Christ. For if these tenets were removed from their form of worship, there would be little of value left. Anciently, they had Israelite-type temples, having most of the features and fixtures described in the temple of Solomon, after which pattern the temple of Nephi was built. This combination of Mosaic and Christian religions was practiced only among the Nephites before the time of Christ. The emperor's emblems of office—called the *San-Chu-No-Jingi*—are the Mirror, the Jewel, and the Sword. These could be likened to the Liahona or director, which guided the families of Lehi and Ishmael through the desert, the Urim and Thummim or seer stone, and the Sword of Laban, which Joseph Smith saw."

Poster board seven read:

JAPANESE LANGUAGE ROOTS

"No viable written language for general use was had among the Japanese before the eighth century C.E. At that time, Chinese professors supplied them with a written language suitable to the Japanese spoken words. Before that time, the spoken word or traditional record keeping was all they had. An author-scientist, James Churchward, writing in one of his books entitled *Children of Mu*, declared that the Japanese language still contained, in 1931, nearly forty percent Quiché Mayan words. The Mayan culture of Central America is purported to be what is left of the ancient Nephite civilization and the only group in the Americas anciently to have a written language."

Meyers tapped the boards with his pointer and said, "These seven pieces of evidence that I present in summary strongly suggest that the Japanese people are actually descendants of the ancient Nephite civilization in the Americas. Other items of interest and comparison could be offered, as we have seen."

Samuel concluded, "Foreknowledge of this essential information concerning any perception of future happenings upon the land of the Americas impacts us as a people, particularly LDS members. There appears to be enough revelation on this matter of the Nephite nation in the last days to allow us to cooperate with the divinely ordered plan."

Now it was Polk's turn again, taking up where Samuel left off. All were surprised at how spry he was. The coughing spells seemed to have disappeared. He peered over the rim of his reading glasses to gauge the interest of those in the room listening to him. There were no comments as he surveyed the group and bowed before them from his chair as if he were speaking before ministers of Japan. His eyes continued to glide from face to face. They waited. No one in the room, not even Dr. Polk—especially Dr. Polk—wanted to break the spell at this moment. They had mentally traversed the Pacific Rim. They had studied the Polynesian people and their culture, they had crossed New Zealand and Australia, then they had moved up the far western Pacific Rim to the numerous clusters of Asian islands, and had ended up in Japan. In each case, it seemed they found evidence of the House of Israel and remnants of the Nephite nation.

The collective minds in the grand salon now had a greater grasp on the escape, nurturing, and possible whereabouts of the seed of Nephi, Jacob, Joseph, and Zoram than any group on earth. Together, the group had offered more interesting and profound insights into the future role of the gathered Nephites and the comparable impact of the Nephites in the last days than any other assembly.

They all agreed, for the most part, with the evidence that pointed to the conclusion that yes, there were Nephites living today. Then, within the past day, they had reasoned that if that were true, a nation or nations must be housing those descendants of the four

Nephite tribes of Lehi. Each person now seated around the salon knew that if the Nephites were, in fact, identifiable, then it was clear from the Book of Mormon that the Nephites of today must receive the gospel from the Gentiles; and, if it were presented with the proper spirit, they would come into the Church and form the core of Nephites that would receive their inheritance. Also, in a cohesive body, the Nephites would lead out in the building of the New Jerusalem.

This was heady stuff, and both Polk and Meyers were aware of its implications on all others in the Church. They also knew that it was not their duty or responsibility to present it to the Church. They were convinced, however, that it meant that the Lord would favor the Nephites as he had favored other select groups in the past. He would begin grooming them for the awesome task ahead. It would make the coming forth of these people more tolerable to the members to know that they were coming, because the spirit of acceptance and cooperation would be everywhere present among the covenant Gentiles and Lamanites. The covenant people would realize that the Lord had carefully told them in the scriptures that this is the will of the Father, that they should receive their inheritance in the days of the Gentiles, and the Gentiles should be numbered among them in full fellowship.

The evidence before them indicated that the time for those promises to commence would be soon. Going into the twenty-first century, the power of the world was shifting from the West to the Orient, a fit movement of prophecy. It was a promise to that seed which would be kept.

At last Dr. Polk broke the silence. "This brings us all the way to the present. We will simply let this report stand. I would like to present it to a couple of people I know among the Brethren, but if you hear nothing of it in the near future, you will know that either it is not timely to bring out these findings, or . . . that they have not been accepted."

With his good-natured smile, Eric was quick to respond. "The problem is that none of us can ever read these scriptures again without knowing the meaning. It will never be the same. You know what it reminds me of?"

"What?"

"Those ink blot pictures. I remember a picture of a beautiful woman if you look at it one way, and a witch if you see it from another point of view. Once the beautiful woman is pointed out from the same design, you can only see the beautiful woman. I will never see the scriptures we've studied in any other light."

"You're right," agreed Dr. Polk. "When we really see the Book of Mormon complete, and we have greater light than we now have, we will all wonder why we overlooked so many things that are still beneath the surface in our reading of the book. How is it possible to overlook so many hidden things? It is the mark of a great piece of literature to continue to give you deeper and deeper insights. The Book of Mormon is great and profound literature. It is also scripture, which means it was written under divine inspiration from the Lord. It is true."

Unable to resist greater clarification of his recent study on the whereabouts of the Nephite nation, Dr. Polk continued, "Let me tell you an interesting thing that happened when Elder Heber J. Grant offered the dedicatory prayer that opened the Japanese mission in the early 1900s. In his prayer he made a unique request that I have not found in any other prayer in the annals of Church history. Truly unusual. While President Grant was offering the dedication, he requested the Lord to assign the Three Nephites—those special servants of the Lord who asked to remain on earth after Christ ascended into heaven following his visit to the Americas—to minister to the Japanese nation. Was the Lord sending a vital message through his servant to tell us something? It was certainly a special request to that nation. Did President Grant know by inspiration that the Japanese were, in fact, Nephites? Just a little something for you to ponder."

* * *

"BRENDA, WE HAVE TO TALK." There was a youthful edginess in Max's voice that signaled a change in attitude from last night.

They had moved to the vacated aft deck. The others who would have been lounging about, sunning themselves on the deck chairs, were inside the yacht, either in their staterooms or the salon. The wind had become too fierce to enjoy the casual relaxation offered by the deck. Max didn't mind it, though, and Brenda followed him out of the salon onto the deck. They sat in two director's chairs with their backs to the breeze and watched the small whitecaps that formed on either side of the vessel. They heard someone say it looked like a storm was brewing, but the air was warm.

"Okay," Brenda said, sweeping strands of her long brown hair from her face, just to have the wind swish it back again. She looked steadily into Max's deep-set blue eyes with anticipation.

"Brenda . . . this morning with Karry—you know, the steward—was an incredible spiritual experience."

"What do you mean?"

"What do I mean?" He shook his head as if he were bewildered by her response. "I mean just that. I have never experienced such a high. You don't know . . . I didn't know. It was really something to explain the gospel and feel the rush of such a great spirit that hit Todd and me."

"Wait, Max. Wait. I'm not on the same wavelength. You and Todd had a wonderful time telling Karry all about your conversion. Is that what you're saying?"

"Yeah. You got it. But it was more. We were *teaching* him," Max beamed.

Brenda was not moved.

"I'm sharing something with you, Brenda. It's something very important to me. I want you to hear and try to understand what's going on. Hey, we spent hours and hours in that little room with Karry, having one of the most exhilarating, time-stopping encounters with . . . what? . . . the Spirit of the Lord, I guess. Some of those same feelings I had when I decided to convert came over me. But this thing this morning was really, *really* special. What can I say?"

Brenda was feeling uncomfortable. She didn't like to hear Max talk this way. It seemed too weird to her, too fanatical. She was unable to respond. She couldn't relate to whatever it was he felt. Not at all.

Max spoke, "I'm dreaming big dreams, at least for me. I have to tell you, Brenda, something is happening to me. I can't explain it as clearly as I would like, but you have to understand that what I want to do is coming from deep inside. I'm thinking about doing something . . ."

"What's that?"

"I know I must sound holier-than-thou to you, but the fever has hit me."

Brenda studied the smooth planes of Max's face. She could barely breathe. Whatever he was trying to say was not good. She knew instinctively that Max was slipping away from her. Even she could see something different about him—a light, almost a glow, in his face. She didn't know how to react. All she could muster was a throaty laugh, a defiant retort.

"Be serious, Max. Listen to yourself."

Max turned his head away, looking out to sea. Finally he said, "My life has changed course, Brenda. Todd and I talked to your dad and Dr. Polk before lunch. We told them about our experience this morning with Karry . . . and they urged us to think about serving full-time missions. Oh, Brenda, those missionaries who taught me were so great." Max spoke rapidly, his voice filled with excitement. "I never even considered that I would be able to be like them. For one thing, I'm not in their league . . . I don't know all the stuff to teach, and I'm not educated. Besides, they told me their folks paid all their expenses, and I sure don't have that kind of financial support. But this morning the Lord helped us . . . He sort of guided us in what to teach. You can't believe what that meant to us. We both felt it. Then Dr. Polk said money would be no problem, that Brother Meyers helps missionaries all the time—financially, I mean. Do you understand what I'm saying?" Max searched Brenda's stony face for even a flicker of empathy.

No response.

"I know we've talked about getting married, Brenda . . . but if they will approve me, and if Brother Meyers will loan me the money . . . uh, well . . . I want to think about accepting a personal mission call."

It was out. Max looked out to sea again and waited. Nothing. After what seemed to be a long time, he slowly turned his head and looked at the girl he loved.

Brenda's face had lost its color and vibrance. She was shaking her head over and over in disbelief. She had known that Max and Todd had been persuaded to hold a heavy religious discussion. It had made her uneasy all morning. When they met for lunch, she had noticed that Max was preoccupied with something that excluded her, but she had not in her wildest nightmares thought he would give up a couple years of his life for this church of his. That meant he would not be around, not be near, not be involved with her. There would be no wedding, at least not soon. How could this be? Why had she ever let Granny Katherine talk them into coming? If she had stayed in San Francisco with Max, they might be talking about totally different things right now. Maybe they would have become officially engaged. Who knows? As it now stood, there was a whole new twist to her relationship with Max. Why? *Why am I the victim of this grasping religion?* she asked herself. She looked away from Max, who attempted to reopen the lines of communication. He reached out and rubbed her arm gently, asking her again if she understood what he wanted to do.

"Sweetheart, I love you. I don't want to lose you. Two years will go by fast. And if this morning's experience is a sample, I'll be a better man when I get back."

Brenda stood up, threw her head back, letting the wind toss her hair to the side of her head. Then with deliberate contempt she walked along the deck to the door of the salon and disappeared.

Max remained seated as the wind began to howl. He had known that there would be no easy way to explain his feelings and plans to someone who lacked the Spirit. Even so, it troubled him deeply that he had hurt Brenda.

* * *

TAKAHASHI STOPPED SAMUEL IN THE PASSAGEWAY from the galley to the staterooms. Instinctively, the two bowed to one another.

Takahashi said, "I wish to ask you something."

Samuel patted Takahashi's shoulder and invited him to his stateroom where they could speak freely without interruption. As they reached Samuel's cabin, the ship dipped to starboard, forcing

Takahashi to grip the brass railing that swept along the entire passageway. Samuel had his hand on the door latch and managed to steady himself.

"Things are getting rough out there."

"I know," Takahashi said, shaking his head. "And I understand the captain is too sick to make it to the bridge."

"Yeah, that's right. It has some of us a little uneasy. But maybe this rain won't get any worse. Come in."

Takahashi sat down across from Samuel.

"Now then, go ahead. What did you want to ask me?"

"Last night while we were talking about my father, you mentioned that you have great respect for his firm beliefs and that he is an honorable man. I have to agree with you, but with one reservation: my father is a proud man who may never accept the gospel. It hurts me that he resists. He is so firm in his resolve to remain steadfast in his traditions. You have opened my eyes to the great potential of my people. Why is it that my own father will not listen to the whisperings of the Spirit? If he is of the tribe of Ephraim, as my blessing tells me that I am, then surely he should be more sensitive to the gospel."

Samuel sat for a moment without responding to the question. He had some of those same concerns about Takahashi's father. In many ways, Kondo, the father, was indeed a proud man. He had resisted every overture to teach him about the Church. Still, he was also a good, decent person.

Samuel replied, "Your father is an example of the old order of things. Simply because he has the blood of Israel coursing through his veins does not mean he will open his mind and heart to the gospel. I believe that his lineage should make it easier for the Spirit to touch his heart, but you must remember, his are the old traditional ways. When I speak of the gospel going to the Nephite nation and the Book of Mormon whispering to the seed of Jacob and Joseph, I can't help but visualize you, your wife and children, and others of your age. You, Takahashi, are the new generation of lively, converted people who will begin to fill up the ranks. It seems to me that it will be your children and their children who will, perhaps, be in the vanguard group that will inherit the land and build the New

Jerusalem. I seriously doubt that your father and mother will catch the spirit of the gospel in this life."

"You do?"

"Yes, I really do. When I met with your father for lunch a few days ago in Tokyo, I was reminded of how set in his ways he really is. He does not want to expand his mind and fill it with new and exciting concepts. He loves his family; he enjoys his life as it is; he honors his ancestors. But, Takahashi, be at peace. The Lord will sort this thing out. The Lord has asked us to be patient and longsuffering. We must heed that counsel when it comes to your father. Remember one very significant aspect to the entire plan of salvation."

"What is that?"

"There had to be those who would endure life up to this time without the benefit of the teachings of the gospel. Your father was born before the message of the restored gospel came to his city. He was raised without a knowledge of things as you know them. You were young and impressionable when you joined the Church. He was mature and his religious patterns had already been formed before he ever heard of the Church. The Lord takes such things into account. There is a wonderful phrase that I've heard in my life. I remember it whenever I get stirred up about someone not accepting the teachings of the Church. It goes: 'Be patient, my son. I am in charge.' Be patient, Takahashi. Love your parents. They were the forerunners to your great blessings. They kept the flame alive."

"That's an interesting concept."

"If it weren't for all the honorable people who came before us, those who lived hundreds of years ago, where would we be? There has to be a plan for them, and there is. We have the great ordinances that are being performed in the temple to take care of those wonderful people whose blood runs in us."

Samuel laced his fingers and said, "You know the story you related to me the other night about your ancestor who refused to cut the neck of the warrior?"

"Fujita Toko?"

"Yes. He knew nothing about the gospel of Jesus Christ, yet he was filled with a righteous spirit to resist taking another man's life. That same spirit of caring is in you, Takahashi. Sometimes it skips a generation or two, but it is amazing how some can grasp the spirit in any age. You must be one of those with a caring spirit about you. I'm sure that if the gospel had been presented to your great-great-grand-father, he would have accepted it. From what I can tell in the account you shared with me, he was that kind of person. You come from a noble family. Don't forget that. Your bloodline goes all the way back to the House of Israel. You are of royal lineage. The Lord will not leave your father and family without making every effort possible for them to understand and accept the gospel. You have my word on that."

Takahashi stood up to leave.

"Wait," Samuel said. "While I was speaking to your father on the phone just before leaving Tokyo, he told me that he had been having a recurring dream for the past few weeks. Did he mention it to you?"

"No, what did he tell you about the dream?"

"He said he dreamed he was in a tropical setting, viewing a large white statue. That was all he could remember about the dream. But let me tell you what I feel impressed to advise you. You will be in Hawaii with your family pretty soon. Why don't you rent a car and take your father for a drive around the island, and end up at the temple? Let him stroll with you around the temple grounds. It may be interesting to see what he will encounter there. Just do it, Takahashi. Please."

CHAPTER TWENTY-THREE

The Storm

Sunday Afternoon
On the High Seas

AFTER LUNCH, ALL THE MEMBERS OF THE CHURCH on the ship held a quiet testimony meeting in lieu of regular Sunday services. By the time they finished, the stampeding black clouds were bloated with rain. Over and over the yacht was swept upward by the waves of the rolling sea, then dropped into troughs. Each time it was like being plunged into a watery crevasse. The storm was dramatic to watch; it terrified Brenda. Each time the ship made one of its roller coaster movements, Brenda held her breath and grabbed whatever seemed to be bolted down. She had never been this far out in the open sea. It was as if Nature with all her power was demonstrating that if it suited her fancy, she could swallow up the yacht that now seemed so insignificant compared to the rolling waves.

Satellite photos on the Net had indicated no storm at sea directly in the path of the *Free Eagle*. There had been little warning, two hours maximum. Because of the captain's illness, the first officer had been at the helm around the clock. When it became apparent at first light that the captain was still not up to resuming his post, Officer Stone had dispatched a crew member to roust the navigator in training from his bunk; he *had* to get some sleep. Soon after Officer Stone had dropped onto his bunk in total exhaustion, the navigator noticed a blip on the radar screen. He had quickly checked the weather forecast. Since it only called for light rain in the late afternoon—not at all uncommon in the tropics—he had not disturbed the first officer. A few short hours later, young Stone awoke with a start when he was nearly flung from his bunk by the tossing waves. Racing to the bridge, he took the wheel, the apprentice navigator nervously standing by. Both hoped that the unexpected storm would be over in a few minutes, certainly not more than a half-hour of rough seas. He would advise the crew and charter guests to take precautions, which meant that all were to stay indoors and secure their life jackets. He didn't want to alarm them, but it was standard procedure in any storm.

* * *

BRENDA GROPED HER WAY into the salon, still troubled by her distressing talk with Max on the aft deck. She had not expected such a change in his plans. She decided not to let Todd know her feelings. He had already warned her of what Max would do if she were not willing to at least take a look at the teachings of the Church.

Seeing Todd, she asked casually, "Where's Max?"

"Guess."

"On the computer."

"Yeah, one of the guys up on the bridge asked him to get further information from the weather satellite, then try to contact neighboring islands that might be on the network. It looks like maybe the crew is getting a little nervous. They want to make sure we have full contact with nearby islands. I guess this storm is really starting to kick up. Anyway, while Max is checking out the computer, the fellow who is training to be a navigator is on the radio. I guess they want to check around about this storm."

Brenda sank down in a plush lounge chair, her gloom as dark as the skies overhead. She wasn't ready to talk to Max—just yet, anyway. She had to think about what she could say to him that might make a difference.

* * *

FIRST OFFICER STONE WAS NOTHING if not confident in his

ability as a yachtsman; at least he had been until early this afternoon. But his confidence was born of pride and arrogance rather than experience. Of course he could manage a little squall, he told himself. He had watched his father weather a violent storm off the coast of Ireland when he was fifteen. He had read the manuals. He knew the proper techniques of seamanship. At least he thought he did.

And if it turned out that he couldn't handle it after all? Well, no one could blame him or hold him responsible. After all, he had been honest. He had told the captain when he hired on for the year that he had no experience at the wheel during an actual storm. *The captain can damn well get himself up here, sick or not, Stone fumed.*

It was common knowledge that the captain had experience under such conditions. He had taken on a monsoon last year and won. With the captain at the helm, they had no worries. Even Stone had been reassured by the captain's record. The only problem was . . . the crew said the captain was too ill to climb the stairs to the bridge. The first officer had dispatched Karry to confirm the captain's current condition. One of the maintenance crewmen had reported that the captain seemed to have picked up some island fever and was completely delirious.

"He's in another world," the crewman had reported.

"You surely don't mean incoherent?" Stone scoffed.

"That's about the size of it."

The crewman, a bulky sort from Hawaii, had leaned over to make sure the first officer was paying attention. With a toothpick gripped between his teeth, he had briefly studied the youthful face of the man in charge. "Last year this ship was out fifty miles from port at Fiji during a big blow," he said, a warning in his tone, "and the captain brought her in safely with only minor damage. You gotta do the same."

Stone dared not mention his lack of skill to any members of the crew. It would needlessly disturb them and maybe filter through the ship to the rest of the crew and guests. He wished the captain had not spoken of it to the Thorns at dinner that first evening. He desperately wished Captain Montgomery were on the bridge. *Damn that fever!*

The first officer struggled at the helm, the yacht twisting among the waves, which continued to grow in volume. Again, he sent word for Karry. He needed to get an update on the captain's condition—now! Just then Karry appeared, struggling to remain upright as he pushed his way through the door to the bridge. Breathlessly he reported that the captain was running a very high fever.

"Mrs. Thorn says he's in no condition to get up and help sail the ship, even if he wanted to. He's chalk white, sir, and as Mrs. Thorn says, delirious."

A sense of numbing fright came over the first officer. This violent weather condition was far beyond what he remembered of the tempest he had weathered with his father on the Irish Sea. There was no one, not one soul to whom Stone could turn, who had experience under these conditions—no one on board . . . except the captain. The situation scared the first officer to the very tips of his toes. How had he ever let himself in for such a heavy responsibility? He knew, struggling to see out the large, curved, rain-obscured window of the bridge, that his life was in absolute jeopardy—as were the lives of the others on board.

Karry stared at the nonresponsive first officer. "Did you hear me, sir? Mrs. Thorn says he can't possibly come up on the bridge. She says he would pass out if he tried to stand up. Besides, he doesn't even know he's aboard a ship. How could he command one? . . . Sir . . . can we make the nearest port?"

At that moment, a large swell with a lip pushed upward directly in front of the yacht. Seeing the surge of water crashing across the bow sent the first officer into a panic.

Karry saw it. For a moment he studied Stone's wild eyes and pale skin, then realized with a cold chill that the man knew next to nothing about piloting a ship in a violent storm.

Before long, all the major swells were sending water swirling over the lower deck. One huge wave hit the starboard side and caught the first officer off guard. He lost his grip on the wheel and it spun crazily, sending the ship sideways like a car skidding on ice.

Most of the alarmed passengers had assembled in the main salon by this time, feeling somehow safer together. The sudden lurching movement of the ship knocked everyone in the salon to the port side of the yacht, slamming them against the furniture in the room. Fear was etched on the faces of Polk's group as they literally clung to whatever they could grab.

The first officer groped for the stainless steel railing in front of the helm, one hand finally getting hold of the turning wheel. Karry, who was not so quick, banged up against the metal siding.

As soon as he could get his footing, Karry scurried back down to the captain's quarters. Anney and Katherine were busy placing ice packs around the captain's head and body, desperate to get his fever down.

"Karry! This is a frightful situation," Katherine exclaimed with dismay. "Isn't there anyone else among this crew who knows anything about piloting a ship in a storm? The captain always has a port in mind whenever the weather is bad. Is the officer at the helm headed there? How far is it?"

"I asked him that very thing moments ago on the bridge, Mrs. Moore. He . . . that is . . . he isn't certain. But I know that Tim, the young man who knows a lot about navigation, is on the radio and searching the charts to determine the nearest port. Don't you ladies worry. I'm sure we'll make it there. We can't be too far away."

The fact was, Tim had told Karry an hour ago that the yacht was at least a hundred miles from any port. Karry lowered his gaze from Katherine's searching eyes and studied the captain, whose condition had been worsening since yesterday afternoon with an ever-increasing fever.

By the time the ship had sailed late last evening, the fever had shot up to a frightening 105 degrees. This morning, the chef and another crewman had held the captain in his shower and poured ice water over him repeatedly in an effort to reduce the fever. Now that the captain was back resting in his bed, the fever had lowered somewhat. They repeated the process each time his temperature spiked. But by noon he had become delirious with fever. As the maintenance crewman had said, the captain was completely out of it.

In the main salon, speculation ran high as to what was wrong with the captain, though no one knew for sure. All aboard hoped it wasn't contagious.

When Stephen squeezed into the captain's crowded quarters, Karry slipped out and made his way back up to the bridge.

"How is he, hon?" Stephen asked Anney in a low voice.

"Oh, Stephen, I'm no doctor, but he doesn't look good. We're trying to keep his fever down. That's all we know to do. We're in the tropics, you know. It could be anything. How's the first officer doing?"

Stephen shrugged. "I'm going to see for myself in a second."

Anney's frightened eyes held Stephen's, both remembering the captain's comment about the first officer's inexperience in rough weather. Both realized that the captain was needed on the bridge to command the vessel through the driving rain and swelling waves.

Stephen left Anney and Katherine in the captain's quarters and made his way back up to the main salon. He slipped repeatedly on the spiral stairs. Each time, he regained his footing and climbed again, finally reaching the landing above. He passed through the salon.

He could see at a glance that his friends were tense and distressed. Takahashi was bent over his wife, trying to help her. Noriko was holding a plastic bag to her mouth; her color was gray. For all her self-assurance, Maria seemed terrorized, almost in shock. Brenda, who was crouched on the floor clinging to the sofa, urgently plied her father with questions about conditions and the captain.

Stephen shouted, "Just stay where you are. I'm going up on the bridge to talk to the first officer. I strongly suggest that all of you put on those life jackets—don't just hold them—and stay in this room. Somebody help Dr. Polk get his on. You guys break out and secure the life rafts." Eric and Todd scrambled out to the aft deck to do as they were told.

Stephen continued to grip the railing as he made his way from the main deck to the bridge. Rain pelted him in sheets on the rolling, slippery deck. He was appalled by the conditions. How could it get any worse? He wondered what he could do to make sense of the dire situation. *I'm no sailor. What can I hope to accomplish by barging into the command center of the ship and confronting that young officer?* Stone had seemed so aloof and superior, Stephen had not pursued a relationship with him after that first day. And, after all, Stephen had been busy with Dr. Polk's needs.

First Officer Stone was a mystery man, sort of a socialite yachtsman whose talents Stephen didn't trust nearly as much as the captain's. But the captain lay ill below. Stephen had just seen up close how sick he really was.

What good would it do to check out this fellow Stone? Probably none. Nevertheless, Stephen felt a great urge to observe the situation on the bridge firsthand. Perhaps seeing the officer confident and in control at the wheel would at least allay fear . . . fear that gripped his own mind . . . fear that he saw mirrored on every face in the group below. He would at least talk to the young officer and get a realistic assessment of conditions as he saw them.

The wind caught the door to the bridge and flung it wide open as Stephen entered. Immediately he could see Stone wrestling with the helm. His shirt was damp and perspiration was beaded on his brow. Stephen knew at a glance that the man was not in control of the vessel. The neophyte navigator stood beside him, shouting directions and relaying his observations of wave activity approaching the ship.

As the ship topped out on each gigantic wave, there followed a swift, stomach-lurching drop to starboard, then another slow roll. Another wave flung the vessel sideways, then suddenly forward. Stephen could only imagine the terror that slide produced in the hearts of those in the salon, and what of Anney and Katherine? Anything loose would be flying all over the quarters below. At least the furnishings in the salon were bolted to the floor, and the crew had quickly stowed all hanging objects and loose pieces of furniture.

"Bring the rudder hard to starboard, sir," the crewman shouted as he observed the next wave about to plow into the side of the ship.

"I can't, dammit," Stone yelled back. "The wheel feels like the screws are out of water. It's too loose." Suddenly the *Free Eagle* listed sharply to starboard. At the top of the wave, her bow plunged deeply into the trough, swooping up hundreds of gallons of water onto her deck.

From where he stood, gripping the railing, Stephen could see through the rain-splattered, heavy-duty glass surrounding the bridge that waves were churning on both sides in a twisting, violent chase of each other. It seemed that the giant waves would sink the vessel. They were crashing against the hull even before they could be detected. It was impossible for Stone to steer the bow into the waves that Stephen knew promised the safest results. The waves seemed to have no consistent direction.

Stephen stood frozen in place, convinced that conditions looked even more ominous from the bridge than from the windows of the main salon. The next large wave struck the ship savagely at an angle to the bow. With growing panic, Stephen seriously wondered if the next frightful pounder would take them down. It was his first real experience with the overpowering fury of an angry sea.

"Sir!" Stephen shouted from behind the first officer. "Sir, I've come up on the bridge to determine the seriousness of the storm and to learn what we should do."

The officer glanced over his shoulder momentarily to see who was speaking, then his attention reverted immediately to the helm and the view of the crashing waves.

He shouted furiously at Stephen, "Please return to the salon immediately and make certain that no one moves about the ship. Get off the bridge! Passengers are not permitted to be here."

Stephen was stunned by the lack of control exhibited by the first officer. "Sir, I must know what to tell the others about the status of this ship. That is not an unreasonable request. What sort of danger are we facing?"

The officer kept his attention riveted on the maneuvers he was attempting to make to keep the vessel pointed directly into the oncoming waves. The problem seemed to center on which of the twisting mountains of white-capped water to dive into as they continued to bombard the vessel from several directions. Again and again, the vessel's starboard took the brunt of odd-angle waves. When they hit the side of the ship, she seemed like a toy splashing about in a bathtub as a whimsical child stirred the water.

How much more could she take before capsizing? Suddenly Stephen remembered the movie *The Poseidon Adventure*. It had seemed pretty far-fetched when he saw it in the theater. But the *Poseidon* got just one giant wave, and that had been enough to turn the ship over. How could this little boat take much more? He feared this fellow Stone as much as he did the sea.

Stone thundered imperiously, "Dr. Thorn, we are presently navigating a serious squall. I can tell you no more. Please do not distract me with your questions. I am doing the very best I can to maintain this vessel in a steady position. Return to the salon. I command you."

Stephen could see that the man was not about to cooperate with him, a mere passenger, and a landlubber at that. Besides, would it make any difference what he said?

"Dr. Thorn," the officer shouted again, "leave the bridge immediately, or I shall have crew members remove you."

"All I want to know is if you can handle this ship."

Stone's roar filled the bridge with anger. "Get out! Get the hell out of here, I say! I may not be the most experienced helmsman, but I'm all we have. So leave me alone and get back to the salon!"

Stephen grimly pulled on the door latch as the wind once again caught the slab of the door and yanked it wide open. He would have to resolve this his own way.

Stephen's face was set as he held to the railing and worked his way down the stairs. As he struggled against the wind and spraying water, it came to him what had to be done. *We've got to get the captain up here to the bridge! This ship will surely go down if we don't.*

Stephen wrestled with the wisdom of being candid with the others. Did they need to know that the ship was in the hands of a thoroughly inexperienced officer? Finally, he decided that they must know the full truth in order to help themselves. Finding Karry near the salon, he pulled him inside and told everyone in hearing distance the blunt facts of the situation. He knew he was frightening them, but he desperately hoped to shock them into exercising faith.

Polk sat on the carpet where Brenda and Max were securing him into his life jacket. It was impossible to remain in his wheelchair with the ship violently twisting and rocking. Everyone was on the floor or hanging onto the railing of the stairs leading to the aft deck, where Eric had located the cabinet that contained the life rafts.

Samuel worked his way close to Stephen. "So what is your suggestion, Stephen?" he asked as quietly as he could over the noise of the crashing waves and the howling wind.

"The captain needs to be at the helm."

Silence.

"Let's go down and see the captain in his bunk, then," Samuel suggested.

Just then the *Free Eagle* gave a groan from her underbelly. It sounded as if the metal beams that supported her hull would twist apart, splitting her seams, allowing water to come rushing into all the entire lower levels. Stephen felt a new stab of terror.

"Stephen," Polk called from his seated position on the floor, "I should like to have a prayer. I know of little else we can do at this very moment."

Everyone murmured in agreement.

Polk asked Takahashi to be voice, adding a suggestion for what he could specifically petition the Lord. "Would you kindly ask our Father in Heaven to bless the man at the helm? Ah . . . and one other thing: while you plead our cause, would you ask that he heal the captain immediately?"

Katherine, who had hurried to the salon from the captain's quarters to retrieve life jackets for the captain, Anney, and herself, was sick inside, feeling responsible for these poor innocents. After all, it was she who had, through her invitation, placed them here in danger. Hearing his suggestion, Katherine glanced up to study the face of Dr. Polk, interested in this turn of events. She wondered if Polk really felt that the captain could be healed of his illness by simply praying. This was new to her. She had never been in a group where such simple faith prevailed. She was all for it, if it worked. But personally she doubted that it would make any difference at all.

Takahashi got to his knees, was tossed to one side, then decided to remain seated. He gripped the arm of the sofa to steady himself.

Again a violent wave sent a rolling shock through the ship. Maria couldn't hold back a scream as she tried in vain to steady herself on the deep-pile carpet. Stephen wrapped his free arm around the coffee table and worried about Anney, below with the captain.

It was a short but reverent plea to the Father. Takahashi used no flowery words; they were simple and profound pleas to a loving God that he would intervene and steady the vessel. Takahashi paused, then with the purity of a child, asked Heavenly Father to raise the captain "from his bed of affliction."

The amens were loud and fervent throughout the salon. Off to the far end of the room, Karry had been listening. He, too, had dropped to his knees during the prayer. Perhaps better than any person in the room, he knew the first officer lacked the skills to take a ship through this storm and come out safely on the other side.

Stephen stood up, gripping the doorjamb. Inspired by the prayer, he said to Polk, "I know that you use oil when someone is sick and you give a blessing. Do you have any oil? Can you give the captain a blessing?"

"Yes, but I can't possibly get down those stairs the way the ship is tossing. Others could give him a blessing, though."

"Hey, don't worry about that. Eric, Todd!" Stephen shouted, looking around him.

Brenda pointed to the aft deck. "They're preparing the lifeboats in case we need them," she shouted back at her father.

"Okay. Max, Karry, come with me." Stephen rose and started for the stairwell. "I want you two to help me bring the captain up here and lay him on the sofa. I think, with all due respect, Dr. Polk, that you should give him a blessing, and those of us who can will assist you. You know better than I what to do. I personally haven't had much experience with blessings, but I saw it work for you when you had your stroke. You stand in good with the Lord. If we ask with good intent, I think he will answer our pleas."

Polk nodded gravely.

"Do you think the captain is going to allow you men to hoist him up and drag him up here in the shape he is in?" Takahashi asked, taken back by Stephen's brash suggestion that they haul him up bodily.

Katherine spoke up. "Who cares whether he agrees or not? He isn't altogether aware, anyway. If Stephen thinks it will do some good, then, boys, go get him. If he protests . . . then remind him who owns the ship."

It was worse than transporting a lifeless body from the captain's quarters to the main salon. Captain Montgomery was not so out of it that he could not protest that they were dragging him from his bunk and up the stairwell.

"I *don't* want another shower!" he was mumbling. Stephen sighed. It was going to take mighty faith to pull off this miracle, but he, Max, and Karry were all in agreement. They had already begun exercising their faith when they descended on the captain's quarters and half carried, half dragged him out over the protests of the chef, who was watching over him with Anney.

"Have you men gone insane?" the chef shouted. "What right do you have to carry the captain from his quarters?"

"Out of the way, man," Max shouted as he pushed past the chef, who stood dead center in the passageway. "If you don't move, I'll flatten you."

Surprised, the chef backed into the galley and watched as the captain passed by, carried by the three men.

Everyone in the salon had remained huddled together as the ship lurched from starboard to port. Polk had instructed them to continue in silent prayer as Stephen and the others retrieved the captain. Entering the large room, they laid the captain out on the long sofa, his pajamas sopping wet. He was awake by the time they propped his head up on one of the cushions. Bewildered, in a whimpering voice, he asked once again why they had removed him from his bunk.

"Captain," Polk advised him, speaking slowly and clearly, as if to a sleepy child, "we are in the midst of a terrible storm and are in peril of our lives. Your first officer does not have the skill or the courage to command this ship in such conditions. You are desperately needed at this time. We have all decided to pray and bless you that you will have the strength to get up on the bridge and steer this ship to safety." Polk turned to address the group. "Now then, this is what we will do: I want every last person in this room to listen carefully to the words of the blessing. I will anoint the captain's head with oil. Then I have asked Samuel to seal the anointing." All in the room recognized that Polk spoke with authority.

Samuel always carried a small cylinder of consecrated olive oil on his key chain. He produced it, steadied himself on his feet, unscrewed the cap, then handed the small container to Dr. Polk, who had been moved over to the sofa and was held in place by Stephen and Eric. With his other hand, Samuel also gripped the arm of the sofa to keep from sliding across the smooth carpet.

Polk glanced around and spoke to his companions. "This is a very serious matter. I'm convinced that the Lord will ratify the blessing pronounced, if our faith is sufficient. These types of blessings rely heavily upon the faith of those present, so I beg all of you, please apply all the faith you have . . . that the Lord may heal this man."

Polk carefully anointed the captain's head with oil, then handed the cylinder back to Samuel. Samuel managed to replace the cap and put the oil in his pocket, then he held Polk's hands atop the captain's head while Polk spoke the words of anointing. Then Eric and Takahashi groped their way closer and prepared to assist in sealing the anointing.

Polk made one more comment before Samuel performed the healing ordinance. "My friends, there is enough priesthood present in this circle to literally lift this vessel out of the water and place it safely in a quiet lagoon." He looked from face to face, the shrieking of the wind the only sound in the lurching room. "Please, Brother Sam."

Samuel took but a few words to pronounce a blessing of healing. He expressed the words with great sincerity and calmness, revealing no hint of doubt that the captain would regain his strength.

After the amens were spoken, the sounds of the wild storm seemed even more frightening than before, with lashing rain and the constant wind whipping the ship about. There were no words needed. The blessing was given, the deed was done.

Katherine, watching and listening from her place across the room, was deeply affected. There was something about these men, sort of like . . . well . . . they had some kind of power she had never felt before. Her mind could not help but see a contrast here. Bob had certainly wielded power, too. But he had applied a different kind of persuasion, one that required microphones and cameras and . . .

"All right, you guys," Stephen said with a loud voice, startling Katherine out of her reverie. "I want Takahashi on the front and Todd and Eric on each side. Pick him up, and let's carry him to the bridge."

"Hey, Dad?" Todd questioned. "He's out of it again. Look at him."

Stephen ignored the comment.

Karry looked at the captain being grappled by the men, then suddenly jumped up. He stumbled over Katherine, mumbling about making his way down to the lower deck. She thought he had suddenly become ill and was racing for a bathroom. Poor kid.

Karry wasn't sick. He moved with haste and entered the captain's quarters where he went immediately to the closet. In less than a minute he had gathered up shirt, pants, underwear, and socks, then picked up the captain's deck shoes that had a special substance on the soles for slippery decks. He stuffed them all inside his slicker to keep them dry.

He was just starting out of the room when the chef stepped into the opening. Noticing the steward in the act of concealing the captain's belongings, he yelled, "What are you doing, you little thief?" Forgetting about the whereabouts of the captain himself, he saw only that Karry was making off with the captain's things.

"Don't get in my way!" Karry shouted. "Not now. I have to fetch these for the captain. He's going to the bridge and needs to get dressed first."

"Sure he is. You saw how sick the man is. Where did you take him?"

"Well, we took him topside, and they all prayed over him in the salon."

"What are you talking about? Put those clothes back. You hear me? Put 'em back."

"Out of my way!" Karry had no idea how he would get around the cook, who had him bested by fifty pounds.

Suddenly, the cook flew forward as if he had been shot from behind. He fell to the shiny floor and slid to the bulkhead before coming to a halt. Karry saw what had propelled the fat chef in his lunge forward: Max had come up behind him, leaped up to grasp the exposed ceiling pipe with both hands, swung both feet into the air, and landed them squarely in the small of the chef's well-padded back.

"I had the same idea as you, Karry. The captain needs his clothes."

It was a struggle to reach the bridge, hoisting the captain up the stairs with the rain and wind whipping at his face and hair. Max and Karry caught up with them and brought up the rear.

The captain continued to protest his treatment. He was more lively than before, though, and angrily insisted that they put him down and let him walk. They refused. He could hit his head on the deck if he fell. No way were they chancing anything. The ship listed steeply to starboard as if it would roll over in the sea; then, while the men carrying the captain clung to the railing and waited, it slowly righted itself and they proceeded to drag him further up the stairwell. At the top, Takahashi let go of the captain, who was now on his feet, though unsteady, and pulled open the door to the bridge.

A shout of protest blasted from inside, loud enough for all to hear: "What the hell is happening here? Are you men out of your bloody minds?"

Together they pulled the captain inside. With Todd supporting him on the left and Eric on the right, they walked him toward the first officer. Stephen was behind the captain. He leaned around the unsteady commander and with the voice of an admiral he shouted to the First Officer, "Sir, step aside. The captain is ready to take the wheel."

The captain was more alert than he had been at any time in the past twenty-four hours. His eyes were wide open and he peered through the glass windscreen, seeming to notice the storm for the first time. Though wobbly on his feet and braced on both sides, he pulled himself up and said with a raspy voice, "Mr. Stone, I will take the wheel."

"You'll what, sir?"

"I can manage, if you will kindly step aside."

Eric spoke with authority: "Man, are you going to do what the captain says, or do I have to help you decide?"

The young officer moved aside, but stood ready to grab the wheel if the captain fainted. A giant wave approached the bow, and with reflex born of long experience, the captain spun the wheel and guided the ship through the crest.

As the ship settled to a more even keel, the captain swayed slightly, clinging to the wheel with his sweaty hands. A puzzled expression passed over his features as he looked down and noticed his wet pajamas for the first time. "Gentlemen," he quipped, with a small embarrassed smile. "This is the first time I've taken the helm in this garb."

Just then Karry burst through the doorway, the captain's clothing in his arms. "Sir," he shouted breathlessly, "I have your uniform right here. Want me to help you dress?"

"Please do, mate," the captain said, his voice growing stronger with every word.

By the time he was dressed, the captain seemed more vigorous. He insisted that he no longer needed the men to hold him up. He was in control. Each wave became easier to detect. Within minutes, he was fully alert and shouting orders.

Stephen looked to the ceiling of the bridge and offered his sincere thanks. Their prayers had been answered.

CHAPTER TWENTY-FOUR

The Sword

Fiji

FIJI'S AIR TERMINAL CONNECTED with the world. Quantas flew into the airport with giant 747s, dropping off and picking up passengers to whisk them in several directions throughout the Pacific. The morning that the group disembarked from the yacht, they rushed to the air terminal, and finally made it through the controlled international gates. The main group was scheduled on Quantas for Osaka, Japan; the others were set to catch flights bound to Hawaii and on to California.

Dr. Polk had decided not to make the trip to Japan; he needed to rest. Anney and Katherine would accompany Polk as far as San Francisco. Roy would intercept them there and escort the good professor back to Provo. Karry was also bound for San Francisco, full of plans for baptism and getting settled into college.

Those heading for San Francisco were scheduled to fly out half an hour ahead of the group bound for Japan.

Max and Brenda sat off to one side of the gate, away from the others. "Brenda," Max said softly, holding her hand gently in both of his. "When I said I loved you, I truly meant it. You are like sunshine and music in my life. Please try to understand."

Brenda listened with total attention, pleased by his words, though fully aware that a "but" would soon follow. She replied. "I believe you, Max. I also know that real love means that you would be willing to give up certain things to be with me."

"Oh, Brenda, why does it have to come down to a choice? I love you *and* the Lord. I have come to know the Lord and love him more fully than ever before in my life. I feel like he wants me to serve him for the next couple of years. I don't really expect you to understand my feelings yet . . . I know it is hard for you. But if you would put your trust in him, you could receive the assurance that things can still work out. We're not very old, you know . . . I mean, we're pretty young to get married. You could finish school while I'm gone . . . and maybe even take a look at the Church. I'm not pushing you . . . but you could just sort of think about it."

Brenda sighed. She half turned, put her arms around Max's neck, and pulled his face down to hers. She kissed him—a sad, tender kiss—then pulled away. "I don't know where all this is going to lead us, but I do know I need time to think about a lot of things. It's not going to be easy. For now . . . well, let's just end this trip as friends. I have to think."

"Brenda, please understand. I want to call you. I want to see you. I really don't want to lose you . . . Please don't walk out of my life."

The first boarding call interrupted anything Brenda might have said, and the two stood up awkwardly, their mutual situation far from reconciled. They gathered their belongings, then joined the queue to board the plane.

Anney had preboarded with Dr. Polk before the bulk of passengers, first receiving Stephen's quick hug, then turning to wave good-bye to their shipboard companions. Then, as Katherine stepped up to hand the attendant her first-class boarding card, Samuel gathered the courage to reach out and touch her arm. Gently pulling her aside while others crowded past, he asked if she would wait just a moment. Katherine, eyes widened with interest, looked closely at Samuel. His face was pale, and he seemed a little agitated. As this short but powerful man spoke earnestly, she felt the rhythm of her heart quicken.

"I know you came searching for answers to eternal marriage, Katherine," Samuel began. "I hope . . . that is . . . I would never try to prevent you from someday being sealed to your late husband, if that were possible. But . . . I would like to urge you not to be hasty. You have a long life ahead of you."

Katherine laughed, not completely understanding him. "Tell me about it," she said merrily. "Who are you kidding?"

Samuel caught his breath. She was so lovely. Her spirit seemed so close to the surface; and again, it seemed so familiar to him. "I think you have at least another twenty-five years," he said huskily. "And maybe more."

Katherine tilted her head charmingly and smiled, still puzzled that he was so serious. "So how does that change anything?" she asked.

"It means you might have time to see me . . . that is, if you wouldn't mind." He pushed ahead with what he wanted to say. "If I were to drop by next week and happened to come up to your place in San Francisco, would you . . . have dinner with me and maybe take in a show?"

Katherine was surprised but pleased. She studied Samuel's strong jaw and small-boy, embarrassed expression. He was nervous. He really seemed to mean it. She hesitated a long moment. *Bob has been gone such a short time*, she thought. *Just the other day, I was wishing I could die, too. I flew thousands of miles to learn how I could be married to him after this life. Now, here I am looking at another man, liking what I see in his face . . . and feeling as giddy as a girl.* Katherine took a long breath, needing time to sort out her confused feelings. Somehow she couldn't give Samuel a direct reply . . . not yet.

"The really good shows are all booked," she teased.

"I have ways to get good seats," Sam persisted with a grin.

Their eyes held. He seemed to be looking into her soul again. What power this man had over her.

"Yes, Sam, I'm sure you do," she said slowly. Without thinking, she reached up and touched his cheek lightly. "All right. If you get to San Francisco next week, I'd be honored to have dinner with you."

In a quick burst, Samuel exhaled the breath he had been holding, and his face flushed with pleasure. He took her free hand in both of his, then impulsively leaned close and brushed his lips to her smooth, fragrant cheek.

Suddenly, both were jolted back to an awareness of their surroundings by a voice over the loudspeaker heralding the final boarding call for Katherine's flight. With a quick smile and good-bye,

Katherine turned around and handed her pass to the young Fijian girl who welcomed her aboard.

Nearly everyone in the international terminal witnessed the mild exchange Samuel played out; they saw his beaming face as he waved Katherine off. He didn't care. He was attracted to this charming, beautiful woman. If she were given enough time, he was sure she would embrace the teachings of the Church. He would certainly work toward that day.

* * *

KARRY WAS OVERJOYED with the turn his life had taken although it was strange how rapidly he had quit his job on the yacht, deciding to stay close to the group he had come to admire. At the end of their missionary discussion, Karry had told Max and Todd that he wanted to join the Church. He knew during the prayer he had offered that he wanted what those two guys had. He even asked if he could be baptized in the yacht's hot tub. Samuel had carefully explained to him that even though there were those on the ship who held the priesthood and had performed baptisms, he would need to be taught a little more, then be interviewed by a mission leader and be baptized with the sanction of that authority.

Before the yacht docked at Suva, Karry was set to go with the Thorns back to California. He had already informed the captain, who had gone back to his bunk to rest when the storm abated, that he was quitting. The captain was in no shape to remind Karry that he would forfeit his month's pay if he left early, so Karry was saved the lecture. He didn't expect to get paid for time he didn't work, anyway. He shrugged off the thought.

Some of the conservative members of the group raised their eyebrows. It seemed a little sudden for Karry to want baptism—after just three hours with those self-styled but earnest missionaries. But Max and Todd didn't think it was odd or too soon. If they had had the authority, they would have baptized him in the hot tub on the spot. It was actually the two of them who convinced Stephen and Anney to let Karry return home with them to Lafayette, try to get a student/work visa, and go to a community college there. He would work to earn his way. From the time he was a young boy, he had always earned his keep.

Katherine, never one to question impetuous decisions, had been caught up in the conversation and assured Karry she could get him into a college somewhere in the Bay Area. "I have friends," she had said. That settled it. Anney had been concerned that things were moving too fast, that the young man was making major decisions he might come to regret. She insisted that Karry call his parents from the yacht and get their permission.

Karry protested that suggestion with a short laugh. He let her know that his parents considered him an adult, and whatever he decided, he was on his own. "My father believes a boy is a man at eighteen and ought to be out working on his own, but I'll try to call them. We don't have a phone. They'll have to go from the pub to fetch my dad."

It took an hour of repeated calls, but Karry's father was finally located. He came on the phone in the local pub and without hesitation, confirmed that Karry was indeed on his own. If he wanted to leave a good-paying job and go to some college, then he would have to suffer the consequences. But his father wished him well.

Karry had never enrolled in college in Australia, and told Todd and Max as much after the discussion, the phone call, and the decision to go.

"Don't worry about it," Todd had assured him. "You can get into a community college in California. Half the students are from foreign countries."

* * *

THE DWINDLING GROUP ARRIVED AT OSAKA International Airport, the second largest airport in Japan, and started through customs. Samuel observed to all within earshot, "Look at this marvelous terminal. This is what I mean by a people with great skills for the twenty-first century." He kept up the praise of the Japanese: "These people can make anything they set their minds to create. Don't ever doubt their ability to build the New Jerusalem."

Through customs, they walked to the outside and were ushered onto the airport commuter bus that whisked them to downtown Osaka. They switched from bus to commuter train and an hour later wound up in Kyoto.

Junko, this time without her Chinese husband, met them at the train terminal in Kyoto in a twelve-passenger van she had rented. She had brought along her dear friend and houseguest, Komae, who was visiting for the week. Komae had immigrated to Oregon after joining the Church. Since she spoke fluent English, she offered to translate for the group. She was more than eager to join in the planned excursion. Takahashi was also ready to help with translation.

Samuel approached his friend and respectfully bowed from the waist. "Junko, thank you so kindly for coming. You are priceless." As each person in the group was introduced, she graciously bowed, smiling her welcome.

The temple grounds at Nara were more crowded than they had been a few weeks earlier when Samuel visited the head priest in his private quarters.

"I have given a second donation," Junko whispered to Samuel in Japanese while the group stepped out of the van and started up the gravel walk to the shrine.

The head priest would see them.

They waited a full ten minutes, then the doors to the lounge inside the head priest's quarters slid open, and the head priest entered with the young priest whom Samuel had met on his last visit. Both priests were again robed in white. The younger priest was holding a long, carved, wooden box that resembled a finely crafted violin case, only longer.

Though some felt a little awkward, everyone bowed to the priests and the priests bowed in return. Through Junko and Komae, the priest welcomed the group. Hot tea followed, served by two young women wearing long kimonos, each with her hair tied up in a knot at the crown. They bowed. All except Junko's cup of tea remained on the table, untouched.

It was not customary to rush anything in the head priest's quarters. He was in charge, and he timed the proceedings as he chose. After all, he waited on the royal family, and they did not press him to rush matters. He made small talk.

Samuel's eyes swept over the case at least a dozen times before the young priest, responding to a nod from his superior, lifted the case and placed it on the low table in the center of the room. His thin fingers worked the latch as the group stood in anticipation. They had all been told of the contents. Each had heard Samuel relate the account of the Seven Blade Sword and the seven tribes of Lehi. On the ship they had carefully studied the reference in the Book of Mormon where Jacob, Lehi's son, refers to the seven tribes: "Now the people which were not Lamanites were Nephites; nevertheless, they were called Nephites, Jacobites, Josephites, Zoramites, Lamanites, Lemuelites, and Ishmaelites." Jacob did not distinguish among the seven, as he explained in his writings; rather he lumped them all into two basic tribes, Nephite and Lamanite. Dr. Polk had shown his students a second reference to the seven tribes of Lehi in 4 Nephi and a third in Mormon's commentaries, each time listed the same way, beginning with the tribe of Nephi.

Slowly, carefully, so as not to harm the contents of the case, the young priest opened the lid. Inside, resting on a purple velvet lining, was the rusted Seven Blade Sword. It was for viewing only, definitely not for touching.

Samuel spent a long time looking at the sword, scarcely breathing, memorizing every part of it. *Whose hands have touched this weapon? Surely they were the posterity of Lehi . . . valiant Nephites, struggling to maintain their heritage in a strange, new land.*

Turning to Eric and Takahashi, who stood next to him, Samuel said in a hushed voice, "There you have a marvelous symbol of the seven tribes of Lehi—a tradition brought two millennia ago by this people to this new land . . . and now we see the visible remains of that dynamic, survival-oriented people here in this object."

Maria and Samuel sat on the wooden bench, removing the straw sandals and replacing them with their street shoes. Maria slipped on her low-heeled, black shoes easily, but Samuel had to tie his lace-up Oxfords. Before he had tied the first shoe, she was ready to stand up and walk to the parking lot with the others of the group who were moving away from the entrance.

"Can we talk for a second?" Samuel asked in a quiet voice. "Now that we have explored the issue of Nephites this far, I want to repeat something I mentioned to the group in our discussion and get your reaction, Maria."

Maria turned to meet Samuel's eyes with a kind, but questioning look. "Sure," she said, "I'm interested."

"I want to let you know some of my feelings about coming here. I'm thinking about the seven tribes of Lehi. I'm sure you're not ready to talk in any depth about the significance of the tribes, but I have been thinking: Why would the great prophet Mormon record their names and identities three times, including his own rendering of the names, if it were of no importance, especially in the very condensed record on the plates? He tells us repeatedly about the extreme difficulty of engraving on plates. There had to be a compelling reason."

"That I would have to agree with," Maria said. She sat down once again on the bench.

"Did you notice that Mormon, Jacob, and Nephi—all prophets—recorded this? That makes three accounts—amounting to three witnesses in the Book of Mormon—indicating that such a tribal designation had endured throughout their history. This is what makes the revelation given to Joseph Smith concerning the fulfilling of a promise made to them anciently by their prophet Jacob, which was to happen 'in the flesh,' so very critical. It appears to me as proof positive from that scripture that all seven of these tribes or families still exist."

Maria did not respond. She looked deeper into Samuel's eyes, neither confirming nor disputing his comment.

"Maria, I tell you, this was underlined and accented in the revelation to Joseph Smith, when he was told that this was the *very purpose the plates were preserved*. What could be more vital for us to know? Joseph was also informed that the knowledge of their Savior should be given to all four tribes of the Nephites through the testimony of their fathers. What testimony of the Nephite fathers do we have except the Book of Mormon? And if they were yet alive in 1828, which would certainly be necessary if they were to obtain the record of their fathers, then they are living today, descendants of all seven tribes! Those seven tribes are Nephites, Jacobites, Josephites, and Zoramites—plus the three tribes of Lamanites: Lamanites, Lemuelites, and Ishmaelites.

"It all comes down to the great mission of the Nephite return. I know you know what it is, but I have to say it again: they are to develop the Zion society and spearhead the building of the New Jerusalem. This is very high on the Lord's list of things that are essential to happen in the last days. I tell you, Maria, the "greater things" are just waiting for us as a people, if we will listen. It is all tied together. I am convinced that the sealed portion of the plates that Joseph Smith was forbidden to translate must contain the blueprints for the building of the New Jerusalem and the detailed instructions for living a Zion society." Samuel had begun to raise his voice, but he hushed it to a near whisper. The others were fifty meters down the path to the van; they were out of earshot.

Samuel continued in a quiet, yet determined voice, "All of this information we have been uncovering about the return of the Nephites and comprehension by the Church membership today is predicated on our belief in the Book of Mormon. It clearly states that unbelief in the book would cause the Lord to withhold the greater things and bring the Church under condemnation."

Maria listened, impressed, but not completely convinced, though she had certainly softened in her views because of the things she had heard over the past few days. She needed time. Time to study and ponder. She was not ready to comment and make any final judgment one way or the other. "Samuel, I still have to work this out in my mind. It's new and I need to spend more time considering it. I hope you understand. I certainly feel you have given it your best shot. For this I thank you."

Samuel touched her wrist with his hand. Sincerely and kindly, he said, "Maria, thanks for staying on. I am aware that I have been troubling to you, or at least what I have presented, but you were good to stick it out."

"Frankly, Sam, I'm glad I did. But as I said, I still have reservations about some of your evidence, and I have mentioned those points. I have to admit, though, I will never study the scriptures you

REFERENCES

CHAPTER 2

Regarding the Seven Tribes of Lehi, Mormon 1:8-9 shows that there are four Nephite tribes and three Lamanite tribes (see also Jacob 1:13-14 and 4 Nephi 34-39). It was the Nephites who received covenants of survival and of an everlasting inheritance in this land, for these were given when no Lamanites dwelt among them (see Jacob 7:24).

The Nephites were also called the "remnant of Jacob" by the Savior (3 Nephi 20:16: 21:12; see Index for *Jacob, House of*). The names of the Nephite tribes are Nephites, Jacobites, Josephites, and Zoramites. The Lamanite tribes are Lamanites, Lemuelites, and Ishmaelites (see also D&C 52:2). This is also mentioned in Chapter 24 and the above references.

CHAPTER 5

See 3 Nephi 20:16; 3 Nephi 21:12; 3 Nephi 23:1.

CHAPTER 9

Alma 62:48–51 and 63:4–8 show that 5,400 families of righteous Nephites left their homes to go to the "land northward." Only one shipload of them arrived there. Other shiploads, also heading toward this same area, were presumed lost at sea or drowned.

The great Nephite prophet, Jacob, had prophesied that the Lamanites would destroy the Nephites, and would come into possession of all their promised land. He then gave them this short but all-important prophecy, saying, *"and the Lord God will lead away the righteous out from among you"* (Jacob 3:3, 4). The story found in Alma appears as the only viable, and the most likely, fulfillment of his prophecy.

Covenants through this same Jacob are recorded in 2 Nephi 9:53, 10:2, and 10:17–19. At this time, the Lamanites and Nephites had but recently separated (see 2 Nephi 5:4–6, 20–24). Jacob 7:24

confirms this complete separation. In the last part of the covenants (see 2 Nephi 10:17–19), God consecrates this land unto the Nephites, and to the Covenant Gentiles who would be "numbered among them" (2 Nephi 10:18, and 3 Nephi 21:22).

In the building of the New Jerusalem, Christ assigned the leading role to the "remnant of Jacob," assisted by the Covenant Gentiles, "and as many of the house of Israel as shall come" (3 Nephi 21:23).

Whereas the ships that left the "narrow neck of land" were headed north, they could hardly avoid the prevailing clockwise currents, now called the North Equatorial and the California currents. These currents join and veer sharply to the west, crossing the entire Pacific Ocean just north of the Equator, and circulate around the entire North Pacific Rim, washing the shores of Japan. This would most likely locate the Nephites within the reaches of the North Pacific Ocean.

The Nephites are also granted this land, as commanded of the Father by his Son, in 3 Nephi 16:16. The Savior quotes a prophecy of Isaiah to show that those who would be given this land would be a united or a Zion People, and that the time of this consecration would be "when the Lord shall bring again Zion" (3 Nephi 16:18).

Obviously the Nephites cannot return to this land, become a Zion People, and be the principal builders of the New Jerusalem if they have perished. Neither can the above prophecy (see 3 Nephi 16–18) be fulfilled. Nor can the Lord gather them in from their long dispersion and establish again among them his Zion (see 3 Nephi 21:1). He shall not then establish them in this land until the fulfilling of the covenant which he made with their father Jacob; and it shall be a New Jerusalem (see 3 Nephi 20:22).

Also excluded from possible fulfillment would be the prophecy given the Prophet Joseph Smith, wherein he promised that all four tribes of the Nephites—Nephites, Jacobites, Josephites, and Zoramites—that the knowledge of a Savior would come through the testimony of their fathers, which testimony can only be found in the Book of Mormon. It was for this very purpose that the plates are preserved which contain these records (see D&C 3:16, 17, 19).

If our disbelief in a Nephite preservation comes from a lack of scriptural evidence, then the chain of covenant and prophecy presented here—when understood and believed—will supply that evidence. If it is lack of belief in the words of Christ and his prophets, then we may, in effect, come close to denying him.

CHAPTER 13

The story of the miraculous transformation of righteous Lamanites is recorded in 3 Nephi 2:11–16.

CHAPTER 14

The quotes from President Benson can be found in *The Ensign*, May 1986, pages 5 and 78.

CHAPTER 17

The day of the Lamanite has not yet come. In D&C 49:24 is this reference: "But before the great day of the Lord shall come, Jacob shall flourish in the wilderness, and the Lamanites shall blossom as the rose." This may, and probably does, have reference to 3 Nephi 21:23, 24. In this revelation the Lord outlines the building of the New Jerusalem, with Jacob (the remnant of) being the principal builder.

Would this not equate to "Jacob shall flourish in the wilderness?" Then in verse 24, the Lord says, "And then shall they assist my people that they may be gathered in, who are scattered upon all the face of the land [perhaps meaning on various Indian reservations] in unto the New Jerusalem." Would this not be a "blossoming?"

CHAPTER 18

Information taken from Jack Seward's *Hari-Kari*, published by Charles E. Tuttle Co., Japan/Vermont, 1968.

CHAPTER 19

"The Nephites will roll through the Gentiles like a lion among lambs" (3 Nephi 20:16). This scripture calls the Nephites the "remnant of the house of Jacob," and it is repeated in 3 Nephi 21:12.

CHAPTER 20

The Lamanites are to be invited into the New Jerusalem. This subject is referenced and discussed in Chapter 16.

CHAPTER 22

The article described appeared on the editorial page of the *Church News* in October 1980. Referring to Poster #2, this reference reads as follows:

"Wherefore, my beloved brethren, thus saith our God: I will afflict thy seed by the hand of the Gentiles; nevertheless, I will soften the hearts of the Gentiles, that they may be like unto a father to them; wherefore the Gentiles shall be blessed and numbered among the house of Israel." (2 Nephi 10:18.)

Please note that this prophetic covenant gives the Gentiles (Americans) the opportunity to be numbered among the house of Israel. All they need to do to obtain this inheritance, as listed in 3 Nephi 21:22, is to "come in unto the covenant," which must refer to both the covenants of baptism and of the temple ordinances. In doing so, they become eligible to join the Zion society of the Nephites and assist them in building the New Jerusalem.

Referring to Poster #4, modern scholarly research has altered the date of 660 B.C.E., the traditional beginning of the Japanese Empire, to a time nearly six centuries later. Using archeological, ethnological, and textual studies, two recognized scientists agree that the birth date of Jimmu Tenno, first Emperor of Japan, was 60 or 61 B.C.E. and his death was 1 B.C.E. This is indicated in *Historical and Geographical Dictionary of Japan*, by E. Papinot (Ann Arbor, Michigan, 1948), pp. 5 and 228. See also *Japan: A Short Cultural History*, by Sir George B. Sansom (New York, 1931). The traditional date, 660 B.C.E., may well be the birth year of the first progenitor of the Japanese—Father Lehi, who may have been about 60 years of age when his family left Jerusalem.

Referring to Poster #6, the San–Chu–No–Jingi are Japan's Emperor's emblems of office: the Sword, the Mirror, and the Jewel.

Similar objects were given to Joseph Smith, together with the golden plates (see D&C 17:1).

The Seven Tribes of Lehi are referenced and discussed in Chapters 2 and 24.

CHAPTER 24

The Seven Tribes of Lehi are referenced in Chapter 2.

ABOUT THE AUTHORS

Keith C. Terry is a popular and prolific writer who has authored a number of fiction and nonfiction books for the LDS market. He is the author of the best-selling novels *Out of Darkness* and *Into the Light*, also published by Covenant.

A perpetual student and researcher, Keith earned bachelor's and master's degrees from Brigham Young University. He has also pursued graduate studies at the University of California. Along with his busy writing schedule, he enjoys jogging, scuba diving, and family history research.

Keith and his wife, Ann, live in Provo, Utah. They are the parents of nine children.

Wesley Jarvis has spent his life researching material on the whereabouts of the Nephite nation. It has been a family tradition passed on from his great-grandfather through his father to seek out this information.

A former employee of Geneva Steel before his retirement, he is a great student of the Book of Mormon and has found many opportunities to share information with others. He is an active high priest and loves the gospel.

Twice widowed, Wesley Jarvis is married to his third wife, Josephine.